The Legacy Series
Volume 1

The Legend

The Guide

The Frenchman

The Prophecy

Sheritta Bitikofer

MOONSTRUCK WRITING

CONTENTS

The Frenchman

Contents   265

The Prophecy

Contents   399

Terms to Know   401

The Legend

Legacy Series Book 1

Sheritta Bitikofer

MOONSTRUCK WRITING

CONTENTS

PREFACE

Because the Romani are a somewhat secretive and obscure people group, some things in the story may not be accurate to their current culture. However, what elements are mentioned have been verified through multiple sources (interviews, historical accounts, and reference websites) about the Romani people. Opinions of the characters in this book do not reflect my own opinions of the Romani, nor are they necessarily the accepted views of the people in contemporary times. However, there have been multiple laws enacted in British history that persecuted the Romani. This book takes place during one period when Queen Mary put the Egyptian Laws into place. They stated that any gypsy (Romani) individual found on English soil would be executed and anyone associated with them would suffer the same fate. Put into law in January of 1555, it had a profound affect on the Romani population in England at the time. Our characters find themselves in such times.

TERMS TO KNOW

Loup-garou – The French translation of "Wolf Man".

Gypsy – A derogatory term for the Romani people, derived from their supposed origins in Egypt. The Romani are divided by sub-tribes and are call themselves by different nationalities. For example, the English Romani call themselves Romanichal. French Romani are called Manush in France. In Germany, they call themselves the Sinti. In most of Eastern Europe, they consider themselves Roma. In Spain, Finland, Iberia and Wales, they are known as the Kale. The people in Ireland that are similar in culture to the Romani, but not considered part of the Romani nation are called The Travelers. Romani are a nomadic people and originate from India.

Vitsa – A clan of Romani, composed of a few families traveling together.

Kris – A Romani court that assembles the elders of a vitsa or family to pass judgement on a Romani who breaks their code of ethics or purity.

Marime – To the Romani, this is a two-fold term. One is an act or taboo that would make one impure or unclean. The second is the state of social banishment that is imposed on a Romani that has committed a crime in their group.

Gadje – Any non-Romani. Males are called "Gajo" or "Gadjo" and females "Gaje" or "Gadji". The dialect and spelling changes between different sub-tribes of the Romani.

Galbi – a gold coin used for decoration in Romani women's clothing to show off their wealth.

Tuppence – Two pennies.

Crown – Worth five shillings, which is sixty pennies. This was the most common coin in circulation and was issued in either silver or gold.

Mysgather – A tax collector

Constable – An appointed official who executes law and order within a town. His responsibilities include upholding the law of the country, arresting criminals, and imprisoning them.

Warder – Prison guard.

Bawdyhouse – A whore house

Wood Reeve – A man paid to patrol the forests for beggars and criminals.

Watchers – A team of men posted outside the city walls to watch for danger so as to alert the constable of the city.

CHAPTER 1

The forest north of Wye was anything but quiet that night. He hadn't known a moment of pure silence since his childhood years. From where he squatted under a sheltering oak, he could hear them all carry on around him as if nothing were wrong; as if an abomination like him never existed in their world.

The laughter of the townspeople in Wye was a haunting reminder of everything he could never have. It was the first day of August, marking the beginning of the harvest. He could imagine them all feasting on the fruits of their labors and celebrating in the Gule of August. If he breathed in deeply enough, he could smell the freshly baked loaves of bread from the dinner tables of the families in Wye and the surrounding farmlands. There was a time when he would have partaken in such festivities, but that time had long past; and now his tongue may never know the rich enjoyment that a slice of bread and butter could bring to a tired and miserable creature.

Some distance away, separate from the celebration, he could hear a lone traveler snoring in his bed sack. He could hear the soft popping of the embers from a dying campfire and the savory smells of a beefy stew. His stomach rumbled, reminding him that he still had not eaten that evening. As wonderful as the traveler's stew smelled, it wasn't what he needed.

An owl called into the darkness, asking the unanswered question of his life. *Who... Who... Who are you?*

He could not answer. For years, he had wandered in the proverbial darkness, lost in his own confusion of what life could afford for a lonely and cursed man like himself. All he knew was that life had little meaning anymore. The child who sat at the table with his family had a future. The traveler had a plan, somewhere to go and maybe someone's arms to run to, but the man who crouched under the swaying leaves of the oak tree had nothing.

The sound he had been waiting for finally graced his ears. It was the frantic rustling of an animal in the deep brush of the forest. He sniffed, breathing in its fear. He took off, weaving through the tall elms and oaks whose branches shaded him from the moonlight.

When he found the fawn caught in a hunter's trap, he ducked into the bushes so as not to alert his presence too soon. It tugged and twisted, but the noose-like knot around its ankle would not loosen for anything, not even its desperate attempts at escape. The grass and leaves around it had been scattered in its hasty efforts to regain its freedom.

Watching the animal, he wondered where its mother could be. Had she abandoned it? Or was the fawn alone in the wilderness? This was the first time he had come to find a deer so young ensnared this way. With the aid of its parent, it might have avoided such a fate.

If he had any mercy within him, he would have turned away and looked for a meal elsewhere. He could have even cut it loose so it could live another terrible day in a world that considered it to be nothing more than a beast to be killed and eaten. He was not so merciful, and the darkness within him needed to be fed.

Slowly, the demon took over his body. His nails grew into claws, and his teeth elongated into carnivorous fangs that glinted in the moonlight. Eyes that were once a deep brown brightened into a golden hue that put the crown jewels to shame. His heartbeat pounded in his ears as his blood quickened at the sight of his intended meal. Nothing else mattered but this kill.

He approached the deer from behind, his bare feet silent in the lush grass. The fawn wasn't even aware of him until it was too late. He grappled the head of the fawn and snapped its neck with a sharp twist. He heard the bones crack and the fawn's thin and gangly legs went still.

He breathed a prayer of thanks to the Lord above for the meal, an old habit that should have died with his humanity long ago. Then, he set to work on the trap and sliced through the cord with a flick of his sharp claw. Lifting the carcass over his shoulder with abnormal ease, he sped deep into the woods to begin his feast.

The demon within him rejoiced at the meal, but the human was disgusted. For every lamb, every cow, every deer, or small woodland critter that had met an ill fate at his hands, he died a little more inside. It was a wonder there was anything left of his sanity.

Even as he swallowed the raw, blood-riddled flesh of the fawn, he hated himself and what the demon had reduced him to. Fangs and claws slashed through the sinew and snapped the bones as if they were as brittle as a crust of bread. Blood dribbled down his chin, tarnishing the cloth of his tunic.

Slowly, the maddening hunger subsided, and the demon slipped away to let the man breathe easy once more. He lifted his head from the steaming belly of the fawn and regarded the bright stars that shined in the clear night sky. They were the witnesses to his beastly display, and they would carry the message to God that he was unworthy of salvation. If only death would take him and send him to the lowest circle of hell for which he was marked. Then, perhaps, he would know peace again.

The world came back into focus as the demon receded from the forefront of his mind. He could hear the gentle snoring of the traveler and the happy chatter of the townspeople once more, but a new sound lured his attention away from the quarry he had stolen.

He listened to the harried voices. To the west and near the slow-moving river that snaked toward the town, there was a man, perhaps two, and a woman arguing. After living on the fringes of society for years, he had learned to distinguish the sex of passersby without the benefit of sight or sound. He needed only a sniff from downwind.

His hands went still over the mutilated fawn as he heard them scuffle on the banks. Robberies were nothing new, but from her feeble words of protest, he began to realize that this was no robbery of money or possessions. The men wanted something greater. With the wind, he could smell their carnal need for the woman. He recognized the scent. It was the same one that drifted out of bawdy houses in the cities and permeated the rooms of newlyweds. Those women gave themselves to men for money, power, or out of pure love. Yet, it was clear that this woman was not a willing giver.

Everything in his rational mind told him to leave the matter alone. It did not concern him. Yet, when her scream pierced the night, he was spurred into action.

He ran toward the distress, swifter than the flight of a hawk as it would swoop down to catch its prey.

When the shore of the river was in sight, he stalled and stayed in the sheltering shadows of the trees.

He didn't need the moonlight to see the struggle taking place alongside the River Stour. The woman bravely resisted the two men who were nearly twice her size. They were dressed in beggar's clothes, loose-fitting garments stained by days spent in filthy, slothful living. Though he could not get a good view of the woman, he could feel her tenacity. She fought for her freedom with a ferocity that astonished him and endeared him to her plight.

He darted from the concealment of the bushes and crashed into the men, throwing them away from their victim with little effort. His inhuman strength could not have been used for anything more admirable than in saving the honor of a woman. With grunts and curses, the disoriented men scrambled to their feet, but he was upon them in seconds with his fangs and claws bared.

Their cries for help and mercy would go unanswered. He slashed into their throats, and the last breaths of their pitiful lives gurgled forth. Blood spilled on the grassy shore of the Great River Stour and dribbled down to pollute its dark waters.

He stood over their bodies, their unblinking eyes staring up at him with horrific expressions, frozen in their last terrifying moments. They were not the first men he had killed, and God knew that they would not be the last. It was his nature, something he could not control, but like the fawn, these kills were necessary. Any man who would force himself upon a woman was lower than even a mangy flea-infested dog.

Without so much as a word to the lady, he turned and ran into the woods to flee. Surely, she would faint or scream and alert others to the sin he had committed. "Wait!" she called out to him, her feminine voice slowing his flight.

He heard the rustle of her skirts snagging on the brambles as she pursued him into the forest. He looked down to his hands and saw they were still caked with blood, both from the fawn and the men that he had killed. His clothes were tattered and tainted by his iniquity, hardly the sight that any lady should behold.

She approached, panting for air. It had been an immeasurable passage of time since he was in the company of a lady for more than a few moments. He immersed himself in her scent and listened to her strong, pounding heartbeat. She smelled of the forest, wood smoke, and pure womanhood with a hint of herbs like jasmine.

For a while, she said nothing. They simply shared the same space, a couple of yards apart from one another, but it was enough to make his hands shake. The demon liked the woman without even knowing her, and that should have been enough to convince him to run again. He stayed. Why in God's holy name did he stay?

She spoke, but he didn't recognize the words. The sounds rolled off her tongue in a musical, lilting way that intrigued him. It wasn't English or even the uncommon barbaric language of the north. She spoke only two words, or perhaps it was one in her language. There was a distinct cadence of French, but the pronunciation was laced with something more foreign – more exotic.

She said it again with a hint of authority in her voice as if she were demanding something of him. The demon responded to her, and the coldness washed over his eyes. He knew now that they were golden, so he would not turn to face the lady. He was tired of frightening those who might have intended good will to him, and he would not let the demon ruin this moment.

His hands curled into tight fists, and he could feel the slickness of the blood on his skin. The woman spoke again, but the words were different now. She wanted something different.

He moved forward to run again, but she hurried to his side. He shied away into the shadows and finally let her see what he was. More than anything, he was curious to see what she looked like instead.

Golden eyes glared through the darkness, the moon's glory reflecting back the demon that possessed his body and soul. The beast gazed upon the woman, who was not what he had expected her to be.

She stood some distance away, her darkened complexion declaring her foreign ancestry. She was not a slave, but neither was she a woman of status like the ladies of the royal court. Her coarse, ebony hair cascaded down her body in bounding waves while her dark eyes penetrated through to his condemned soul.

Her bare feet were set wide in a confident stance, hardly the posture of any respectable lady. A long and heavy skirt draped from her waist, obscuring any curves beneath. Yet, the collar of her blouse dipped low to expose soft skin. A wool vest hugged her breasts in place, while golden rings adorned her ears. A bandana held back her hair from tumbling into her face as the winds whipped through the trees. Coins that hung from the cloth dotted her forehead, contrasting sharply with her dark skin and glittering in the moonlight.

Her brows knitted together as she looked upon him, but he sensed no fear in her. When she stepped forward, he stepped deeper into the shadows. A low, warning growl rumbled from his throat, but he would not bare his teeth at her like the animal that he was.

She shushed him, her full lips puckering as she came closer. He wanted to flee. He should have, but the longer he gazed into her eyes, so mystic and enrapturing, he found that he couldn't move. She was beautiful and alluring beyond all reason. Never before had he seen a woman so entrancing.

The growl faded on her command, and a new sound drifted through the air that sent his body into a panic.

The woman, whom he now knew was a gypsy, began to hum a sweet tune. He shuddered, and his knees gave way beneath him. He collapsed to the ground under her spell.

"Away from me, witch," he demanded.

They were the first words he had spoken to another soul in ages. He rejected her company, but there was no ignoring the way she made him feel. Defenseless, exposed, weak. His demon no longer liked her, and for once, they were of one accord and wanted to flee from the woman.

She would not let them. Her gypsy song floated through the air and wrapped itself around his head, making him dizzy and breathless.

She crouched down to him, and her hands caressed his face, her fingers grazing over his beard and the blood that had dried across his jaw.

Upon her touch, the demon quivered and withdrew, taking the golden eyes with it to make him look a little more like a man and less like a monster.

His chest heaved for air as tears wanted to spill from his eyes. This couldn't have been a gypsy. She was an angel. Who else could wield so much power over a man such as him? He had visited priests and begged for absolution that none could provide. He had slept in the tombs of saints all across England, searching for a reprieve from the darkness that encased his soul, but he would always wake with the same sickening feeling in his gut that he was not cured. This woman could control the demon, which no one could do; not even himself.

The corners of her lips tilted into a gentle smile, one fraught with pity and her song ended on a final note that lingered in his mind.

"Who are you?" he whispered. The words came out stuttered and clumsy as if he had forgotten how to speak.

She did not reply but tucked a strand of unruly hair behind his ear to unveil some of his face. He reached up with an unsteady hand and grabbed her wrist, feeling the throbbing of her pulse in his palm. "Who are you?" he repeated more urgently.

"It does not matter who I am," she said, and he could hear the heavy influence of French in her words. "What matters is that you are loup-garou and I need your help."

He peered at her, his brown eyes narrowing in bewilderment. Loup-garou? What was that?

"What is your name?" she asked.

Unlike her, he would not hesitate to give her what she wanted. He would give her anything after the miracle she had just performed. "John. John Croxen."

CHAPTER 2

He was unlike any loup-garou she had ever seen. Though her experience was somewhat limited, the last loup-garou she met wore finer clothes and looked like more of a gentleman than John Croxen. His stench alone was detestable. His dark hair was unkempt and slick as if he hadn't washed in weeks. His beard, scraggly and tangled with blood, was not as long as some, but it was clear that John hadn't shaved in quite some time.

Yet, there was no denying that he was loup-garou. The way he tore the vagrant apart and how his eyes had glowed an animalistic gold was enough to confirm her suspicions. He was loup-garou but where was his pack? Why was he so alone and clearly detached from civilization? It was not their way, to live like beasts. Yet, here he was with a film of blood on his hands and around his mouth and nose.

Any other woman would have run in terror at the sight of him, but Annalette knew better. She saw through to the core of his strength.

"How did you do that?" he asked, each breath coming out in rasps as if he were afraid to upset the balance she had put into place.

"I know how to do many things," she replied with a smile. "And I know many things about you, loup-garou."

John's hand tightened around her wrist, and she knew that the blood of those men would make her unclean. She was unclean just for being close to this creature. If her father were to see her now, he would rage about her disregard for their way, but this was a matter of life and death. It could not be helped.

"I don't know you," John said, his deep eyes narrowing into tiny slits of distrust. "I've never met you before. How could you know anything about me?"

Annalette sat back on her heels, and John slowly released his hold upon her. "No, we have never met." It was a shame they hadn't met sooner. The way the moonlight slanted across his features, Annalette knew there was a handsome face beneath the layers of grime and filth.

She looked down to the dark red handprint around her wrist and swallowed hard. Such an impurity wouldn't have bothered her years ago, but she had forced the doctrines down her own throat, and it had paid off.

Slowly, she rose and walked toward the direction of the river with the unde-terred need to rinse away the shame. "Where do you come from, John Croxen?" she asked, keeping in mind to talk as if he were standing next to her. John could hear for miles away. There was no need to shout over her shoulder.

As she expected, John scuttled to his feet and followed her through the trees. "Why should I tell you? You won't even tell me your name."

No, she wouldn't. Not yet, anyway. The old ways were still ingrained in her thoughts. To give her name would be giving him power that he didn't deserve; not because he was a loup-garou, but because he was a *gajo* – a non-Romani.

"In time," was all she said as they came upon the spot where the two vagrants had been murdered.

The sight of their mangled bodies would only make her ill, so she turned from the corpses and traveled up river, to the north, where the water would be the purest. "My camp is not far away," she told him as she knelt by the water. "In the morning, I will tell you everything."

As she began to scrub and rub away the bits of blood upon her hands, she heard John throw the bodies into the river. It was not a proper burial, and the villagers downstream would certainly be shocked to see what floated their way overnight, but like her impurity, there was nothing to be done.

This had been an ordeal from the start. Leaving her family, following the trail of a loup-garou to the east, manipulating those men into thinking she would be a willing victim... Annalette could hardly believe she had stooped so low.

She took a deep breath, expelling the fear just as she washed away the last of the blood from her hand and wrist. If she was to succeed in her mission, she had to be the rebellious Romani girl that she once was. Her disrespect for their customs was excusable as a child, but she was a woman now and could not so easily push aside the ways of her people. Not anymore.

It had to be done. When she returned to her family, they would hear nothing about the loup-garou or the men she had placed in death's path. They would know nothing as long as she had anything to do with it.

She looked downstream and watched John scoop the river water in his hands and splash his face. Droplets dripped from his beard as he continued to clean away the blood. Annalette opened her mouth to warn him that he was washing with polluted water, but she bit her tongue.

The *gadje* did not need to know all of the Romani ways, and she could not expect a shameless people to consider such things. They would bathe with horses if the water were agreeable, regardless if it was contaminated or not.

When he dried his face with the hem of his shirt, she caught a glimpse of the strong body that lay beneath his beggar clothes. He certainly had the physique of a loup-garou. It was unlike any she had ever seen on a mortal man. Not even the most handsome man in her clan could boast such a body as John had.

Daily labor and hard work could not produce muscles so defined. It was as if he were the masterpiece of a sculptor. It was only a glimpse, but Annalette felt a wave of heat course through her. It was as if she had been left outside in the snow all her life and then suddenly brought inside to warm herself by a roaring campfire.

Her body flushed even greater when he looked to her with a clean face that could not disappoint. She quickly turned her eyes away, but the damage had been done and could not be reversed. A bit of her childish innocence had been chipped away by his roguish looks. It frightened her, at first, to think that there was something waiting underneath her pious concern for customs. A wildness, perhaps, that she had once known in her youth, but buried away for years.

Only John could hammer away the rest of her defenses, but she could not let him get close. He was too valuable and her mission too precarious to allow herself such indulgences. Her father always told her that the Romani never associate with the *gadje* unless it was absolutely necessary and only for a short time.

Well, this was necessary and if Annalette had her way, they would be on their way to Canterbury right then and there. She had to draw him in slowly. To give him all the answers now would be to give up her leverage in the bargain that would need to be made.

Strengthening her resolve, she looked back to the loup-garou. "Will you sleep by my camp?"

John sighed and looked to the forest, indecision and unease in his eyes that sent a streak of panic through her. If John didn't consider her to be worth his time, then he could easily leave, and though she could track him, there was no telling what it would take to gain his interest again.

It was already clear that he was lost, confused, and if she were any judge of character, Annalette would have ventured to say that he was frightened. Of what, she didn't know, but she would have the answer he needed more than anyone else.

"No," he finally replied, his deep voice crashing through her mind with foul news.

"It's not far," she offered. "Just upstream."

"I will sleep at the edge of the wood." He turned his eyes upon her once more, and she tried to breathe again. "Do I have your word that we will speak in the morning?"

She could already see the questions forming in his eyes. Though she wanted to rejoice in her victory, it would be premature. John needed to trust her, and right now, he was curious more than anything. She could accept that.

With a nod, she stood and set herself upon the path to her campsite along the river. Whether she would get any sleep was uncertain.

Dawn brought with it the dew of the morning that settled over the leaves and blades of grass. Fog drifted over the River Stour as frogs and other creatures stirred from their nests. Birds chirped their cheerful morning song, but it did nothing for John's troubled heart.

He sat under the shade of a twisted and knotted oak and watched the gypsy sleep. All night, his stare was fixed upon her slumbering figure, his mind hard at work to solve the mystery before she awoke but nothing made sense anymore.

Whoever she was, she refused to give him more information. John didn't even know her name.

John should have left her the moment he knew she was asleep. He should have moved on from this place before the bodies of the two vagrants were discovered downstream. Villagers might try to investigate and search for the killer along the river. He stayed for only two reasons.

She called him something. *Loup-garou*. He knew now that it was French, but what little French he had learned second-hand from the tutors at the manor had fallen out of his head a long time ago. The word seeped into his thoughts like a poison and begged him to stay. If he remained with the gypsy, perhaps she would keep her promise and tell him everything, but how much could he trust the word of a gypsy?

Perhaps she would tell him what a loup-garou was and why she had called him one. There was hope in this; that she could explain his sickness and perhaps provide him a way to redemption like no other priest could. If he could escape hellfire, he would stay by the river for the next one thousand years waiting for the answers.

The other reason he stayed was far more enigmatic. The woman, whoever she was, had an ambiguity about her that he couldn't turn away from. If she was a gypsy, where was her clan and why was she traveling alone?

Queen Mary had decreed last winter that all gypsies were to be executed and anyone known to be harboring gypsies or associated with them would be punished severely. If this woman was fleeing for her life, John should have been the patriotic Englishman and brought her to the constable in Wye, so she could receive her punishment.

It was commonly known that the gypsies were a wicked people. From what he had heard, they were nothing but thieves who could twist the minds of ignorant peasants for their own purposes. Their women were sultry and seductive, while their men could kill and maim without mercy.

He had only seen gypsies from afar. They hardly seemed to be the same people that gossipers whispered about in the streets. The gypsies danced and sang around campfires, but it was not in tribute to some pagan god. They celebrated life and the company of their clan. Perhaps it was this bias that stayed John's hand of judgment upon the mysterious gypsy. He had to know why he felt the instinctive need to protect her and why she needed his help.

Perhaps it was how her body curved in such an alluring way. It called to his manhood with its siren song, but he resisted, even as he watched the way her chest rose and fell with each steady breath. He could not let himself fall into the trap of lust. Otherwise, the rumors about the gypsies would be true.

He heard her heartbeat quicken as she rose from her makeshift bed. The thin blanket couldn't have been comfortable, but perhaps she was used to sleeping on the ground just as he was. John grew still as the gypsy looked around and cast her captivating gaze over her shoulder.

They locked stares, and John's chest ached. Even in the daylight, he couldn't deny that she was a handsome woman, even if she was a foreigner.

"Sleep well, gypsy?" he asked.

He didn't mean it in offense, but her dark eyes shot daggers at him, pinning him where he sat. It was clear that she did not take kindly to something in his tone or his question.

She stood and straightened out her thick skirt before moving toward the river's edge. John rose to follow as soon as her gaze released him.

"Will you not speak to me?" he questioned.

As soon as John realized that the woman was disrobing, he staggered backward and fled to the tree line once more. He averted his eyes out of respect, but he would not give her peace.

"The least you could do is give me your name now that it's morning," he called out to her.

Even a single word would have been better than silence. He had lived so long with only the sound of his own demons circling in his head. An utterance from any kind soul would be like the ringing of church bells to frighten away the evil.

He listened to the whisper of fabric dropping to the earth and the sound of the river receiving her naked body. Water sloshed, but he would not turn for anything, not even if she asked, though every sinful need begged him to steal an eyeful while he had the chance.

Resigned to silence once more, John sighed and leaned against the trunk of an elm to wait.

It was some time before he heard the woman take up her clothes again.

"How long have you been loup-garou?" she asked, her sweet and lyrical voice like a balm to his tired spirit.

"What is that?" he questioned hastily, his gaze turning to the blue morning sky. "I don't know what a loup-garou is, much less how long I have been one."

She approached, and he could smell the tang of river water in her long hair. When she came into view, he was grateful to see that the gypsy was fully clothed, though the fabric clung to her damp skin.

"You are loup-garou," she said, her hands wringing out her hair that had been tossed over her shoulder. "You are a man and a wolf in one, are you not?"

John scoffed at the very idea. "I am possessed by a demon. I am not a loup-garou."

The gypsy giggled and shook her head, the golden earrings tapping against her jaw. "No, the wolf is not a demon. It is an aide."

John passed a hand over his face and rubbed at his eyes. "You're talking rubbish, gypsy. I don't understand."

She stomped her bare foot into the grass like a defiant child. "Do not call me that. I am not gypsy. I am Romani."

He recognized that term from pieces of conversation and understood it was what the gypsies called themselves. John jerked his chin at her. "Then give me a better name to call you. Do you have a name?"

The woman seemed to debate with herself as if wondering whether to trust him or not. If she didn't trust John, then it was a wonder she let him stay with her while she slept. Any vagabond could have stolen what few goods she had, or taken her in the carnal fashion as those men tried to do. Yet she allowed him to remain. Why would she not trust him with her name?

"Annalette," she said.

For a moment, he wondered if it was another foreign Romani word. "Does that mean something in your language?"

She flipped her hand at him, and a stray droplet of water cooled his cheek. "That is not important. What is important is that you help me."

John shook his head. "I'm not doing anything for you until you explain to me what a loup-garou is."

"I told you," she insisted. "It is a man and a wolf in one. You are a loup-garou. Your eyes, they were like a wolf's last night."

"I'm telling you, it's not a wolf. It's a demon."

She sighed and cast her eyes heavenward. "You English and your demons and angels. The wolf is not a demon. It is a spirit of nature."

John looked away, frustrated by her lack of understanding. They were from different walks of life, different worlds entirely, but how could he explain to her what he had known to be true for so long? "Wolves are beasts. They don't possess a person. Demons do."

"A loup-garou embodies the spirits of both man and beast." She moved to stand in his field of vision. "Once a month, you shift into a beast, yes?"

John swallowed hard, remembering all the times he had fallen senseless. He would wake up next to a fresh kill, normally something larger than his usual prey, and he would be naked. Each month he had to steal new clothes or think ahead to undress before the shift took hold. Such a painful and frightening change.

At first, it took him by surprise. Then, over the many years of living with his demons, he learned to predict their movements and when they would choose to emerge and wreak havoc on his body. There were signs that hinted to the coming of the devil in him. Thankfully, he had a few weeks left before it would come again.

He nodded to her question.

"And you cannot eat as you once did, yes?"

"I get sick if I eat anything that grows from the earth besides fruit." He wasn't too afraid to admit that much. He had known of others who could not eat certain foods because it would disagree with them. Just one bite of a potato would weaken him for days.

Annalette nodded and smiled as if she were excited that he might finally understand. She would be disappointed. "Yes, and you can hear and smell things over long distances."

"The demon makes me do all of those things," he pleaded, still unconvinced that it was a wolf or beast of any kind. The demon made him behave like a wolf, but that was not the same.

"It is not a demon, John. You are a loup-garou. Isn't there a name for this in your language? Wolf-man?"

His face wrinkled in disgust. "Werewolf? The full moon has no sway over me," he explained, recalling the frightening legends and stories that the old, grisly cook used to tell him. They were stories to make him behave, nothing more. Werewolves devoured babies and disobedient children on the nights of the full moon. Although he had woken up to plenty of severed heads of sheep and deer, he had never awoken to stare into the lifeless eyes of a child or infant.

"That does not matter," she said. "The wolf doesn't care about the moon. It only cares about the hunt and once a month, it must run free. Do you remember anything when the wolf comes?"

John paused, his lips parted as he was ready to tell her that he remembered nothing during those dreadful nights. He thought it was because God didn't want him to know what terrible sins he committed, or that the devil wanted to keep him blind to his atrocities to maintain his power over John.

"How do you know any of this?" John asked, his tone fraught with frustration.

Annalette crossed her arms over her chest. "My uncle was loup-garou. I helped him keep it a secret from our family. When they discovered that he was impure, they renounced him as a Romani."

She spoke so coldly as if it meant nothing to her, but he could sense the deep sadness in her as keenly as if she were weeping to his face. It was another of the "gifts" from the devil.

John wanted to pity her uncle, but there was little left in his heart for such petty emotions. "You have my condolences," he said with a complete lack of sympathy.

"I learned what he could and could not eat; I learned how he controlled the wolf spirit, so he could live a normal life. He was bitten by another loup-garou before I was born and left for dead. But the wolf spirit healed his body, so it could live inside him. Were you bitten?"

Her eyes roamed over John's body from head to foot, but she would find nothing to answer her question. There was a flicker of some emotion in her eyes that caught his particular attention. It wasn't the scrutinizing look of an inspector, but the leering gaze of a harlot.

"No," he replied with a sneer, wondering why she assessed him so.

"So, you were born a loup-garou?"

John clenched his fists as his lips drew into a grim line. "I was not born anything. When will you understand that it's a demon, not a wolf?"

Annalette threw up her hands and bowed her head in dramatic expression, the coins on her headband clinking together. "Very well. You are possessed by a demon. It is pointless to argue with a *gajo*."

"I thought I was a loup-garou?" John blinked at the new and unfamiliar word.

Annalette flashed him a cunning smile. "I thought you said you were demon-possessed?"

A muscle in John's jaw tensed at her sly trick. He had to admit that some of her story was compelling, but how far could he trust a gypsy? They were known to be thieves and murderers, hence why the queen wanted them expelled from the country. Such vermin had no place in civilized society. Then again, neither did he.

"Why do you need my help?" he asked, folding his arms over his broad chest.

Annalette turned and walked away to her makeshift camp with a look that challenged him to follow. "My brother has been arrested. I've heard that he's being held in Canterbury and will be executed soon. I must go to save him."

John wanted to laugh at her arrogance. "Do you really think you can just walk into Canterbury as a gyp-"

She shot him a fiery glare, and he avoided his blunder.

"... as a Romani woman and simply ask for them to release your brother?"

Annalette began to gather her supplies and roll them methodically into her pack. "No. That is why I need your help."

He watched her skillfully fold her blanket and slip it into her bag, mindful to keep her cooking utensils away from her bedding. "What can I possibly do?"

Annalette stood and shouldered the bag with a grunt. "You have what I don't. You can go into town like any other man and negotiate. If being a man will not suffice, then you will be a beast for me."

John looked down to his soiled clothes, discolored with the stains of blood and earth. "If I walk into town wearing this shirt, no one will speak to me. You do realize that I haven't been a member of respectable society for a long time?"

Annalette tilted her head to the side, gazing at him with a wistful look of curiosity. "How long?"

John stared at her, wondering how much he should divulge to a perfect stranger. She was the first woman to show any hint of compassion for his plight. There was no fear in her eyes when she faced the demon that lurked within him. Loup-garou or demon-possessed, she seemed to accept him. For that, he knew he could tell her more.

"One hundred years or more. The demon has kept me alive this long, my soul bound to the world of the living until judgment day."

Annalette smiled and shook her head ruefully, not showing a hint of surprise at his confession. "You will not live forever, John Croxen, but the wolf is keeping you alive for a purpose. You must find it."

She turned and began to walk upriver, headed northeast toward the road that led to Canterbury.

John stood by the river and watched her walk on, her hips swinging with each step.

He had heard rumors that the gypsies could tell one's fortune. It was their gift from the devil himself. If she had a second-sight, or if she was also bound by a pact with Satan, then she understood him better than anyone else in the world. Yet, if she were a mortal like any other, and if she were telling the truth about her uncle, Annalette would be a valuable source of information. She could teach him far more than he could ever learn on his own. Her talk of purpose was intriguing, but the wealth of knowledge that she could provide was more so. If a century of roaming the countryside like a bitter ghost would not yield answers for him, perhaps this gypsy could.

John rushed forward with his inhuman speed and snatched up Annalette's pack. He bore the load and walked alongside her.

Her beguiling lips curled into a knowing grin, and they journeyed along the river toward whatever fortune or destruction awaited them.

CHAPTER 3

"You have been loup-garou for over one hundred years and only changed once a month?" Annalette cried, disturbing a flock of birds that were perched in the canopy of trees over the trail John had led them to.

John shot her a heated glare. "Why would I let the demon take dominion over my body more than once?"

She pinched at the corner of her eyes as she tried to keep a tight hold of what little patience she had. "If you don't shift enough, the wolf will become unruly and discouraged. It will cease to give you life. Do you want to die?"

"Dying would be better than living in this hell," John retorted as he adjusted the pack's strap over his shoulder. She couldn't ignore the way his words were saturated in self-loathing. "Do you know what it's like to have this immense evil inside with no way to rid yourself of it?"

In all truth, she did not, but she knew how torn her uncle, Nicu, had been before he found some solace in another loup-garou. She remembered the way Nicu would stare into nothingness, his thoughts far away from the *vitsa*. His heart had never been in their celebrations. The wolf made him long for the wild, which he resented. To a Romani, family was everything, or at least it was supposed to be.

Annalette turned to him and held up her hand to stop him from continuing down the path. "We must remedy this," she asserted. Before he had time to argue, she reached out and gripped the sensitive part of his shoulder that Nicu had shown her long ago.

John closed his eyes tight and roared like a beast as the pain must have coursed through his body. If he would not willingly shift, then Annalette would have to coax the wolf into the open. She had heard the stories of loups-garous who could not shift after a certain age because of their negligent years where they did not nurture and encourage the wolf within them. If John did not make sure his wolf was satisfied, he would not live as long as most in these desperate times.

The formidable man who was nearly twice her size, crumbled to his knees and dropped her pack to the ground. To see him kneel before her was oddly rewarding. To know that she could make a man so defenseless with just a touch sent skitters of pleasure down her spine.

If what Nicu said was true, pressuring this one muscle would inspire the shift. However, if what John said was true, he would be uncontrollable in his loup-garou form without the experience he needed to command the wolf spirit.

It might not have been wise, but Annalette was the only one who could teach him to control the beast. She was the only one who could show him what he had gone without for so long and it was her key to gaining his trust. With her knowledge of loups-garous, she was sure that she could defend herself, but he could easily kill her in one powerful swipe of his claws.

In the midst of his pain, John reached out and tore her hand away from his shoulder. With a look of utter bafflement and shock, he held his tender flesh. His golden eyes lifted to stare at her. Such beautiful eyes, more beautiful than they had been on her uncle or any other loup-garou she had met.

In fact, everything about John was beautiful from his sturdy body to the soul that personified it. She saw it gleaming from him like a beacon of wholesomeness in a sea of depravity. Even in his wild state, Annalette couldn't help but admire the one who was more in balance with nature than any other human in the world.

Ever since Nicu came to her in her youth and revealed his secret, she had become enamored by the power and mystery of the loups-garous. There was so much she could show John if only he would let himself believe that he was not cursed. Indeed, he was blessed, though the Romani would never admit that.

"What did you do?" he questioned.

"It's a trick my uncle taught me. It can cripple a loup-garou, but it can also bring the wolf out into the open. The wolf only comes out when it feels threatened, or it needs to hunt, but, if you can make peace with the animal, you can command it to come out by your own will."

She took a few steps back to let him breathe and recover.

"How do you know so much? Are you a loup-garou too?" he asked, gasping from the pain.

Annalette smiled and shook her head, her black hair swaying around her shoulders. "No, I am not. Though, I envy you and all other loups-garous like you. Females are not born loup-garou, even if our fathers were, and we cannot be bitten or we will die. My uncle tried to turn his wife into a loup-garou and failed."

It was before she was born, but the way Nicu told the story, one might think that it happened just yesterday. Though he was loup-garou, there was no limit to his grief and compassion for life. Killing her had forced him to admit that he needed a companion; someone to look after him and ensure that he never attempted to kill again.

Annalette fulfilled her job well, but it was not enough to save Nicu from her family.

John cleared his throat and stood on shaky limbs. "Did you learn all of this from your uncle?"

"I did. He learned it from a loup-garou alpha. Though, some things we learned by accident."

He propped his hands on his hips and looked to her, his murky brown eyes glimmering in the sun. His eyes reminded her of the color of rich, fertile soil. "An alpha?" he asked.

Annalette crossed her arms over her stomach, willing the aching in her lower belly to subside. John could send her heart reeling with just a subtle look that meant nothing, and yet everything to her. "Yes. Just as wolves have a pack, so do loups-garous. In a pack, there are those who are more dominant, more powerful. They are called alphas. Below the alphas are the protectors, the betas. They protect the pack and the alpha from danger."

John eyed her as he reached down to take up her pack, the one he had dropped when she grabbed his shoulder. "I thought the alpha was more powerful? Why does he need a beta?"

"The alpha is concerned with internal affairs. He must keep his pack in order and under control. The beta is concerned with external affairs, keeping the outside world from harming the pack. Below all of them is the omega and he is sometimes the most important. He keeps strife from destroying his pack from the inside."

"Isn't that what the alpha does?"

She shook her head, realizing how complex the loup-garou pack was, now that she tried to explain it. "Not exactly. Here is an example. If you are the alpha of a pack and there is a disagreement between a few other pack members, you can try to settle the conflict. If you are unsuccessful, the omega can step in and distract them from the problem. Or, if the alpha is becoming overbearing or harsh, the omega can bring the error to his attention."

John sighed and glanced away. Annalette could sense his annoyance, but she also knew that he was listening. He needed to know just as badly as she needed to tell him. Though, she had to be careful not to reveal too much too soon. If she told him everything, then he might leave her before they arrived in Canterbury.

The idea of John abandoning her to the forest was almost more than she could bear. She took a deep breath to quell the anxious thoughts and waited, watching the way his face pinched into a thoughtful look. It was as if he were trying to make sense of so many things at one time.

"So, there are more like me? More loups-garous?"

She drew closer, stepping slowly as if she were approaching a nervous horse. "Yes, many more. But they're in hiding, just as you are." Annalette stopped when she realized that John was keeping his distance from her. For every step she took forward, he took a step back. "What is it?"

John cast her a wary gaze, his lovely eyes looking her up and down. "You do strange things to me. Last night, you bewitched me with your song, and today you try to bring out the demon. You can command this evil better than I can with your gypsy trickery."

That word. Annalette fumed at the mere sound of it. She heard it muttered by the peasants under their breaths and shouted as insults from across the streets. The word was synonymous with evil and a false conception of who the Romani people were, but she couldn't expect a *gajo* to know the truth. She would have to show him that the Romani were not as they appeared. Not entirely.

"It's not trickery. My uncle taught me how to soothe the wolf. That was the song you heard last night."

"Your uncle taught you many things, but how can you be certain? How do you know it's a wolf and not a demon?"

Annalette inhaled deeply, remembering the long nights she stayed up with Nicu while he hunted across the Scottish moors under the light of the moon and stars. She remembered his loup-garou form and how monstrous it had seemed at first. As she grew accustomed to its shape, she thought it to be magical and one of the most wondrous things she would ever behold. That was until she saw John. He would learn to embrace the beast as well. He had to, or he would die.

"I've seen a loup-garou transform," she proclaimed as if it were a thing to take special pride in. "It is a wolf. Surely, you must suspect that it is not a demon?"

John shook his head, but she could see the hesitance in his stare. "What this evil asks of me can only be the product of the devil."

She gestured to him, beckoning for the details. "Like what? Tell me what the demon says to you, and I'll show you it's a wolf instead."

The determined set of John's jaw told her that she had ventured into a den of serpents.

"To start, it forces me to eat the uncooked flesh of animals. No Christian man would consume so much blood and flesh unless he was possessed."

Honestly, Annalette expected a stronger argument. "The wolf needs you to eat as he does. You can eat cooked meats, but it will not give you the same nourishment as raw meat. While some loups-garous do kill and devour the flesh of humans, most do not. I know you haven't eaten a human."

A deep frown creased his forehead. "How do you know?"

Annalette smiled, glad that he asked. "I can see it in your eyes. If you did, you would not be so stable in your mind. Eating the flesh of a human can make a loup-garou insane. He becomes merciless and far more aggressive than a loup-garou who has not."

A shadow passed over John's face, and his gaze became distant, just as Nicu's had so many times while sitting around the campfire. Back then, Nicu had told Annalette that he was dwelling on the tragedy of his own life and existence. She would have given anything to know what John was thinking in that moment as he whispered the word, "Insane."

Annalette knew that she wasn't wrong. John had not killed a human, but something had pulled at his heart when she spoke of it. Something deep within her heart begged her to charge forward and wrap her arms around the loup-garou until the pain melted away, but it was far too soon for intimacy. He wouldn't even let her get close.

"Did your uncle eat human flesh?" he finally asked, dispelling the dark thoughts from his mind and returning from the miserable place he had briefly visited somewhere in his past.

She tossed her hair over her shoulder. "No. But the alpha he met with knew a loup-garou who did. Such loups-garous become reckless, and hunters track them down."

"Hunters? Like the royal hunters?"

It occurred to her that they weren't progressing down the path and time was slipping through their fingers. The longer it took for them to get to Canterbury, the slimmer her chances became of saving her brother. They had to reach the outskirts of the city before nightfall, or her plan would fail.

She turned and continued northeast. The road they walked upon had once been a busy trail, but now nature was reclaiming what man had paved through its heart.

Just as she predicted, John obediently followed like a trained dog. "No. There are hunters who search out the supernatural. There are those who know how to kill you and will stop at nothing until every loup-garou is dead."

John came up alongside her. "How can a loup-garou be killed?" he asked.

Annalette kept her eyes on the trail ahead, though she longed to meet his eager eyes. She didn't want to believe that John was only interested in what she knew. It had been a long time since any man had the faintest attraction to her, but the longer they talked of loups-garous and the more diffident he was to be near her, the clearer it became that he was using her just as she was using him.

She had to gain his trust, just as she had gained the trust of the men the night before. Their lifeless faces flashed in her mind's eye, and she quickly pushed back the images. No amount of reasoning in the world could justify her facilitation of their deaths. They were dead because of her. They lived upon the fringes of society, but they did not deserve death, especially by the hand of a loup-garou.

She couldn't think of that now. She had to stay focused on her mission. Earn the loup-garou's trust so she could free her brother. That's all she wanted, and even if it meant killing hundreds more, she would get what she wanted.

"You may have noticed that you can heal from most anything. If your skin is cut, it heals. If your bones are broken, they will mend without the aid of a physician. But if a limb is severed, it will not grow back. If you are decapitated, you will die."

"I heard that silver hurts a werewolf," he said. "Is it the same for a loup-garou?"

She nodded. "Yes. It burns you like fire. And there are plants, such as wolfsbane, that are poisonous to your kind."

Annalette stopped. "If you were not bitten, then you were born a loup-garou," she reflected as she looked to him. "Where is your father? He should have told you all of these things."

John's brows lowered in hatred and looked to Annalette with brooding eyes. "I did not know my father. If I did, he might have taught me these things. But God has not been so kind as to give me a life of ease and comfort."

There was something more. She was not the only one withholding the truth.

Annalette's heart bled for the loup-garou. There was much pain and sorrow within his heart, and although she could teach him many things, she had come so late. Decades had been spent in darkness, and every voice in his own head screamed their lies that he was not worthy of salvation. If only he could understand that he was forever transcendent beyond salvation. The favor of God did not matter so much for a loup-garou as it did for a mortal man.

"We are many stars scattered in the sight of God," she said. "He has been more than kind to you. This is a gift. A blessing. Not a curse."

John scowled. "Is that what your uncle believed when he was cast from your family?"

Her eyes searched his for the kindness that he had once shown her, but something of the wolf had finally emerged, though his eyes were no longer gold. He had never been part of a pack, but it was clear that he would be an alpha one day. Despite his biting question, she smiled and slowly set back on the trail.

"My family saw him as unclean. He was *marime*. It is a word that our people use to describe someone who has committed a sin or defiled themselves. Like the hen, who is a bird that doesn't fly; or the frog who both swims and walks on land, they saw the loup-garou as an unnatural blend of two things that should never be blended."

"But, you still helped him. Why would you do that if he was unclean?"

She smiled to herself. "Because I did not care about the traditions at the time. I was an obstinate child. When my father told me not to climb a tree, I climbed it anyway. When my mother wanted me to help with washing the clothes in the river, I would wander off and chase bugs."

"It sounds like you were quite the handful," John remarked with an amused upturn in his voice.

"Yes, I was. And it was my wildness that convinced my uncle that I would be a good companion for him." She sobered quickly when she thought of his trial, when they called a *kris* to decide his fate within their *vitsa*. "I do not agree with my family. They didn't see how magnificent he was as a loup-garou. They only saw the beast and scorned it because they thought it was a *mulo* – an evil spirit."

"A demon," John corrected.

Annalette looked to him and saw a sparkle of humor in the way the corner of his lips tilted upward. He tried to turn the tables, but she would not fight the current as he did. She rolled her eyes. "I suppose they would agree with that, but I don't. He was not possessed, and neither are you. *Mulo* or demon."

"Did they know you disagreed with their verdict?" he asked, kicking at a rock along the path to send it rolling through the grass ahead of them.

Finally, their conversation had turned to her. For how long, Annalette wasn't sure, but it was a good sign that John wanted to know more about her. Perhaps he would drop his defenses just long enough for her to squeeze through.

"No," she replied. "Under my uncle's warning, I did not speak my mind. Besides, a woman cannot speak during a trial. I haven't seen him since, but I'm sure he is well. He had talked about traveling across the sea to France, where our family is from, but I'm not sure if he ever made it."

A beat of silence passed between them before John inquired, "If you're from France, then why are you here? You must know about the edict that all gypsies are to be deported from the country."

Annalette sighed. "I know," she said. "The Romani roam. It's what we do. We find where we are welcome and Scotland offered our people a safe place to exist. The only reason we have come this far south was because my other uncle, on my father's side, has fallen ill."

She looked to John, wondering how much she should divulge. It might have been reasonable to assume that if she confessed more of her own past, then he would feel more open to disclosing the secrets he had kept hidden.

"It's customary among our people to come to the bedside of an ailing family member. It helps the spirit transition from this life into the next. If there exists any animosity between the dying, it's expected for the offender to go and ask them for forgiveness. Before I was born, my father and his brother did not agree on coming to Scotland. The *vitsa* – our clan – was divided. My father wanted to come to his bedside to ask forgiveness for splitting up the family."

"But how did your brother get arrested?"

Anger burned in her chest for the injustice and disgrace to her *vitsa*. None of them had been captured, but one simple mistake became their undoing. Now more of their family was scattered, and Annalette could feel the weight of the strain on her family ties.

"We were separated from the family for a few days looking for work around Canterbury, and one of the townspeople reported him to the constable. He was arrested and thrown into the Westgate prison."

"What about your family? Why aren't they helping you?"

She didn't have to see his face to know that John was growing indignant at the idea of a woman traveling alone.

She looked heavenward, remembering the terrible fight she had with her father before she left their camp. "They have already given up hope that he can be rescued. According to our customs, I cannot say the name of the dead, but I know that Gallius is alive. I will not mourn his death until I see his body. Against my father's wishes, I have decided to go after him on my own."

John was quiet for some time until a single sound roused him from his silence. "You're hungry," he stated.

There was no use denying it. With his keen hearing, he surely heard her belly growl. "I have not eaten since yesterday afternoon."

John pointed ahead. "If we continue on the Pilgrim's Way, we will come to Chilham. There's bound to be a bakery there that you can steal from."

Annalette huffed and reached up to unfasten one of the gold coins from her bandana. "Contrary to what you have been told, my people do not steal. We don't take bread that we can easily make ourselves." She handed him the coin. "If we need something, we buy it honestly."

John took the coin and examined it, letting the sunlight glint off its polished face.

"Of course, if you're to go into town, we may need to clean you up a bit," she remarked, looking up and down the loup-garou's ragged appearance.

His clothes needed to be washed, and though there was no time to mend the tears and holes, she would make time for him to shave the thick beard that covered the lower half of his face. If he walked into a bakery looking like a vagabond, they would not serve him, money or not. Though they hadn't reached their destination, she needed him to look as inconspicuous as possible.

CHAPTER 4

John brushed his hand against his shaven cheek. The dagger Annalette had supplied him was sharp, but still left behind a shallow layer of stubble. Yet it was an improvement upon the scraggly beard that he had grown over the last year or so since he had shaved last.

His clothes, though still worn thin in some spots and torn in several others, were clean and free of the blood and dirt stains that had accumulated from weeks of living in the forest. Annalette's superb washing skills aided him in looking presentable to the villagers he walked amongst.

Chilham was a quiet town along the River Stour, but still a far cry from the secluded nature to which he had become accustomed. Mothers with their babies in tow walked past shops whilst running errands. Craftsmen such as tailors, cobblers, furniture makers, and leather tanners toiled away in their shops and tended to their customers.

Merchant carts rattled through the streets, their mules hauling the heavy loads of wheat and other goods waiting to be sold. He could hear the ping of a hammer striking an iron anvil as a blacksmith on the other side of the town worked diligently at his trade, with the hissing and crackling of firewood in his forge to keep him company.

It had been a long time since he had ventured this deep into any village. Most of the time, he kept his distance from humans, and skirted around towns to avoid being seen. He had little reason to visit a village unless it was to steal – for lack of a better word – what he needed. A shirt here, a pair of trousers there, but nothing that was irreplaceable.

His memories of the last town he visited for an extended period of time were not happy ones. He could still hear the screams of the women as he ran through the streets of London, half naked and crazed with the broken chains attached to shackles clinking against the cobblestone with each step. When he fled to the safety of the woods that night, he vowed never to step foot amongst the humans again. The risk was too great. How the tables had turned.

John had swiped a cloak from a homestead just outside the town and turned up the collar of the coat to conceal some of his face. Though, with his wild hair pulled back by a cord Annalette had loaned him, he still didn't look the part of an average citizen.

He spotted a young child turn and point at his appalling appearance as he pulled on his mother's skirt. John could hear the boy's hasty and childish babbling words from across the square, but he pretended not to notice the ridicule. Adults gave him similar looks, but they were prudent enough to keep their opinions to themselves. In the past, he would have cowered under such scrutiny, but, today, his once raw and sensitive disposition had been hardened by a life of solitude. Their opinions no longer mattered.

While John followed the scent of dough and flour, he thought of Annalette's words and how her simple, yet firm grip on his shoulder had pulled the demon so close to the surface. He had been terrified that he would hurt her, that he would lash out with gnarly claws and slit her throat. He had never felt the demon come out in the daylight. The evil restricted itself to the dark hours of the night.

It made him second guess everything he had known, everything he had been taught as a young boy sitting in the church pews. With his mother on one side and grandmother on the other, he had listened to the booming voice of the priest and his sermons on hellfire and damnation for the wicked. When he was possessed, he was sure that only an act of God would save him from the hell that awaited him behind the veil of death. He knew that demons took the body for its own and would not subjugate itself to any other authority.

When Annalette gripped his shoulder, John felt the fear of violence rise in him. He took hold of the demon, and for the first time, he made an effort to force it back into hiding. He succeeded, meaning that the demon was not the all-devouring plague of the soul that he had once believed.

After over one hundred years of struggling to understand the demon and his special affliction, John found himself thirsty for more knowledge about these loups-garous.

John took another step toward the possibility that he was a loup-garou, just as Annalette had said. If that were true, he was still cursed. Not as a bastard, susceptible to the influences of the demonic realm by the unfortunate circumstances of his birth, but in another way that still had much to do with his absent father. His sins were still John's to deal with.

He found the bakery marked by a plaque that swung above the door. An image of a steaming pie was carved into the wooden panel. It was common enough, but when John placed his hand on the doorknob, a strange sensation passed through him so suddenly that a gasp escaped his lips.

It was as if a thousand needles were gently pricking into his skull. A surge of alarm rushed down his spine, and he released the handle. The sensation did not fade as he stood near the threshold, staring at his mucky feet, but the longer he waited, the feeling did not pass.

For a moment, he wondered if it had something to do with the effects of the shoulder grab Annalette had exacted upon him earlier. This, however, wasn't painful and though the demon in him stirred, it did not writhe or jolt into action as it had before. This was something entirely different that he had never suffered before.

"Come in, whoever you are," a voice called from beyond the door.

John braced himself and entered.

The scent of freshly baked bread permeated the air, mingling with the spices of custards and fruity jams. Shelves against the walls were stocked with rolls and loafs of all shapes and sizes. Two brick ovens were in full operation toward the back of the shop, while a long table had been set out, covered in white flour and littered with the assorted tools of the trade.

A man stood behind the table, a rolling pin between his hands as he flattened out a white ball of dough. His sleeves were rolled up to reveal his thick arms and his apron was dusted with excess flour. Dark locks of hair were pulled back behind his head, but some flour had managed to make its way onto his cheeks and in his hair.

John stood still as the baker's blue eyes fixed on him with an intensity that set him on guard. Though there was a wide window that allowed the baker to watch the streets, John had not passed by it, and there was no way the man could have looked through the solid door. How could he have known that John was standing there a moment ago?

The baker smirked and stopped what he was doing to wipe his white powdered hands on his apron. As he straightened, John realized how well-built the man was. One didn't become so strong by kneading dough all day.

"Can I help you?" the baker asked.

John moved forward and took a long loaf off one of the shelves and approached the baker with the gold coin that Annalette had given him. "I just need this," he said.

It had been a long time since he had been a customer to any merchant or artisan. Mostly, his mother or the manor's cook had sent him into town to fetch a head of cabbage or package of beef from the local market, but back then he didn't need to speak to the vendors. They knew what he needed, and the exchange was made quickly. They didn't want to talk to the runty boy who had no father and served a local landlord in Shrewsbury.

The baker gave him a peculiar look and then examined the coin. "I'm sorry, I don't take gypsy money."

John looked at the face of the coin, but couldn't see what denounced it as gypsy money. It appeared to be like any other gold coin. Then again, it had been a while since he had seen any form of currency up close. He offered it back to the baker. "It's not gypsy money," he asserted.

Piercing eyes narrowed on John. "Sure, it is. It reeks of gypsy hands. You should have known that. Either way, a crown is far too much for a single loaf of bread. I charge tuppence."

John curled the coin back into his palm and gripped it tightly. He wanted to ask how the man could smell Annalette on the coin and why he even cared that it belonged to a gypsy at all.

When he didn't reply, the baker leaned his hands against the edge of his work-table. "Friend, if you're trying to protect the gypsy, you need not fear me. Only ask, and it shall be given."

"Given?" John questioned.

The baker sighed. "There's another of our kind who is a mysgather in this town. I happen to know that he checks all of the coinage that comes through his station. If I pay my taxes with a coin that smells of gypsies, the constable will be told, and my business will be confiscated from me," he explained. "Not only that, but I know you don't need the bread and if you are desperate enough to use tainted money to buy this gypsy food, I admire your courage. Take what you want, as a token of brotherhood."

John's face wrinkled in utter confusion. He spoke of brotherhood, but John knew he did not have any siblings. And when he mentioned *their kind*, John was completely lost. "What do you know?"

The baker's smile faded. "Isn't it obvious?"

Blue eyes began to glow the devilish gold that he had known for over a hundred years. He had seen similar golden eyes stare back at him from the reflection in rivers and lakes in his wanderings. John staggered back and gaped. He had never seen the demon manifest that way in one besides himself, but the baker remained in full control of his faculties. He didn't snarl like a beast or launch himself at John to tear out his throat. He simply stood there, staring with the eyes of the demon. The eyes of the wolf.

"Impossible," John whispered as he tried to quiet his thundering heart.

"It is quite possible, my friend." The golden hue spiraled back into the black-ness at the center of his eyes to reinstate the human blue color. "How long have you been a wolf? If you're shocked by my display, you must be fairly young. Were you bitten?"

John snapped his teeth together. The baker was not the first one to ask such a strange question that day. His eyes darted toward the door and storefront window.

"Don't worry," the baker laughed. "No one is around to hear our conversation."

John looked back, but shook his head, too dazed to even consider having a conversation with the man. "I can't stay, I'm sorry."

And with that, he turned and hurried out of the shop. In his quick getaway, he nearly collided with a well-dressed lord and his consort.

"Watch where you're going, peasant!" the pompous man shouted.

In a fury, John growled and sped away. He could hear the baker calling out to him from the open doorway of the shop, but he would not stop. Not for man and not for a werewolf.

He was soon out of town, the bread loaf tucked against his side underneath the coat to stay warm. The heady scent of rain had descended over the area less than an hour ago, and he knew that a shower was soon to come.

He found Annalette by the riverside, tossing stones into the water from where she sat on the shore. She didn't turn to see him coming, but if she had, the Romani woman would have seen the distressed look in his eyes.

"Why didn't you tell me that your money wouldn't be accepted?"

Annalette looked up, her face alive with puzzlement. "The baker wouldn't take the *galbi*?"

John pulled out the loaf and handed it to her. "Be glad that he was another loup-garou, or he might not have been so generous."

She slowly took the bread from him. "Another loup-garou? I didn't realize…"

John loomed over her, casting a shadow over her. Somehow, he didn't believe her. He had learned to tell the difference between the truth and a falsehood. "How did he know who I was? Is it the way I smell? Something in my manners?"

Annalette tore off a portion of the loaf and smiled to herself. "I'm sure your manners would need improving after wandering in the forest for a century."

"Do not toy with me, woman!" he raised his voice, feeling a bit of his composure slip as his world was sent spiraling into a realm of uncertainty from which he couldn't begin to find his way back. "What was it? How did he know?"

She looked to him without fear or anger. "Did you not feel what he was? My uncle described it as if someone had pierced his skull, but it wasn't painful. Did you feel that?"

John sighed and tried to put back his mild discontent. He felt as if he had been plunged into a situation for which he was unprepared, and it was all Annalette's fault. "In a way, I did. But I've never felt it before."

"Then that was your first time meeting another loup-garou. Congratulations." She took a ravenous bite of the bread and chewed it with all the flair of a female with a distinct deficiency in etiquette.

"And he made his eyes turn gold, but he didn't become as a beast. How did he do that?"

Annalette answered with her mouth full. "It takes practice. He might be as old as you are, perhaps younger." She swallowed. "If a loup-garou has proper training, they can control the wolf well enough to let it show on command."

John knelt to her, his hands out in a beseeching way. "Show me. Train me. Help me control this beast."

He had never been a proud man, but the last century had taught him to not trust another soul for fear of being hanged as a witch or turned away as a condemned soul. He did not rely on anyone besides himself, but when he saw how the baker had such command over the beast, he knew that he could no longer live his life that way. He had to learn, to adapt, and get control over this invisible force that dictated his existence.

More than anything, he was tired of living in fear of the things he could not see or fully understand. The wolf inside of him was real, he knew that now, but he could not ignore it any longer.

Annalette looked to him, her gaze full of sympathy. "I cannot teach you every-thing, John. Only an alpha can show you how to control your wolf."

"Then lead me to an alpha. Where is the one who trained your uncle?"

She shook her head. "I do not know where he is now. We met him in Scotland, but he was from another country, and that was years ago."

John pounded his fist into the ground, forming a crater around his knuckles. "Then take me to your uncle, damn it!" he bellowed. "I have to learn."

A smile crept over her lips, but he could not read the emotion behind it. Haughty? Victorious? Is this what she wanted from the beginning? For him to grovel and beg for the answers? Whatever it was, he had given it to her and John couldn't fight the roiling anger that she would behave so despicably. It was not becoming of a beautiful woman, Romani or not.

When she didn't reply, he stood and stormed away toward the direction of the village. If she was going to play the tease, then he would too.

"Where are you going?" she called to him.

"Back to the bakery," he replied. "If the baker knows so much, then I will learn from him. He would be of more use than you."

She let out a sound of protest, and he heard her give chase. "You promised to help me."

"That was when you said you would tell me more about what I was. Now, you won't tell me what I need to know, so I don't have to hold up my end of the bargain."

John knew he could escape faster than this, but he allowed the gypsy to catch up and come to his side. He noticed that her pack was still back where she left it by the river.

"But, what about my brother?" she complained, true panic discharging from her like an aromatic perfume. His ruse was working, and this time, he would see *her* beg.

"You're a strong woman. You can find another way to get him out of prison, I'm sure."

Annalette skipped in front of John and slammed her hand against his chest to stop him in his tracks. "I need your help, John. If you help my brother escape, then we will try to find you an alpha."

John looked down at her fingers spread across his chest, the tips just barely touching his bare skin around the edge of his tunic collar. Tiny rain droplets began to fall, pattering against the leaves of the canopy above them.

The rain was not the only thing in the air. He could smell Annalette's worry, even if it weren't written in her wide, dark eyes. He was tired of her games and almost regretted saving her from the vagrants who were ready to make her submit to their needs. If he had let her go and minded his own business, he would have lived another hundred years in blissful ignorance. He would have known nothing of loups-garous and accepted his lot in life as a demon-possessed bastard with no future and nothing but a miserable past.

Instead, a discontent was slowly building. She had let him peek behind a door that led to a new world of which he could not take part. It was a cruel torture as she still taunted him with the keys to that door, bartering for the right to learn what he should have known all along. She was no longer an aide. She stood in his way to gaining control of his humanity.

Then again, her company had worked a miracle in him that he never thought was possible. Staring down at her lovely face, he felt his spirit awaken. No, he couldn't regret saving her, but he did regret feeling this way about her. No woman should have had such control over a man.

"You're not only going to help me find an alpha, but you're going to tell me the truth." He waited for her to quietly question him before continuing. "What is it that you have been hiding from me? It has nothing to do with loups-garous or your brother. I could tell you were lying when you talked about your family."

Annalette slowly lowered her hand and took a step away from him as the rain began to pour down, drenching them both.

A silence stretched between them, seeming to last for an eternity as her mystic eyes fixed on his. He would not give an inch or let her run. She wasn't the only one who had the power to make their prey yield to their demands.

"My family knows that I've gone to find Gallius, but they may not be so concerned about my return."

John lowered his brows. "Explain."

Annalette took a deep breath. "The life of a Romani woman revolves around her family. She is expected to be a good wife and mother but, I am well past marrying age."

John shrugged. "So, you may never marry. There is no crime in that."

She pressed her palm to her forehead and closed her eyes. "No, it's not a crime. When a Romani woman marries, the husband is to pay her family a sum of money to compensate for her upbringing. My father has never been compensated, and along with my brother and his family, they have to take care of me as well. I can never leave them."

"So, you've become a burden to your family," he said, his voice softening.

Annalette only nodded and lowered her hand to her hip. She would not look him in the eye, probably out of shame for her spinster status, but John would not judge her because he knew exactly how she felt.

As a boy, he had heard the bitter whispers from his mother. She didn't know he had been listening behind the cracked doors when she complained that her wages were going to feed him and clothe him, a child she never wanted, a child that brought misfortune upon her and ruined her chances for a happy life.

"As a child," she explained, "I was always running off and breaking the traditions of our people. A bride is chosen based on her character. No family wanted a wild and unruly woman for their son. Then, I spent so much time with my uncle that I had no time for marriage or suitors. I was past the marrying age when he was cast out from our *vitsa*, and the fee that my father set for my hand was far too great for any family who was willing to take me."

She finally looked to him with despondent eyes. "I may never marry; therefore, I will never fulfill my role as a Romani woman."

It wasn't a foreign concept. It was nothing new that a spinster or husband-less peasant was not looked upon favorably by English society. Even his own mother was considered damaged goods and always the last choice for any man looking to take a wife.

"Will you return to your family when you've rescued your brother?"

When she spoke, he could hear the distinct resentment laced in her words. She was not pleased with her place in her clan, but there was still a resignation there as if she had accepted it long ago and there was little that could be done.

She shrugged her slender shoulders. "I have nowhere else to go. The Romani are not welcome in many places. I could return to Scotland, but then what would I do? No. I must return to my family. One day, perhaps I will find a husband."

They were brave words for one who knew there was an unlikely chance for happiness in her future. He admired that courage, that strength of will, but at the same time, he could still sense her brokenness and longing beneath the tough veneer.

Whatever drove him to speak, whether it was the look in her eyes or the way her tragic story moved him so, John knew that it was only fair to share some of his own misfortune. Perhaps in admitting his own unworthiness, he could let her know that she was not alone.

"My mother never married either," he said. "At least, I don't know if she ever did. I told you before that my father was not involved in my life and that was true. My mother was taken against her will by a man that she didn't know. When she told her father, he went after the cad to force him to marry my mother. He never came back. They found my grandfather's body torn to pieces by a wild animal three days later."

Annalette crossed her arms over her chest. "Your father must have been a loup-garou."

John nodded, knowing that it all made perfect sense now. "With my grandmother a widow and my mother heavy with child, they went to Shrewsbury in search of work. They were farmers by trade, but my mother knew how to spin wool. They found jobs at a manor. My grandmother washed clothes, and my mother did the only thing she knew. As I grew up, I also became a servant at the manor. Not a day went by when I wasn't reminded that I had no father and I was the reason my family suffered."

"You were not the reason. Your father was the one who raped your mother."

Her words were less than gentle as if the truth had to be pounded into his head, but John could not undo years of self-loathing in the time it took her to utter that one sentence.

"I believed it was because I was a bastard that the demon chose to possess me. I was already unworthy in the eyes of God by my unholy conception. It only made sense that I should be cursed for bringing misery upon my family."

"But, you did not sin, John," she pleaded. "You did nothing but live."

He gave her a hard look. "And you have done nothing but live your own life how you choose, and you are being punished by thinking you are a burden as well." He would return fire with fire.

Annalette blinked, but if she accepted his words, he could not tell. A curtain had been drawn once more, but John would not let them be separated so easily. They were from different walks of life, but in this, they had found common ground. If they could just build upon that ground, then the capacity to trust one another would soon follow. John was aching to trust another person again, even if it was a Romani.

John watched her as the rain continued to pummel down. In an act of compassion, he slipped off the coat he had stolen and draped it over her, letting the thick wool block out the rain. She gripped the edge of the fabric and held it in place like a shield against the forces of nature while he continued to get soaked. He was used to being without such protection against the elements.

What he wasn't used to was the warmth that grew in his gut. He pitied the gypsy, who was alone in the world for the time. To be so out of reach from her role as a Romani and a daughter to a Romani family, Annalette must have felt the weight of loneliness descend on her, whether she would admit it or not.

Incongruous with their previous conversation, she cracked a mirthless smile.

"What is it?" he asked.

She held up the fabric of the long cloak. "This. Romani don't wear such garments. It does not honor the distinction between the body halves. It is unclean." She rolled her eyes. "I would be *marime* to even touch this."

There were multiple facets to their traditions and cultures. It would take a lifetime for John to learn everything, but he was at least willing to listen, whether he understood it or not. "Perhaps you should take this time to break a few of your *marime* rules. I won't tell."

His words came out more suggestive than he anticipated, but it elicited a giggle from Annalette, and that made it all worth it.

CHAPTER 5

With every yard they traveled down the path toward Canterbury, Annalette could hear her voice of conscience screaming at her that her plan had taken a sour turn. She hadn't planned on telling John so much about her past. She should have lied and told him that she had a husband and children waiting for her in Dover while her family attended to her dying uncle. She should have said that her life was the closest thing to perfect.

Everything about John had stolen away her common sense. It took every ounce of willpower she had to keep her mind focused on the mission they had set out to do. Yet when he looked into her eyes, so full of that inexplicable alpha dominance that could demand the moon and stars to bow at his feet if that's what he wanted, Annalette could not lie to him about her family again.

They had walked in silence for a couple of miles, and Annalette couldn't help but feel uneasy in the quiet. She gazed out over the River Stour, watching the ripples of the murky water as it flowed downstream. It was not a better sight when compared to John's handsome, somewhat shaven face, but it was far safer.

The rain continued to fall, but its force had lessened significantly from a few hours before when they left Chilham. The river was anything but calm as the raindrops peppered its surface. A family of ducks swam to the shore where the mother led her babies to the shelter of the thicket.

The river reminded her of a time in her childhood when playing games with the other boys wasn't some terrible transgression. Back then, they could wrestle and tease one another without risk of pollution by each other's touch.

Annalette remembered the exact day when all of this changed, and her best childhood friends could no longer tussle with her outside of camp. Just one touch to her skirt and they would be unclean. They would be *marime*. It was not as appalling a crime as being a loup-garou, but it was enough to ruin one's day.

That was also the day that her father began to advertise her worth as a potential daughter-in-law to the other families with whom they traveled. None would have anything to do with her wildness. Now it was too late, and she would never know the intimacy of a man unless she stepped outside of the traditions of her people.

She desperately wanted to heed John's advice and push aside the purity laws for just a few days while they rescued her brother. It would be far easier on her soul if she did. It'd be like the old days when she could run free without the eyes of the *vitsa* watching her like a hawk, waiting for her to make one more mistake.

John suddenly stopped and his gaze lowered to the grass. His nostrils flared, and Annalette wondered if the wolf was letting him know that tonight would be his night to shift. She recognized that disturbed, concentrated look.

"What is it?" she asked.

John's head lifted and swiveled to the north as he looked across the river. He grabbed her hand and pulled her - none too - gently into the forest. Trusting him completely, she followed and did not ask another question.

They ducked behind an oak tree, whose girth was wide enough for them to stand behind and not be seen by whoever John sensed coming, but they could not stand side by side. Instead, John had positioned her with her back pressed against the rough bark of the tree, and he stood in front of her. He was so achingly close that she could smell his warm, masculine scent. It made her slightly dizzy to know that she only had to reach out and she could touch his chest like she did earlier when she tried to stop him from abandoning her in the wilderness.

She turned her head away to reject the temptation and listened. She heard nothing, but that didn't mean a great deal. If John could hear it, then there was certainly someone there.

"Who?" she whispered.

"A wood reeve," he replied with his eyes fixed toward the river. "He's patrolling on the other side."

Annalette nodded slowly. She knew the wood reeves well. They had been the bane to the Romani ever since they came to this country. The constables were responsible for their own jurisdictions, but these wood reeves were the watchers of the forest. If they found a beggar, a Romani camp, or even a corpse, they were the first to report back to the nearest village. In Scotland, they weren't so much of a problem, but England was rife with prejudice against the Romani and the wood reeves were not to be taken lightly.

Slowly, John edged away from Annalette, and it was then that she realized he was still holding her hand. It had felt so right that she barely noticed it. He guided her away from the oak and deeper into the woods until the river was completely out of sight.

"Have you had many dealings with the wood reeves?" she asked once she knew they were a safe distance away.

John released her hand, but his gaze continually reverted to the north as if he were still looking for the reeve. "Quite a lot, actually."

There were so many things Annalette still didn't know about John. None of it should have mattered, though. Her task was to rescue her brother, not become friends with a *gajo* loup-garou. Yet perhaps asking more probing questions could get her what she wanted. If he chose to answer her, that could be a sign that he trusted her. After the slight blunder outside of Chilham, she needed to try and make herself valuable again.

"Out of the one hundred years you have been a loup-garou, how long have you spent wandering the forests? Surely, you haven't lived your entire life out here."

John adjusted the pack strap on his shoulder, and his lips pulled in a belligerent look as if he didn't want to tell her, but at the same time, he did. "It's hard to tell the passage of time. Perhaps a few decades."

"And before that?"

John bowed his head for a moment, then looked to her, assessing her for something. Whatever it was, she wasn't sure if he found it before he answered,

"The day the demon... the wolf... took over my body, I ran from the manor. I left my mother and grandmother without any warning. I thought that the demon would hurt them and I didn't want to give it that chance. I searched for help to rid myself of the demon. I went to priests and the tombs of saints, hoping they could drive it out, but they couldn't.

"When I found that none of them could help me, I knew I had to keep myself from hurting others." He took a deep breath. "I went to London. There's a place where they keep people who are not fit for proper society. They had the means to lock me away. I was there for three days. I sat in my cell and listened to the screaming and deranged wailing of the others who were there. They were the slow, the mad, the insane. Bethlehem Hospital was a place to keep them all so the outside world wouldn't have to deal with them. It proved to be no place for me."

Annalette forced herself to watch the swirling emotions in his eyes as he told his story. Annalette had spent most of her life in the fresh air and open spaces. To be locked away behind stone walls seemed unthinkable. If she were not already out of her mind going in, she would be crazy coming out.

For a loup-garou, it would have been the same. The wolf needed freedom. It needed to run and hunt, but John wouldn't have known that.

"Did you leave after the three days?"

John cleared his throat, and his voice dropped into a deep tone. "I did, but not as a man. I wasn't due to shift for another few weeks, but I could feel the spirit growing restless. It changed, and I found my way out. By the time I came to my senses, I was standing naked in the streets. The chains the guards had bound me with had been broken by the beast, and there was blood on my hands. Under the darkness of night, I fled the city and vowed never to return until I knew I wouldn't hurt anyone."

"So, you fled to the woods."

He nodded. "I knew that was the only place I could go where the spirit – the wolf – would not cause too much trouble. Those two men who attacked you were the first I had killed in years."

Annalette blocked the impulse to think of the men and hardened her heart against the guilt. "You didn't seem too bothered by it."

John was silent for a few moments before he replied, "I'm not bothered by it because I haven't allowed myself to be bothered. The wolf is the one who killed them, not me. When I heard you scream and I saw that you were in danger, I let the spirit take control and do what needed to be done."

"You saw that killing them was necessary?"

"The wolf did," he said. "But that doesn't make it any less of a sin."

Sins and demons. That's all he had ever thought of or talked about. The sin of being a bastard child. The sin of being demon possessed. The sin of murder. There had to be something else to his life. Something else to look back upon with fondness. From what he had told her, there was nothing but darkness and sadness.

Annalette wished that she could have changed that in some grander way to show him he was not possessed. It didn't help him that the foundation upon which he had staked his claim for the last century was crumbling beneath his bare feet. Now he had more questions and more worries. Annalette might not have been helping at all.

That should have been none of her concern. After her brother was safely back with her *vitsa*, she would not see John again. She could not leave her family to go on a wild goose chase for an alpha or her uncle. She had never heard of another loup-garou in England besides the baker whom John told her about. If the baker didn't know an alpha or was not an alpha himself, it would be near impossible to find another. She was not willing to give up her family for an impossible mission such as what John wanted.

However, she would not let John know that. As far as he knew, she would go to whatever lengths were necessary to help him. It was too bad that despite her growing attachment to him, she could not save his soul.

"You speak of sins, but your heart is pure," she stated.

John chuckled, hoping it would hide the storm within him. Annalette's words, her mannerisms, everything was threatening to unravel him. Telling her about his time in London had pried open his heart further than he was comfortable. "What do you know of my heart? Is it true what they say of your people, that you can see the future and know a person's deepest secrets just by looking at them?"

She shrugged. "There are some who claim to have such powers, but I am not one of them. I just know that you have been kind to me, which tells much about your character. The English hate the Romani, and despite your first hesitance, you seem to be... content with me."

Content was putting it mildly. When he threatened to leave her just outside of Chilham, John realized how much he had grown accustomed to her company. He would sorely miss her wild scent and the sound of her heavy skirts that whispered with each step.

Thankfully, she had promised that their journey together would not end after they reached Canterbury. Though he still wasn't sure how they would get her brother out of prison, he consoled himself that his reward would be within sight.

All he had to do was keep his thoughts from slipping into the forbidden place that her eyes beckoned him to explore. He had never known the love of a woman, but he desperately wanted to believe that Annalette could show him.

"I will admit that I can't understand why no man would want you. Surely money couldn't be the only thing to stop you from taking a suitor?"

Annalette crossed her arms in the same way she did whenever she talked about her inadequacies as a Romani woman. "As I told you, it's not just about the money. I would be a disgraceful wife. As it is, I'm a disgraceful daughter, too. I don't do my fair share of work in the camp sometimes."

"If I had my way with this country, no woman would work."

She huffed. "So, we would be forced to stay home with the children?"

"Not necessarily. But I would make it so no woman would be forced to work. They could if they chose, of course."

"If we do not have children and work, then what are we supposed to do with our lives? Twiddle our thumbs until the husband comes home and then pamper him?"

John rubbed the back of his neck and tried not to feel uncomfortable in this conversation about husbands, wives, and marriages. "You can do whatever you want." He looked to her. "If you didn't have chores like washing or cooking, what would you do with your day?"

Annalette thought for a moment and then smiled. It was a beautiful sight. If only she would smile more often. "I would travel, as I have always done, but I would leave England. I'd go to France, perhaps Italy and the countries to the east. There is so much to explore and see."

Her zeal was contagious and John returned her smile. "And what would you do when you arrived at those places?"

She looked to the sky and spun as she walked with her arms stretched out. "I'd do just this. I'd walk. The forests of Scotland are different than here, so they must be different everywhere else. I want to see the forests and know the creatures of it."

For a brief moment, he saw the child she must have been years ago before the responsibilities of adulthood stole her joy away. "Have you always wanted to do this? Or was it your loup-garou uncle who inspired such a desire?"

"He encouraged it, but I've always wanted to travel this way."

John grew bold. "Then you should. You should travel and see the forests of the world."

The smile faded from her lips, and it was as if the sun had been hidden behind a dark rain cloud. If only John had the right wind to push away the sadness once more and bring back the light. "It's not right for a woman to travel alone. See what it got me in Wye? The world isn't safe for a woman, especially me."

"Then I'll make it safe." The words slipped out so fast that John hardly knew they were spoken until Annalette shot him a curious look. "I mean, I can go with you. England has always been my home, but I know it too well. Perhaps it's time for a change. If we traveled together, I'd make sure no one would bother you."

Annalette gave him a strained smile and then looked away.

"Unless your dream of roaming does not involve a partner."

"It's not that," she said. "It's that I had always thought I would travel with my husband, not a stranger."

John tried to keep his heart from slipping from his chest. "You can hardly call me a stranger anymore. And by the time we get your brother out of Canterbury, we would be far from unacquainted."

"That may be true," she sighed. "But it is a fantasy. I can never leave my family, no matter how much I'd like to travel."

John wanted to take her in his arms and squeeze her until she admitted that she didn't need her family, that she could live without them, but he could not force her to say the things she didn't mean. No matter how wonderful her dream was or how much it meant to her, Annalette would not let herself be free of her family bonds. He understood that, but it didn't mean he had to like it.

"If you ever do decide to break away, promise you'll find me?"

She looked at him, a soft and carefully neutral expression written on her face. "I promise... As long as I'm not married before then, of course," she added with a witty shrug.

"Of course," he replied and watched the way the sunlight gleamed in her raven hair as she looked away.

Chapter 6

The evening sky blazed with bright pastel shades of red, orange, and magenta. It was a spectacular sunset to chase away the storm clouds from earlier that afternoon. Though John was content to keep moving, Annalette had convinced him to take the detour she had been planning.

"How do you know they can be trusted?" the loup-garou asked as they approached the quaint cottage that sat upon acres of farmland just outside of Canterbury. They were less than a half hour's walk from the edge of town, and despite the short stop due to the rain, they made excellent time.

"My brother was with this family just before he was arrested," she explained as she gazed up at the humble home. "We came to do some work for them on our way to Dover. They were the last to see him and treated us well."

She looked to John, who appeared leery of the idea of staying with the family, despite her assurances. Annalette wasn't so sure of the plan herself, mostly due to the raging emotions that boiled within her. Staying calm was crucial to the plan. Their talk from earlier had laid a dangerous groundwork for digressing thoughts and unholy ideas.

"Think of this as a way to practice your etiquette," she said. "You will need to learn how to talk to people again."

John sighed, and though the sun was dipping below the tree line, the dim light cast his face in a glow that made her heart pound a little faster. She couldn't push aside the memory of how he had loaned her the coat to keep out the rain, though it was meager in the way of adequate shelters. It was the gesture that grabbed her attention.

Just moments before he revealed such sensitivity, he had been willing to leave her alone in the wilderness. The only reason he seemed to care now was that he knew she was more than just alone in the countryside. She was romantically alone as well.

That, and she was willing to give him something for his troubles, something that he couldn't get elsewhere, but the deed wasn't done. She had to give him something more to keep his interest, though it would go against everything Romani women embodied.

Then there was the way he talked of traveling the world together. It would have been forbidden by her people. They were not married, and he was not Romani. It was *marime* just to think of such things, and yet, she had fallen in love with the idea of having him by her side. It was *marime* just to be associating with a loup-garou and a *gajo*. It was ridiculous, and her heart beat wildly against the unfairness of her people's traditions.

Her uncle had made her realize how flawed their culture could be. There was nothing wrong with being loup-garou, yet her family believed him to be cursed and impure. John believed something similar, but they were both wrong. Why would she want to be part of a people who would exile such perfect creatures from their world?

If she found her own way, then perhaps she would have a chance for a better life. What could the world offer her? What could John offer her?

She had heard of Romani who purposefully disengaged themselves from their own *vitsas* to seek better lives. They did not survive. The law of the land did not permit them or any other homeless vagrant to go unpunished. Though Annalette believed herself to be strong and capable of living outside of the safety of her *vitsa*, she knew that it wouldn't be enough. She needed her people, flawed as they were.

They stepped up to the threshold and Annalette took the honor of rapping upon the heavy pine door.

The farmer's wife, Mary, greeted them. Her dark eyes went wide at the sight of the Romani. "Annalette! It's so good to see you!" she cried, but Annalette saw straight through her hesitance. It was likely that Mary never expected to see her again.

Mary's bright eyes looked to John, and she seemed to struggle to keep the fake smile on her lips. "Who is your companion?" she asked. More than likely, the farmer's wife might have been wondering where their chaperone was, as well. She would need to know how many the town watchers would need to capture before the night was through.

It took her utmost composure to speak civilly to the woman. "May I present, John Croxen," Annalette replied with a respectful gesture to the loup-garou. "John, this is Mary Thompson."

John looked just as tentative as Mary and bowed his head. "A pleasure, madam."

Annalette grinned, happy to see that he still remembered something of being a human gentleman.

Mary curtsied and moved aside to allow them inside. "Please, come in." The cottage was small, just big enough for the farmer, his wife, and their young son who was sitting on the floor of the common area playing with a wooden horse toy.

Annalette greeted the boy with just as much warmth as she had with Mary, but John was at a loss for what to say or do.

"Henry should be coming in from the fields soon," Mary said as she moved toward the kitchen area where a fire was blazing beneath a pot of stew. "He's rounding up the last of the flock."

"What livestock do you raise?" John asked.

Annalette froze. Had so much changed in just a few days? "I thought you grew cabbage, Mary?"

Mary let out one of her bubbling laughs. "We do. Henry was struck by this odd notion to expand our income by herding sheep, as well, but I have yet to see the usefulness of it."

Annalette nodded. So that was it. The family needed money.

She looked to John who didn't seem bothered by the fact that there was potential game outside the house, but perhaps he had learned to temper the hunting instinct over the years. Though, she knew that John would need to eat soon, and the stew, though it smelled hearty and delicious, would not satisfy the belly of a loup-garou.

"Everyone eats lamb," Annalette remarked with a helpful upturn of her voice to hide her growing disquiet about being under Mary's roof. "And you could always sell the wool at market."

Mary shrugged as she lifted the pot lid to stir the soupy contents. "This is true. It might be too soon to tell, but I feel as if our cabbage patches put food on the table, more so than those sheep."

"Why are you so big?" cried Daniel, the little boy who had snuck up behind the visitors in the kitchen.

John quickly turned and stood as a giant in front of the gangly youth with bright blonde hair. As a loup-garou, he could have easily broken the boy's body in two. The images of those two men from the night before, mangled and lifeless, came to Annalette's mind. She knew exactly what John was capable of, but judging by the obvious awkwardness exchanged between the two, she knew that the burly man wouldn't harm a hair on the boy's head if he could help it.

"He's a blacksmith, Daniel," Annalette replied, knowing that John wouldn't have been prepared for such a question. All loups-garous were strong and powerful, able to crush a skull with their bare hands or fell a tree without the help of an axe. John was no different, and the bulging muscles beneath his tunic were a testament to that.

"A blacksmith? Gallius wasn't as big as him, though."

"Daniel," Mary scolded. "Stop being rude to our guests."

"It's all right, madam," John said before turning back to the child. "I used to cut timber as a boy. I've done hard, honest labor all my life."

Annalette knew it was a lie, but she crouched down to be at eye level with Daniel. "And if you worked hard, you could be just as big as John one day."

The look in the boy's eye told her everything she needed to know. Reluctance and disgust. His parents had taught him something of the harsh world, and the Romani would never look the same to him.

"Daniel," Mary said, "go see where your father is and let him know we have company."

The boy nodded to his mother and raced out the door without a second look back. Annalette wondered if Daniel was truly going to fetch his father or run into Canterbury.

The woman straightened and wiped her brow on the back of her arm as Annalette came to stand with her by the hearth. "I apologize for his rudeness. He's becoming wilder each day. He's a help to Henry in the field, but he's restless." Mary sighed. "We heard about Gallius. We're so sorry for your loss. Henry saw him being taken away to Westgate."

Annalette mitigated her rage and shook her head, the coins on her bandana jingling. "He's not dead yet, Mary."

By the pinched look on Mary's face, she braced herself for foul news. Annalette had not prepared her heart if she arrived in Canterbury too late. The woman said nothing and glanced to John, who was wandering around the common area. He looked to be casually inspecting the furniture, though Annalette knew he was trying to appear calm and not as uncomfortable as he really was.

How long had it been since he stood under a thatched roof and walked across a wood-planked floor? The Thompsons were fortunate, more than most, but their home was far from luxurious. They could never put on pretenses that they were wealthy or an affluent family. Not for long anyway. How many more Romani would they call on to work for them under the impression that they were safe?

"Is he traveling with you?" Mary whispered to her.

Annalette pursed her lips. She knew that John would be able to hear every word they said, no matter if it were in the softest whisper, but to brush away Mary's question would be impolite.

"Yes, he's going to help me get Gallius out of prison."

Mary gasped. "Out of prison? Dear girl, you can't be serious."

She nodded. "I'm quite serious. He is my brother, and I will not be the one to abandon him."

"Do you understand how dangerous it will be? The fort is heavily guarded. How do you intend to get in?"

Annalette slid a look toward John whose hand lingered on the back of a wooden chair. "Worry not. I have a plan."

John's head perked up at a sound that neither Mary or Annalette could detect and she suspected that he heard the approach of the flock.

She looked to the broth swirling in the cast iron pot and grimaced. "Is there meat in that stew?" she asked Mary.

Mary laughed. "Of course, dear. We slaughtered a lamb just a few days ago and have been slowly picking it apart to eat."

"Do you have a leg or slab of meat that you could roast for John? He's not fond of stew. It upsets his stomach."

Mary hissed in regret. "No, I'm sorry. What is in the stew is the last of the lamb. I have some bread if he would prefer that."

Annalette watched John's hand tighten over the back of the chair and heard the sharp crack as the wood splintered. "No, I don't think that will do," she said.

John huffed out a breath of air as if giving in to the unpleasant consequences that were to come. "I'll have the stew, Annalette."

It was the first time he had uttered her name, and he had spoken it in such a way that made her body tingle. If there was one thing she hadn't known about loups-garous, it was their uncanny attraction.

The only two loups-garous she had ever met were her uncle and the alpha who abetted him. She had been a young girl then, and her head was still full of butterflies and daisies. As a woman, her mind was preoccupied with other things and none of them were so innocent as making wishes on a dandelion before blowing their seeds to the wind.

Annalette bit her lip as the rest of the world carried on as if John hadn't just seduced her with the mere use of her name. It was why she had been so careful not to give it to him so readily. Names held power, and John now wielded such power over her.

She wrapped her arms around her churning stomach and turned to the simmering stew in the pot. It certainly smelled good, but how would it affect John?

A few moments later, Daniel preceded his father into the house. Mary greeted her husband, a tall and lanky fellow with a sparkling look in his eyes.

He greeted his feminine guest with familiarity, while he eyed the stranger with the same suspicion that John must have received everywhere he went. He was not built like the typical Englishman, and his powerful presence must have set some on edge.

Yet, from the very beginning, Annalette had never been afraid of him. The idea that he could easily kill her never crossed her mind. Instead, plenty of other thoughts paraded around inside of her head, and none of them could be spoken in the open. She was sure that no one, especially her family, would want to hear the unholy daydreams that she had entertained ever since she met John. She would use them to her advantage, if they could last through dinner without getting arrested.

John could already feel his insides seize and rebel against him. He had been careful to avoid the chopped vegetables in the stew and slurped the broth slowly, knowing that the essence of the things that made him sick was what made the soup so dangerously delicious. Even after eating the chunks of lamb, he was left feeling ill and nowhere near satisfied.

The deer he had killed the night before should have lasted much longer than this, but with the added excitement of meeting Annalette and learning of his true nature, his body no longer reacted the same.

The voices around him became dull and grating to his ears. Even Annalette's soothing cadence couldn't abate the queasiness that overtook him so violently. His vision blurred as he cast his eyes to the table. Fixating on something usually calmed his nerves enough to withstand this kind of sickness, but he could no longer focus on the flow of the wood grains or see the fine splinters that jutted out from the surface.

He had been sick like this before, and it never ended well. When he told Annalette that he would eat the stew, he thought he could make an attempt at controlling the beast inside of him. Though it would take him a while to consider the strange spirit as a wolf instead of a demon, he couldn't fight against it just yet.

"John?" he heard through the haze. "Are you all right?"

He had the clarity to shake his head and pushed himself from his chair. His muscles ached and were given to fits of spasms. It was a wonder he could walk to the door at all. "No... I'll be right back," he assured before disappearing into the night.

John moved around to the side of the house and braced himself against the stone wall as the stew made its way back up his throat and spewed out of his mouth to puddle in the grass at his feet.

It was better than the last time he became ill from eating what he shouldn't have. He had eaten a whole carrot in his quest for food just a week after he first changed and fell unconscious for an entire day as his stomach rejected the once healthy food.

When the poison had been expelled from his system, John felt the gold wolf eyes come forward in a cold rush. His nails, once trimmed with a bit of dirt underneath, grew long and sharp like claws, and scratched against the gritty texture of the stone until tiny bits were broken off. His sharp teeth pricked at his lips as he gasped for air.

In the times that he had starved himself, he thought the demon came forward to force him to kill and devour raw flesh. He understood now that the wolf needed nourishment, just like Annalette told him. The lamb he had just consumed was not the only meaty bits amongst the bile. Some of the fawn he had feasted upon had been ejected from him as well. Now, he was even more hungry, and his belly was empty.

The frightened bleating of the sheep reached his ears, and without another thought, he moved around the cottage toward the pen where the flock was corralled. The yews and rams skittered away from John as he approached the fence. They all knew that he was a predator, but this predator wasn't just a wolf. He was a man and John fought to stay that way. His golden eyes shone through the dark, regarding the sheep with a hungry glower.

"No," he growled to himself. John shook his head sharply to rid himself of the thought, but his stomach would not listen. It returned his growl with another that was more convincing than his own.

Before John realized what he was doing, he had vaulted over the split-rail fence and snatched one of the sheep from the flock. He snapped its neck and quickly sliced into its belly to let its guts spill into the soil. The rest of the herd became frantic and cleared the spot where John cut into the carcass to feast, just as he had on the young deer the night before.

The warm and bloody flesh slipped down into his stomach and eased the pain of hunger. The wolf was contented, as well. His senses returned to him, and he could hear the desperate flock pushing against the wooden planks to escape the corral.

A dog, one that was used to protect and herd livestock, darted underneath the split rail. The animal barked at John and bared its jowls in threat against the predator. When the dog saw John's golden eyes and blood dripping from his chin, it whimpered and ran away to safety.

There were human shouts coming from the cottage. Amongst them was Annalette, and that was enough to pull him back from the precipice of beastly insanity.

His heart hammered against his chest as he looked down to his prey and hands that were covered in the evidence of his crimes. He had snagged livestock before, but never from someone with whom he had become acquainted.

With wide eyes, he looked to the house and saw a lone figure running through the darkness toward the corral. John sprang to his feet and fled over the fence, and into the forest. With only the moon above to light his path, it was unlikely that the human would get a clear glimpse of him, but, with John missing from the dinner table and the suddenness of the attack, all fingers would point to him. He had been guilty of many things, but never convicted.

Taking shelter in the woods, John took deep breaths to calm himself, but it was no use. The wolf had not retreated, though its belly was full and satiated. His golden eyes still glimmered in the darkness like two bright sparks of savagery while his claws dug into the bark of the tree on which he had caught himself.

John tried to drive back the beast, but it was to no avail. It was as if the wolf laughed in his face and pushed harder to force the shift upon him, though it wasn't the right time of the month for it. Never had he changed outside of his cycle, so why did he feel so provoked now?

Pain flooded through his body, just as it had when Annalette gripped his shoulder. His blood was set aflame, and he cried out in agony as the shift began to take hold. One noise, a presence, blasted through, and John found the strength to hold it back for just a little longer.

"John!" Annalette called. "John, where are you?"

He shoved himself from the tree and was able to take a few staggering steps before he stumbled to the ground, overcome with weakness and pain. He crawled away from her voice, knowing that once the wolf took hold of his body, he would be powerless to stop it from killing anything in its path.

His nails dug into the dirt as he clawed through the weeds and grasses. He could already feel his bones popping and twisting out of place, but he jammed them back by tightening his sore muscles around the inflamed joints.

John found a protruding root from a nearby tree and held onto it as the shift lurched his body into unnatural positions.

His name was whispered, so soft and sweet. Annalette's voice, though danger-ously near, gave him a little more courage to battle against the shift. He pulled himself up to the tree, his hands bracing against the trunk and his head hung low. His legs continually tried to buckle beneath him, but he kept his knees locked tight to remain standing.

Grunts and groans escaped from between his gritted teeth as he continuously counterattacked the wolf. He had gone over a hundred years without knowing how to control the beast, but tonight he would show the animal who was in true control.

A hand touched his shoulder, and he jerked away. "Leave me," he said, his voice gravelly and guttural. The words were untrue in the sense that he wanted her close to ease the pain, but it was unwise for her to stay.

She touched him again, and this time, he didn't shy away. Her hand traveled from his quivering shoulder and down his arm to his elbow. When she made it that far, he sensed her move under his arm to stand in front of him, trapping herself against the tree.

John lifted his head and leaned away, but couldn't bring himself to launch off the tree to escape her. Annalette's scent clouded his judgment, and for a moment, he was ready to give into anything and everything. Needs, both feral and eternal, gripped his soul and John continued to fight it all.

Annalette shushed him as she had the first night and began into her song. John would not allow it, and he took her throat in his hand to silence her. Her steady pulse beat against his palm.

"No," he commanded. "I want control. I will have it. Do not interfere."

John looked to her with his golden eyes, and she nodded in understanding. With his fingers wrapped around her neck, he could have easily killed her, but she was no sheep. She did not fear the wolf, and the wolf did not want her dead. Both of them, the man and the wolf, wanted Annalette very much alive.

He released her and began to slowly pull away, but this time she reached out to him. Annalette's hands tugged at the front of his bloodied shirt. Her fingertips brushed against his chest and stomach as she trailed down to the edge of his tunic.

"The best way for you to learn control is to let go," she whispered, her breath a sweet aroma in a world of rancid chaos.

"I don't want to hurt you."

"You won't," she assured as she lifted the edge of his tunic. "You don't want to tear this."

John succumbed to her influence, though he had no intention of doing as she said. He raised his arms to allow her to pull the tunic over his head. The night air crawled across his skin, but he didn't feel the chill as Annalette's hands fell to the front of his trousers.

A new primal need took hold, and his body became flushed with heat in response to her. Afraid that she would feel the throbbing at his crotch, John jumped and fell on his backside as he scurried away from the temptress.

"You're not helping," he rebuked as he widened the distance between them.

John knew what women could do to men, how they could whisper a few words and make the stronger sex crumble in a heap. He understood what they did behind closed doors under the cloak of night, but feeling Annalette's tender touch and seeing the sly look in her eyes had suddenly made him as nervous as an adolescent boy who was just discovering that girls were useful for more than just washing and cooking.

Her scent, her dark and mesmerizing eyes, her very spirit drove him mad with a new desire. The wolf hungered for it too. He denied himself the chance. He would not be like his father, who took a woman against her will.

Annalette watched him flee, a look of coquettish glee on her face. "Is the wolf truly afraid of a petty woman like me?"

John let out a mirthless laugh, all the while still feeling the wolf lurk, waiting for the right moment to strike. "You're no woman. You're a vixen."

She sauntered forward, her bare feet gliding over the blades of grass with such grace that he had to stop and stare. "I only want to help, John." She knelt down by his side and placed her shaking hand upon his heaving chest. "I know you're in pain."

John swallowed hard and felt the arousal in every part of his body that mixed with the aching of the coming shift. How could two sensations exist so simultaneously? "You cannot heal this. Just leave me."

Annalette sat back on her heels and grinned.

"What? What is it?" he asked, tensing to run if he needed. Could she sense something that he could not?

"Your eyes," she said. "They're red."

John peered at her and edged farther away. "Red? They've never been red before."

A light-hearted giggle bubbled from her lips. "It means you are..." She glanced down to his crotch, now hard with desire.

John leapt to his feet and tried to escape her feminine power, but she took his hand to silently beg for him to stay.

"You act like a child, John," she laughed. "Please, don't go."

The shift surged forward again, slashing through any erotic thought he might have had. His fingers bent and stiffened, but that didn't stop Annalette from tightening her hold on his hand.

John had been thrown off his guard, and there was little use in preventing the spread of the shift any longer. Still John would try until the last possible moment. He fell to his knees, and she was by his side instantly.

"Please," he pleaded. "Leave me."

"I will not," she insisted. "A wolf should never turn alone."

John roared as his body convulsed, but he would not allow it to shift. Not yet. He pounded his fist into the earth and bellowed in rage. "I will not turn!"

"Don't resist, John. You need to shift outside of your cycle. You must stay balanced."

John spun and glared at her with fangs bared. "Does this look like balance to you?"

She did not run in fear but crawled forward as if he had invited her closer. "You are only in balance when you and your wolf are in one accord," she replied. "Do not demand control of it, but compromise."

He snarled. "There's no reasoning with a beast."

"There is if you try." She cradled his face in her hands like she had the first night they met, when she had calmed the beast for him. "Reach within yourself, John. Make it know who you are."

Everything she said was outlandish and impossible. How could John communicate with something he could not see? How could he speak with a spirit as if it were a breathing being?

One thing was for certain. This was the longest he had ever held back the shift, and it wouldn't be much longer before he had to let go. Then Annalette would be the one to pay for the gift of enlightenment that she had bestowed upon him.

"Focus, John," Annalette coaxed.

He shook his head against her hands. "I can't," he whimpered.

Too quick, even for him, Annalette leaned forward, and their lips met.

The wolf howled, and if John weren't otherwise occupied, he would have howled with it. Pain gave way to bliss in a single moment of intimacy.

He shuddered and then every muscle went slack. He would have crumbled to the ground if it weren't for Annalette. Their lips moved together as if they knew exactly what to do, though John had never been this close to a woman in his life.

The wolf no longer held authority over him. His eyes returned to normal, and his teeth and nails were no longer sharp. The entrancing Romani woman that he barely knew, now dominated his soul, and the shift was no longer the threat. What he would do with her was what occupied his thoughts.

His arms enveloped Annalette and he took her to the ground, straddling over her as they continued to drown in the passionate kiss that made him feel more like a man than ever before. Her hands roamed over his body, going places that had never been touched by a loving caress.

She arched her back, pressing herself into him and he could smell her arousal as an intoxicating fragrance that elicited a moan from both of them.

His own hands explored down her sides, to her hips and legs that had been so hidden by her heavy skirt. He had never realized how shapely they truly were. Skin so soft and smooth seemed to have been blessed by the Holy Trinity.

Annalette's hands paused in their exploration just long enough to unbutton her vest and open it to let loose the breasts beneath. His hands cupped against her blouse as he moved between her legs, preparing to do what nature had intended for the sexes.

He could feel the heat of her desire seep through the front of his trousers, and he didn't have to second guess whether this was what she truly wanted. Her nails scraped down his back as she offered her neck to him. John took it greedily, letting his lips and tongue trail down the sloping curve until she shuddered and sighed beneath him.

Everything about being with her felt right. What they were about to do was pure sin for both of their beliefs, but none of that mattered. Feeling her supple body respond to his every touch was something to which he could become addicted. In every sense, the Romani woman was addicting, and John knew he could never let her go after this night.

A twig snapped, tearing him away from Annalette for a brief moment to listen. The wind carried a distinct scent his way, but his mind was too clouded by lust to make sense of it. She wouldn't let him be distracted for long. She pulled him back down onto her and worked at the fastener on his trousers.

He let himself believe it was an animal or faraway traveler on the road.

The scent came to him once more, and he heard the sound of footsteps approaching.

John pulled away, and this time, he climbed off of her. She let out a cry of displeasure. If only she could realize how disappointed he was as well. It would be difficult to shake her off.

"What's wrong?" she asked.

This time, it was his turn to shush her, and he stared into the night to find the source of the footsteps. Annalette looked around and pushed down her skirts before she set to buttoning up her vest once more, concealing that which he was ready to claim for his own.

John breathed deeply to clear his head, and then sniffed for the scents. There was more than one. Perhaps five men encroaching in from every side.

He pulled Annalette to her feet and in one direction, but it was too late. Ahead, he saw the glint of metal in the moonlight and knew it to be a saber. He tugged her in another direction, but a militiaman came at them in a mad dash.

John prepared to battle, but Annalette stepped in front of him as the men surrounded them. If he were alone, John would have found a way to escape and suffer the cuts of the swords, but Annalette could not heal as he did. Even if he lifted her onto his back and bolted for an escape, she might have been hurt.

"By order of the Queen, you are under arrest, gypsy," shouted one of the men carrying a constable's air of authority, as he wielded his sword to point at Annalette's heart.

Now would have been the opportune moment to let the beast out of the cage, but even if he knew how to summon it, he could not. Annalette held fast to his hand and squeezed it, beseeching him to not do as he was thinking. Fighting the men would not have been a challenge, but for whatever reason, Annalette did not wish it.

John glared at the men who had been saved by the Romani's benevolence, and a couple of them stepped back in trepidation. No matter if Annalette was there or not, John refused to go quietly, and he vowed to instill the fear of the devil in them before the night was over.

CHAPTER 7

The prison was more grotesque than she had imagined. Her nose was assaulted by scents that she could barely stomach. As the warders dragged her down the corridor, her bare feet scraping against the stony floor, Annalette gagged and retched with each breath. Human waste, blood, and death hazed her senses.

She had to hold onto the truth that she wouldn't be there for long or she might go mad. Peeking into the occupied cells, she could see the torch light gleam against the void and despondent faces of prisoners who were also awaiting their gruesome fate.

Annalette cast her gaze to the floor to avoid meeting their desperate stares. She could not save the miserable souls trapped in the Westgate prison. They traveled down a few more winding corridors until they reached a secluded part of the tower with fewer cells and fewer occupants. The warders threw open the iron bars and tossed her inside, as if she were nothing more than a piece of trash to be disposed. In their eyes, all Romani must have been worthless.

The warders left after locking the cell, and Annalette picked herself up off the dank and filthy floor. With only a few torches to give light to this gloomy wing, it was hard to see anything besides the glinting bars of her cage and the light that reflected off the puddles of stagnant water from the leaks in the ceiling.

Looking around, she saw the shadowed figure of a man huddled in the corner. "Gallius?" she asked, hope sparkling in her words.

The figure moved and let out a sputtering cough. "Annalette?"

She fell on her knees before him and reached out for her brother's icy hands. Though he smelled like a corpse, she kissed the back of his fingers.

"You shouldn't be here," he croaked.

"And neither should you," she replied. "But we won't be in here for much longer."

Gallius sat up, and the amber light of the torches fell across his bruised face. The warders had not been gentle with him, but she wouldn't have expected them to be kind to a foreigner. She touched his cheek and grimaced. As soon as they were free of the English brutes, she would tend to his swollen face and whatever other wounds had been afflicted upon him during his captivity.

Everything was going according to plan. All she had to do was wait for John. Nothing had been spoken between them, but she knew that he would come for her.

"How did you get here?" he questioned.

One side of her mouth turned up in a humorless smirk. "Same as you. The Thompsons called the authorities."

His one good eye went wide. "Why did you go to them if you knew they had betrayed me?"

Annalette sat back on her heels and surveyed his torn and wrinkled garments. As her eyes adjusted to the dim light, she saw some places where blood had soaked through the fabric of his tunic. "It was part of my plan," she replied. "I know how careful you have been around towns and there would be no other explanation for your arrest. When you didn't return to camp the other day, I simply pieced together the only possible answer. I knew if I went to the Thompsons, they would turn me in, as well, to get their reward. They needed the money." She shook her head, wishing she could forgive their deceitfulness. "But it will be fine, now. We will be out of here within a day, I assure you."

Gallius' face went blank in confusion. "What do you mean? How – "

She held up a hand to quell his questions. "All you need to know is that we have an ally on the outside and he will do anything to rescue us. He's not above killing everyone in this prison to do it."

Her brother gave her a dubious look. "What ally? What have you done?"

Annalette could fool everyone else, but she could never fool her own brother. They had shared a womb, after all. It was only natural that he would know her better than anyone else. She brushed back a strand of dark hair that had fallen in her face. "I found a man like our uncle. A loup-garou. I convinced him to help me."

There was so much more to her explanation, but Annalette knew that she could never tell her brother about the sins that had led them to this place. He surely would have turned from her in disgust if he knew that she had almost laid with a man to whom she wasn't married, loup-garou or not.

Gallius sighed in disappointment. "Annalette, my dear sister, why would you defile yourself with his company? He is worse than a *gadje*."

A fire of indignation burned in her. "You're wrong," she defied boldly. "He is a kind man. How could you say such things about someone who was willing to rescue you, a perfect stranger?"

"If he is what you say he is," Gallius spat viciously, "then he is an unholy monster. He is *marime*, Annalette. Why can't you see that?"

Her hands balled into fists on her knees. "Because I have not let the traditions of our family cloud my sense of loyalty. I wouldn't have made it this far without him. Always help a brother and always pay when you owe. That's what father always told us."

His nose wrinkled with disgust. "That thing is not my brother, and I owe him nothing."

"He saved my life, Gallius. You can't ignore that."

"For that, I will be thankful, but I will not break bread with him or with you."

Annalette gritted her teeth. "Me?" she hissed. "I have done nothing but try to save you, and you reject me? You are blinder than I thought you were."

"By associating with this loup-garou, you are *marime*."

Annalette gasped at the insult. "How dare you! After I traveled miles over the countryside, endured the company of a stranger, was arrested and thrown into prison for you. I have suffered more than any Romani woman should, and you aren't even thankful for my sacrifice. If anyone is *marime* here, it is you."

Gallius pointed a finger at her. "You see, this man has already polluted you. You would never be so brazen if we were with our *vitsa*."

"No, brother. I have always been this brazen." She shook her head. "I had buried it deep to make myself into what our family wanted me to be. But if this journey has taught me anything, it's that being myself is no crime. I will never be *marime* as long as I am true to myself."

The cell grew silent as Gallius turned away. He was a proud man, a man dedicated to family and tradition. Though Gallius and their uncle had been close, he still turned his back on his own blood. Now that she had come all this way, would he forsake her? Would he refuse her help just because she spent the day in the company of a loup-garou?

When his silence became more than she could bear, she reached out and took him by the shoulders to bring him out of his thoughts. "When John comes, will you be ready to flee with me?"

Gallius looked to her once more, scorn in his eyes for the woman who had risked her life to save him. She had tracked the loup-garou for days, manipulated the vagrants to attack her the night she met John, endured the beast's company all the way from Wye, and put herself in the hands of traitors all for the chance to see her brother again. Would he honor her efforts? Or spit in her face?

Finally, he nodded, but she had a strange feeling that all would never be right between them again. If Gallius could just meet John and get to know the loup-garou, perhaps he would see that not all loups-garous are *marime* at heart. Knowing their uncle should have taught him that, but the years that had passed since their childhood had expunged the truth from Gallius. Only Annalette remembered.

Gallius took pride in his Romani roots and followed their laws to the letter. There wasn't a single more pious man in their *vitsa* than her brother. No doubt, he considered the mere act of speaking to her to be some sort of sin, but one could not look for the devils in everything. Otherwise, they would never see that angels and goodness surrounded them.

Annalette sat back on her heels as a blood-curdling shriek rang and ricocheted off the stone walls of the prison. She winced and tried to block out the sounds of John's anguish. She couldn't know for sure if it was John, but something instinctively told her that it was.

A force deep within her pulled at the scream. It had been tugging at her heart since the moment she parted with the loup-garou. Something unspeakable had taken place earlier that night in the forest, though Annalette couldn't explain it.

When she lay with John, his hands gliding across her skin with feathery softness and the gentleness of a true lover, Annalette felt a spark in her spirit. At first, the sensuous kisses had been part of her scheme. If she could make John care for her as more than a helpless maiden, if she could play the part of a lover, then he would be more inclined to free them.

She had known that they would not be in the same cell once they were brought to Canterbury. The authorities dealt with the associates of Romani differently, and the evidence could be clearly heard by all in the prison. So, if she were to be free, John needed to be on the outside and rescue them from their cell.

Her plan had dire consequences. Those brief, passionate moments with John were nothing but pure bliss, and she would cherish them for the rest of her life, even after they parted ways. Annalette neither knew where her uncle was, nor where an alpha might be. She couldn't hold up her end of the deal and John was the one who would be fooled. As soon as they escaped the prison, she and Gallius would have to flee from the loup-garou before he caught onto the truth.

She hated herself for wanting to feel him against her body one more time, knowing that she might never get the chance. Simply remembering the way he touched her made her cheeks flush and core ache for more.

Cold strategy had turned into true desire when John reminded her that she was indeed a desirable woman. No man may ever touch her that way again, especially if she never married. John showed her intimacy like no one ever could, and her heart no longer beat for her Romani family, but for the loup-garou who was being tortured because of her selfishness.

As she sat there, listening to the cries of the man she wanted to trust, as the whip scored into his flesh, Annalette knew that leaving John would not be easy. A bond had formed between them, and she hardly realized it until it was too late. Leaving him would be the hardest thing she had ever done, but it had to be done. She had no future with him. Her future was with her people.

John screamed as he felt the tight knots of the cat o' nine tails lacerate his skin. The blood from his gashed flesh dripped all the way down to the back of his heels and he continued to slip on it as his feet met the cold stone. His torturer repeatedly whipped him, slashing into his back and sides too many times to count.

"I don't understand," he grumbled to his partner. "He's either got some tough skin, or this whip is useless."

John could feel the edges of his filleted flesh begin to mend as the punishment continued. The warder didn't realize how resilient his prisoner could be. They would be in that cell until judgment day and John would still walk out with a flawless body, but that didn't stop him from feeling every lash of the deep cutting whip.

His lifeblood ran in a pool on the floor, the backside of his pants soaked through until the fabric clung to his legs. His hands wrapped around the chains that bound his wrists and spread his arms out wide to receive his just penalty for being associated with a gypsy.

The whip went still, and John hung his head, his breaths ragged as he sensed another man enter the room. "Is he dead yet? It's been an hour since you began."

Time had passed by in a blur for John. It had been an hour filled with nothing but ceaseless torment at the hands of his captors. One thought kept him awake and vigil. Annalette was somewhere in the prison, and he could smell her fear beneath the congesting odors of bile, blood, and filth.

"Not yet, milord," the warder replied.

Footsteps came close and his muscles tensed as the wolf readied to strike back. The animal in him had been caged, but John knew that now was not the right time. He had to wait for the perfect moment.

The men gasped and fingers pressed into his flesh. "There are no cuts!" one exclaimed. "How is that possible? Look at all the blood!"

The new man, who smelled of riches and finery, stepped around to face the prisoner. John closed his eyes, knowing they were a deep and fierce gold in response to the immense agony he had been subjected to.

"How can you bleed, but not have wounds?" the man asked. He recognized the voice and scent as belonging to the constable, the one who had put them under arrest in the forest. "Speak, you swine!" he bellowed, but John would not give in to the need to retaliate.

After a moment, the constable walked away. "Bring me the hot iron," he ordered.

John groaned, knowing what awaited him.

One of the warders came back, and he could hear the hot metal sizzling. There was no warning as the iron was passed to the constable. The fiery tip penetrated his side, and he could feel it scorch his flesh as it jammed up beneath his ribs and pierced a lung.

He roared like a beast and pulled on the chains until the links snapped. John fell to the ground, and the constable yanked the iron from his body. The warders muttered to one another, and he heard them shuffle backward to put distance between themselves and the beast.

The constable leaned down and observed as John's wound healed over, leaving behind little more than a streak of dark blood that ran down his side to prove that he had been injured. There wasn't a scar or blemish to verify it otherwise.

With his legs still shackled together, he couldn't run, but he turned to the constable and let out a sinister growl to make his displeasure known. Golden eyes shone through the darkness and the constable held up the iron as if it would protect him from the monster he faced.

John eyed the white-hot tip of the weapon and how it trembled in the constable's hands.

"Someone get the priest!" he shouted.

The warder that had been tearing into John's flesh for an hour dropped his whip and scuttled out of the cell. John snapped his fangs at the constable and sent the man scurrying to the cell doors.

"A priest cannot save you from me," John thundered, a bit of the wolf's words slipping through in an effort to terrify the humans that gaped at him. For once, they were of one mind. They both wanted freedom and to take revenge upon those who had hurt him.

More than anything, they wanted to free Annalette. It was as if her soul and his were tied together somehow, and until Annalette was in his arms again, he could not rest.

Through the fetid and moldy air of the prison, he could smell her below him in cells where the other prisoners were kept, awaiting their execution or other punishment. He had overheard talk that she and her brother, along with a few other gypsies they had collected, would be hanged at dawn on the gallows by Canterbury Castle. First, they would be paraded through the streets for all the townspeople to jeer at them from afar, degrading them to something less than human.

There was no time to waste, and morning would bring with it worse horrors.

"He must be in league with the devil," he heard the constable whisper to his warder. "The priest will know what to do with him."

John, on his hands and knees, crawled around to face the men who plotted his fate. He could smell their fear, and his wolf basked in it, relishing his victory over his captors. They were powerless, and they knew it. Weapons would do them no good against a loup-garou and chains could not bind him.

Even though his wolf was ready to tear them apart, his strength had not fully returned. The last hour weakened him more than he wanted them to know. He would use every means at his disposal to dispirit them. He snarled and behaved like a caged beast until the priest arrived.

The man looked tired as he entered the cell, probably awoken from a deep slumber to come running at the constable's request. As soon as the holy man's eyes fell on John, he fished out his crucifix and crossed himself as protection against the profane demon before him.

He uttered Latin phrases that John knew all too well. It was what he had heard each time a priest tried to exorcise the demon from his mortal soul. It failed every time, and this would be no different. What the human didn't know was that this was no spirit that could be wished away. The wolf was part of him and always would be. He realized that now, thanks to Annalette.

When his words proved useless, the priest shook his head in disbelief. "He must be a witch. He must have given himself to Satan, and he is beyond salvation. No confession is necessary. He must be burned and beheaded."

At the mention of beheading, John paused and slunk into a corner, daring any of them to try and detain him long enough to even get close to severing his head from his body. He would fight until his claws and fangs became dull, but he would not die that night. Annalette gave him a reason to keep breathing, and he would take firm hold of the hope she had given him.

CHAPTER 8

I t seemed as if half of the town had gathered to watch his execution. John had heard once that they hung the witches before they burned them, but the constable and Justice of the Peace did not impart such mercies. It would have done little good anyway. He had tried to hang himself on the sturdy limb of an elm decades ago, but his neck was too strong and the wolf too determined to live.

He looked to his right where the gallows stood just outside of Canterbury Castle. If his plan failed, Annalette and her brother would be dragged to this very spot in the shadow of the great castle at dawn. If he still had breath within him, he would not allow it.

John's trek through the center of the city had drawn out the sleeping villagers. Some were roused by the sound of the heavy chains scraping against the stone pavement. Others, however, were summoned upon orders. Wards banged on their doors and called them out to witness the execution, though John had hoped this would be a quiet affair. He should have known better than to wish for such a thing. The execution of a criminal was an exciting event in quiet towns. Next to gossip, it was something villagers practically lived for.

As the pyre was mounded high with wrapped bunches of branches and dried hay, John silently waited on the platform with his hands tied in chains behind his back. His feet and torso were also bound to the post so tightly that his digits had nearly gone numb. The iron links bit into his belly and the crook of his elbows.

An executioner, with his face shrouded in a black mask, stood nearby with his heavy axe in hand. Once John's body would begin to burn, his head would be relieved of his neck, but he had a plan before the eager axe-man got the chance.

The warders and constable should have known that these chains couldn't hold him.

His keen ears listened closely to the hushed and anxious conversations of the crowd. The women asked why he was being executed so strangely. The men had their own theories before the constable would make his announcement. Children with sleep still crusted along their eyelids clung to their mothers' skirts, probably wondering why they had been dragged out of bed at such a late hour.

John's eyes were brown once more, and the wolf paced back and forth within him, just as nervous as he was, but he used such emotions to his advantage. In the Westgate prison, on the other side of Canterbury, was Annalette, who had no idea about her impending death. She depended upon him, needed him to succeed, or else they would all be dead. No one else was going to come to her rescue.

Slowly, he began to look inward, just as Annalette had said. He reached within himself and found the wolf. With his eyes closed, he focused upon it. A primal, savage being that was both willing and ready to come out and greet the people who dared to try and kill him. This time, John would not force it back.

There was no one in the crowd, no one around the pyre that he personally cared for or wanted to preserve. The only person he cared about was the woman locked away in a cell, who neither deserved to be killed nor the persecution she faced. The world had been a cruel and unfair place, and Annalette was his shining star that lit up the darkness inside. He would stop at nothing, until he knew such a light would be his and his alone. The world owed him that much.

John's lips moved as he silently made supplications to the wolf, making a verbal pact with it. If he could just have control, just for this moment, they would no longer be at war. He recognized the wolf for what it was and vowed to respect it as Annalette had been trying to teach him.

In just a few moments, he would find out if the wolf heard his blasphemous prayer.

"This man," the constable began as the crowd fell into a hush, "is possessed by a demon. He is in league with the devil himself!"

A gasp rippled through the crowd. Some jeered and shouted insults to John, speaking to the demon as if they had any religious right to do so, but he let their jeers roll off his shoulders. They were just as ignorant as he had been.

"We shall burn the demon from his body so that his soul may be saved by the Almighty God in heaven." He turned to the priest who was standing by, holding a rosary in his shaking hands. The constable gave a quick nod to hand the assembly to him.

The holy man approached the unlit pyre and turned to John. He could hear the priest's teeth rattle together as he spoke. "This is your final chance, demon," he shouted with his pulpit voice. "Leave this child of God now, and you will be spared the fires of hell!"

John closed his eyes, and when he opened them again, he knew the gold flickered through brighter than the torch that was waiting to be dropped at his feet. "I am no demon," he proclaimed. "I am loup-garou!"

Those who must have known French shrank back. Those who didn't were soon given the translation. John was a werewolf, half man and half beast. What they didn't know was that a meager fire would not stop him, and whatever attempt to save his soul would be in vain. It didn't need saving.

The priest, with eyes wide, crossed himself and turned away to give the torch-bearer the cue to light the pyre. There were cries of fear as John's gold eyes surveyed the crowd that came to watch his demise. The men stepped in front of their women who clutched their babies tighter. As soon as the fire of the torch kindled the first of the wood bundles, they changed their tune and were grateful that they would be rid of the beast soon.

John felt the heat around his legs first, and then it crept up his chest to warm his face. Sparks and embers floated to the dark sky and faded with the stars as the wood and hay ignited.

He writhed against his iron bonds, but the smoke he inhaled made him weak, and the chains would not budge. He gritted his teeth as he watched the fire spread around the platform. It was only a matter of minutes before his clothes and skin would be licked by the flames.

The crowd cheered, hastening the blaze with their hateful words. Produce like cabbage and tomatoes were thrown at him and tumbled into the pyre, but it would not deter his concentration. He breathed in the smoke and sputtered a cough, as the flames grew higher around him and washed his body in a tawny glow.

He growled in his throat and supplicated to the wolf once more. If it didn't come forward, they would both perish. He could still see the glimmering of the fire in the metal blade of the executioner's axe.

When the first patch of skin on his ankle was seared, the wolf came alive. John roared, his sharp fangs bared for the spectators that wanted the monster dead. The executioner flinched, but would not drop his weapon.

John struggled against the bonds until the iron links finally snapped. He stood, free and surrounded by the vindicating fire. To them, he must have looked like the devil himself, but his transformation wasn't complete.

The wolf melded into the man, amalgamating with his body until they were truly one.

John began to shift.

The pain was intense, but not nearly as agonizing as it had been in the past. He let the wolf have reign and didn't fight the shift. He had spent countless nights fighting against the spirit he should have embraced from the beginning. Now, it was time to make amends.

When it was over, the crowds were screaming and running for the safety of their homes.

John looked down to his new form through the eyes of the wolf. He had been a large man to begin with, but he grew nearly twice in size, and a thick layer of ebony fur covered his body that was slightly singed by the flames.

For the first time, he was conscious of the shift. He looked to his hands. His palms and the undersides of his digits were crusted in thick and calloused skin like the paws on a dog and tipped with vicious claws to match. His upper body kept the same structure as a human with arms and a broad chest, while his legs, feet, and head were that of a wolf's. A tail swung behind him and bumped against the post he had been tied to. His torn clothes were slowly being reduced to ash upon the platform.

John turned to his executioner who had lost control of his bowels and shrieked before darting into the darkness. The priest took shelter in his church while the constable and Justice of the Peace were left standing, staring at the beast. Wards and militiamen fled to the burning pyre with their flashing sabers in hand, ready to take on the devilish beast.

John was too quick. He bellowed and leapt from the podium to come crashing to the cobblestone square. The brave men rushed forward, but with a powerful sweep of his arm, he sent them and their swords flying. A few blades found purchase and sliced into his skin, but it would not slow him down. Within seconds, his flesh bound itself back together, and not a single drop of blood fouled the ground.

When the immediate threats were pushed aside, he dropped to all fours and galloped his way to the prison. His wolfish head ducked low and lips pulled back into a determined snarl. They could follow all they wanted, but they would not catch him at full speed.

If he thought he was fast as a human, he was doubly fast on loup-garou legs. It explained why he had sometimes traveled dozens of miles in one night while under the influence of the wolf. Now, he had complete control of his destination. Houses and shops flew by in a blur as he retraced his path back to Westgate, following the wild scent of the woman he had to protect.

The warders in front of the prison gates stood their ground with their swords, but once they realized that it was no giant stray dog or a bear barreling toward them, they abandoned their posts without further hesitation.

Instead of taking the path that had been cleared for him, John leapt onto the side of the stone tower where Annalette was being held captive. With his sharp claws latched into the rock, he scaled the wall until he reached the very top, and climbed through the archer's port.

After slamming aside a few daring guards who had been posted there, John traveled down the spiral stairs to the place where the prisoners were kept. It didn't take him long to find Annalette, but she was not alone. The wolf balked at the presence, but John remained in control and did not show his annoyance.

When he came to her cell, he found her at the bars, gripping them tightly with her delicate hands. Her lips parted, and eyes widened as she stared at the beast that had come to save her. He detected a trace of fear, but it was soon gone when John stood to face her.

An energy passed between them that stunned him for only a moment. The aching in his soul subsided when he laid eyes upon her, and even though chaos exploded within the prison, his world was perfect now that she was near.

Though he could not speak with a human tongue, he could impart what she needed to know without words. He took hold of the cell door and snapped the lock with a quick tug. It was time to leave.

Annalette did not come at first but turned to the other man in the cell that John didn't know. The stranger rose to his feet, transfixed by the loup-garou. Only upon Annalette's bidding, he came to the open door and followed her out.

They were slow in comparison to John's long gait as they escaped out of the prison. While he bounded down the stairs, six steps at a time, they struggled to keep up. When they arrived at the main floor of the tower, the other prisoners stared and shrieked in horror.

Several guards tried to intercept them in the narrow passages, but John dealt with them easily enough and slammed them against the stone bricks until either the rock or their skulls cracked with the force. They were no match for his strength and size. If they had silver, then they might have had a chance.

Once outside of the prison, they avoided the main thoroughfares, and made their way to the safety of the forest. It was hard to say whether anyone would follow them. Some peasants, warders, and watchers scoured through the trees with their torches and pitchforks to find the beast, but John and his Romani allies were smarter and traveled south, away from the town and river, deeper into the downs. Annalette had mentioned her family was in Dover, and that's where they would go.

None had spoken a word since their escape, but John deduced that the man in their company was Annalette's brother, Gallius. They had a similar scent, no doubt from the family blood they shared. He was injured and weak but kept up with the party as they fled far away from Canterbury and the civilization that wanted them all dead.

John would not stop until he could no longer hear the searching villagers or the frenzied warders who were still trying to make sense of what happened back at the castle and Westgate. They were already past the village of Nackington when Annalette and Gallius stopped and collapsed against an obliging tree. They did not have his unending stamina to travel for miles on end, especially as tired and weary as they were.

The loup-garou padded to their side and brushed his muzzle against Annalette's shoulder. The man and the wolf needed to know that she was there, safe and out of danger from the world that hated both of them.

"I'm all right," she answered to his mute question. "We just need to rest."

John understood and turned to patrol the area while the humans made their beds in the leaves and slept. They were free at last. Free to stay or to leave the country, but they would not face death at dawn as the law had demanded.

Somehow, the loup-garou was not at ease. Not completely.

After groping into the void, lacking the understanding of what he was, John had finally taken hold of himself, even if it was a loose grip. He felt what it was like to walk as a loup-garou and not a frightened man who thought he was possessed by some evil spirit. The wolf was not evil, only wild and untamed. It needed guidance, but so did John.

Annalette was the one hope for both man and beast. Now that he had held up his end of the bargain, it was her turn. They would roam all of England to find her uncle or another alpha who would be willing to train him. He remembered the baker in Chilham and knew that would be his first choice, but there was a chance that the alpha would not trust a stranger into his pack. If he could find Annalette's uncle, then the initial meeting might not be so tense. They had the young Romani woman as a mutual connection, which would be something in his favor.

As he stalked the woods, he thought of the world that had opened up to him. Now that he was no longer crippled by ignorance, John felt as if he could live again.

More than that, he wondered how many others like himself were living in darkness. How many more sons had been abandoned by their fathers too soon? How many men and adolescents had been bitten and turned into loups-garous, and had no direction from those that turned them? What were they doing? John had survived a hundred years without knowing the truth, so how many more had been living the same way for much longer? Was it a rarity for an uneducated loup-garou to live as long as he did?

Something began to burn in his chest. It was a need to find them, to tell them that there was hope and a way out of the gloom and cursed life into which they had been thrown. His wolf agreed and longed for the companionship that only a pack could offer. He might not have known how to fully control his body just yet, but he would. Once he did, there was nothing to stop him from helping those who could not help themselves.

The sun had risen over England, the threat of death finally behind them. Though the queen still wanted all gypsies out of her country and every peasant and nobleman was willing to turn in old friends for the ransom she offered, Annalette knew that her stay there was not over. Danger lurked in every village and behind every smiling face, but she couldn't leave. Not yet.

That was why she hid behind the oak tree, watching John as he bathed in the shallow creek near where they had stopped to rest for the night. Sunlight sparkled off the rippling current and the water droplets that speckled his skin. He faced away from Annalette and her eyes caressed the strong curve of his back.

A pair of trousers were neatly folded on the bank, probably stolen from a nearby cottage or traveler. The shift had rendered him naked, and without her pack, she was without supplies as well. That's why it was important for her and Gallius to leave soon and find her *vitsa*. Once she was reunited with them, all would be well, and she could put the unpleasant business of abandoning John behind her.

She couldn't leave without seeing the loup-garou one last time. It was a risk to leave John, knowing that her end of the deal had not been fulfilled, but she had no way of tracking down her uncle or any other alpha for that matter. John was a clever man, and now that he knew there was a new world waiting for him, he would find a way to carry on without her. Could she?

Her heart tugged in two drastically different directions. All she wanted, since the beginning of her scheme, was to bring her family back together and perhaps prove her usefulness. Now, she had fallen hard for the man she thought she could deceive. So far, her trickery had worked, but she hated that it worked so well. She hated how she felt about John and everything that had transpired in such a short time. He had turned her life upside down, which was never in her plans.

Annalette watched as he cupped water in his hands and tossed it down his shoulders before dipping his head below the surface to rid himself of the grime and dirt from the night before. The part of her that admired John for what he was, burst with pride for his accomplishment. He took control of the wolf and worked with it to achieve what he wanted. No victory was ever sweeter than to see a man succeed.

A deep frown formed between her eyes as she thought of all the triumphs he would have without her. One day, he would be able to shift back and forth at will more fluidly. He'd be able to shift into his purest wolf form and command the golden eyes of the loup-garou, but she would not see it. She would see none of it.

When she turned, her chest heavy with a loss that should never have been hers, she heard him speak.

"I know you're there," John called.

Annalette froze and listened to the water slosh as he turned and climbed back onto solid ground. Like a fool, she turned and beheld the loup-garou in all his magnificence. Her blood sang with the familiar lustful tunes that she had hoped to never hear again.

Even when she was awaiting her rescue in the cell, sitting in filth and listening to the moans of the other prisoners awaiting execution, the memory of John's kiss and touch invaded her thoughts. If Gallius could have sensed her impurity, he would have been utterly disgusted – more than he already was. To Annalette, it was the most natural thing to be so drawn to a man like John.

After just a day, she knew that he was everything a man should be. Bold, caring, and selfless beyond explanation. He would make a great leader, and Annalette knew that she would have no part in the long future for which he was destined.

As he approached, river water drizzling down his limbs and chest, Annalette couldn't help but want to be part of everything he did and everything he was. It was out of the question, but her heart would not listen to reason.

She turned away again, but his hands gently gripped her hips to prevent her exodus. Her body hummed with expectation and the war between her heart and her mind resumed once more. A soft breath escaped her lips, and her head tilted back until it made contact with one of his broad shoulders.

His hard arousal pressed against her skirts and she flinched for only a moment before melting into his warm embrace that encircled her torso. Her hands, trembling as they were, found his and gripped tight to keep them still, before he could do something they would both come to regret.

"Please, don't," she whispered.

Instantly, John dropped his arms and moved away. A coldness passed over her as his absence was keenly felt. If she weren't pretending, she would have urged him to take her in his arms once more, just to fill the void he had created by pressing his way into her heart and then withdrawing.

"What's wrong?" he asked, his deep voice rumbling in her chest.

Annalette swallowed and shook her head. "You're making this difficult for me," she admitted.

She didn't have to see his face to know that it was crinkled in confusion. He still had no clue about the torment she endured.

"What? What am I making difficult?"

Though every part of her wanted to turn and face the man she had tricked, she couldn't. If she did, she would be lost and beg for what neither of them could have. A future, a life together, a love that was scandalous and forbidden by her people.

The kiss from the evening before had been a ploy to afford the militiamen more time, as well as to seal the fragile trust between them. Annalette had been desperate to get to her brother, up to forsaking her own innocence and virginity. She allowed John to touch her in places that should have been kept consecrated for marriage. She let herself drown in him, but it was a dying ember that could never be rekindled. Not now, not ever. She would be unsatisfied until her dying breath.

"I must leave," she finally said, a slight quake in her voice as she let the words float through the morning air.

John was silent for a moment, before he quietly stepped around to stand in front of her. Annalette's legs would not obey her command to flee. She felt like a child standing before an angry parent, but John was not angry. He appeared even more confused and heartbroken with his brown eyes narrowed upon her.

"Leave?" he repeated. "But, you said – "

"I know what I said," she snapped with a flick of her wrist. "But, I cannot stay. I must find my family. Gallius is safe, and if we hurry, we can arrive before our family passes into mourning. You did what I asked of you, and for that, I will be forever grateful... But, I can't stay here."

John stepped closer, and that subtle move spurred Annalette into action. She hurried to pass him by, but John grabbed her by the arm.

"I will go with you."

She shook her head. "No. Gallius knows what you are. If you go with us, he will tell my family. You wouldn't be welcome in the camp."

"The forest isn't safe for the Romani, especially now that militia from Canterbury will be looking for two escaped prisoners. I can escort you through to Dover."

She shook her head again, her dark hair tumbling around her shoulders as hot tears stung at the corners of her eyes. "No, John. Gallius will not allow you to join us. He is not like me. He sees loups-garous as unbalanced beasts. He sided with my family when they exiled my uncle. I cannot put you through such persecution."

John's grip tightened on her arm, but not with bruising force as she had expected. "I can follow from a distance."

She stamped her bare foot in the lush grass and slashed her arm through the air as if trying to push away his constant rebuttals. "I cannot bear your company, up close or from a distance. Don't put me through this torture," she cried.

The tears flooded down her cheeks. It was hard to leave her family. It was hard to allow herself the dishonor of being arrested and thrown into prison, but, to leave him was the hardest challenge she ever had to face. If she had to break his heart to get away, then so be it. She would not leave these woods with the loup-garou in tow. Yet, the knowledge that she would never see him again was enough to shatter her spirit. How could she live without him?

John released her, but Annalette did not run immediately. She walked ahead, her chest and shoulders quivering with the silent sobs. He did not follow, at least not that she could tell.

Annalette must have made it only a few yards before the weight of her sorrow descended upon her like a heavy mantel, and she crumbled to the forest floor. John was there to catch her, and she cried into his chest, her fingers spread across his skin.

Tender hands brought her in, but it was his warmth that soothed her soul and provoked her to explain her hysteric show of emotion. For once, her brokenness was not a trick.

"I've lied to you," she said through her whimpers. "I've lied to you from the beginning. I can't continue with you, knowing that I've treated you so vile."

"What did you lie about?" he asked. "Is Gallius not your brother?"

Annalette laughed through her tears. "Nothing so harmless. I knew you were a loup-garou before we ever met. I heard rumors about something that was stealing captured game from traps, and when I investigated, I recognized that it wasn't any ordinary beast taking the game. There was intelligence behind it. So, I knew it must have been a loup-garou.

"I took a chance letting those two beggars harass me. I provoked them into trying to force themselves on me, because I knew you were close by. I had no idea you would kill them. I knew from experience with my uncle that I could use you to help me get Gallius out of prison. I took us to the Thompson's homestead because I knew they would tell the authorities that I was there. They betrayed my brother, and I knew they would betray me."

Annalette sniffled back a fresh wave of regret. "I deceived you into helping me, and now I am no better than what they say about gypsies. I cannot take you to my uncle or to an alpha. I don't know where to begin searching for them, and nor do I want to. I need to be with my family. I can't travel as you have encouraged before. There are so many things I should have never done with you, never told you. I have lied and cheated you." She looked into his face, mustering every ounce of dignity that she had left in her. "But, you have done something far worse. You have stolen my heart."

She expected John to rage, to roar like a beast and toss her into the dirt like the sinful vixen he had accused her of being the night before. He did nothing of the sort. He gazed upon her with a look that Annalette couldn't distinguish.

John pulled her in tighter and kissed her lips that were seasoned with her tears. Annalette did not beat against his chest or struggle to get free of his hold, but gave into the kiss and sighed against his mouth without question.

The kiss was as fervent as it had been the night before, but now there were no secrets between them, and she was not compelled to carry on the charade. He was aware of her treachery and what she had done to him, but his kiss told her plainly that he was not furious with her. Why? She might never know.

That honest kiss and every caress that followed sent Annalette into the storm of passion and longing that she had tried to avoid since the minute she realized that she could come to care for John as more than a pawn in her ruse. It overtook her and rendered her defenseless against the loup-garou.

He lowered her to the ground, and they finished what they had started the evening before. With her vest open and skirt hiked to her waist, John pleasured her in every way that a woman could wish. In a blur of fiery desire, his hands and mouth moved across her body to places that had never been awakened before, sending her deeper into the depths of passion and thrilling her body from the tips of her toes to the untouched recesses of her mind.

She raked her nails across his skin, and he shuddered as he let out a low growl against her neck. It was a growl of pleasure and not of anger. She explored his body, touching and stroking in as many places as he would allow, and he did not bar her from anywhere.

His hard arousal slid up her thigh and she gasped as the heat of expectation flooded between her legs. One of his arms hooked around her back, lifting just enough to receive him with ease. The energy, the tingling between her legs, continued to build as he teased her with his kisses that traveled down her neck, to her shoulders, and then to her chest.

She gripped his hair, silently begging him to linger there until the world ended, but there was more to experience, more to savor.

His lips seized hers once more as he moved closer and closer to the center of the heat. The unbearable wait for the moment when two would become one was more than she could bear.

John pulled back to meet her feverish gaze. A question lay there, but he should have known the answer. Annalette wiggled against him in just the right way to show that she was eager and waiting. His body went rigid as a groan rattled his chest. Just to hear that she could please him so, thrilled her just as much as his caresses.

When he entered her, filling the core of her desire, they moaned and spiraled higher and higher together. The bliss of every movement sent her soaring, and Annalette wanted nothing more than this moment to last for all eternity, suspended in the glorious union of two people in love.

There was an end and what a superb ending it was. She shuddered as her body and flesh burned with the yearning for release. When it came, Annalette dug her nails into John's arms and let out a shriek of pleasure and let herself go limp in his embrace.

At the same time, she felt him swell inside of her, pulsating with his own release as they came to the climax of their passion together.

Breathless and weak, they laid in each other's arms as the world carried on around them, as if nothing magical had just taken place in the forests of England. Annalette could feel her heartbeat throughout her body, making her limbs twitch with the residual effects of John's love.

There was no accurate way to describe the euphoria Annalette experienced, nor the joy that filled her soul with the knowledge that John seemed to have forgiven her, though she had completely betrayed his trust. There was no hatred in his lovemaking, nor resentment in anything he did to her. Everything was saturated with love and longing. How could they go their separate ways after this?

She rolled her head to the side and met his lips one more time. John brushed his nose against hers and grinned at her in that dazzling way that made her core tighten with eagerness for more.

"I will follow you both from a distance," he whispered, his breath pluming upon her face, "and make sure that you arrive to your family safely."

Annalette reached out and found the strength to take hold of his arm. "But... what about you?" she asked, searching his expression for any hint that he wasn't serious. How could they do what they just did and part ways so casually? She couldn't do it. Not anymore.

"You belong with your family," he said, his smile fading. "If that is your choice, I will find an alpha on my own."

She squeezed his arm. "Will you come back?" she asked, her voice thick with emotion.

He nodded. "If you'll allow me."

Annalette pressed another kiss to his lips and rolled onto her side. "If my *vitsa* could accept you too, would you stay?"

"Gallius already knows what I am," he reminded her, his words laced with remorse. "If he tells them, it'll be just as you said. We would be no better off than if I had never stepped foot in your camp."

Her bottom lip quivered as her chest clenched with dread. John was right, but Annalette didn't want it to be so. She couldn't lose him, not after all they had been through. "I can't do this."

John bent his head to hers. "You are Romani," he said slowly, enunciating each word as if they were the bread of life made especially for her. "You belong with your family, and I belong in a pack."

"Then I'll come with you."

"I could never ask that you leave your home and family for me."

"What if I offered? What if I said I wanted to?"

It went against everything she had been taught to believe. Family was everything. It was why she risked her life to save Gallius. It was why she defended Nicu. It was why she had tried so hard to be everything they expected her to be and why she failed so miserably at being a Romani woman.

John had shown her another way. There was a whole world out waiting to be seen. Their talk about traveling no longer seemed so impossible now that they had each other. Perhaps she was naïve. Perhaps she was placing her heart in his hands too readily. But she knew what she felt, and if he asked her to, she'd pull down the very stars in the heavens just to make him smile. He had become more precious to her than any family she had.

He shook his head. "You're not thinking clearly."

Annalette sat up and placed her hands upon his chest, feeling his heartbeat drum against her palms. "My mind has never been this clear, John Croxen. Whether it's pure or not, I love you."

His lips parted, but he did not return the sentiment as she had predicted. It was then that she second guessed herself. Did he not feel the same all along? The passion they shared just moments before, had it been nothing to him? What about the bond that connected them? Was that not real too?

Gazing deep into his eyes, she knew that what they shared had been true. It was not a trick to gain acceptance. Annalette bared herself, wholly and completely. John, on the other hand, was still hesitant, and she could only guess it was because of her previous deception. It would take more than a few mawkish words to earn his trust again.

Silence passed between them before John sat up and took her hands in his. "If living for this long has taught me anything, it is to assess yourself more carefully before making a decision. Wait until we find your family and see if you feel the same way once you see them again."

Annalette took a deep breath and then nodded, knowing full well that it would only waste more time. She knew her mind and what she wanted now.

CHAPTER 9

John perched himself on a high limb of an oak as he watched Annalette make her way back to the place where she and Gallius had spent the night. His eyes followed the way her hips swung with each step, and he dug his claws into the bark of the tree to bring himself back to the task at hand.

Yes, John was upset that Annalette had lied to him and used him so dishonestly. It had been a trick since before they even met, but her tears were genuine and heartfelt. The plan had changed since they started out together just outside Wye along the River Stour. Her regret was palatable, almost as much as her fear of rejection by his hand. John could not be mad as she came to this stunning revelation that she had fallen in love with him through the course of their short journey.

What hurt more than her deceit was the realization that he could not keep her. This had all been so she could return to her people, to her home. John could not, in good conscience, bar her from that right. Just as he had told Annalette, she was blinded by the feminine impulses to run after love with abandon. Once she realized that she would miss her family too much, she would change her mind and leave him, and his loup-garou heart broken.

She was a wild creature who had caged herself for all the wrong reasons. Now that she had a taste of freedom, she wanted more. Regret was something he knew well, and because John cared for her, he would not let her make that fatal mistake. The life of a vagabond suited him, but he could not drag her down with him.

John had never experienced love, nor knew it intimately as some did. He did not have the love of a family to support him as a youth. His mother, as kind as she was, hesitated when it came to loving her own son. She told John that he reminded her of why she no longer had her father, why she was reduced to a servant and could never be free. She did not once express the warmth and caring that mothers usually showed to their children.

To have Annalette confess that she loved him was a startling thing. John could not return the sentiment because he didn't know how. He wasn't even sure if he loved her in kind. He cared for her more than any other human alive, and he couldn't deny the bond that had formed during their lovemaking. He wasn't even sure what had driven him to the sinful impulses that overtook them near the river. Maybe it was the way she looked so beautiful, even when she cried, or perhaps the way she bared her soul for him so candidly. Whatever it was, that was one thing he would never regret about her.

The Romani woman in the clearing below had subverted his spirit, and with every breath, he knew that it would be painful to leave her, more painful than any bodily transformation he would ever undergo.

Below, Annalette stood and turned in a circle, her dark eyes sweeping the trees and bushes. "Gallius!" she called out, cupping her hands around her mouth so that the sound carried farther into the woods.

There was no response. John sniffed the air for the Romani, but his scent was faint, as if he hadn't been in the clearing for hours. He leapt from his hiding place and dropped down to join Annalette.

She gasped and turned with her hand to her chest. Seeing it to be her lover, she relaxed and let out a long breath. "I didn't know you were so close," she said.

John glanced over his shoulder to the branch from where he had jumped, which was nearly fifty feet from the ground. "Where's Gallius?" he asked, surveying the clearing with her.

She shrugged and held out her arms with a flair of exasperation. "I don't know. When I left, he was asleep... or, I thought he was asleep."

John sniffed again and caught onto Gallius' scent. He followed it from the direction they came the night before, to the place he had laid for the night, and then to the south. He had left behind a scattering of tells that led him to believe that he ran through the thicket. Judging by the fading traces, he was long gone.

He heaved a sigh and turned to Annalette. Her distraught expression told him enough.

"Maybe he tried to look for me when he woke up, and I wasn't here?" she offered. "Or maybe he went to fetch firewood to make breakfast?"

"Without cooking gear?" John asked with a hint of disbelief.

Annalette crossed her arms over her chest, but would not confess what she was truly thinking. And John would not say it either.

He wrapped her in a hug and whispered in her ear, "We will find him."

He would, even if he had to trek across the whole of England to find the man that caused his beloved so much pain.

The Romani camp was somber. There was not the usual music, laughter, and singing that she was accustomed to in the evenings. It was clear that her paternal uncle was extremely close to death's door or had passed over the threshold into the world of the dead. She could just barely make out the faces of the men and women who talked softly amongst themselves around the campfire. Some drank ale from their mugs, others pushed around the food upon their tin plates as deep frowns crinkled their foreheads. The mourning phase was long and structured for the Romani, and close kin would continue to mourn for years after the funeral was over.

The urge to run into the camp and proclaim her return was indisputable, but John held her in place, his hand gripping the back of her vest to keep her from plunging forward too soon. They had traveled all day, tracking Gallius' scent until they came to the southern edge of the Kent Downs in the heart of the lower region of the county. They knew Gallius was amongst them, but they did not know how he had been received or what he had told them already.

"I have to go to them," she whispered to John.

He nodded. "I will be close by. I won't leave until you tell me to."

She turned to meet his gaze, so soft and yet also hopeful. "I would never want you to leave, John."

Standing beside him in the shadows of the forest, she couldn't believe she had come to this place, forsaking her roots for the love of a man that they would never truly accept. If Gallius had any mercy at all, he would stay silent and let her family believe that John could be a viable husband for her. That was the only way they would let a *gajo* into their family. If they knew he was loup-garou, there was no chance. She had to know either way.

A smile spread over his lips, as he reached out to tenderly touch her cheek and slip a lock of dark hair behind her ear. "I will wait until I hear word."

She knew that he was still hesitant to accept her decision. Coming back to her camp had reminded her of the love and loyalty she felt for her family, but she hadn't changed her mind yet. The dream of seeing the world with John at her side was still irresistible, but if she could have both John and her family, then she might have preferred that.

She took his hand and kissed his palm before she turned to the Romani camp. She trod softly forward, both unwilling to startle them and understanding the reality of the grief they must have been experiencing.

Her mother was the first to see her. The older woman, dressed in a bright blue skirt and flowing blouse, was feeding the scraps from dinner to the dog that followed their camp across England. Her face was wrinkled from age and the weary work that motherhood demanded, but Annalette could see the deep lines around her mouth from the millions of sweet smiles she had given freely over the years.

The Romani's sparkling brown eyes went wide when they laid upon An-nalette. Instead of rushing forward to embrace her daughter, Annalette's mother turned and hurried to her father who sat on the other side of the campfire. He was in mid-sentence with another man that she didn't recognize when her mother grabbed at his shirt and pulled him to his feet.

Annalette froze as she watched them exchange some frenzied words and her heart began to pound in her throat. This was not the welcome she had anticipated. Her father looked in Annalette's direction before hurrying away toward a group of older men who congregated by a nearby wagon. She recognized some of them as the *vitsa* elders, but they were joined by more men, probably from her uncle's own *vitsa* with whom he had traveled.

When her mother finally approached her, eyes downcast. It was the same look she had given Annalette whenever she had done something improper or *marime*. The old woman who had shaped her into the person she was today was ashamed of her.

"You should not have come, Annalette," she spoke in her husky Romani tone.

Annalette surged forward to take her mother's hands, but she backed away and made a displeased gesture as if her daughter were some wild, contaminated beast.

"Mama," she whispered, "why not? Don't you want me here?"

It was then that she saw a tear glisten at the corner of her mother's eye. "Dearest, I do. But... your brother said things that we can't ignore."

She froze in place, her hands trembling at her sides. Was there any way to salvage this? "Mama, whatever Gallius told you about the man who helped us escape, I assure you it's false."

Her mother lifted her glare and shook her head. "He didn't speak only of the loup-garou. He spoke of you."

John leaned against the oak and listened to the trial. From his place in the shadows, he could hear their voices clear enough, but he couldn't understand their words. They all spoke in the Romani tongue, but he did hear a few words that Annalette had taught him. Loup-garou. *Gajo. Marime. Mulo.*

The elder men spoke with a haughty coldness of the most heartless judge while Annalette pleaded animatedly for her case. She spoke his name many times, and each time the men sneered with contempt. It was clear that they were not willing to listen to her side of the story.

Her brother stood nearby with a group of other younger Romani men, shouting phrases in an accusatory way. The women and children kept their distance and had retired to their wagons or played outside the camp, away from the drama that unfolded around the campfire.

If he had no respect for her people or her customs, he would have barged in and defended her. No one else was going to. Though he wasn't sure what exactly she was being tried for. He crossed his arms as a cold wind passed through the woods.

A man, dignified with his white shock of hair, stood above the assembly and all fell into a hush. He made one statement and then turned his back to Annalette. One by one, they all mimicked him. She fell to her knees and began to weep. Such a terrible sound that he couldn't bear to hear.

He fidgeted in place as he watched the scene and realized that she was the one under fire, not John.

There was a man, tall and dark haired, that bore a resemblance to Annalette. He was the last to turn away, but John could see the heartbroken look on his face. None would come to her side to comfort her, though many of the women who stood on the edges of the camp, seemed to pity her plight.

John swallowed hard as he had to watch her stand on her own and walk away from her family and the people she thought she could rely on.

One woman did show her mercy. The one who came to her when Annalette first entered the camp, hurried forward with a sack brimming with fabric that John assumed was clothing. There were some emotional words exchanged, and the old woman embraced Annalette. One of the men shouted at her, and they parted.

Her face streaming with tears, Annalette ran from the camp and into the forest on the other side.

John ran to catch up with her but refrained from touching her until he knew that she wouldn't push him away. No doubt this was because of him. If she rejected him in the same way that her family just rejected her, John wouldn't know what to do. The entire time he waited for her to return, he wanted to hope that she would still want to run away with him, despite his previous insistence that she wait. He had hoped they could have some sort of future together, but was this what she had in mind?

"He told them everything," she whispered. "He told them all about you and me... and what we did." She fell to her knees once more, and a hand stifled her wails. "I am no longer Romani. I am forever *marime*."

At first, he was shocked. How could Gallius have known what they had done? Was he watching from a distance? Did he hear Annalette's moans? Or did he simply make a good guess? Once the shock wore off, John began to shake with rage. Every muscle in his body tensed and he was more than ready to kill every last ignorant, staunch Romani in the camp until they repealed their judgment.

"I'm sorry, Annalette."

John took a step back, but she looked to him with imploring eyes and reached out. He was the reason for her misfortune, and yet she still wanted him. It was the unconditional love that he had been denied as a child. This woman, beautiful and brave, covered the scars on his heart and in one simple gesture, healed a lifetime of bitterness.

He did not hesitate to enfold her in his arms. Annalette could have resented him for being the reason her family turned her back upon her. If he were any normal man, perhaps they would have forgiven her for having a relationship outside of the union of marriage. Since he was half animal, her sin of bestiality would not be overlooked so easily.

She looked up into his face, and though sadness marred her beautiful features, John never thought her more perfect. "I'm yours, John," she said. "I have no family to return to. Where shall we go?"

He took in a deep breath and let it flow out through his flared nostrils. "Wherever you want." She had sacrificed everything for him. It was only fair that he gave her everything she wanted. "We'll go to Scotland, or France. Germany, Italy, the far east. You name the place, and we'll go."

Annalette let her hands rise to his chest and tried to smile. "We should find you an alpha."

He bent his head low to touch his forehead with hers. In the midst of everything, she still thought of him. He didn't deserve her. "But, is that what you want to do?"

She laughed. "If you're with me, John Croxen, I'll go anywhere."

His lips spread into a warm smile and he kissed her in the dark one more time before he led her away from the life she once knew. Unlike the first time she walked away from her family, this time she wasn't alone.

John kept a vigil watch outside the baker's shop. Annalette was asleep by his side, her body concealed by a long cloak they had commandeered from a sleeping traveler on the Pilgrims' Way just before they arrived in Chilham.

She no longer wore the bandana of the Romani to hold her wild and thick ebony hair back from falling in her face, and they would need to procure some more suitable clothes for her to wear. With some skill and finesse, they could make her appear as a mere foreigner rather than an illegal gypsy.

The village was awakening from its slumber, and he could hear the voices of families in their homes as they washed and prepared for the day ahead. Merchants all around were opening the shops for business, and if his loup-garou senses were correct, the baker was coming downstairs to open his shop any second now.

John pushed himself up and waited for the front door to open. The baker, whom he knew to be loup-garou as well, stood at the threshold and grinned to them both.

"I was wondering when you would show up again," he said before stepping aside to let them through.

John smiled to the kind stranger and gently shook Annalette to wake her. They had traveled through the night to come back to Chilham, sometimes down unmarked trails that tore at the hem of her skirt, but she never once complained.

He had been gentle with her and several times John suggested that they stop to rest, but she would have none of it. She wanted to arrive at Chilham before dawn so they could come into town under the cover of night. Losing her family and her Romani status did not diminish her spirit in the least.

Once inside the bakery, the owner locked the door behind him, and Annalette tossed off the hood that had masked her features from any curious strangers passing them by on the streets.

"I hope bringing her here won't put you in danger," John said as the baker set to preparing his ovens and worktable for the day ahead. Bowls of rising dough were scattered over the floor and every available surface.

"As long as her scent is gone by the time the mysgather comes around, I should be fine. You left so suddenly the other day. I hope I didn't startle you."

John ran his fingers through his hair. In all honesty, the baker did frighten him with his talk about bites and age. Now, he wanted to know more, and he was ready to hear it.

"I apologize," John said as she guided Annalette into a nearby chair that wasn't occupied by dough. "I do need your assistance."

The baker straightened from picking up a couple of bowls off the floor by the window and turned to John. "What would that be?"

John gathered up his pride and tossed it aside for the moment. "Who is your alpha? Do you have one in Chilham?"

It took a moment for the baker to comprehend his question and then he shook his head. "No, not in Chilham," he said. "I was born a loup-garou, so my father was my mentor. Are you in search of an alpha to train or to join his pack?"

To hear that they had come all that way for nothing would have disheartened any man, but John would not give up so easily. "I need a mentor," he said. Then, in an act of faith, John told the baker about his life thus far. He told him everything from being a bastard son of a nameless father to a man who thought he was possessed by a demon and not a loup-garou at all.

The baker nodded in understanding as he listened and collected his dough bowls. "It would seem you are in a dilemma, my friend."

"Do you know of an alpha nearby?" Annalette asked as she rubbed the sleep from her eyes.

The baker pondered for a moment. "It's hard to say. Our kind have learned to hide so well over the centuries. The general populace considers us to be witches or demon-possessed. Sometimes, we hide in plain sight, as I have learned to do and how the local mysgather does. Others have taken to the woods and live as hermits. I know of an alpha in the highlands to the north, but he does not allow just anyone into his pack. Englishmen aren't welcome in his territory."

John came forward and gripped the edge of the worktable as the baker slathered his hands in flour. "There must be someone. What about your father?"

"He was killed some years ago by a hunter," the baker informed with a sigh, "and he wasn't an alpha."

"Then perhaps you can teach me?"

The baker laughed. "Alas, I cannot. I know many things, but to teach is a different concept entirely. I have never had a pupil or apprentice for a reason. Besides, you need someone more dominant to break you into a pack, and I can already tell that you are far more dominant than I am."

John looked down, wondering how the baker could discern that so readily. "There has to be someone."

He could not comprehend why it should have been so hard to find others of his kind. Alphas and packs should have been on the lookout for those who needed their guidance. It seemed only right, yet here he was without a network to turn to. It was one more reason he needed to take a mentor so that he could be one for others.

The baker paused for thought, a ball of dough between his hands. "There may be someone, though I can't recall if he was dominant. His name was Nicu and he was a gypsy as well."

Annalette bolted from the chair and rushed to the table. "My uncle?" she exclaimed. "He was here?"

The baker smiled to her. "Yes... I can see the family resemblance. He was here for a few days a few years ago. He said he was going to France, back to the place he was born."

"Albi," Annalette said. "He spoke of it often. It's just north of Toulouse and along the River Tarn."

The baker nodded. "He was the last werewolf to pass through town besides you." He offered out his hand in friendship. "My name is Bartholomew, but my close associates call me Bart."

John happily shook his hand, acquiring some of the flour from the baker's palm. "John. John Croxen. Thank you for your help, Bart."

The baker nodded. "My pleasure. Will you be going to France, then?"

John looked down to Annalette. A glimmer of hope shone in her face for the first time since they made love near the river the previous morning. She grinned at him and never looked more beautiful with her black tousled hair and clothes that were in need of a good washing.

"I'd like to see my uncle again," she replied.

"Then we will go to France." John turned to Bart and gave his profuse thanks one more time before he ushered Annalette from the bakery.

She slipped on her hood, and they stepped into the morning sun. The streets of Chilham were filling, and John knew they needed to escape into the forest before the townspeople grew suspicious.

Once they had made their way down the River Stour, a safe distance from the town, John turned to Annalette. "It won't be easy to get passage across the channel."

She gave him a wicked smile. "It wasn't easy to escape the prison in Canterbury either, but we did."

John chuckled. "I don't think shifting into a beast will help us gain passage."

"Then perhaps it's my turn to rescue us from danger."

He gave her a reprimanding look. "I thought Romani were not thieves and murderers?"

Annalette nodded. "Yes, but I am not Romani anymore, and just because I am not a thief doesn't mean I don't have a few tricks up my sleeve."

It was then that he knew everything was coming into place. He had been taught as a child that God ordered the steps of his children and had mapped out their lives from birth to death. The pain, the rejection, the loneliness, it all led to this moment with Annalette.

Perhaps he had survived the last hundred years alone so that he could know the true bliss of having a companion. Perhaps he was denied love as a child so that he would know its full power when it crossed his path.

Staring down at the crafty and stunning Annalette, John realized that what he felt for her could be nothing short of love.

He took her in his arms and kissed her, letting that love pour out with every subtle movement of his lips upon hers. They would travel to France and seek out her uncle. God had ordained these days, aligning the pieces of this game so perfectly that John could not deny His handiwork any longer.

"I love you," he murmured when they finally pulled apart.

She giggled. "I love you, too."

God had not sent him an angel, but a gypsy who would love him and lead him out of the darkness to fulfill his purpose.

The Guide

Legacy Series Book 2

Sheritta Bitikofer

MOONSTRUCK WRITING

CONTENTS

TERMS TO KNOW

Wepwawet – Egyptian deity, depicted as half man and half wolf. His images on the walls of temples and tombs throughout Egypt have sometimes been mistaken for Anubis, but they hold the distinct difference that Wepwawet's head is purposefully painted white or grey to resemble a wolf. However, Anubis and Wepwawet share funeral process duties such as guiding the dead through the various gates of the underworld after death. Wepwawet, which holds an epithet of "opener of the way/path" is attributed to the creation of the Opening of the Mouth ceremony which is essential in the embalming process so that the "ba", or life essence, can find its way back to the mummy in order for it to continue on into the afterlife. Wepwawet has also been honored in the pharoah's hunting parties, serving as a scout for various missions and called "the one with the sharp arrow who is more powerful than the gods." He has also been symbolically attributed as uniting Upper and Lower Egypt, both for religious purposes and political. Scholars believe this because his standard is sometimes paired with the standard of the Apis Bull, which represents Lower Egypt. Wepwawet is also the god of the thirteenth nome of Upper Egypt and his main temple is buried eight meters below the capital city of the name, Asyut.

Hem-netjer-tepi – Literally means the "first servant of the gods" and holds the position of high priest in the temple.

Duat – Ancient Egyptian underworld

Aaru, Field of Reeds – Ancient Egyptian's form of heaven, where a righteous soul goes to spend eternity.

Ammit – Egyptian god with the body of a lion and head of a crocodile that devoured souls that failed the Weighing of the Heart in the afterlife.

Feather of Ma'at – Ma'at, the goddess of order and morality. Her feather is weighed against the hearts of those who died. If their heart was lighter than the feather, they would be permitted into the Field of Reeds as a reward for living a good life. If their heart was heavier than the feather, their soul would be eaten by Ammit, the devourer of souls.

Anubis – God of the underworld (Duat) and the one who weighs the heart against the Feather of Ma'at on the scales.

Padrone – An employer, protector, or provider role in a dependent relationship. Padroni is plural.

Jerkin – A leather vest worn over top shirts.

Piacere di conoscerti – Italian greeting for "pleased to meet you"

Amico mio – Italian "my friend"

Buona sera – Italian for "good evening"

Benvenuto – Italian for "welcome"

Signorina – Italian for "miss"

Signore – Italian for "sir"

Lupo Mannero – Italian term for werewolf or wolf man.

Grazie – Italian for "thank you"

Ragazzi – Itialin for "boys"

Istanbul/Constantinople – Central trading hub in Turkey. The capital became officially known as Istanbul in 1453.

Asena – In Turkic mythology, Asena was a grey wolf who rescued the survivor of a raid and nursed him back to health. He later impregnated the wolf and she gave birth to ten half-wolf, half-man sons. One of which, Ashina, is said to have founded the Ashina clan which ruled over the Göktürk and other Turkic nomadic empires.

CHAPTER 1

IN THE DESERT OUTSIDE ASYUT EGYPT, 1570

The bright sun emerged over the eastern horizon, bathing a golden glow over the sands of Egypt. As light hit the brilliantly painted limestone of the temple's outer walls, Tor awoke in his private chamber. Slowly, the rays of the life-giving sun passed through the pillars, through the courtyard, and into the inner sanctuary that faced east.

His dark eyes watched as the beam of light slowly traveled across the stone floor, passing over the cracks and worn edges of the bricks that served as a reminder that so much time had passed since they were first lain. Yet here he was, carrying on the traditions of his forefathers that had been passed down since time began.

With stiff movements, he sat up from his bed, a mere wooden frame with braided straps that kept his sleeping body off the dusty floors. The wool pillows that might as well have been as old as the temple itself were in great need of new stuffing.

Tor gripped the edge of the cot and looked down to his bare feet. His skin was tanned by years spent in this isolated desert. His hair, a few shades blacker than his eyes, was slicked back by oils to keep it clean and out of his eyes.

The sun couldn't have come at a worse time. In his dreams, he roamed foreign lands covered in luscious greenery. He could even smell the exotic food he had never tasted and saw the faces of strangers from all walks of life in clothing that appeared so strange and alien to him. Such dreams were coming more frequently. If his father were here, he would have told Tor that it was an omen, a prediction of the future to come. His father knew such things of the future that no other did and his guidance would have been invaluable to Tor now.

As Tor's eyes swept over the painted walls and inscriptions of the temple that overflowed into his private room, he couldn't see how such premonitions were possible. He was bound to this place where he was born and raised, and if he was any judge of fate, he would die here as well. His soul ached for exploration, but his mind confined him within these walls. He had a duty and he would take pride in it until his dying breath.

He sighed and rose from his bed. With heavy, lumbering steps, he prepared himself for the morning rituals. He cleansed his body with anointed water and oils that he had blessed himself. He took the incense and set it to smoldering, so its fragrance would permeate the temple.

Then, he donned his linen robe before stepping out into the secondary chamber of the temple, where the priests were permitted to carry out their daily tasks. With his bowl of burning incense in hand, a tiny wisp of smoke rising from the herbs, he wrinkled his nose just as he had done as a child. Some things, no matter how often he did them, were never easy. The aroma was always too strong for his keen nose. All priests that came before him had to bear the stench, and so would he.

The chamber's high walls were covered in the images that told the story of creation. Rich and vibrant colors showed Ra drawing the earth from the primordial ocean to begin the process of life with the other gods of old in attendance to the momentous event.

Tor looked to their faces in profile, their eyes unblinking. They reminded him of his duty, of the task that he had been born into just like his father and grandfather before him. The gods scolded him for his dreams and secret longings for other lands. He was Egyptian and Egypt would always be his home. Why should he want anything else?

He approached an adorned set of doors that were coated in the precious golden metals of the gods, which led to the innermost sacred chamber of the temple.

As he stood alone, the only beating heart for miles around, he could have given a thousand reasons why he should leave. Yet under the stares of his deities, the will to escape left him for now. He set the bowl of incense on the small altar table beside the doors, and what was left of the resigned priest bowed his head and lifted his hands in supplication.

His lips moved, forming the ancient words of the gods. His voice droned on, reciting the spells that he uttered every morning and every night for the last three hundred years.

When he was finished, he reached out and opened the two glittering doors just as the sunlight struck its gold embellishments.

Inside sat a statue of his god, of his ancestor, Wepwawet. Meeting the stony eyes of the half-man, half-wolf god, Tor was struck once more by the gravity of his position. He alone was left to summon the god from his resting place each morning so that the daily cycle of rebirth would not be broken.

If he was not here, who else would maintain the balance between chaos and Ma'at? Certainly not the native people of his country. They had given up on the old ways. They were no longer a proud people, but weak and submissive to the powers that had invaded their lands and stolen their way of life. Tor knew better that their link to the past was the only thing that could preserve their future.

Ma'at, order, must be maintained for the universe to continue as it had been. If he did not, Wepwawet could not be the last functioning god, fueled by Tor's dedication. Upon the god's shoulders, he carried the burden of the ignorant people as he battled the demons of the netherworld and kept the waters of the Nile from consuming the cities.

He slowly backed away from the shrine and began to strip off his linen garment so he could complete the next phase of the ritual. Standing bare before his god, he stretched out his arms to embrace his own wolf, the one that had been passed down to him through his ancestral line. It was his personal gift from Wepwawet. It was why he, more than anyone else left in the world, had to be the last priest of Egypt.

Before the wolf could claim his body, a sound came to Tor's sensitive ears. He turned his head and listened to the slow approach of camels. Their grunts and stamping hooves in the sand outside the temple were unmistakable.

Camels were not an uncommon occurrence in the desert, but the rattling of saddles that clanged in time with each step was not so common this far out. It had been many moons since he had an intruder dare to try and enter the temple. The people of Asyut should have known better than to try and come to a place that was supposedly cursed. The natives had given up on their gods, but not their superstitions.

Instead of slipping back into his clothes, Tor slunk into the inner chamber that was lined with painted columns on either side of the center walkway. In one swift jump, he perched himself within a recessed ledge along the edge of the ceiling that was just tall enough for him to duck into and practically disappear. Perfectly concealed by the shadows, he could watch them as they entered the sanctuary.

He listened to the men, three of them, enter through the temple gates. They all spoke in the common language of the day. He understood Coptic well enough, though he had been raised on the language of the ancients.

His father had taught him many languages, including the sacred form of picture letters that covered the walls of the temples and tombs throughout Egypt. Such knowledge had been lost by the human inhabitants, but the priests of Wepwawet kept the language alive, along with their traditions and rituals.

The men dismounted their camels in the outer courtyard, which would have been as far as any priest should permit them. To enter the inner chamber was blasphemous and disgraceful to the gods. Only those whom the pharaoh himself permitted were allowed to enter here.

Tor allowed them passage, but only because he was curious. One of the men who entered, was not a native. He was a foreigner, much like the ones he had seen in his dreams with pale skin and odd clothes that clung to his frame. Through the incense that was still burning on the altar, Tor could smell the foreigner's acrid sweat, telling him that the man was not used to such a hot and dry climate.

The two others, natives with their long tunics and heads wrapped in turbans, gazed around the chamber with eyes of wonder. The foreigner did as well, but he was more interested in the carvings than the structure of the temple.

Looters had come here before and each time, Tor drove them away. The statue and incense bowl alone would have been a valuable prize to sell on the market. Gold had once been a plentiful resource and the ancients were master craftsmen of the metal, able to mold it and use it in magnificent ways. Now, the natives were greedy and cared nothing for the religious significance of the gold.

"This is incredible!" the foreigner said as he shuffled to a depiction of Wep-wawet and the goddess Isis. His fingers dusted the inscription below it and he grumbled in another language that Tor did not know. By the man's inflections, Tor could tell that he wasn't pleased.

"We should leave," one of the natives said.

"Nonsense," said the foreigner. "Do either of you know what these symbols mean?"

Neither of the guides were paying attention as their hands gripped the hilt of their khopeshes. The sickle-shaped blade glinted off the sunlight as one of the men turned, and it flashed in Tor's eyes. He backed away from the glare, causing a tiny fragment of the ledge he perched upon to fall to the floor. The soft tap of the impact echoed in the temple.

Both Egyptians spun in his direction and looked to the source of the movement. Tor did not waste time. He leapt from the ledge and used one of the columns to propel himself forward, with his eyes glowing a seething gold and sharp fangs bared.

Tor landed close to them, well within striking range of their blades, and let out a terrible and earth-shaking roar that loosened the dust and sand from the uppermost crevices of the temple ceiling.

The men screamed and immediately fled out of the temple, abandoning the foreigner.

The pale man turned and stared with wide eyes at the naked priest, but did not move. Tor growled and snapped at the intruder, but still he didn't flee as the others did. Either he was fearless or too stupid.

Instead, the man did something that Tor was not expecting. He spoke.

"Warm greetings," he said as he placed his hand over his heart and gave Tor a deep bow.

It startled Tor enough that he ceased growling and took a few steps away. This man greeted danger with such openness. No human had ever been so bold when they faced his wolfish golden eyes.

"You are not welcome here," Tor snarled with an underlying promise that if he didn't leave, the foreigner might find himself dead.

Still, the man did not run. "I know this is a sacred place. I only came to learn. I've traveled far to be here and see this magnificent – "

"This is not a place of learning," Tor interrupted. "This is not a place of worship. This is a house for the gods. Mortals are not to be here."

The man paused, his lips parted as if he were ready to speak again, but didn't have the words. His shoulders slumped and there was a brief look of disappointment in the stranger's brown eyes.

"I thought – "

"Whatever you thought," Tor snapped, "you were wrong. Leave!"

The man sucked in a breath and then turned back to the portrait on the wall. "I'll leave after you tell me what this means. Who is this?" He pointed to the image of Wepwawet with his white wolf head and body of a man.

Tor squared his shoulders. He supposed that he could give something to this man for showing such brazenness. "That is Wepwawet and this is his temple. I am a son of Wepwawet, and therefore his hem-netjer-tepi. The high priest. It is my duty to take care of him and his temple."

The foreigner frowned and lowered his arm to his side. "So, this is just a temple?"

Just a temple. Tor wanted to spit at the man's disregard for the sacred. This wasn't just any temple. It must have been the best preserved temple in all of Upper Egypt. Nowhere else would he find images in such striking, vivid colors, nor a place that hadn't been reclaimed by the sands of the desert. Tor had served as the high priest, as well as every rank of priest below him, to ensure that the temple and Wepwawet were well cared for. He worked hard every day to make sure that this piece of his faith was preserved, whether anyone else wanted it to remain or not.

"What were you expecting? Your guides should have told you that this place was a temple."

The foreigner cleared his throat. "I was hoping this place would be a little more than just a temple. I'm searching for a place that was said to be the seat of a great civilization. One where people like you and other preternatural creatures lived together."

Tor balked and sneered at the stranger. "People like me?"

A tiny spark of hope flickered in the foreigner's eye. "Yes. There are many, many more like you around the world. Didn't you know that?"

Tor balled his hands into fists against the very idea. Perhaps this is what his dreams were all about. All he had ever known was the priesthood of Wepwawet. The priests were the descendants of the god, his emissaries on earth. They were his chosen people because they shared his gift of transformation. The blood of the wolf coursed through his veins and it was evident in the way his eyes still gleamed a brilliant gold instead of their usual nearly black hue.

But he was the only one left. His father told him of some in the past who had moved on from the priesthood, convinced that carrying on the old traditions was a fruitless effort in the wake of foreign religions like the cult of the Nazarene. The rest, like his father, had died at the hands of men who knew their secrets. Tor, alone, had survived the onslaught and stayed the course of the destiny he was gifted, plagued by the deaths of so many other priests. This temple didn't just house the great god, but the ghosts of those who were no longer alive because of a fatal mistake.

Now, this man was telling him that there were more like him outside of Egypt? More sons of Wepwawet? He was sure that those who strayed from the faith were no longer alive, perhaps killed by other hunters or dead because they could not survive without the support of others like himself. This stranger spoke of there being many of his kind, many priests. It couldn't be possible.

"You are lying," Tor sneered.

He laughed. "I assure you, I'm not lying. My padrone is similar to you, but with some notable differences." The foreigner's gaze swept over Tor, examining his naked form from the crown of his head to his bare feet. "Very notable differences, in fact."

Tor eyed the man with suspicion. Was this a plot to get him to leave the temple so the locals could ravage the place with their money-hungry hands that so often snatched the past from its rightful place? Or was he telling the truth? Were there truly more like him beyond the land of the Nile?

He listened closely, ignoring the howling winds of the desert outside the walls of the temple, and tracked the heartbeat of this stranger. It was steady, constant, and slow. The man was not lying.

"This civilization you speak of. What is it?"

The foreigner shrugged and offered his hands as if to show the priest that he had nothing to give. "That is why I'm here," he answered. "My benefactor told me to come to Egypt and search for evidence of a werewolf or vampire. Egypt is such an ancient country that he suspected the civilization would be here somewhere. When I asked the locals in Cairo and Thebes, they directed me here, saying there was a god who was half-man and half-wolf. This must be your Wepwawet." He gestured to the temple painting behind him.

Tor's eyes drifted to the carving of his deity, feeling his chest tightened with dread. His life had not been a lie, but neither was it completely true. He had long since believed that Wepwawet had once been a man that existed before time began, and then canonized for his unique qualities. He suspected that was how all the gods, including Ra and Amun, were idolized. Never in his life would he have thought a creature such as himself and his ancestor existed outside of Egypt.

"You will not find such a civilization here. I have never heard of a werewolf or a vampire. There are only gods and mortals here."

The foreigner took a few steps forward, his polished shoes scraping against the dirt on the stone floor. "No, you see, you are a werewolf. Wepwawet is a werewolf. Surely you have a myth about vampires; creatures that drink blood?"

Tor retraced his memory to when his father taught him about the countless gods and demons of their world. He remembered each one and their stories and many matched what this man was describing, but none so specific. "There are many gods and demons that devour the living and the dead, but they were not called vampires."

"Is there anywhere in your religion that speaks of a place where these gods resided? A heaven or hell, perhaps?" the foreigner asked.

"There is Duat, the world of the dead, but not all of the gods reside there." Tor paused in thought. "There is, however, a place I read of once in the ancient texts." Perhaps it was the need to get this man out of the temple, or it was his own fascination with this new revelation that made Tor's tongue a little looser than it should have been. "There is a place that Wepwawet was said to visit. My father wondered if it was his place of birth. It is far outside of Egypt. The text told where it might be, but the places are unfamiliar to me."

The pale man's countenance lifted in a look of utter glee. "Can you show these texts to me? Perhaps I can interpret the places for you. We could even go there together."

That was when Tor grew rigid and he glared at the man. "I will never leave the temple. My place is here, serving my god."

The man who must have known nothing of true religious piety sighed. "This is no place for you, my friend. A werewolf needs a pack. A family. It won't do you any good to be alone with these relics of the past. The world has moved on from the ancient ways. We can cross oceans and deserts. I am a scientist and an explorer, and I can tell you that there is more to life than serving a god. There are so many places to see, so many things to do. There's wonders that..."

Tor tuned out much of the man's speech after he mentioned oceans. His eyes traveled once more to Wepwawet on the temple wall. His name, written in the ancient symbols, was engraved above the deity's head. One symbol of which showed a wolf standing at the prow of a boat. The god was known as the Opener of the Way, leading the pharaoh into battle or going ahead of long journeys to make the way safe for royalty.

Each time Tor had been permitted to travel on the Nile, he felt a special connection with Wepwawet. More than that, he longed to sail over the waters once more. Because of his responsibilities, he hadn't been afforded the time to visit the Nile for long, before he was needed back at the temple.

"Cross the oceans…" he mumbled in the language of his ancestors, a language long dead and forgotten.

The foreigner stopped in the middle of his dialogue and watched Tor, perhaps waiting for him to translate what he had just said or for a different answer than he had previously given.

Tor looked to the man who dressed in strange clothes and reeked of a place he had never been. They were the embodiment of two separate worlds. One of the old and one of the new. They had nothing in common, no shared beliefs, no shared ancestry, nothing to bind them in friendship or comradery.

Yet, before him stood the answer to his dilemma. With this man, he could find the origins of his god. He could travel and visit those places that he had only seen in his dreams.

It was then that Tor wondered if it was Wepwawet himself that gave him the dreams. Perhaps this was the god's way of telling him it was acceptable to move on from the temple. Perhaps there was an element of his destiny that he had not yet discovered, but awaited him to the north east, where the ancient scripts described a plentiful land fit for the gods alone.

He turned to look toward the inner sanctuary where the massive statue of Wepwawet stared at him from his stony throne. As the only priest left, he was the one to interpret the will of the gods. With the dreams and the arrival of this stranger, this must have been the god's approval.

Tor looked to the man and nodded. "I will help you."

Florence Italy, 1570

Giovanni gripped the reins tighter as he steered his black mare down the country road toward the towering villa. Candlelight flickered in the tall windows that overlooked the front lawn and massive gates that were already open and ready to receive guests.

Beside him rode the wary Egyptian, Tor. After spending many hesitant hours with the werewolf in his pagan temple, the two became better acquainted. It made the ten day sea voyage back to Florence much more bearable.

The easiness he felt with the werewolf was a stark contrast to the knotted feeling in his stomach as they approached the Villa DiGennari of his padrone. After serving Michael Gennari for nearly a decade, Giovanni had never quite overcome the awkwardness of working for a vampire. Perhaps it was less Michael, who was the even-tempered benefactor with his gentle cadence and wise brown eyes, but more his apprentice, Yaverik.

The latter had been bitten by the former, but they were nothing alike. Brash, cold, and sometimes rather vindictive, Yaverik had an uncanny way of making his flesh crawl. Michael was not the predator of the dark featured in cautionary tales mothers told their children to make them behave. Yaverik, on the other hand, could have been the very inspiration for such stories.

Giovanni looked to Tor and studied the way he balanced himself upon the steed Giovanni had loaned him for the journey. Apart from his dark skin, one might have never suspected he was a foreigner until he opened his mouth to speak.

Giovanni fashioned him in the clothes of a middle-class Italian gentleman, but the tailors of Cairo were nonetheless impressed by his broad and burly physique.

He had never met a werewolf in person, though Michael had spoken of their kind often in their long evening discussions.

Tor had a look about him that exemplified strength and dominance, but the look in his dark eyes told another story. Ever since they left Asyut, the Egyptian seemed distant and thoughtful, and Giovanni could only guess as to why until they reached the Mediterranean Sea.

The morning before they set sail, he found Tor staring out over the warm waters. Giovanni finally gathered the courage to ask his new traveling partner if something was bothering him. Tor rambled on and on about gods and temple duties, how he felt guilty for leaving but somehow sensed it was his destiny to do so.

Giovanni never believed in destiny, though he had been raised to think that the Almighty God ordained the paths of His children. If meeting Michael and Tor taught him anything, it was that everything he had learned about God and the Christian world was not the only truth.

What he did know was that Michael would be pleased with his discovery. Giovanni might not have found the civilization he was so determined to discover, but he did find the guide that could take them there.

With numerous papyrus scrolls safely tucked away in a pack upon Tor's saddle, they made their way from the coast to Florence. Their long journey was not finished. In fact, it was just beginning.

They passed through the stone pillars and down the gravely path rimmed in trimmed bushes and trees, punctuated by marble statues reminiscent of Greek and Roman masterpieces.

"Your padrone," Tor said, "he pays you well?"

Giovanni was proud to hear him speak in Italian. Days spent on the ship had afforded them time to teach him the language. Though Michael knew more languages than Giovanni could keep track of, it would make communication easier on all of them if Tor could accustom himself to their ways. Tor was a fast learner and absorbed the language like a dry sponge.

"He pays fairly," he said softly, wondering how far Michael's sharp senses reached.

The truth was not so passive. In all reality, Michael was not the most generous of padroni. Giovanni was a well-known explorer in this region of Italy and could have gone to any baron, or even the king, and offered his services for a handsome salary.

His mistake was associating with Michael too soon in his career. While his contemporaries were scouting the far east, and sailing the Atlantic to the west, the vampire lord had him trekking around the globe in search of anything but riches and fine trade goods. Michael had always told Giovanni that he was on the hunt for something far more precious. The truth.

The truth he learned all too well was that once he learned Michael's secret, he could never leave his payroll. Only a change of heart or death could part them now and with Giovanni's growing debt, something had to be done.

Giovanni looked to Tor once more and the staff that he held firmly in his right hand while he guided his horse with the other. "Do you wish to leave your staff on the veranda?"

Tor shot him a hard look and Giovanni turned away. He should have known better than to ask it, because not once since they left his temple, had the staff been anywhere other than by his side.

Topped with the mysterious cross that sported an elongated loop for its uppermost prong and inscribed with even stranger symbols, Giovanni knew it must have had some spiritual significance. He called it an ankh and though Giovanni burned with curiosity, he sensed Tor's growing impatience with each probing question he asked about his world and ancient culture.

When they reached the stone steps that led into the front courtyard, both Giovanni and Tor dismounted. Tor shouldered the pack full of scrolls and parchments while Giovanni lugged his travel pack from the back of his mare. He struggled up the steps with the heavy load of clothes and study materials until Tor obligingly took the burden from him and easily coupled it with his own.

Each day, Giovanni learned something new about the werewolf. He witnessed his incredible strength just two days into their trip when he pulled their barge laden with supplies from the waters of the Nile without breaking a sweat. Only yesterday did he find out the range of his extraordinary senses when he detected an approaching boar nearly half a mile away. He proceeded to seek out and kill the beast to feed them both for the evening.

Michael's courtyard was a splendid garden full of radiant flora and fauna, with many exotic specimens from countries to which the wealthy vampire had traveled. With only the moonlight and stars above to light their path, it was nearly impossible to realize its particularly brilliant landscaping style. Giovanni sometimes wondered why Michael spent so much time and money into creating a magnificent villa when he would never see it in all its daylit glory.

Before they even reached the veranda, a servant opened one of the massive doors that led into the inner vestibule of the villa. With his eyes downcast, the servant invited them in.

The vestibule was lit by several lanterns, their glow gleaming off the polished mosaic floor they tread upon. Grecian pedestals against the walls boasted the carved figureheads of philosophers, emperors, and explorers from around the world. Doors on either side led to connecting rooms while a staircase ahead ascended to the second floor of the stately home.

Michael was a man of refined and sophisticated taste. Though he had never divulged his true age, Giovanni knew he must have been fairly old, despite his youthful appearance. He envied the vampire for the many stories he told of his travels and interactions with infamous artists and noblemen from the past. He was sure there was no place the vampire had not been, besides, perhaps the New World to the far west. It was only a matter of time before Michael sailed there and brought back some other artifact to add to his vast collection.

As if his thoughts had summoned the lord vampire himself, Michael appeared at the top of the stairs and opened his arms wide to his guests. "Benvenuto, Giovanni!" he greeted, his deep voice booming against the cedar rafters above them.

Michael's dark beard was trimmed close and covered his jaw and around his lips, which was the common style of the day. He was not sporting a hat this evening, so his ebony hair shined in the lantern light as he greeted his guests. Dressed in clothes worthy of his noble status, he must have been quite a sight to Tor.

His brilliant blue leather jerkin, trimmed in gold with a high collar, was laced together with a cord and buttons over his broad chest. His jerkin revealed the rigid sleeves of his doublet beneath, and the ruffles of his linen shirt accentuated his wrists and around his neck.

Giovanni watched Tor's baffled expression as the vampire made his way down the stair to reveal his paned, billowing, trunk hose, embroidered in fine silk, and the stockings that clung to the lord's legs. Though Giovanni and Tor were dressed in similar garb, the elegance of Michael's attire far outshined their simply constructed style.

Giovanni bowed to his padrone, but Tor remained upright. Not once since they left Egypt, had the high priest followed his lead in any of the customary etiquette of the day and he prayed that his lord would not take offense.

When he rose, he saw Michael inspecting Tor closely.

"And who is this you have brought with you?" Michael asked.

"May I introduce Tor, the high priest of Wepwawet in Asyut."

Tor said nothing as his eyes were fixed upon Michael, a mixed expression of hesitance and revulsion.

"Piacere di conoscerti, Tor," Michael said, giving a slight nod to his foreign guest.

So far so good.

"Buona sera," Tor returned, bringing a smile to Michael's face.

"Have you been to Italy before?"

"No," Tor replied in nearly perfect Italian with a hint of his mother-tongue flavoring the words. "This is my first time out of Egypt."

"I hope Giovanni has been treating you well?"

They exchanged simple pleasantries and Giovanni told the story of how he came to find Tor in the nearly abandoned temple outside of Asyut.

"And I believe you'll be quite pleased to hear what we found."

"Did you find Arnathia?"

That name. Giovanni had heard nothing but that name for years as he criss-crossed from Greece to England to north Africa, searching for this strange, lost civilization.

"Not exactly, but we found a series of texts that can help us find it." Giovanni turned to Tor and motioned for him to relinquish his sacred scrolls. The priest had been reluctant to share the texts at first, but he seemed intrigued enough by this place called Arnathia that he was willing to cooperate – if that could be the correct word for it.

Giovanni received the saddlebags upon his thin shoulder and staggered under their immense weight. Centuries of knowledge were entrusted to his weak frame and Tor was less than pleased. Michael helped to steady him.

"Why don't you take those to the library, Giovanni, and prepare them for us. I'd like to have a word with our guest." Michael must have seen the cautious look in his eyes, because he gave an encouraging smile and guided him toward the library to the left of the vestibule. "No need to worry, amico mio."

Giovanni knew better than to ask too many questions of his padrone and proceeded with one of the servants into the library with the scrolls in tow.

CHAPTER 2

"Signorina, we should not be spying on your father," Francesca whispered.

Jane swatted at her blood servant as she kept her gaze fixed on their dark-skinned visitor from behind the sitting room door. "Silenzio," she hissed. It was difficult to block out the potent stench of Francesca's fear, while Jane strained her senses to assess the strong looking lupo mannero standing in the vestibule.

She appraised his tall stature and the way he held himself with pride and confidence. Everything, from the way his arm muscles flexed when he gripped his staff more tightly to the way his shirt and form-fitted vest stretched over his back and chest, made her weak.

"I imagine you have many questions," her father said as he approached the man who called himself Tor. Michael's boots tapped loudly on the tiles, his hands behind his back and chin high to assert his own importance. Tor did not seem fazed.

"Many," Tor replied and Jane had to catch her breath. She had never seen a lupo mannero before, but if they were all like Tor, she knew she would like them immensely. She liked him already and she hadn't even seen the golden eyes for which they were so famous.

Her father grinned, showing his sharp vampire fangs. "And I will endeavor to answer each of them." Tor leaned forward, his eyes narrowing upon her father's face. "Something wrong?"

Tor straightened. "Giovanni said you were a vampire, one who drinks the blood of the living."

Michael rocked back on his heels. "I am," he replied with a nod. "You will also meet Yaverik, my apprentice. He is otherwise disposed at the moment, but I imagine he will turn up soon to discuss the plans... What else did Giovanni tell you?"

"That you are a fair padrone. You have sent him to find this place, Arnathia. May I ask why you are in search of it?"

Michael let out a long breath and Jane prepared herself to hear the old story she had heard almost daily for the last forty-eight years.

"This civilization existed long ago. My father told me of it when I was a boy and his father told him. Not many know of it, but it used to be the birthplace of our kind; the vampires and the lupo mannero – the werewolf. The civilization thrived for millennia before it collapsed and our two races could no longer coexist. I endeavor to find it and discover how our races came to despise one another."

Tor tilted his head. "You mean to say, there is a war between our kinds? Between the priests and vampires?"

Michael chuckled. "Not just your priesthood, but all werewolves. There are so many more of your kind in the world and there are many of mine as well." Michael flattened his hand upon his chest. "I come from an ancient line. My family were some of the first citizens of Roma, but before that, we came from Arnathia, I'm sure of it. I imagine that your own ancestors must have come from Arnathia as well."

Tor shook his head. "No. I am a descendant of Wepwawet, a god of Egypt."

Michael held up a finger to point out his guest's error. "Yes, but where did Wepwawet come from? Suppose he once came from Arnathia as well?"

"You question my faith, signore," Tor accused, his voice dropping so low that Jane's fingers began to tremble.

Michael made a sign of resignation. "I attempt to do nothing of the sort, but consider for a moment that everyone must come from some place and I am endeavoring to find it. It's my birthplace as much as yours. I know the answers lie in Arnathia, as long as we can find it." Her father dropped his hands. "I simply wish to know my origins and why our people can't seem to make peace."

"If our kind are at war, then why do you show such hospitality?"

Michael nodded. "Because I hold no grudge or hatred toward your kind. I have associated with werewolves in the past and have had nothing but pleasant dealings with them as long as they were willing to cooperate with me as well."

"And if they didn't?" Tor asked, a silent question tacking itself to the one he uttered. He wanted to know what became of those who didn't decide to play well with Michael.

Her father shrugged. "In general, if I show trust and amiableness to a werewolf, he returned it in kind. I have not met a werewolf that wished to harm me for no reason. Now, I cannot say the same for humans or other vampires, which is why I extend the hand of friendship to all werewolves, but reserve my judgement on other races."

Tor jerked his chin toward the closed library door. "I presume Giovanni has earned your trust, then?"

Michael paused and looked toward the library. "He has served me well. I don't see a reason to not trust him for now, but humans can be fickle creatures. I'm sure you understand this." He looked Tor over. "By your looks, I guess you are perhaps... three hundred or so?"

Tor lowered his chin in a look of skepticism. "How did you know?"

"Like I said, I have met many of your kind... I'm sure you have other questions, but for the moment, we should attend to our friend, Giovanni, and map out our quest to find Arnathia." Michael turned to stride toward the library, but Tor did not budge.

"Arnathia is not a place to be exploited," he said, his voice echoing off the high ceilings and vibrating against the doorknob Jane grasped tightly.

Michael looked over his shoulder and nodded. "I can assure you that it will not be. This is an expedition of knowledge, not of wealth."

"No one outside of our party is to know about it. The scrolls say that it is a sacred place and I expect you to respect it as such."

It had been a long time since anyone demanded something from her father in that way and Jane had to suppress her grin.

Michael's nostrils flared as if he were ready to charge, but he made no other signs of aggression. "I can respect your protectiveness over Arnathia. It is sacred to me as well. I would not allow anyone to desecrate it; human, vampire, or werewolf."

Their eyes locked and a tremor of tension passed through the vestibule. Behind Jane, Francesca could feel it too and she shivered. Jane, on the other hand, reveled in the feel of power that exuded from Tor. She wanted to draw closer, to feel it course through her.

Almost as soon as it came, it died away, and Tor bowed his head for the first time in veneration for the padrone. "Grazie."

Michael said nothing and entered the library, the door left open to admit their guest when he was ready to join them. For an aching moment, Tor stood in the vestibule, silent and motionless. Jane waited, watching with such intensity that her eyes watered. She could hear her father and Giovanni already pouring over the scrolls they had brought.

"I know you are there," Tor mumbled, his eyes sliding directly to the cracked sitting room door to meet her anxious gaze.

Francesca gasped and jumped away, but Jane bit her lip, ready and willing to meet her father's guide. She opened the door, letting the light from the vestibule flood through before she entered. Her heavy skirts rustled with each step as she came to face Tor.

With her hands meekly held behind her back and long blonde hair braided around her head and interwoven with bright ribbons, Jane knew she was attractive. Michael spared no expense to make sure she had the finest silk garments and all the luxuries that a woman could ever want.

Yet, when Tor beheld her for the first time, he didn't smile as other Italian men did. His eyes didn't alight with interest, yet what could she expect? He hadn't even shown a hint of happiness since he walked in. Lupo mannero or not, Jane was determined to find out why he was so placid.

"Buona sera," she greeted, sure to make her voice drip with sweetness. All the ragazzi loved to hear her speak.

Tor bowed lower than he did to her father just moments before. "Buona sera, signorina."

Jane's lips twitched and pulled as she tried not to let her face split into a grin. He might have been speaking perfect Italian, but there was still a hint of his Egyptian accent that snaked through the way he formed each sound.

Up close, Tor was so much more than just a werewolf. He must have been the most handsome man she had ever laid eyes on. His exotic and unique scent alone made her head spin. She could imagine him wrestling a scaly and vicious crocodile along the banks of the Nile, his bulging muscles glistening with sweat in the hot sun. Not only that, she could imagine him wrestling with something a little softer and between silky sheets.

"You are a vampire as well," he said. Jane was slightly grateful that he seemed so open to conversation. When Giovanni was in the vestibule, he was as silent as the grave.

"I am," she replied. "Many are misled by my youthful appearance."

Tor's eyes drifted to the hem of her skirt and back. Yes, Jane was nearly half a century old, but many disregarded her as a mere adolescent of sixteen, perhaps seventeen, years. It was only when she carried on a mature and intellectual discussion that they might wonder how old she truly was.

"I was born a vampire," she continued. "My father and mother are both vampires as well."

As soon as she let the word "mother" slip from her lips, she immediately regretted it. It had been years since she let herself think so much on the memory of her mother and it brought with it too many emotions to count.

Jane had learned to push it all aside, just for a moment, to worry about the grief some other day. If she didn't, she'd surely go mad.

Tor watched her and he must have seen the flash of feeling in her eyes. "Something wrong?" he asked and she could sense his sincerity. It was clear that he wasn't quite attracted to her, but he did care.

Jane rolled her eyes. "I envy you and Giovanni. You're going to see the wondrous Arnathia."

"You do not sound so impressed."

She scoffed. "I'm not. Father's been talking about Arnathia for as long as I can remember. It's nothing special anymore. It's just a place I've never been."

Tor's eyes penetrated through her half-truth to see the reality of her sarcasm beneath. "You do want to go."

Jane slowly paced around Tor, but he did not turn to follow her movements. "A caged bird would gladly fly into hell if it meant it could escape the confines of its prison." She let her eyes wander over his body, seizing the moment to be so close while it lasted. "I used to go with father on his trips across Europe, but I haven't left Italy in nearly fifteen years. I'd gladly go to Arnathia if he would let me."

"He let you go with him on voyages before, so why not now?" he asked as she made her way back around to face him.

Jane shrugged and looked away, casting her smoky gray eyes to the intricate pattern mosaic on the floor. "I don't know. He doesn't answer me when I ask." She looked to Tor through her thick, dark lashes. "Maybe he's worried that a certain wolf may be bad company for me."

She saw the slight waiver in Tor's defenses and she was ready to pounce upon it.

"Jane," her father snapped from the library door. She jumped and turned to face Michael's hardened gaze. "Leave the signore alone," he ordered.

Without hesitation, she fled from the vestibule to return to Francesca who was still waiting in the sitting room. Her father could command obedience, but Jane's wild spirit pulsed for the chance to get closer to the Egyptian.

At the door, she turned back and locked eyes with the high priest once more. His defenses, thick as the walls of Jericho, were restored and he slowly walked away to join Michael and Giovanni in the library. Her father gave her a reprimanding look that promised a harsh scolding later, and then disappeared with the lupo mannero.

Everything about Italy and its people set Tor's teeth on edge. The smells, the sights, their language, it was all too foreign for his tastes. The oaky scent of the vast vineyard behind the villa had been overpowering upon their arrival. His senses were assaulted by the countless blooming flowers that he didn't recognize. This place, with its sprawling farmlands and towering trees, was nothing like his home in Egypt. Not even the lush banks of the Nile could compare to the green and flourishing landscape that met him with every turn. Without a doubt, this was the place his dreams had taken him on so many nights.

The vampires, Michael and the young woman in the vestibule, were even stranger. He had only seen such pale skin on the faces of various other deities in his temple. They were even paler than Giovanni. Their eyes, limpid and penetrating, were also enchanting, and try as he might, Tor could not tear himself away from their gaze. It was like being caught in the stare of a cobra with its hood fully extended and head bobbing just before it would strike.

Apart from their hypnotic presence, Michael and his daughter seemed pleasant enough, though he could have done without the slightly rotten odor that emanated from them, nearly suffocating the fragrant oils and perfumes which were obviously applied. He wondered if Giovanni could smell the death upon them as well.

For the time being, he would accept their hospitality, but he kept a tight fist around his staff, evoking the gods for protection against the creatures. As he entered the library, however, he wondered how dangerous they truly were. He sensed no deception in them, nor any malicious intent. And if Giovanni had been able to work for Michael for so long without being harmed, it was likely that they would not pose a threat to him either.

Giovanni was still in the midst of arranging the papyrus scrolls across the polished wooden surface of a massive table in the center of the library. Tor tried not to breathe in too much of the musty scents of old paper and leather that surrounded him on all sides.

A quick glance around the library told him all he needed to know about Michael. He was a man of knowledge. His extensive collection of bound books and framed maps that hung on the walls were testament to that. Tor's meager assortment of dusty scrolls in a chamber beneath his temple was nothing compared to this corner of the modern world.

Oil lanterns burned on the table tops around the room, splashing the ribbed spines of the tomes in the amber glow. It was a wonder that Giovanni could read in such light, as he pointed to the slightly faded black ink letters on the papyrus.

"Tor, correct me if I'm mistaken, but is this the correct scroll?"

Tor approached and stood between the two men, Giovanni on his left and Michael on his right. He peered and shook his head. "No, it is this one," he replied, pinching the edge of the coarse, fibrous paper and pulling it from one corner of the desk to lay flat in front of them. "This details Wepwawet's yearly journey to the Realm of Plenty and Peace."

"Is that what your people call Arnathia?" Michael questioned, his eyes transfixed upon the symbols that he would not be able to decipher without Tor's help.

"It is the closest in description, yes. There is no other mentioning of a place where Wepwawet would go outside of Egypt. If he would go anywhere else, it would be your Arnathia."

"Not just *my* Arnathia," Michael corrected, his voice hushed in reverence. "Yours too. It's for both of our kind."

Giovanni jabbed his finger at the paper. "And this details exactly where we can find it."

Tor turned back to the sacred text. "It says that Wepwawet passed over a barren desert that belonged to his enemy, and across a great sea."

Michael turned and strode toward an expansive map of the known world framed upon his wall. Tor had never seen anything like it. Sprawling countries adrift in a blue sea. The vampire pointed to a spot in the top eastern corner of a land mass near the center.

"If Egypt is here, and Wepwawet says he passed through a desert, he could have been talking about the desert to the south."

Giovanni joined him. "But beyond this sea is a land colder than Africa. Arnathia couldn't possibly be there."

Michael stroked his beard. "The west is a possible choice. What if those from Arnathia traveled from the New World?"

"This is possible," Giovanni concurred..

Tor walked up to the map, marveling at its many lines and inscriptions. "Wepwawet's enemies were not to the west. Egypt's enemies came from the east."

Michael nodded and traced his finger from the land they designated as Egypt, and went eastward. "That would mean Arnathia could be in Arabia."

"Their names are similar," Giovanni offered.

Tor waved his hand over the map. "No, no. The text also says that the Land of Plenty and Peace did not reside in the land of the enemies. It was past it."

Michael jabbed his finger on Egypt one more time. Slowly, he slid it northeast, over the thin strip of land that connected what was labeled as "Africa", past Arabia, and over a body of water labeled as "Mar de Bachu."

"Here," Michael said. "On the other side of the Caspian Sea."

Giovanni whistled. "That's far away, signore. It will be a long journey."

"Then we should leave as soon as possible," Michael replied with a grin, undaunted by the distance. If it took nearly a week and a half for Tor to journey from Asyut to Italy, it will take over twice as long to get to the Caspian Sea. At least he will have a chance to sail again.

The air in the library shifted and Tor felt the wolf spirit within him raise its hackles, fur bristling in agitation. Even Tor couldn't help but feel the hairs stand on the back of his neck, a low growl rumbled in his throat. He had been on edge, that much was true, but there was a new threat with which to be concerned.

He turned and glared at the doorway, waiting for whatever it was to enter and challenge him. His wolf begged for the fight to break the tension.

A man appeared, dressed in the same fashion as Michael, but with no aristo-cratic flair to his demeanor. His dark hair was pulled back by a tight cord, his cold and calculating eyes fixed upon Tor with a look that he could only identify as pure maliciousness. There was nothing obvious in his appearance that would suggest he was capable of harm. The man was slight and tall, with broad shoulders, but Tor was far stronger and could easily snap his neck if he pleased.

Tor's wolf was right to want to fight this man, this new vampire. Somehow, he knew this man could do bad things, and his thoughts drifted back to Jane. An instinct to protect her, as well as Michael and Giovanni flared within him like nothing he had felt before.

Yaverik opened his mouth, revealing a set of sharp fangs that put a crocodile to shame. A vile hiss told Tor all he needed to know. Tor took a bounding step forward.

Michael slid between them and held out his hands to stop them from tearing one another apart. "Signori," he said, his voice deep and rigid with authority. "I will not allow such hostilities."

The other vampire lifted his chin and sneered down his nose at Tor as if he were nothing but a mangy animal. Behind him, he could almost taste Giovanni's unease.

"You brought home another pet, Michael," the vampire remarked, his accent heavy with a foreign lilt that Tor did not recognize.

"Yaverik, this is Tor. He is our guest from Egypt."

"This is the one who will take us to Arnathia?" Yaverik asked, doubt plain in his eyes, as if he didn't believe the Egyptian could be their ideal guide. It was clear this vampire didn't know who he was looking at.

"I am. Yet, it seems you are not interested in whatever truth Arnathia may offer."

Michael, once more, interceded. "Yaverik is my apprentice, Tor. He will be coming with us on the expedition. I expect both of you to cooperate. Can I trust you to do so?"

Tor watched Yaverik, waiting for the vampire to concede first. He was not well versed in working with others to achieve a common goal. The life of a high priest was not intended to be solitary, but it became that way for him. Too many years had passed and Tor would have to refresh himself in how to collaborate with others. He could be a lone wolf no longer.

But, so help him, if Yaverik did anything to harm Jane, or Giovanni, Tor would not hesitate to kill the vampire by whatever means necessary. Yaverik did not yield, but Tor gave the padrone a short nod and tucked away his pride for another day, for another fight. The wolf would shed no blood this night.

CHAPTER 3

MEDITERRANEAN SEA, 1570

Michael found him leaning against the railing at the forecastle of the ship. The moon's glorious light rippled off the calm, dark waters of the Adriatic Sea. It was good to smell the salty air once more, and feel the light spray of the sea against his skin. It had been far too long since Michael stepped foot onto the deck of a vessel of this magnitude, but the experience was empty.

Ever since they left the villa at dusk, he felt as if he were missing something, though they had spent meticulous hours packing every provision they would need for this long journey. Michael knew precisely what he was missing, but there was no way he could have taken it along with him.

The void within him would remain for the rest of his nearly immortal life. This was only the beginning of an era without a bride, without his Caterina. By now, Michael had been accustomed to death. He had lost his father to the ravages of time, his mother since his boyhood years, and many of his mortal friends had been long gone. Yet, to lose his wife, his lover, and best friend, had been more than his spirit could bear.

This expedition, this pilgrimage to the ancient city of Arnathia, would be his maiden voyage into a new life. Thirty years was more than enough time to grieve, and he had to set a better example for his daughter.

He climbed the steps to the forecastle, moving with the ship's gentle sway as it cut through the waves ahead of them. They were a few hours into this journey and making good time. The only souls above deck were the lookout, seated above in the crow's nest, the helmsman, who was a loyal friend of Michael's from many years back, Tor, and himself. Though some would dispute if a vampire had a soul at all. He had studied with the greatest philosophers of the century, and even Michael was unsure of the answer to whether his body housed a soul.

The werewolf's hands were loosely laced in front of him over the railing, as he gazed out over the sea. The tips of his dark hair fluttered around his ears as the breeze whipped at his face. He had shed his civilized garments, wearing only a pair of loose fitted breeches that one of the sailors had loaned to him for the trip. His dark skin seemed to absorb the moonlight, giving him an air of strength and confidence.

Michael sensed a calmness in him that wasn't there in all the time they had plotted their course and discussed the finer details of the expedition. Even as they boarded the ship, Tor was sneered at by the ship's crew and captain for his exotic appearance. He seemed out of his element. Here, however, in the presence of the sea, there was nothing but tranquility. As a vampire, he could sense this. He could feel every emotion of those around him as if they were his own at times, and Tor radiated such strong emotions.

Tor was uncomfortable in the company of vampires and humans, that was made perfectly clear. Michael couldn't blame him for feeling that way. Many of the werewolves he had met were wary of his intentions. Some were raised to hate all vampires, no matter how friendly they may appear. Others might have had unsavory encounters and threw up their guard before they even let Michael speak to them.

Tor was also a rarity. He had never met a vampire before, but the werewolf could sense the difference between Michael and Yaverik. Despite Michael's good intentions and his attempts at indoctrinating Yaverik into his humanistic and philopatric idealism, the young vampire maintained a streak of disobedience and violence. He had already lost a dozen servants to his unreasonable rages.

Without even seeing Michael's apprentice, Tor felt the darkness in Yaverik. Though the werewolf might not have known it, there truly was a drastic variance between Michael and Yaverik. Michael was born a vampire, raised amongst them and trained from an early age to cope with the demands of his bloodlust.

Yaverik, on the other hand, was bitten. He was born a human and lived as any other boy would. It was only when it became necessary to bring him into the nocturnal world of the vampires that Yaverik had to become one himself. The teenager had seen too much one summer night, and though Michael wanted to give him a chance, it became evident that he could not be trusted with their secret unless it became his own.

That was over fifty years ago, but some distasteful quirks were hard to kill. Michael could only hope that Yaverik's aggression and short temper would not create problems for them on this journey.

"Beautiful, isn't it?" Michael asked as he came to stand beside Tor.

Tor did not move or turn to acknowledge the vampire, though Michael was sure that he heard him. "Giovanni told me that you enjoyed your voyage from Egypt to Italy."

"I had never been to sea before, but always wanted to," Tor replied as he lifted his head to regard the distant horizon. "The Nile cannot compare to this."

Michael still marveled at the way Tor picked up the Italian language so quickly. It was true what they said; werewolves possessed sharp minds and quick wits.

"I remember the first time I sailed with my father," Michael said. "We were journeying from Naples to Sicily to conduct trade. I climbed onto the bowsprit and liked to imagine I was flying."

Michael didn't have to see Tor's face to know that he had cracked a tiny smile.

"I did the same on our way from Egypt. Of course, it was daylight then and the sun was warm. Nothing like this cool night."

Michael unclasped his hands from behind his back and leaned against the railing, just as Tor did. "I do apologize for the inconvenience of traveling this way."

Tor shook his head. "It is no inconvenience."

The vampire chuckled. "There is no use lying to me, Tor. As a vampire, I can see your memories."

Tor looked to him, eyebrows arched. "Truly?"

"Indeed. I know you said to Giovanni that you wished we could travel during the day, because then you would be awake with your gods."

Tor looked away. "I said that before we ever arrived to your villa. I apologize if I have offended you."

Michael waved his hand and made a sound of dismissal. "Pah. It is fine. I hate to impose my limitations on others, but sometimes it cannot be avoided. Those who work closely with us have to change their entire schedules to accommodate."

"Such as with your slaves?" Tor asked, his gaze turned back to watch the crests of the waves foam white against the darkness.

Michael knew he was speaking of the two humans they brought on board with them. Marco and Angelo had served them for many years now as their blood servants. Both trusted companions and fully versed in the ways of the vampire. Sometimes, they were more than just servants, but extensions of their own family. Marco, especially, was protective of Michael and had been ever since the vampire admitted he was over four hundred years old. The blood servant sometimes treated him like an old man, though he barely looked a day over thirty.

"They are not slaves in the traditional sense. It is not an unbalanced arrangement. In return for giving them a comfortable life, a handsome allowance, and relative freedom, they allow us to take sustenance from them once a day. We never take more than we need and we give them plenty of time to heal." In fact, that was what Marco and Angelo were doing right then. Both Michael and Yaverik had taken their portion soon after they left Italy and the blood servants were resting to regain their strength.

Tor visibly shivered. "Forgive me, but I cannot imagine drinking the blood of a human."

"It is not in your nature to drink blood as much as it is to eat their flesh."

"Neither have I done so."

Michael nodded and made a face of approval at the note of disgust in Tor's voice. "This is good. I have met werewolves who feast on nothing else and suffer for it. There is something about consuming human flesh that disturbs the mind of a werewolf. They become unruly and violent."

Tor sighed and shook his head. "Werewolf... It is hard to get used to hearing that word."

The vampire nodded, understanding Tor's point of view. He had known nothing of life outside of Egypt, nothing outside of his lonely priesthood to understand how big the world truly was. "Your kind go by many names. Werewolf, Lupo manero, loup-garou, bodark, rakshasa, varkolak... No matter the nation, the religion, or the country, your kind have existed everywhere."

The priest of Wepwawet was silent for a moment. The only sounds came from the flapping of the mainsail, the creaking of ropes as they strained against the pullies, and the splashing of the waves against the bow. Michael found the melody of sea travel soothing, especially when the deck was clear and the moon shined brightly overhead.

"I never knew that men like me existed outside of Egypt," Tor muttered.

Both his innocence and naivety were endearing. He was a pup who had ventured outside of his den for the first time and Michael could already see the seeds of adventure take hold in Tor's mind. "Yes, they are everywhere, and so are my kind. The only way you could know this is if you traveled as much as I had."

"You are an explorer like Giovanni?"

Michael smiled. "Not exactly, but I know many men who were. Magellan, Vespucci, Columbus. All of them were pioneers. The edges of our world are expanding and it's becoming increasingly difficult to hide. Things that have been around since the dawn of time are finally being given names. Things that have been able to live in the shadows are being thrown into the light and those like us are powerless to stop it."

Tor turned to him. "You mean, most humans do not know about us?"

Michael tightened his fingers over the tops of his hands until he could feel the bones beneath his skin. These were daring times indeed. Just taking a journey of this magnitude was risky in itself. The windowless carriage stowed away in the orlop deck beneath them would certainly turn heads, but there was no other way for them to travel in the daylight hours without it. Michael would be trusting Giovanni, Tor, and their blood servants to keep them safe and as inconspicuous as possible.

"Giovanni has been privileged with knowing me and Yaverik. I do not extend such invitations lightly because of the superstitions of the people. Of course," he shrugged, "the world is becoming wiser. Every day, the humans are understanding more about their world and the dark days of fairytales and monsters are fading out of sight."

"So, there are no more hunters? No more assassins?"

Michael looked to Tor and saw the hope in his eyes. It was a shame that it could not stay there. The look of a stern and heartless Egyptian priest did not become him. "Alas, there are still hunters. Perhaps, not as many, but they still exist." He frowned at the memories that flashed through his mind's eye as he reached into Tor's past to understand. "I know your father was killed by hunters. I wish I could tell you that you have nothing to fear, but it would be a lie."

"Do you make it a practice to invade another person's memory?" Tor questioned with a flair of irritation that Michael read as non-hostile.

He gave the werewolf a helpless look. "Sometimes, it is better to know where one comes from so you can better predict their future intentions."

He was especially aware of the growing threat that loomed over their party, the scheme that would follow them to the east like a looming cloud. He hoped that the outcome he predicted would not come to pass, but Michael knew that he could not reveal what he knew, lest the expedition be ruined for it.

"Does Yaverik have this skill?"

Michael reached out with his senses to track his apprentice and found him playing a game of cards with Giovanni and some of the crew below deck. The crew were too tipsy with drink to fear the vampire with whom they played. "My apprentice was not born a vampire, so he does not."

"Then Jane can?"

There was a tenderness in the way Tor asked that Michael tried to ignore. Whether he was amiable toward werewolves or not, Jane was still his daughter. Many men had asked for her hand in marriage, but he turned each of them away. More correctly, he asked for Jane's opinion on the man and she denied them all. They were wealthy enough that Michael did not have to marry his daughter off for the sake of money or convenience. They had a stable family reputation that assured he didn't need to align himself with any other, and he wasn't willing to use his daughter as a bargaining chip. Jane would marry for love, just as her mother did, and Michael expected nothing less.

If Tor happened to be the one she fancied, however, Michael would have to give the matter a little more thought. It was clear when they were alone together in the vestibule the night before that she felt something for Tor. Because he respected his daughter, he made the decision not to pry. He could have searched Tor for any hint of affection, but so far, he had seen only a willingness to protect. Nothing more.

"Yes, she has the ability, but she is still young and doesn't understand how to use it just yet."

Tor opened his mouth and paused, as if debating whether to speak or not. "You do know that she is in the cargo hold with her servant, correct?"

Michael grinned. "Yes, I know."

"And you will do nothing?"

He sighed and looked out over the sea, remembering how Jane had thrown such a tantrum when he said she couldn't go with them at first. "I traveled often when she was young, but she and her mother accompanied me. When my wife died, it was a while before I left Italia, but I never took Jane with me. It's been long enough that I think it's time we traveled together as a family again. I did not tell her this, because I wanted to see what she would do. I knew she had come to the end of her wits with boredom and I suspected she would do something this daring. Also, I think she should see Arnathia, which is why I let her think I didn't know she and her blood servant were in that trunk. She should have known those breathing holes would give them away. Even if I didn't smell her, I would have known something was amiss."

Tor gave a great belly laugh and Michael was gladdened to see the werewolf more at ease. "Why is this place so important to you?" he finally asked when he was finished. "Is it still inhabited?"

Michael knew that he spoke of Arnathia. "I wished that it was, but I doubt it. It was a place of peace and that seems like an aloof concept to some now. No one wants peace when one can make money on war."

Tor flipped his hands so his palms were facing the stars. "Then what can you possibly gain from visiting a place that has been abandoned?"

Michael looked to Tor, wishing there was a better way to explain his intentions. He needed to know that such a place still existed. "We all need to know where we have come from, so we know the paths we need to take. I have spent too long on the sidelines. My family prided themselves on their heritage, and we have always been prosperous, but for as far back as I can remember, we never accomplished anything. We did not contribute to anything but war and helping to widen the gap of differences between our kinds. My father told me how his ancestors fought in the war against werewolves, but they didn't know for what they fought. To combat the hatred, I must know what happened."

"What if you find something you do not want to know?" Tor asked. "What if your ancestors fought for a just reason?"

Michael had long debated this, but he had no answer. If the vampires were at fault for the war, he knew that he would dedicate his life to rectifying the injustice committed by his race. If the werewolves were to blame, Michael was still unsure. He was inclined to believe the best of all. One cannot condemn the son for the sins of the father.

"We shall see when we find Arnathia." Michael pushed himself away from the railing and walked toward the stairs that led down to the main deck. "I'm going to go have a talk with my daughter now."

"Do not be too harsh on her."

Michael looked over his shoulder, astounded by Tor's candid petition. He knew nothing of his daughter and their relationship, but must have sensed their closeness already. At least he could be assured that Tor would not cause much strife.

"I can assure you, I will not..." He turned away and continued down the stairs. "By the way," he added, "be careful of Jane. She's quite fond of puppies."

Istanbul, 1570

The smells and sounds of Constantinople crowded in around Tor as he walked beside the carriage. Giovanni, whose hands gripped tightly on the reins of his mare, rode not far behind him, while Marco steered the carriage through the bustling streets. Angelo and Francesca, the other blood servants to the vampires, rode on the other side, making sure that the pedestrians gave the carriage a wide berth.

Tor had given in to Michael's insistence that he have a steed of his own, but while the vampire was asleep, he lent it to Francesca. Her accompaniment on the journey, along with Jane's, was unexpected and Tor would gladly give up something he clearly did not need in order to accommodate the ladies.

However, he wished he had the horse now, if only to make a quick getaway from the city. Even his wolf itched for open spaces and freedom to run. This had been the longest he had ever gone without shifting into his truest form, either for recreation or for ceremonial purposes. Unfortunately, from what he could tell, there seemed to be no end to this pivotal trading center. All around, he heard languages he recognized and others that were far more foreign. Faces pale, dark, black, and yellow met him with curious stares everywhere he looked.

The chanting of prayers, ringing of bells, shouting voices of peddlers on the streets, tinkling of metal harnesses as carts made their way down the lanes, children and babies crying in their homes; all of it was enough to make Tor's ears bleed, if he let his focus waiver. He pushed out the sounds, letting them become like the dull roar of rushing water. Instead of overwhelming him, it became a mild annoyance.

Smells, both reeking and aromatic, vied for control over his nose. A few times, he had to resist the urge to retch, out of respect for the locals who passed them by. To anyone else, this looked like a procession of a wealthy merchant. They all bore the appearance of nobility or affluence with their private horses and clean clothes with fine embroidery that practically glittered in the sunlight.

Tor wore the garments he had been given for the trip, though they chafed and itched in places. He had been accustomed to the freedom of a linen robe for so long that he had forgotten how confining proper clothes could be. Most of all, he missed the feeling of the earth beneath his bare feet. These polished leather shoes were hardly practical to him.

For all the clothes and accessories they gave him, Tor still looked out of place walking with the party. With his dark complexion and obvious exotic features, anyone might assume him a slave of the Italians. Yet, none dared to look upon him as a slave, as long as he still carried his staff and retained the sneering look of a man willing to murder on the spot. With how irritated he was in this hectic, harried territory, Tor didn't doubt that he would stoop to such lows. If one man so much as got in his way or jostled him, Tor was liable to break.

Beside him, the black and windowless carriage wobbled along the uneven streets. The wheels, sturdy as they were, bucked and dipped over every little obstacle in their path. He couldn't imagine how Michael, Yaverik, and Jane could sleep under such rough conditions.

A softly spoken word confirmed it.

"You're upset," Jane said.

In the noise, it would have been a wonder if any human ear could pick up her voice. Tor, however, was no ordinary man. He moved close to the side of the carriage and nearly missed stepping over a pile of fresh horse dung.

He and Jane hadn't spoken a word to one another since they were at the villa. Tor had heard Michael give her and her blood servant a strong reprimand for stowing away on the ship. He took advantage of the nighttime hours to sleep and rest up for the land journey ahead, so he didn't have the chance to spend any time with Jane.

"I have never been in a city this... big," he said, searching for the right word to describe Constantinople. It was the capital of the Ottoman Empire, an important stop along the trade routes that connected the west to the east, but Tor longed for the quiet markets and scarcely populated towns along the Nile. Cairo and Alexandria rivaled the magnificence of Constantinople, but the air was vastly different.

"Are Yaverik and your father resting?" Tor asked.

"Yes," she replied. "They're both asleep. I was asleep until your unease woke me."

Tor's brows knitted together in confusion. "How could I have woken you? I haven't spoken a word."

"When you're born a vampire, you can sense the feelings of others. Sometimes, it's strong enough that the emotion becomes your own."

Tor glanced heavenward. There were still so many things he didn't understand about this world. "And now, you are uneasy, too."

"Only a little," she said, but he could hear the strained smile in her voice. "It's like being pressed in on every side, but unable to move or breathe. Am I right?"

She couldn't fully appreciate how right she was. "I've spent most of my life in a temple with only the scarab beetles and cobras to keep me company. This is..." he could not find the word in Italian, so he said it in his native tongue.

It brought a giggle out of her. "I love the way you say things. Say something else like that."

Tor sighed, thinking of what Michael had advised him on their first night on the ship. He understood the vampire perfectly and Tor was not inclined to return Jane's affections. Whether she had a fondness for puppies or not, Tor could not reconcile the image of a young girl with the fact that she was far older than she appeared.

To play along, however, he said in his own language, "The Nile is life. The Nile is death. Forever let its waters run strong and proud."

It was a saying his father sometimes chanted to remind himself that with every blessing comes a curse, but as long as it exists, it should continue to do so. It was his father's last words and Tor vowed never to forget them.

"It sounds lovely, whatever it means."

He was tempted to tell her, but thought better. If Jane truly favored Tor, he had to make it clear that he was not interested in intimacy. She was Michael's daughter, and though Tor was being paid a handsome sum for his services as a guide, he would never say that Michael employed him. He might have been Giovanni's padrone, but not Tor's. They were acquaintances, and nothing more, but he didn't want to upset Michael by making a pass at his daughter by accident. Everything, including friendliness, could be misconstrued.

"Are you angry that I came along for the journey?" she asked, true curiosity laced in her words.

"I am not angry," Tor replied. "I am... indifferent."

"Indifferent? Do you mean you would not care if I was here or not?"

Tor let out a snort as an unpleasant, rancid smell crossed his path. "That is not what I meant," he replied, perhaps a little too brusquely. "Like your father, I would have preferred that you did not endanger yourself by coming on this pilgrimage." He looked to a few unsavory characters who were too busy inspecting long, curved daggers in their hands to notice that the Egyptian was glaring at them. "But, since you are here, nothing can be done, so there is no use being angry over it."

He heard Jane shift in the carriage, as if she were drawing closer to the barrier of painted wood and padding between them. From what he glimpsed, the inside of the carriage was quite comfortable with lounge beds and pillows for the vampires to recline on.

"You don't think like most men," she acknowledged.

"How is that?" he asked, looking ahead to a turn in the street that led under a canopy of clotheslines. Blankets and tunics were spread out along the lines, dragging down to graze the tops of the pilgrims' heads who were riding their horses instead of walking.

"Father was angry, so was Yaverik and the captain of the boat. Some of the men didn't seem too upset, but they were too interested in other things about me to be upset."

Tor tightened his grip on his staff, and had to remind himself that there was no other staff like it in the world, so he needed to be careful not to break it.

"But," she continued, "you don't seem mad, and it appears that you refuse to get mad at all."

"I have trained myself to suppress my emotions unless absolutely necessary."

Jane edged even closer. "For times like in the library when you nearly attacked Yaverik?"

Tor shook his head. He remembered how he felt. Violent, ready to tear the vampire apart simply for existing in the same space as he. Yaverik was a threat, whether Michael said so or not. However, that did not excuse his outburst. "You were watching from some hidden place?"

A young boy ran toward him and bumped into Tor's side. He glanced back at the rangy youth, but the boy sped on into the crowd without so much as looking back.

"No," she said. "I felt it from across the villa and heard the way you growled at him."

Tor heard the shiver in her voice, but knew it couldn't be from cold or fear. She was intrigued and aroused. Even through the carriage wall, he could smell it mingle in with the other scents of the marketplace they traveled through now.

"Jane, I –" he was prepared to scold her for having such thoughts and feelings toward a man that she would get nowhere with. Tor found her pretty enough, and as much as he was fascinated by her interest alone, it could never be.

It wasn't hesitation that stopped him from reproaching her. A sharp pain pierced through his gut that made him stagger on the path. Giovanni's mare shuffled to a stop, but Tor refused to be the reason they slowed down. He took another step as the pain snaked through his limbs and numbed his fingers. He hadn't felt such an urgency in many years.

Once a month, the spirit of the wolf needed to take control. On those days, Tor simply changed into his beastly form in the morning and stayed that way all day and night until the following sunrise. His father had told him that was when Wepwawet was the most connected with his priests. Tor didn't think that the need to turn and be one with Wepwawet would come during their expedition while he was away from the temple. Yet, here he was, feeling the throbbing need to shed his clothes and run free.

"Tor?" Giovanni questioned from behind.

"Are you all right?" Jane whispered.

He looked from one to the other and nodded. "Yes, I'm fine. I just need…" He patted at his belt. His sack of dried meats was missing. Often times, the excessive eating of meat could hold the wolf back for most of the day if the change became inconvenient. He looked to the ground around his feet, then behind him, but could not see the pouch through the scurrying feet of the locals and traders.

"I need my meat," he muttered.

He knew that Giovanni might not have heard him, which was a good thing. Tor wasn't sure how comfortable Giovanni was around, what he called, werewolves just yet. Despite their awkward first meeting at the temple and long talks on the forecastle deck of the ships as they traveled the Mediterranean, there was a bit of hesitance in Giovanni. If Tor made too quick of a movement, the scholar flinched. He might have thought if Tor was hungry enough, perhaps the werewolf would resort to human meat instead of the dried beef they had packed before leaving Italy.

"Meat?" Jane questioned, a note of panic in her voice. It couldn't be possible that Jane felt the same way. A creature who drank blood afraid of another who ate raw meat?

"I had a pouch of meat and it is gone…" An idea came to Tor and he struck the ground with the butt of his staff. "That boy," he growled through his teeth.

He was no stranger to theft, especially in the marketplaces back home, and he should have known that a place this size would be a breeding ground for thieves and orphans looking for an easy meal.

Not this time.

Tor immediately turned and handed his staff to Giovanni. "Hold this and keep going. I will return." He pointed a cautionary finger at the curious scholar who scrutinized the carvings in the wood. "Do not let anyone else touch it."

He would permit Giovanni to carry it, but no one else. It was too precious to be trusted into the hands of a stranger.

With that, Tor turned away and darted into the crowd.

It didn't take long for him to pick up the trail of his beef, and followed it through the mass of humans, pushing some aside and gliding past others without knocking them to the ground. He found the boy running down a narrow alleyway between two tall buildings.

Tor hurried forward just as the entryway became blocked by a cart. The merchant stopped and hopped down from his wagon to talk to a trader. Tor growled and found a neighboring alley. With the aid of some barrels and crates, he leapt onto the roof with great ease. He had spent a lifetime climbing over the structures of the temple and a bustling city was nothing in comparison.

He found the boy exiting the alley into an adjoining street that was slightly less busy than the first. Tor followed him along the rooftop, leaping over the chasm between the homes with his inhuman agility, and dodging under clotheslines. Several of the locals saw him from below, but he didn't care. He would have caught up with the runt sooner if his clothes were not as binding. If he had no respect for Michael, he would have discarded them long ago.

The boy ducked through another alley on the other side of the street. Tor ran and jumped from the building. Upon landing, he rolled across his shoulders, tearing some of the fabric across the back of his vest against the sandy ground.

Pedestrians shrieked and shouted as Tor pursued the boy into the alleyway, which wasn't an alley at all. Wooden planks that bridged the space between the two buildings on either side of the corridor blocked out much of the hot sun. At the end was a door.

Yet, as Tor grew closer, he felt something he hadn't felt since his father breathed his last. The back of his skull tingled, alerting him to the presence of another priest of Wepwawet. Though, it was vastly unlikely that another priest would exist this far from Egypt. Unless, it was one of these werewolves, the ones Michael and Giovanni had told him about.

He heard the voices of men just beyond the door and charged forward. Werewolves or not, he needed his meat. The whiney voice of the boy met his ears and then a sharp crack as skin met skin with considerable force. Tor snarled and all went still.

A voice called out, but he didn't know the local language enough to respond. Instead, he gripped the loose handle on the door and ripped it open to let himself in.

Inside, a group of men stood around the boy. Other youths, a little older, stood to the sides and against the walls of the room. All dressed in the torn and tattered garments characteristic of beggars and street rats. The older men, the ones who were werewolves, looked to him with suspicion, their dark eyes narrowing.

From the looks of them, Tor knew they must have been locals. They weren't so unlike him, except their skin was a few shades lighter than his own. They were dressed better than the boys, in clothes that didn't sport holes at the elbows and seams, but neither were they wealthy.

This must have been their den, a private place to store their loot. Glancing around, the room seemed sparsely furnished with colorful pillows and rugs laid across the ground in no particular order. Light from above was provided by a loose lattice work with vines weaved along the struts.

The one who exuded the most confidence stood in the center. All of the werewolves were muscular, just as Tor was, but this man was half a head taller than the others, with a harder look in his eye. Tor was sure that the only reason they tolerated his presence was because he was also a werewolf, like them. If he were human, they would have thrown him out already, or worse.

The leader jerked his chin at Tor and asked something, but again, he did not understand.

"The boy stole my meat," he said in Coptic, perhaps the only contemporary language that they would understand.

He was wrong. The leader shook his head as the others peered at Tor and his strange clothes.

Tor repeated himself, this time in the ancient language of the Egyptians, his father's language. Again, they did not reply.

If they were werewolves, then perhaps they would understand the language of Wepwawet. It was a different formulation of sounds that Tor knew was distinct from any other language in the world. It had been passed down through the priests, created at the dawn of time by their god. If Michael was anywhere near correct, they would understand this language.

Tor tried one more time and the leader's brows perked up. He looked to the boy who clutched the open pouch in his trembling hands. The leader snatched the meat away and approached Tor.

He almost wanted to pity the boy for the bright red mark on his cheek. It was clear that he had failed his leader in some way.

"I apologize for him," the leader said in the ancient language. "He thought he had stolen money."

Tor glanced at the boy's dejected face. "I don't know if I should be relieved."

The leader, whom would have been considered a high priest in the temple back in Asyut because of his stature and dominance, chuckled. "He also should have known not to steal from his own kind."

"He is still young, he wouldn't know."

The boy still had quite a bit of growing up to do before he would receive the wolf spirit gift from Wepwawet. He could tell that some of the other youths in the room had just as long to go. Others, might have turned fairly recently, judging by the way they stood away from both factions, one of the group, yet not belonging to either childhood or adulthood. He knew their pain and sympathized.

"Yes, but in times such as these, we all need to learn quickly." Tor wasn't quite sure what the man meant, but nodded anyway and cinched up his pouch. "Where do you hail from?" the leader asked.

"I am from Egypt. My traveling companions are from Italy." It might have been foolish to give so much information, but there was a kindred spirit about this den of thieves and the werewolves within it. "I ask that you not harass us as we make our way through Constantinople."

"Istanbul," the leader corrected.

Tor gave a short bow of his head. "My apologies."

"It is fine," he said with a flippant wave of his hand. "Many foreigners do not know the difference. Some do not care. Either way, we will stay clear of your caravan."

Tor thanked him and turned to leave, but the leader grabbed Tor's arm to stop him.

"Friend, I must warn you that there are greater dangers in the city. We are the only pack, but there are other groups of men that will not be so lenient with you."

Tor's mind quickly snapped to the unthinkable. "Hunters?"

The leader nodded, his dark and bushy brows knitting together. "Yes, and humans who will not know what you are. They may attack your caravan."

Tor took a deep breath and let it out slowly. A large city as this was bound to house a few disagreeable characters, but he never imagined there would be hunters. There was one thing he did know, and that was that there was safety in numbers. Tor took one look to the others, the pack as the leader called it.

"I have a favor to ask then," Tor began.

At first, the leader did not seem pleased, but he nodded. "For a fellow brother and son of Asena, anything."

Tor opened his mouth to question the leader's words, but there was no time. "May I ask for an escort through your city? You may keep your distance from the carriage and my companions, but I would greatly appreciate your protection."

The leader rubbed at the thick, dark beard that covered his chin. He debated the idea for a few moments, and then nodded. "Yes, we can do that. We will follow you on the rooftops and in the crowds. If a hunter comes close, we will alert you, but we cannot interfere. I have already suffered many losses in my pack and we are all that's left. We will escort you to the borders of the city, but you are on your own beyond that point."

"I understand. You have my many thanks." The panic in Tor subsided only a little. He would have some level of protection as they traveled, but it was no guarantee for safety. If they came across a hunter, Tor would have to defend his party on his own. He wasn't so sure that he could.

Based on how well he did the last time he came into contact with hunters, Tor hoped that time had changed him enough so he could be wiser and stronger.

CHAPTER 4

OUTSIDE ISTANBUL, 1570

By the time they were out of the city and well into the countryside outside of Istanbul, night had fallen. They stopped for a short time after Jane, her father, and Yaverik awoke from their sleep, so that they could take their daily blood meal and allow their servants to rest before continuing.

A small tent was erected for the modesty of the females of the party, while the others huddled around a small fire out of sight from the opening. Jane could smell the roasted meat they rotated on a spit over the flames, but it was nowhere near appetizing. It was food for the humans to help revive their strength for the journey.

She sat on the rug that her father had laid down for them, so that they wouldn't have to rest on the hard ground. With her legs curled up beside her and leaning upon her hand, she thought of Tor. He wasn't in camp. All she knew was that he had to leave, but he would keep up with the others once they started moving.

When he came back from reclaiming his meat in Istanbul, there was something different about him. He seemed wary, but when she asked him why, he wouldn't answer. Perhaps it had something to do with the appearance of more werewolves like him. She could sense them outside the carriage, though they never spoke or approached the group at any time. They kept their distance and as soon as they left Istanbul, the pack dropped away and Jane did not sense their presence again.

However, that couldn't explain the edge in Tor's voice when he spoke, because the aura persisted, even after the other werewolves left. Her father would give her no more details when she asked where Tor had run off to. That was nearly an hour ago and he still hadn't returned.

"What do you think of Angelo?" Francesca asked from her bedroll deeper within the tent.

Jane turned and gave her blood servant a look. "You should be resting."

Francesca propped her chin in her hand, her green eyes sparkling. Jane always did love her green eyes, especially when they lit up with excitement. "I know, but I wanted to know what you thought of him."

Angelo wasn't the most handsome man, not like Tor. Given her choice of humans within their close circle of acquaintances, Jane would have preferred Marco far better. He was strong, mature, and had been with her father for quite a while. Angelo was still relatively new to their odd family, having served Yaverik for three years so far, and Jane hadn't spent enough time around him to form an opinion. In fact, she kept her distance from Yaverik too when possible, which was why she hadn't spent time with Angelo.

"He's fair, I suppose," she replied, knowing full well that both her father and Yaverik could hear their conversation. At least they would be aware of Francesca's feelings for her fellow blood servant. Perhaps they already knew. Her father had a way of knowing things before anyone else and it infuriated Jane at times. She wanted to learn his secrets, but he still insisted that she was too young.

"He's been extremely friendly with me the last few weeks," Francesca said, her free hand stroking the coarse fibers of the rug beyond her plush bedroll.

It was not uncommon for the blood servants of covens to fall in love, get married, and even have a child who would be loved and cared for by their masters as devotedly as the parents. It happened once when Jane was a child, between the blood servants of her parents. Michael released them to live their own lives, which is when they took on Marco, who was a little older than her at the time. If Francesca and Angelo should enter into such a relationship, Michael was sure to be lenient.

Appraising Francesca, Jane realized that if she could find love in Angelo, then she should grasp it with both hands. An unmarried signorina of little wealth over the age of twenty would have a hard time finding a lover. Francesca was not so old, but she would be soon. She had faithfully served Jane for almost a decade now and had become her closest confidant. It would be heart wrenching to let her leave, but Jane was not one to stand in the way of true love.

"You should ask him what he thinks of you," Jane advised.

Francesca's eyes went wide. "That would be improper."

"Nonsense." Jane leaned toward her blood servant as if to share the greatest secret of the universe. "Men are dense. They need to be told everything. If you fancy him, then you should tell him. He will give you a quick answer if he thinks the same of you."

Now it was Francesca's turn to give Jane a look. "Then what's holding you back from Tor?"

Yaverik would never have stood for such a bold rebuttal, but Jane and Michael were far more tolerant with their servants.

To be honest, Jane wasn't sure what was holding her back. Each time she thought of telling Tor exactly what she wanted from him, her stomach and chest would twist in knots until it felt she would never breathe again. She knew full well that Tor didn't care for her in the same way. It was debatable whether he even liked her.

For all her vampire abilities to read emotions, she could not penetrate the thick walls that Tor had built around his heart. Why they had been erected in the first place, she couldn't say. The only way to know anything about Tor was to plainly ask, so there was no confusion in the matter. Yet Jane could hardly bring herself to ask the burning questions that demanded answers.

Jane pushed aside her heavy skirt and shuffled over to Francesca on her hands and knees. The blood servant giggled at the impish look on Jane's face. "I'll make a deal with you," she whispered. "If you agree to tell Angelo how you feel, I'll tell Tor how I feel."

Francesca shot her a dubious look. "Promise?"

Jane held out her pale little finger to her friend. "Promise."

She accepted the oath and hooked her own pinky around Jane's.

"In fact," Jane said. "I'm going to go do it right now."

Before Francesca could reach out and grab her mistress's hand, Jane was already at the tent opening. "I thought Tor went away?"

"He did. I'm going to find him," she replied with a simpering grin.

Francesca made a sound of disapproval, but it was too late. Jane slipped out of the tent and crept toward the horses. The fires of determination had been rekindled, but for how long?

On the other side of the tent, she could hear the men talking around the fire. If she weren't wearing her full skirt, she might have been able to sneak out of camp completely unnoticed by human or vampire. She was fairly confident that her father would hear her at the very least.

She found Giovanni's horse where Tor's staff was securely tied to the horn of the saddle. With a single touch, she focused on the crux of the staff and the bond that tethered it to its owner. Werewolves had their sense of smell for tracking. Vampires had what her father always called The Sight. It was the collective ability to feel another's emotions and see their memories, as well as follow the spiritual essence of a soul left behind in small traces as it traveled across this earth.

The latter ability was reserved for only the most powerful of born vampires, but Jane's heritage was pure and strong. If her father could, then she certainly could.

It only took Jane a few moments before she could sense the pull of Tor's soul on the staff. It snaked through the forest, away from the camp. Jane slipped off her heeled slippers and took off into the trees.

The branches and bushes snagged at the delicate fabric of her skirts, tearing at the stitching and embroidery that her father had paid a hefty price to have completely perfect. Jane was done with perfect. Done with tame and proper.

Her father scolded her for being blind to the truths of the world. She was too young, far too young to know of the dangers of stepping outside of the normal parameters of their culture and society. Jane had been yearning to bust out of her tight and itchy clothes for years now, longing for something wild, something savage. Something like Tor.

Tonight, she would get a taste of it. Only then would she know if she wanted more.

Jane smelled him before she ever saw him. A musky scent of fur and forest that beckoned her in for a closer look.

Slinking closer toward the row of shrubs that separated them, she knew he must have known she was there. Her skirts, if not her scent, would have been a clear giveaway. Stealth was not a skill she possessed, nor was it something her father would care to teach her. After all, what use would a lady have for sneaking about?

She peeked over the bushes and her eyes went wide. Tor was just as she had imagined him to be. Massive. Neither man nor beast, but a functional mix of both. Magnificent, and yet intimidating.

Jane wasn't afraid when he turned his wolfish head and stared at her with the golden eyes that seemed to burn through the darkness of the night. His nostrils at the end of his long muzzle flared as he passively sniffed the air.

With movements so fluid and graceful, he rose onto his hind legs, his shiny, dark pelt reflecting the few rays of moonlight that filtered through the trees. His tail disturbed the fallen leaves behind him as his broad and muscular shoulders squared to display the chiseled chest and stomach. Seeing him in the light, she saw streaks of brown and silver across his back and chest.

She likened his body to that of a statue that had been crafted by one of the masters of the arts. Regardless of his beastly appearance, with vicious claws tipping his humanlike digits and strong arms hanging at his sides, Tor was like a god.

Jane rose from her hiding place and pushed her way through the bushes, drawn to him so completely that all the rest of the world faded away. Tor did not flinch, run, or even growl at her presence. Yet, she could sense that he was not entirely pleased to see her. She didn't care.

She had never before laid eyes upon a werewolf in its greatest form. She wanted to touch him, to feel his fur beneath her fingertips and explore every part of this amazing and wondrous body.

Tor slowly lowered himself back down onto all fours and slowly padded toward her. Despite his displeasure, he was in full control of himself, and seemed to understand exactly what she wanted.

With a hand, trembling with excitement, Jane reached out and weaved her fingers through his thick mane, caressing around his neck. This form was twice the size of his human form and he had to bend his head down to graze his wet nose against her cheek.

He snorted and shook out his mane. Jane giggled and would not be deterred.

"I hope you know how magnificent you look," she whispered.

The intelligent look in his eye told her that Tor heard every word she said. Yes, now was her chance to say everything, even if he was a wolf.

"Tor, I – "

His head snapped to the side, his ears erect and swiveling to listen to something in the distance. Jane went silence and listened as well. She heard the pop of the gunpowder first, then the yelp of distress from Tor.

He staggered into her as the scent of blood filled her senses. She hastily caught him and looked in the direction of the assailant. Why hadn't she detected him first? So wrapped up in everything about Tor, she had been oblivious to any danger.

The man, cloaked in black and half of his face concealed in a shroud, she couldn't identify him, but her intuition told her this man had murder on his mind. This wasn't some case of a hunter mistaking Tor for sport. This man specifically wanted Tor dead. He lowered the barrel of his smoking pistol and holstered it into his belt before he turned away, obviously thinking that his job was complete.

The fur around Tor's shoulder became caked with his blood and it was slick to the touch. He should have healed by now. Upon quick inspection, she saw the edges of the bullet wound burn and sizzle. A wisp of smoke curled upward from his flesh. Silver.

He was alive, but if the silver wasn't extracted soon, he might not be for long. Her father had told her enough about werewolves to know their weaknesses and their many strengths. Tor looked to her, dazed with his lips curled back in a snarl. It wasn't directed at her, but at the immense pain. Jane felt it too, seeping through her own body and searing her skin. If only her abilities allowed her to take away his suffering.

She hissed toward the assassin. Blinded by the need to vindicate Tor, she left him where he fell and darted through the trees. Her skirts tore even more and snagged on the unforgiving brambles around her. The assassin did not flee in the face of a female who was running far faster than any human should be able to.

Instead, he pulled out a stick. No, a stake. Jane skidded to a stop and noticed the man also wore a cross around his neck and it caught the moonlight just enough for her to finally see it against his dark clothing.

Whoever this man was, he knew nothing of vampires. Their hearts did not beat, so there was no use in plunging a stake through her chest as the myths dictated. Neither would she be deterred by a simple cross.

Completely untrained in the art of martial combat, Jane charged the man and slashed at his face, her eyes blazing a deep red and black as the fury took control, and fangs glistening between her lips. The man dodged a few blows, but her nails managed to slice into his shoulder. Several times, he tried to stab her chest with the stake, but she evaded every attack, and finally knocked it from his hand to render him defenseless.

He let out a long whistle that was half-muffled by his face mask. Jane lunged at him, ready to see how deep her fangs could sink through his flesh. Her father had taken pride in the fact that he had never killed a human, but Jane was not above taking the life of this stranger. He hurt Tor and that was all the reason she needed.

Before she could grip his neck, she heard a faint disturbance in the air and then felt a sharp pain in her side. She fell to the ground and looked down to see the arrow pierced through her bodice and embedded in her ribs. With each move, a burning spread through her body, the source coming from the arrow tip.

Jane hadn't much experience with garlic, except when she passed a bakery or house where cloves were hung in the kitchens. The smell alone made her sneeze and cough. To feel it coursing through her veins was a different sensation entirely. Everything felt as if it were swelling, growing thick and tender. Her flesh pressed against her tight stays and rubbed against the seams of her chemise. The very blood in her veins congealed and her limbs convulsed as the poison reached to the most outer points of her body, which were growing rigid and immobile.

She let out a scream, hoping it would alert her father in time. She looked to the assassin and he was joined by two more men, one holding a crossbow. Her vision went blurry as the searing pain intensified. She swayed and the world began to tilt. Just before everything went black, she heard the angry and helpless roar of a werewolf some distance behind.

The men stooped down to collect her, and Jane lost her grip on consciousness.

Giovanni didn't have the faintest idea what roused Michael and Yaverik. One moment, they were talking about a particular fashion trend that was making its way through Europe, and the next they had looked to the west and darted from their seats around the fire.

Given no word to stay where he was, Giovanni ran after his padroni into the forest. Slow and encumbered by the thick shrubbery, Giovanni arrived to the scene, gasping for air. Yet what he saw next stole the breath from his lungs once more.

A massive beast, a monster neither man nor animal. Perhaps it was both. Yaverik jeered at it, as if it were nothing more than a flea infested, rabid dog. Michael, however, stooped beside it, assisting it to rise on its four limbs.

Giovanni could only guess that this creature was Tor. The werewolf had dismissed himself from the party around sundown, but gave no explanation. The scholar looked to the sky, but the moon was not full. So, the myths were false. Werewolves were not dependent upon the moon for their unholy change.

With wide eyes, he watched Tor reel and stagger.

"Jane has been taken," Michael announced.

The last he had seen of the young vampire, she was in her tent. Giovanni knew that the girl would bring trouble upon their voyage. What was worse, they had two females to look after now. If Giovanni had any say in the matter, he would have ordered them to board another ship bound back for Italy the moment they docked at Istanbul. Yet Michael was in charge and he permitted them to follow for whatever mysterious reason.

"I thought she was in camp?" Giovanni questioned, his voice little more than a raspy attempt to speak.

"She snuck out," Michael replied, one hand against Tor's furry chest that glistened with blood. The wound in his shoulder appeared deep and one whiff of the burning flesh told Giovanni it was no normal bullet.

"I shouldn't have let her leave camp," Yaverik added. "I heard her by the horses."

Tor lifted his wolfish head and stared at Giovanni with penetrating golden eyes that froze him in place. He admired the Egyptian, probably more than either of the vampires that were present. Giovanni was still wary of him, since their guide was not human, but he preferred Tor's company over any of them, even the blood servants. Finally seeing him this way, as a beast and not a man, however, made him question that.

On the outside, Tor appeared just as normal as any other man most of the time. The vampires had their unusual paleness to set them apart from the crowd, but the werewolves could hide in plain sight. Perhaps that was why Giovanni could forget what Tor was when they talked of philosophy and the history of the Egyptian civilization. Standing before the werewolf now, Giovanni could not forget that he was still a dangerous, preternatural monster.

"I knew she would come looking for Tor," Michael said, pulling Giovanni out of the trance. "I allowed her to go." He looked over his shoulder, his eyes searching the forest. "Her kidnappers are long gone. Whoever they were, they must have gone back to Istanbul."

Tor's lips curled back into a sinister growl, and Giovanni jumped, wondering if the beast even knew who he was.

"We will get her back," Michael assured the group. "Whoever these men were, they knew our weaknesses."

Giovanni knew this couldn't be his doing. Not yet. Those men weren't supposed to intercept them until much later in the journey. Whoever these men who attacked Tor were, must have had their own agenda.

Tor's muzzle opened, his white fangs flashing as he tried to form words. Even as a beast, the Egyptian was intelligent and cognitive. Giovanni couldn't help but be both astounded and terrified.

Michael shushed him. "We have to get you taken care of first."

"I will find her," Yaverik proclaimed, taking a step forward like some valiant warrior. The vampire was far from that. No doubt he was putting on a show for his mentor. One would have to be blind not to notice the way Yaverik looked at Jane. If Michael thought him a brave and courageous man, perhaps he would grant Jane's hand to his apprentice. Giovanni prayed to the merciful God in heaven that He would not permit such a thing.

Tor snapped and snarled at Yaverik, and the vampire repaid him in kind with a hiss.

Michael slashed his hand through the air between the two enemies. "Enough!" he snapped. "The three of us will go after her once we get the bullet out of Tor's shoulder."

It was a wonder that Michael could stay calm at all. His daughter had been spirited away by men who clearly harbored malintent for the supernatural. She could have been dead already, but Michael must have known something the others didn't.

"Perhaps I may be of assistance?" Giovanni offered, following the other men as they made their way back to the camp.

Michael waved him off. "It is too dangerous for a human to take on men who know how to kill things more powerful than you."

Giovanni wasn't sure whether to be touched by his padrone's concern for his mortal soul, or insulted that Michael didn't think him capable of staying alive. It was true that Giovanni was more at home in a library or safely exploring the known world with a team of guides and protectors. He was not proficient with a sword, but he knew things that others did not. He was a man of knowledge, not of strength.

He banked the argument for later as Tor let out a shrill whine. The silver must have been excruciating.

"Why wouldn't the men make sure he was dead before taking Jane?" Giovanni asked as he watched the way the powerful werewolf swayed and stumbled through the brush.

"They might have thought he was alone," Yaverik answered. "A wolf without his pack would surely die from a wound like this. The silver would ensure the wound would never heal and Tor would bleed out before morning."

"It's a good thing he's not alone then," Giovanni said with poignant emphasis.

Yaverik caught his hidden meaning and slid a threatening glance his way.

"Yes," Michael said. "While we are on this journey, we are responsible for one another." The elder vampire shot his apprentice a look and Giovanni felt as if he and his padrone, were finally on one accord, when it came to the reckless and spiteful manner in which Yaverik behaved at times.

If nothing else, Giovanni would have loved to tag along on their rescue mission, just to witness the mayhem that would unfold between the werewolf and vampire.

CHAPTER 5

Sneaking past the perimeter guards was easy enough. Convincing Yaverik to slow his pace and stay with Tor and Michael was another matter entirely. As soon as they caught onto the hunters' trail, the younger vampire sped ahead of his mentor at every available chance. Speed proved to be a useful tool in evading the notice of the guards, but Michael had made it perfectly clear that he wanted them to work as a team. Tor begrudgingly agreed, while Yaverik continued to contest the wisdom of bringing so many along to rescue Jane.

For once, Tor wanted to agree with him. He should have gone alone and left the rest at camp. It was Tor's fault that Jane was captured. The silver bullet in his shoulder pierced through the thin wall of consciousness between him and his wolf and the pain was keenly felt by both. It had been years since he felt such agony. Not since his father died. Not since he had caused another catastrophe like this one.

Before they left, Michael had tried to console him as he pried out the round pellet of silver from Tor's wolf flesh, but nothing could persuade Tor to believe that any of this was not his doing. As Michael said, they were all responsible for one another on this journey and Tor was the only one who could have saved Jane. Over and over in his mind, he replayed his mistakes and berated himself for his foolishness.

He should have stayed closer to camp. He should have known that the hunters were close. He should have kept Jane from running after his would-be executioner the moment he knew the bullet was silver. He should have pushed through the pain and attacked the hunter himself. It would have vindicated not only himself but in some way, the death of his father as well; yet another death that could have been avoided if he had done better. If he had *been* better.

Now in his human form and dressed in a loose linen shirt and pair of trousers, Tor squeezed his eyes shut as they crouched behind a band of shrubs within sight of the fortress wall. He couldn't let the guilt resurface or everything would be compromised. He could hear his father's words hammer in his ears. *Stay focused. Stay focused.*

Michael's hand gripped his arm, cold fingers latching over his bare skin so suddenly that Tor started. They locked stares and Tor knew that Michael could sense his grief. He could fool Jane, Yaverik, and even Giovanni into believing that he was too proud and strong to feel anything but loyalty and duty to his priesthood. However, Michael knew better. He would always know that Tor was not all right beneath his cool exterior.

Hearing Jane scream earlier as he lay bleeding had splintered the hatch that he had kept shut over his remorse for so long. Up until just a few hours ago, he had been able to lock away the tragedy that left him alone in the world. Yes, he had revisited the memory a few times, grazing over it like a bug would skim over the calm surface of the water, but never dwelling or delving deeper into the truth. Tor's father was dead because of him. If they were too late, Jane's blood would be on his hands as well.

He gave a quick nod to Michael, confirming that he was good to carry on with the mission. Yaverik, who stooped on the other side of Michael, was jumpy and eager to dash toward the stone stronghold where Jane's trail led.

Across the top battlement were guards – hunters – wielding crossbows, whose tips flashed in the moonlight. Each of them were covered in black clothing, almost indistinguishable from the darkness around them. Only the light of the moon that shined upon their heads and shoulders gave them away. Tor listened, but the inside of the hunters' headquarters was fairly quiet. Some operatives were snoring, while others talked softly. Tor could still not understand their words, but Michael appeared to.

Michael turned to Tor to relay their conversation. "They took the garlic out, but she's still unconscious. They don't know for how long." Michael shook his head. "These men don't know what to do with a vampire," he said. "Those who hunt us wouldn't have kept her alive."

"Obviously, they were expecting her when they came after me," Tor said. "One doesn't bring something they think they will not need. Either they intended to come after her as well, or these hunters are not as they appear." He looked back to the fortress, searching their high walls for any sign of weakness.

He guessed it might have been an ancient palace or castle centuries before, but had been abandoned and taken over by the hunters to suit their own purposes. In Egypt, those who assassinated his fellow priests hid away in recessed caves on the rocky outcroppings in the desert. They preferred to have the higher ground and it put his priesthood at a disadvantage, since the only way to reach them would be to climb the face of the cliff. Tor could still see two of his father's closest friends being picked off with arrows before they even reached halfway.

Here, the guards still had the strategical advantage, but Tor could dodge their crossbow bolts far easier on the ground. Both Michael and Yaverik could match him in speed, so the question remained how they would infiltrate the compound.

"Where is she being kept?" Yaverik demanded, glaring at Tor as if he should have known already.

"In the cellar beneath the courtyard," he replied as he ignored the apprentice's disrespectful tone and took a deep whiff to find her vampiric scent through the cluster of humans.

Almost predictably, Yaverik leapt over the shrubs and plunged forward into the open field between the forest and the main gateway. Michael started to reprimand his apprentice, but Tor pursued Yaverik before the mentor had a chance.

Sure enough, the hunters' quick reflexes caught the swift movement of the vampire and turned their crossbows upon Yaverik. The trajectory of the arrows was positioned just right that they would have pierced his chest, if Tor hadn't intercepted.

Tor overtook Yaverik and tackled him to the ground. The razor edge of one arrowhead sliced into Tor's upper arm, but continued on its path to stick into the ground. His flesh burned for a moment and blood seeped into the crisp cloth of his tunic sleeve just before it began to heal.

"Fool!" Tor growled in Yaverik's ear as the vampire struggled against him to rise again.

On the battlements, the hunters were reloading for a second volley.

He grabbed Yaverik by the collar of his rigid vest and tossed him against the wall of the fortress, so they would be somewhat out of range from the crossbows. The hunters could only aim down so far.

He heard Michael come up behind them. Tor turned just in time to see an arrow pierce into the vampire's thigh. Michael grunted and managed to press himself against the cool stone before another volley rained down.

The alarm had been raised, all because of Yaverik's impatience. Tor would have beaten him to dust if they had the time. The apprentice didn't even bother to check if his mentor was all right. Instead, Tor was the first to Michael's side to assess the damage.

Michael snapped the arrow's shaft and with painful force, slid it from his flesh. Blood gushed from the wound on both sides of his thigh as he hissed, his long fangs bared. When he lifted his eyes, Tor flinched away from the red glare he hadn't seen before. The whites of his eyes were completely blackened, while the usual gentle brown was replaced by a menacing crimson.

Tor gave him a wary look, wondering if the change in his eye color was anything similar to when his own eyes changed to gold. It meant the beast within was close, ready to strike. Would Michael attack in his rage and pain?

His lips closed over his pearly teeth and jerked his chin toward the gate, showing he was ready to continue. Tor looked over his shoulder, but Yaverik was nowhere along the outer wall. The acrid stench of blood filled the air, and Tor knew well enough that it was human blood spilled, not Michael's.

Less than a second later, Tor heard a scream shatter the chaos. Michael cursed in his native tongue and limped toward the open gate that was blockaded by a band of hunters. Yaverik stood in the center, holding a severed head by the scalp. The mutilated body of the hunter lay at the vampire's feet. Tor didn't think the arrogant vampire who dreaded getting his hands dirty on this expedition could be so brutal. To Tor, it gave slightly more credibility to Yaverik's character, that he was willing to kill for a cause. Yet, was it the cause he fought for, or the blood lust?

The air was electrified, like during a thunder storm, alive with clashing hatred, both sides with their own goals to destroy the other. Both thought themselves righteous in their mission, that they were doing what was good for the betterment of the whole.

The hunters raised their crossbows to fire upon the three ill-prepared invaders, their eyes blazing behind the black shrouds that cloaked their faces.

Faceless and nameless, but Tor knew their kind just as well as they knew his. They wanted nothing more than to see Tor and his companions dead, the world a little safer because there were a few less monsters in it. In the same way, he knew that he couldn't allow them to live. He thought of the pack of werewolves in Istanbul, of the boys who had not yet grown into their gift. If the hunters had their way, every last one of them would be killed, no matter the cost, just like those of their creed killed off the priesthood.

Images flooded back, of a skirmish and white linen robes stained by the blood of his friends and family. Mangled bodies, their wounds coated in the sands of the desert that slowly buried them. They were forgotten by time, surrendered to the harsh and unforgiving land that had once given them life. His father lay in his arms, choking out his last words as he bled out from the gash in his neck that was incapable of healing because of the silver blade that had cut him down.

He would not let this end in disaster.

In the time it took for one of the hunters to blink, Tor's shirt was off and he charged ahead of Yaverik. He felt an arrow lodge in his side, but the shift into his beast form loosened it and the shaft dropped from his body.

He roared, the wolf and man now one as it had been earlier that night. The change was much less painless and more seamless than it would have been on any other night. This was the beast's time to roam, to hunt, and to be free. The wolf remembered Jane's scream and feeling her soft touch in his fur. There would be no man or vampire alive who could stop the beast from seeking his revenge.

The hunters fired and Tor felt the silver sear into his flesh, but he continued. In a flurry of fangs and claws, Tor tore into every last man who tried to detain him. Arrows, knives, and swords all found purchase but still he raged.

Tor was vaguely aware of Michael and Yaverik joining the battle behind him, though there was nearly no need. Within a matter of seconds, the hunters were slaughtered, their lifeblood consecrating this ground as a moment of absolution for centuries spent in regret.

Tor's father could not be brought back from the afterlife, his soul far past into Aaru, the Field of Reeds. Yet he could save the souls of countless others who might fall prey to these predators who were far more ruthless than any werewolf. Here, on this ground, his sins were expunged, and when his heart was weighed against the feather of Ma'at to decide his fate in the afterlife, it would be a little lighter because of this day.

Tor collapsed forward onto his elbows, willing himself to stay conscious, despite the numerous throbbing lacerations and crossbow bolts protruding from his chest. He was sure a few silver bullets had found a home in his back somehow.

Yaverik ran off toward the stairs on the other side of the courtyard that led him down into the cellar. Michael came to Tor's side, his feet wading through the puddles of blood that were now beginning to soak into the earth. The vampire tried to help his comrade stand, but Tor growled and trembled with the effort to rise on his own.

The pain was too intense, clouding his mind with a thought that plagued him for years. Many times, he wondered how long it would be before he joined his father in Aaru. How many centuries, perhaps millennia, would go by before he could pass on to be with his fellow priests in the land of eternal plenty? As Tor and his wolf struggled to hold onto their combined strength, he knew it would not be long.

Finally, his muscles giving way to the heavy weight of his massive form, Tor rolled onto his side, his fur inundated with the blood of the fallen. Michael shook him, but the words were muffled and distant. His golden eyes stared vacantly ahead, though all Tor wanted to do was close them and sleep.

Two more figures emerged, blurred and unfocused as his lids dipped and jaw went slack to emit his shallow breaths. Jane weaved in and out of sight, her cries and pleas sounding shrill in his ears. Her arms looped around his neck and she lifted his head to her face.

One thing he knew through the haze of coming death, she was crying. Jane sobbed like a woman who had lost every good thing in this world. She cupped his face as if she were holding the last dying embers of life itself. One false move and he would be lost forever.

Yet as she pressed her face to his, the fronts of their skulls touching, he felt something new. It blasted through the pain and numbing release of death. A coolness touched his muzzle. A drop, not of blood, but of water. Tears poured from her eyes and into his fur. The coolness spread across his skin like a welcome breeze on a hot day.

It started slow, but then it grew. His wounds began to heal, his flesh pushing out the bullets and arrow tips as if by magic. His senses returned to him, but he couldn't bring himself to move. Not yet.

Neither Michael nor Yaverik interceded and kept their distance as Jane continued to cry.

"She's actually doing it," he heard Michael marvel.

"What?" Yaverik asked.

"She's healing him."

Tor closed his eyes, letting the relief consume his body. In moments, there was no pain, no more open wounds. He bucked his muzzle against Jane's chin to get her attention.

When she sat back, Tor licked at her damp cheeks to taste the salt and magic from her tears. She smiled and embraced him as he slowly pushed himself out of the rivers of blood that flowed around them.

"We must go," Michael advised. "If the hunters have allies in the area, they will soon find out what happened."

Tor turned to his combat partners and saw they looked just as ragged as himself, their clothes torn and speckled with blood. Jane stayed close by his side as they quickly made their way out through the fortress's main gate to disappear into the forest.

They would all live for another day, and though death had stretched out its withered and decrepit fingers to seize Tor's spirit, Jane pulled him from the brink. What power did she have that could ward off death itself? Clearly, Michael knew of it, but did not expect Jane to wield it so effectively.

As they ran, Tor looked to Jane and her soiled clothes that were stained with dirt, her torn dress hem dripping with the blood in which she had knelt. In all the years he had been alive, he knew of no one that cried for him. There was no one alive that cared for him so deeply that they would shed a tear if he passed.

Yet this girl, this vampire, cared enough to weep over his body. They hardly knew one another, but she appeared devoted. Perhaps Tor had been too hasty in his assumptions of her. Jane was, after all, more than just a girl. She was a woman at heart. A woman who craved the love of a man she could not have. She deserved that love, but Tor still wasn't so sure he could be the one to give her what she needed.

After this night, however, Tor would never see her the same again. That was certain.

Tehran, modern day Iran, 1570

"We can't leave the carriage," Tor insisted as he squatted by Giovanni on the ground. "They won't be protected if we leave it."

Giovanni tapped the end of his stick at the rough, impromptu map that he had drawn in the sand. The evening sun in Tehran beat down on the backs of their necks as the commotion of the marketplace behind them droned on.

It had been a long trek from Istanbul. The days were long and hot as they traveled through Ankara, Cappadocia, Tabriz, and finally to this trading town just south of the Alborz mountains. Besides Michael, Giovanni was the only one who could speak the local languages, but what he learned from a silk merchant was not what any of them wanted to hear.

"The way through the mountains is too dangerous for the carriage," Giovanni reiterated. "There is plenty of space to ride horseback along the Haraz River banks, but the carriage wheels won't last long."

Tor leaned forward on his knuckles, glaring at the lines and wavy marks. Giovanni had the entire way memorized, but the height and rocky terrain of the mountains was unexpected. He and Michael had discussed the route around the mountains, but that would take longer and their supplies were dwindling at an alarming rate since they had not planned on the accompaniment of Jane and Francesca.

"What do you suggest?" Tor asked, the frustration in his words building.

If anyone was having a difficult time on this trip, it was Tor. Several times, he had to escape away from the party to change into his wolf form to release the knotting tension. The nights were worse when Jane was awake enough to cling to him.

Whatever happened the night they rescued Jane, it changed something in Tor. Giovanni wasn't the only one who noticed, because he heard the blood servants whisper about it occasionally. Tor was more open to conversation than he was before, more relaxed in dealing with the others, except when he had to turn. Michael encouraged the shifts, perhaps aware that he was used to changing far more frequently than he had over the course of this journey.

This was the first time Giovanni had seen Tor angry in days.

"We have to take inventory," he replied. "We can only carry what we need between here and Amol on the other side of the mountains. We should sell the carriage and try to find a camel trader. We can sell the horses as well."

What he wasn't telling Tor, was that he had no intentions of returning with the others. When he came back through Tehran, he would be alone.

"What will the others do to protect themselves from the sun? Traveling only by night isn't feasible."

"I agree. We will have to purchase more clothing for them. Turbans, shrouds, shawls, anything."

Tor wiped the sweat from his brow and nodded. "Very well. I will inform them of the plan while you procure the supplies. We can move out at dusk when it's less dangerous for the others."

"I'll take Francesca and Marco. They know how to haggle better than me. We should be able to find everything we need. If we can't, this is a poor excuse for a trading hub. It is fortunate that most of the towns we have visited are used to seeing foreigners, otherwise trade would be far more difficult."

Giovanni stood and tossed his stick to the side before kicking the dirt to erase his map. It was a risky plan, especially since they were just a little over halfway to their destination – if there was a destination at all.

He looked to the north, to the snowcapped mountains that stretched across the horizon. Beyond them, the Caspian Sea awaited and hopefully would disclose her secrets. Giovanni desperately wanted there to be a civilization, for Michael's sake. It would be one last gift to the vampire.

Turning, he caught Tor's thoughtful stare pointed toward the north as well.

"Something wrong?" he asked as he pulled out his pouch of coins to count how much local currency he had left.

"I've never seen such white sand on top of mountains."

Giovanni chuckled and clapped his werewolf companion on the back. "My friend, that is snow."

"Snow?"

"Si. It is as cold as ice, and sometimes soft to the touch."

"Ice?" Tor looked to Giovanni in puzzlement.

He waved his hand in dismissal. "Never mind. You'll see soon enough. We will pass Mount Damavand on its eastern slope and you will see it more closely."

"There is still so much about this world I don't know."

Giovanni cinched the pouch opening and secured it to his belt once more. "Just wait until you see the rest of it. Deserts and mountains are just the beginning."

It was a lie. Giovanni didn't know whether Tor would ever see such things as the Great Wall of China, the Atlantic Ocean or the highlands of Scotland. If his contacts were correct and they were making good time, they would meet the party on the eastern edge of the sea. From there, Giovanni almost didn't care what happened. There was no money in his pocket that exclusively belonged to him and there were more trusting padroni waiting in Italy for his services.

However, his heart was saddened by the thought that Tor might share the same fate as Michael and the others. Tor was an unnatural being, a werewolf, but he did not always behave as such. The Egyptian priest was generous and kindhearted, though perhaps a little less amiable than others due to his lack of exposure to sophisticated society. Tor was a dying breed of an ancient world, just as Michael was.

Yet, the course of events could not be changed. Amol and a few trading posts along the coast would be the last bits of civilization they would see and there was no telling where his contacts were, so communication was impossible now. There was no turning back from the decision he had made. Giovanni could only hope that time would prove he had made the right one.

"I have a question," Giovanni said after a moment of thought. "Michael told me how you nearly died to save Jane. Is there something more between you two?"

A muscle jumped in Tor's jaw. "No," he replied through his teeth.

Giovanni held up his hands in surrender, as if to beg for mercy from the werewolf who was able to tear apart a small army of men. "I was just curious. Men usually don't go so far for people they hardly know."

Tor let out a long breath through his nose before speaking again, making solid eye contact with Giovanni. "I wasn't doing it for Jane, or even Michael. I did it for my father."

Giovanni lowered his hands and wrung the neck of his coin purse. "May I be so bold as to ask what you mean?" The way Tor talked about his father along the journey, Giovanni knew that he was no longer alive. There must have been something deeper, something hidden under that tough exterior that for which Tor seemed to pride himself.

"When I was young, just a short time after I became a priest, I caught the attention of a band of travelers. I had changed and run out into the desert around dusk. They spotted me and spread rumors about beasts in the desert around our temple. Soon, hunters came and..." Tor shook his head, his expression melting into a show of regret. "The hunters tracked us down. One by one, they picked off the other priests. Most fled, but my father elected to stay. We defended our temple and my father sacrificed his life for it.

"It was my fault that he was killed," Tor said. Giovanni could almost taste the sorrow in his words and it terrified him, almost as much as Tor's wolfish form. Such emotion, such brokenness was not like him. Giovanni wasn't sure whether to be flattered that the hard and calloused priest was finally opening up, or to be worried that Tor might have been losing his mind. Such a solid foundation was rocked and suddenly unstable.

"So, you killed those hunters as retribution for your father's death?"

Tor nodded and Giovanni saw the reverse in his countenance. Suddenly, his walls shot back up and with a snort, he pushed away the misery that nearly crushed him just seconds ago. "In a way, yes. They weren't the same men, but knowing I killed them gave me some satisfaction."

Giovanni had never killed a man. Not yet, and not directly anyway, but he couldn't fully imagine how Tor must have felt. His own father had died of disease years ago, but if he could do anything to bring a little relief to the ache in his heart over the loss, he was sure it would have been a glorious feeling.

CHAPTER 6

Jane started at the sharp rap on the carriage wall. She had been sleeping soundly for the last few hours, despite the constant noise of traders and travelers outside of her dark sleeping place.

"Michael, we need to speak."

The drowsiness instantly left her the moment she heard Tor's deep, husky voice. She sat up and scrambled to the other side of the carriage, crawling over her father's legs as he was just beginning to stir from his sleep.

She grabbed the handle and cracked open the door just enough for the bright sun to spill over the back of her hand. Tor struck the door hard enough to close it once more and he grumbled a word that Jane had recognized as a rather harsh expletive in his language. She had heard it several times on this journey already.

Though the sun was no longer touching her skin, the burning did not subside right away and the scent of charred flesh filled her nose, overpowering the musty smell of upholstery and wood. She could feel that the top layers of her skin had flaked away like old, peeling paint on a neglected wall, leaving the raw and bloody flesh beneath to throb and sting.

Jane hissed at the pain, wondering how she could have been so foolish to not ask if it were night yet. When Jane came of age as a young girl, Michael had let her experience the terrible effects of the sun. Exposing one's skin to an open flame was nothing in comparison to how a vampire suffers in the sun.

Michael sat up and grabbed her hand to check the damage. It was only a second or two of exposure and it had already begun to heal, but nothing would hinder him from being the devoted father that he was. All along this trip, he stayed close to her, just as he had when they traveled with her mother so long ago. He had rarely showed this kind of attentiveness inside their villa and Jane somewhat resented it. She was not a child anymore, but he still treated her like one.

There was something to be said for her father's commitment to his family. Tor had told her about the arrow Michael took to his thigh when they had come to take her from the hunters, and how bravely he fought alongside them. She loved her father dearly, but knowing that Tor had nearly sacrificed himself to save her trumped it all. Jane had only cried one other time, but those tears were not enough to save her mother who had been stolen from them so many years ago.

Michael gave her a chastising look and then turned to the carriage wall where Tor stood on the other side. "Si?"

Tor proceeded to tell Michael about Giovanni's plan to sell the carriage and the change in routes. Yaverik fumed on the other side of the carriage as he awoke.

"We'll surely die if we give up the carriage. It's a ridiculous plan," her father's apprentice shouted. "We will repair the carriage if it's needed."

"It will delay our arrival to Arnathia," Michael countered. "It is a reasonable exchange. Tor, see that we get everything we need. As soon as night falls, we will be ready."

Jane listened to Tor's feet shuffle across the sand as he walked away. If the sun wasn't out, she would have leaped from the carriage and followed him, eager to assist in procuring the new supplies. Alas, she had to stay in the darkness, where it was safe. Oh, how she hated to be safe when she could have been by his side.

Tor's heart opened up a little more to her each day. Though she never carried through with her plans to tell him how she felt, Jane knew that it was only a matter of time before he would be more receptive to her affections. It was likely that if she confessed to him that night when she was captured, Tor would have disregarded her as silly and nonsensical. In just a few days, however, he might come close to feeling just half the same as she did. A few more long talks about Italy, a few more lighthearted giggles, and a touch of the hand here and there, and Tor might be hers.

"Honestly, the way you pine after him," Yaverik groaned, "it's revolting."

Jane's lips puckered angrily. "I don't see how my relations with Tor is any of your business."

"It's unnatural!"

"That's a matter of perspective," she sassed. "Some would say that a frog was unnatural because it can swim and walk on land too."

Yaverik sneered. "You are speaking of a frog. A better comparison is a flea-riddled dog trying to ride below the crupper on a thoroughbred."

Jane was not an innocent child, but she gasped at his euphemism. "I'll thank you kindly not to speak of such things in my presence."

"Silenzio, both of you," Michael interjected. It was not the first time her father had to break up an argument between them and it certainly wouldn't be the last. At least she was solaced in the knowledge that she did not start it. "Yaverik," he continued, "Whom Jane fancies is not your concern."

The apprentice would not be quieted so easily. "She does not need to be chasing after beasts. She needs to find a husband who is a vampire also."

Jane rolled her eyes. "Find a vampire worthy of me and I'll gladly consider it."

There was a pause of silence before Yaverik continued. "There's myself."

She shot him a look. "Now, *that* is revolting."

"What in hell's name do you see in Tor? He's a savage."

Jane lifted her chin. "Perhaps that's why I find him attractive. He's wild, unlike most men within our circle." Out of the corner of her eye, she saw her father begin to scratch his beard, deep in thought. "He's also kind and heroic."

"Need I remind you that Tor wasn't the only one who came to your rescue?" Yaverik questioned.

"He was the one who was dying from his wounds," Jane pointed out. "There's nothing more romantic and genuine than a man willing to die for his friends. I don't recall that you were injured in the least."

Yaverik sat up a little straighter and was ready to match her rebuttal, but Michael interrupted once more.

"Jane, Tor does not have any intentions with you. He has told me so and his emotions tell the same." Her father grimaced. "It isn't right for you to wear your heart on your sleeve in this manner."

She made a sound of disbelief. "You just told Yaverik that it was none of his business whom I fancy."

"Yes, but it is my business. I don't care if Tor is a werewolf or vampire. I do care that you are chasing after a man that doesn't want you."

Jane's chest seized, her father's words echoing in her ears. "Perhaps he just doesn't want to tell you that he cares for me, because he fears you will turn him away."

"I know you can feel his emotions as well as I can," Michael said with a shake of his head. "You know I speak the truth."

She shrugged, trying to hold onto her hopes, which was exactly what her father warned her against. "There's time. He's changed over the last few days. It's possible that he will – "

"Jane," he snapped. "Please, do this as a favor to me. Do not try and manipulate him into loving you. If it is meant to happen, then it will. You should not be so hasty in finding a blood mate. You are still young and you have not met all of the eligible men out there."

"You're saying you want me to wait until another vampire comes along," she replied with a snide twinge.

Michael held up a cautionary hand. "No, I'm not saying that. I'm saying wait until the right man comes into your life. Whether he be vampire, werewolf, or human, it does not matter. You should find a mate who loves you in the same way. Don't try to force fate."

Jane went silent and sat back against the carriage door, her legs stretched out across her father's like a child. With her arms folded over her stomach, she tried to ignore her better judgment that her father was completely right on all accounts.

It was wise to wait, to see what else the future had to offer. Yet, what if Tor was what the fates had in mind for her? What if he was her true blood mate? What if they parted after this expedition and never saw one another again? How long would it be before she found another like Tor that could make her feel so light headed and alive? Worse yet, what if she never found the one to hold her heart? She knew that she couldn't settle for just anyone, and even if a man as noble and wise as her father came along, Jane wasn't sure she would want him either.

The heart within her chest constricted with impending sorrow until Jane was ready to fling herself into the loathsome sun. If she couldn't have a man like Tor, if he couldn't learn to love her, then what was the point of living a thousand years? If she didn't have someone to share it with, would it still be a life worth having?

She shook her head. No, she would not act like a spoiled child who balked if they didn't get what they wanted. Surely, though, Tor's raid on the hunter headquarters meant something more? It must have been a sign that he cared for her as more than a traveling companion. She had to know for certain. She would not believe anything else until she heard it from his own lips that he did not want her.

Outside Amol, modern day Iran, 1570

Night had fallen and Tor was more than glad for it. Each moment spent in the daylight set him on edge as he constantly watched over the three vampires to make sure they were well.

Draped in cloth from head to foot, they should have been safe from the sun. Their eyes were covered in a thin muslin veil so they could still find their way with the rest of the party down the Haraz river banks. They were active enough, but Tor could see them sway in their saddles as the camels rocked them side to side with each step. In the interest of expense, he elected not to have a camel as the rest did. Their purses were too light to waste money on an animal that he did not need.

On their first night in the pass, Michael told him that the sun took much of their strength, which would prove to be a taxing obligation upon their blood servants. They could only feed so much, and though Tor was disgusted by it, he made sure that they fed at every given opportunity as long as the humans were able. Giovanni even offered his blood when Michael was especially struggling and Marco was still recovering from the last feeding.

At night, however, they were more alive, more vigorous. Tor didn't worry about them as much once the sun went down. It was strange to him, that he would come to care so deeply for this band of creatures he had never known existed before a few weeks ago. Apart from Yaverik's typical bitterness and arrogance, Tor was growing fond of them; Jane in particular.

Over the few days that it took to trek through the mountain pass, she braved it well. Each time she felt as if she would fall asleep, she hopped off her camel and walked alongside Tor in relative silence. Her quietness bothered him to no end.

Ever since they left Tehran, he knew something was weighing upon her thoughts. She was far more distant and introspective than usual. Even when he tried to elicit a conversation from her, which was out of the norm as it was, she didn't seem interested in talking just yet. There was still a lingering urgency that he could sense, though, to say whatever it was that was truly on her mind. She wanted to talk, but simply wouldn't allow herself.

It was a few hours into the final night of their journey through the Alborz Mountains when Tor spotted the glowing lights of Amol. He alerted it to the others.

"Grazie Dio!" some of them shouted. The scenery along the river was spectacular with mountains framing the sky, but they were all more than ready to refresh supplies and perhaps rest a little longer now that the longest part of their expedition was over. The hardest part, however, was just beginning.

Tor looked behind and saw Jane leaning against the trunk of a tree some distance from the others. With her turban undone and blonde hair plastered against her damp forehead, he knew she was not well. He turned to Michael, who was watching his daughter just as carefully. They both knew she hadn't fed since that morning, almost a full eighteen hours.

She tempered her feeding, much to Michael's frustration. When the others were taking two to three feedings a day, Jane restricted herself to her usual singular feed. Tor could sense her weakness and agitation with every passing hour, but he also knew that her hunger and fatigue did not have a bearing in it completely. Even his wolf could feel that she had come to the end of her limits.

Tor came to Michael's camel as the blood servants attempted to race their stubborn camels down the hill toward the city's edge.

"Let me speak with her alone," Tor requested. Michael gave him a wary look. Before he could ask, Tor clarified, "You probably know as well as I do that she has wanted to speak with me for a while. We will catch up with you in Amol."

Michael paused in consideration, then nodded. "Very well. I suppose I don't need to tell you to be careful, do I?"

"No, signore."

The vampire then clucked at his camel and carried on with the others to follow the speeding blood servants.

Tor heard the faint rustle of the grass from behind him as Jane fell to her knees. He hurried to her side. With her eyes closed and breaths raspy, as if she had been running for miles on end with no water, Tor held her face in his hands.

"Jane, look at me," he demanded.

Using the skills his father taught him, he sent out a slight but firm pulse of dominance to get her attention. His father always said it was another gift from Wepwawet, useful to claim the respect of the commoners, but his father found it particularly handy when dealing with an unruly priest.

Jane's eyes snapped open, grey eyes staring at him with a vague flicker of acknowledgement.

"You need to feed," he said, his eyes skimming from the dark rings under her eyes to the way sweat dripped from the edge of her jaw.

She shook her head, her cheeks pressing into his palms. "No," she whispered. "Francesca..."

"Is gone to Amol," he finished for her. He briefly let go to roll up his sleeve and reveal his wrist to her. It was coated in a light layer of dust since he hadn't bathed that day, but the blood beneath would be enough for her. "You have been pushing yourself far too much."

He offered himself to her, bringing his skin to her lips the way he had watched them do countless times. Jane fought it, jerking her chin away, only to bring it back with a lustful, crazed look in her eyes that were beginning to glow black and red, just as Michael's had back at the fortress.

"I don't know..."

Tor had enough of the waiting and grabbed the nape of her neck to pull her down. He didn't care if there would be consequences. He didn't think about how his blood might affect her. She was ill and he had the cure, that was all he cared about.

Jane gave in and sank her fangs into his wrist. He looked away and waited for her to finish, even though is wolf raged against what Tor was subjecting them to. He felt neither pain nor dizziness that usually came with losing so much blood. All he could feel were her lips gliding and sucking along his skin, her tongue lapping up the blood that seeped steadily from the two puncture wounds she had created with her teeth.

She not only took from him, but gave something in return that he couldn't describe. A lightness washed over him, almost euphoric, that turned into a tingling that creeped down his spine, through his core and limbs.

All at once and in a shocking revelation, Tor needed her in a way he never had before.

He gripped his free hand into a tight fist until his nails made his palms bleed. Her fingers found this new stream and brought his other hand to her mouth to taste. The tip of her tongue swirled across the half-moon punctures and Tor gritted his teeth, resisting the way she seduced him so easily. He hated the way his member ached between his legs and began to throb, wanting something he couldn't have.

Was she doing it consciously, or was this what every blood servant felt when their master or mistress fed upon them? He had never witnessed this kind of change in them as they let the vampires feed. Surely, she knew what she was doing. She had to.

When she finally released him, Tor watched the wounds slowly heal, leaving only her cool saliva upon his skin. He refused to look up, knowing that his own eyes would be a lustful red. It was the color that was forbidden to all priests who took the celibate vow. Tor had not taken such a vow, because he never had the chance, but there was something tainted and illicit about feeling so strong of an emotion so suddenly.

"Thank you," she said, her voice wrapping around his mind like a whore's caressing embrace. Tor gripped his knees, but couldn't bring himself to stand and distance himself from her.

He sat there, floating on the border between taking her and running into the mountains to disappear forever. Damn the expedition.

She was a child, not in heart but in body. It was her mind and soul of which he had grown fond of. The vessel that contained it shouldn't have mattered as much as it did, but Tor couldn't shake the feeling that it would be wrong to take her, mated or not.

"Tor?"

"Please, get away from me," he whispered, his eyes squeezed shut to force the longing away.

She moved closer and he could take it no longer. Tor pushed her down and positioned himself over her, breathless and impetuously close. He could feel her chest push against his and her legs part to receive him. Yes, she knew exactly what she was doing.

Tor hesitated from taking the opportunity she offered so willingly, though the carnal lust drove him to near madness.

He finally looked at her, showing exactly what she was doing to him. A droplet of blood remained on her lips, coloring them red, just like their eyes. Jane neither shied away, nor resisted him, but weaved her fingers in his slick hair. The heady scent of arousal drifted up to him, adding kindling to the steadily growing fire in his chest.

Over and over in his mind he said he couldn't do this. He couldn't take her. Then why did it feel so right to be so close?

He wanted to feel her skin, explore, and discover if every part of her was as cold as her hands or face were. He wanted to lick off the bit of blood that lingered on her lips and taste for himself why it was so appealing. He wanted to give her exactly what she had silently begged for since the moment they met in the vestibule of her father's villa.

Jane's fingers loosened from his hair and fell upon his chest, her fingertips pressing through the fabric to feel the tense muscles beneath. "I want this," she assured him as her hand came to rest over his heart. It beat strong and fast, the only heart beating between them.

"It doesn't matter if you want it," he said, his voice tinged with a growl. "I can't do this."

Just as he had to coax her to drink his blood, she coaxed him to take everything from her.

She gripped his tunic and pulled him down until their lips met. As soon as he tasted the blood from her mouth, the wolf within Tor broke free of his bonds to release them both from this oppression.

Tor growled and the red of his eyes plumed into a blazing gold. Jane shrunk back as the dominance radiated from him, hotter and more powerful than any force of nature until the air around them hummed.

He scrambled off her, dropping to all fours, his back hunched and teeth bared in aggression toward her seductive intentions. She stared at him, eyes wide in fear. For the first time, she was truly afraid of him and the wolf was well aware. He fed on it, breathed it in, doused his mind in it until the lust and need for carnal satisfaction was completely gone.

"You did that on purpose," Tor roared.

Jane blinked and shook her head. "I don't know what you're talking about," she replied, almost in a whisper that trembled like leaves rattled by the wind.

Tor snapped and growled like an animal, and watched her flinch and shuffle backwards in the grass. "Don't lie to me!" he bellowed. "You made me want it, didn't you!"

Her lips quivered as she blubbered out, "Tor, please, I didn't mean to. I swear it!"

The humanity within Tor reached out to restrain the beast. Though he was just as angry with the girl as the wolf was, he could not bear to see her suffer in fear. His lips closed over his teeth and he sank down until his knees and elbows hit the ground, but he would not let her come close if she tried.

Slowly, Jane rose to grip her knees and gather her skirt in her hands to press the material tighter around her shins. "Father told me once to never take blood from a man, unless he was my husband... I didn't think that this would happen."

Tor pondered it a moment, and then understood. This wasn't her fault. It was his. Once more, his fault. "That's why you have Francesca as your blood servant instead of Marco or Angelo."

Jane nodded as the tear dried on the edge of her jaw.

If Tor hadn't made her drink his blood, he wouldn't have almost lost his self-control. Yet how could he have known? There was still much more to learn.

"I'm sorry," he whispered as he took a few deep breaths to clear his mind once more of the primal urges to take or to kill. Tor didn't know which was worse, the sensation of being out of control because he wanted to lay with a woman or to rip her to shreds for her misdeed as the wolf wanted.

Jane looked away, but would not accept his apology. Nor would she extend her own. They simply sat there, surrounded by the sounds of the night and only the moon and stars to witness what almost took place between them.

"Tor, I... Surely you know that I..."

He didn't need to hear more. He knew exactly what she wanted to say now. "Yes, I know."

Tor watched her face, but there was no surprise, no shock, or even dismay. Her eyes lowered and he watched her throat work out the next carefully chosen words. "I've never met a lupo mannero before. I've never met a man like you, but I know I never will again. It's plain that you don't care for me in the same way, but can you at least explain why? Is it because of what I am?" she pleaded.

"No, it's not that." Tor was mindful to keep his tone soft and inoffensive.

Jane looked to him, imploring an answer. "Then what is it? Am I ugly? Is it because of my father? Tell me!"

He sighed and shook his head. "It's none of those things, Jane. You are beautiful, I assure you. But... it's not easy for me to look at you and see you as a potential mate."

To say it aloud didn't seem quite right. It wouldn't roll off the tongue as easily as another explanation might. Jane was too young. Just a child. Tor couldn't see him with her, not this way, not right now. She might have been nearly half a century old, but she still appeared as an adolescent, just beginning to blossom into a young woman.

After a moment, a spark of understanding came to Jane's face. "Damn this body," she snapped. "This isn't who I am. Can't you love me for who I am as a woman and not as I look?"

She was the one who wondered if her looks had anything to do with it, and now she wanted him to disregard them anyway?

"I cannot," he affirmed. "It would feel wrong. It's not that simple."

"Human women younger than me marry every day to men who are twice their age and society doesn't so much as bat an eye at it."

"That was not how I was taught," Tor argued. "Our ancestors married their own siblings, but that didn't make it right. We know better now that such unions don't always turn out for the best."

Jane sniffled. "So, if I looked older, if I looked like a woman, would you want me?"

Tor pushed himself up to sit back on his heels. "That depends on the kind of woman you turn into. People change over time. Boys turn into men, girls turn into women, and they don't always stay the same. Surely you've seen this happen in your own life?"

She looked away and he knew she thought he was right. If Jane retained her bold spirit and perhaps matured a little, Tor might have deemed her the perfect mate. There were still many obstacles and many years to go until they could arrive at such a perfect place and time that would make it feasible.

"For now," Tor continued, "I will gladly be your friend and your guide, but I can be nothing more."

He expected Jane to sob, to cry out that life was unfair and that he should love her anyway. Yet she remained silent and resigned to their fate. Tor somehow wished that things could have been different. He wished that he could have just given her what she wanted so that she would smile again, but he could not abandon his integrity so easily. No one would have known if they made love. No one would even know what truly happened, unless they chose to tell the others.

The thought occurred to him that perhaps Michael would find out. He could read his memories, after all. He would know everything, and perhaps applaud Tor's strength of will? Would he be so lenient and forgiving with Jane?

Tor rose to his feet and when Jane didn't join him, he offered out his hand, the one she had licked and caressed so tenderly to slurp up the blood that he had drawn with his nails. At first, she didn't even acknowledge him. When he showed her that he was going nowhere without her, she finally took his hand and they made their way down the hill together toward Amol.

CHAPTER 7

DESERT EAST OF CASPIAN SEA, 1570

M ichael didn't want to invade his daughter's mind. He saw the way she slumped over her camel as they continued east from Amol and the way Tor seemed to look to her with immense pity in his eyes, but Michael refused to pry. If she had wanted to tell him what happened on the hill, she would tell him in her own time.

When they turned north, leaving the lush land behind them to trek across a vast desert, Jane still hadn't spoken. Only then did he peer into her memories. What he found, what had been consuming her for days and nights, sparked a fury in him that he thought he had left behind long ago before his daughter was born.

Michael was a peaceful man, a vampire who refused to take a life, even if it meant starving to death. When it came to family, however, he might have been willing to rationalize murder. He offered respect and goodwill to all who came into his acquaintance. But when he saw Jane's memory of Tor straddling over his daughter like a man without restraint, without shame and control, it was enough to make Michael want to kill the werewolf.

He probed further and found the cause for such passions. Then he wanted to turn his ire upon his daughter. How many times had he warned her to never take a man's blood? How many times had he scolded her as a child for trying? Michael had been careful to tell his own male blood servants to never let her drink, even if she begged and pleaded. The passions that were instilled through the touch of her mouth upon an open wound was too great for many men to resist. Whether she wanted him in that way or not, he would take her virtue. It was a common mistake almost all female vampires made. Even his wife had done this before they were mated.

Yet Tor did not take her. The werewolf, somehow, had enough power to resist. This was why Jane was despondent and Tor so morose. Michael understood them now. Tor felt regret for how far he had let himself be driven in the first place, while Jane was embarrassed for her show of impropriety. So she should be.

Michael wouldn't tell either of them what he now knew. Their self-imposed torture was sufficient enough. As much as he detested what his daughter allowed to happen – and he did place sole blame upon her shoulders – he wished, as a father, he could have saved her the heartache. She was still young, as vampires were concerned, but he had never seen her fawn over a man like she did toward Tor. Her emotions were too conflicted to understand, but Michael wondered if she did love the werewolf. In his heart of hearts, he wanted Jane to find love, but it was clear that it was not with Tor.

Michael watched the two of them from his place in the caravan line. Giovanni led the way across the endless sand, Yaverik behind him, Francesca, Angelo, and then Tor with Jane riding by his side. Marco brought up the rear as the sun beat down ever harsher.

It was only their second day across the desert and for the first time, Michael wondered if it was a mistake to travel this far without proper protection. He understood that it was necessary to leave the carriage behind, but their thick and heavy clothing wasn't enough to keep away the fatigue.

Yaverik, as always, feigned his resilience, though Michael could sense his growing weariness. They had already fed once that day and the nutrition it provided was not enough to sustain them. Even Michael, as old and experienced as he was, could barely sit up straight in the saddle. He gripped the reins, the texture of the rope biting into his palms, but it would not keep him awake.

There was no telling when they would reach Arnathia. They could stumble upon it later that day, or perhaps it lay on the far north side of the sea. They didn't know how far the coast stretched. This was still an uncharted land and the only trade routes snaked much farther east than where they were. Perhaps it was folly of him to think that they could find such a place, or perhaps the hateful sun was putting doubts into his mind.

Michael closed his eyes as his muscles began to ache. His chin dropped to his chest, feeling the heat seep into his skin and suffocate his spirit. The cloth absorbed the sweat that poured from his body, making the fabric cling to him and chafe as he rocked upon the camel from side to side.

He could feel his defenses drop and the emotions of everyone in the party came crashing in, adding to the burden from the sun. Their doubts, their fears, their worries, their anger, everything smashed against his skull and squeezed his heart until it hurt. It wasn't just Tor and Jane's dilemma, but the blood servants, and even Giovanni's conflicted interests pounded at Michael's soul.

He gritted his teeth, wishing he could block it out somehow, but he was too weak, too tired.

"Jane!" Tor shouted.

Michael looked up and peered through the muslin that covered his eyes. His daughter had fallen from her camel, calling the entire procession to a dead stop. Tor chased after her as she rolled down the sandy bank of the hill they had been traveling on.

Her turban unraveled from her head and blonde hair gleamed in the sunlight. Francesca gasped and the blood servants instantly dismounted to give what aid they could. Michael could only watch, too drained of energy and motivation to move, though he felt much more than any man or father could possibly bear. He could never stomach to see his child suffering so.

Tor scooped her up and held her close to his bare chest as he hunched over her to shield her face from the sun. The damage had been done. Jane's fair skin was charred and burnt, nearly as black as Tor's eyes. Her eyes were closed and Michael knew she was unconscious by the way her stream of emotion had so suddenly been cut off from the rest.

On his way to them, Marco scooped up her turban. Frantic fingers bound her head and neck once more just as the skin was beginning to heal. Tor's grief and worry was proclaimed loud and clear to Michael, though his face would not betray him to the humans in the party.

Tor was used to this kind of climate, much more than any of them. His tunic had been shed and stuffed in a pack long ago and it was as if the sun itself gave him the strength to carry on while the others dragged. He could travel like this for days without rest, but even Giovanni, who had trekked across Europe, could not go on like this.

With Jane nestled in his arms, Tor returned to the caravan. The werewolf looked to Michael, a hint of an apology in his eyes as if this entire journey were his fault. Never would Michael blame Tor for their troubles. If anyone could be blamed for the hunters, for Jane's injuries, or for the fate that awaited them, it was Michael. It was his idea to bring them out here, not Tor's. The priest only did what they asked of him.

"We cannot continue," Michael declared.

Marco and Angelo shot him perturbed looks. "We've come all this way and now you say we can't continue?" his blood servant questioned.

Michael shook his head. "I mean that we need to camp. We cannot travel this way." He motioned feebly to his daughter, who lay sleeping in Tor's embrace. "Soon, we will all be like her. The sun is our enemy and we can no longer fight it."

Tor approached Michael. "Setting up camp, even for a few hours, will slow down our progress."

Giovanni steered his camel around to join them. "Perhaps we could let the vampires sleep while we continue? We have been traveling in one direction this whole time without giving thought that the civilization might be a little farther west or east."

Tor nodded in agreement. "Yes. We can split up into pairs and cover more ground to the east and west while one of us stays with the camp."

They both looked to Michael for approval. He could see nothing wrong with their plan and nodded. As far as he was concerned, Michael was finished making decisions. He needed rest and whatever would give him that, he was in complete concurrence. It wasn't what was best for the others, but it was better than what they had been doing. The sooner they could find the civilization, the sooner they could return home.

Then again, what would have been best for all was for them to have never left Italy. Michael knew how insane this expedition was. He was chasing a fairytale, a myth, nothing more than superstition. He had to know it was real; he had to know that the relations between the supernatural world were once not so out of balance as they are now.

Just watching the way Tor and Jane interacted, he knew that hate for each other's races was not innate. They could coexist, and if Tor and Jane could get along, so could everyone else. Michael just needed to find the key to peace. Hopefully, it was in Arnathia.

The coast of the Caspian Sea stretched farther north than any of them had expected. Nearly a week had passed of trekking across endless desert and rocky terrain. It took even longer, now that Jane and the others were forced to sleep during the day to conserve their energy. At night, they traveled by the stars with Tor leading the way. Even though the vampires had impeccable vision in the night, Tor's eyes were keener and his senses sharper than any of them.

Jane lagged behind on her camel, bringing up the rear with her father and Marco as the others preceded them. Supplies were running low and the blood servants were growing weaker as their rations were cut. Even Tor, whose diet was made up of the dried meat that he carried with him, was feeling the pressures of starvation.

Yaverik, more than either Michael or herself, was growing restless over the lack of sustaining and nutritious blood available. Even Jane could taste the difference in Francesca's blood as the young woman became thinner and sickly with each passing day. If they didn't find more water soon, or reach the other side of the desert, Yaverik had muttered a vow that he would drain one of the blood servants dry to preserve his own life. Though Michael would stop at nothing to prevent such a thing, Jane feared for the safety of her friends.

Out of all the roiling emotions of the expedition party, Giovanni was the most nervous. Jane watched him constantly look over his shoulder and whisper to himself about how tragic it would be to be eaten alive by the beasts with whom he traveled. Though, she could sense his anxiety ran even deeper than that. Something else was troubling him and she had a feeling that her father knew more than he let on.

It was early one morning, nearly at dawn, when Jane wrapped herself in her protective garb and stepped out from the thick-walled tent where her father and Yaverik rested. Giovanni and the other humans were taking a short nap in their tents before they would split up and search for Arnathia to the east and west, as they did during the day.

Tor, however, was not with the others. With quiet and precise movements, he was collecting the canteens and water sacks from each of the tethered camels. Treading upon the unsteady sand, she made her way toward him.

The sun was just beginning to peek over the rocky horizon, chasing away the dark night and its fading stars. Jane had seen many sunsets and sunrises, and even through the thin fabric that veiled her eyes, she admired its colorful and glorious beauty. When she was younger, before she came of age as a vampire, she would rise early just as her parents were retiring for bed, and go out to the balcony to watch the sun rise over the vineyards. Even in this harsh, merciless land, such beauty could always be found if one chose to look for it.

Tor shouldered the water containers and turned to meet her, his staff clutched in hand. This was the first time they had been truly alone together since she unwittingly seduced him outside of Amol. How she regretted her carelessness and loathed how foolish she had been to think that he actually wanted her when he pinned her to the ground, his body so close to hers.

Thinking of it now brought both pain and pleasure that she was ashamed to feel. They could probably never have a future together, but she still wanted him so badly. Over the long days and nights since her mistake, she tried to put it all behind her, to move on and think of something else besides his intense stare and taut muscles. It was all in vain.

"You should be sleeping with the others," he said. "The sun will be up soon."

Jane hardened herself. "I want to go with you. I feel so helpless just laying around or riding a camel while everyone else contributes."

Tor gritted his teeth and then looked toward the east and the steadily rising sun. "There's a reason you shouldn't help."

"Because I'm a woman?" Jane countered, propping her hands on her hips.

He turned back to her. "No. Because of your..." His gaze darted over her body, as if inspecting her to make sure every bit of skin was concealed before the sun's rays could burn her.

Michael told her about how she had fallen off the camel and Tor came to save her. If she were the silly girl that she had been when they first started this journey from Italy, Jane might have thought he did it out of love. Now she understood that Tor cared for all of them equally. He would have done the same for Francesca, for Angelo, perhaps even for Yaverik.

By the way he seemed to be a natural leader, a natural alpha, Jane knew that his compassion had little to do with her and more to do with him as a man. Tor didn't act in love when he scooped her out of the sand or came to rescue her from the hunters. He did it because it was in his nature to defend and protect. Nothing more. Jane wished she had realized it earlier.

"Because I'm a vampire," she sighed. He nodded and moved around her to begin his journey toward the sun. "Will you not wait for the others?"

"I am going to find water. I do not need assistance."

Ignoring his refusal, Jane hurried after him. "Let me come."

"You will only get in my way."

"I can help carry the canteens."

Tor shot her a look. "As soon as the sun rises, you will be too weak to carry yourself, much less a bladder of water. Then I'll have to carry you and the water together."

Jane hustled over a dune, matching his foot holds as the loose sand poured down the slope. "Please, Tor. Let me try."

Her foot slipped and she slid down the dune on her belly. Sand found its way through the seams of her garments and she could feel them scratch against her skin with the friction. She let out a squeak of distress, but Tor only turned to watch her slip all the way to the bottom.

Once there, she sat down and stared up at him, feeling completely pathetic. Tor cracked a smile and shifted his feet only minimally to dislodge his stance just enough to slide down without falling, as if he were skiing on the sand, using his staff as a rudder to keep him descending in a straight line. He was used to this land and the way it was formed. Sand, mountains, parched earth, this was home to him, just as the lush vineyards and rolling hills were home for her.

Tor stood before her as the sand continued to trickle down after him, pooling at his bare and dusty feet. Since they started to make their way across the desert, Tor stripped down to just his trousers that hugged his thighs a little too tightly for her to ignore.

He offered out his hand, a spark of humor still glittering in his eyes like the stars that shone above. She placed her hand in his and let herself be lifted to her feet.

"If you feel weak, please let me know and we will stop to rest."

Feeling bold and daring in the face of adventure, she replied, "I'll do nothing of the sort."

He might not have been able to see the smile behind her veil, but perhaps he could hear it in her words and Tor smiled wider before they made their way back up the slope.

Tor breathed in the hot, dry air, following the faint and fleeting scent of water. It had been hours since they headed east and the sun was already climbing into the sky at an alarming rate. If he didn't return to camp with good news and fresh water, there would be more at risk than just the expedition.

Jane dragged her feet behind him, sloshing sand with each step and heaving from exhaustion. Just as he predicted, she would not last long. Ahead he spotted a tall plateau that seemed to stretch for miles onward, its rocky slopes gleaming almost white in the sunlight and steep inclines mocking their fatigue. If Jane had to traverse such an obstacle, she would surely trip or stumble. He didn't know if vampires could die from a broken neck, but it certainly wouldn't be pleasant.

He instantly regretted allowing her to come along. Not because he didn't enjoy her company and their light conversation, but because she wasn't safe here. None of them were and he wanted to curse the day that Giovanni shattered his complacency with the proposition of seeing the world outside his temple. This was not the world he would have wished for them to experience. This was not what his dreams had promised. They could not match his endurance and they would all pay for it dearly, unless they found some sign of civilization soon.

He stopped and glared at the foreboding cliff as he waited for Jane to catch up. If she were not with him, Tor might have used his speed to cross the desert and find the water that seemed to elude his grasp. Waiting for her slowed him down significantly, but he had to admire her resilience and spirit. Despite everything she had been through, she still had a kind, caring heart. His wolf saw this and adored her for it. Perhaps that was why, against everything that made sense, he let her come along.

Jane fell to her knees beside him and lifted her head to regard the cliff and plateau. Tor heard a vicious hiss from behind the heavy scarfs and veils that protected her face. She didn't revel in the idea of scaling the heights any more than he did.

In a move that he might come to regret, he shifted the canteens from one shoulder to the other so the straps ran across his chest, and crouched down in front of her. "Get on my back. I'll carry you."

There was a note of hesitation in the way she said, "But, what about you?"

"Don't worry. I will be fine."

With no further prodding, Jane carefully climbed on. With her arms and legs wrapped around him, Tor stood and bore the load. She was surprisingly light, he thought, as he took the first steps toward the mountains.

Slowly, he picked up his pace, being careful not to jostle her. Yet, the further he went, the more Tor realized they would make no progress this way. The land was too rough, Jane was slowly becoming a greater burden, and even his two legs were not going to climb this mountain easily while he was slightly weakened by hunger.

The promise of water called to him, along with something that transcended deeper in his soul the closer he came to the white slopes. Even if there was no water on that plateau, he had to reach it. Both him and his wolf agreed that there was something waiting beyond the point where he could just see over the plateau's edge.

He set her down and looked at the short distance they had crossed. It wasn't far enough and though he had told himself he wouldn't change in front of another soul, Tor knew he had to make an exception. The transformation was a private rite amongst his priesthood. He had never even seen his father shift before ceremonies. Yet, with the help of his wolf, they could conquer the cliff and reach the plateau to discover whatever lay on the other side, so he had to do the profane and change without the aid of concealment.

So, with Jane watching, Tor set down the canteens, his staff, and stripped off his pants to stand naked under the glorious and hot sun. He shifted, not so smoothly as in the past since his belly ached with hunger and his mouth felt dusty and dry from thirst.

When the shift was complete, his dark fur coat bristled in the wind. Any other animal with a pelt as thick and heavy as his wouldn't survive in the heat of the desert. However, Tor was raised to withstand this kind of climate. It was home to him and his wolf. He turned his golden eyes toward Jane, who stared in awe at his beastly form.

With fluid, humanlike movements, Tor hung the canteens around his neck since his shoulders were now too broad for the straps to fit across, and carried the staff in his mouth so all four limbs would be free to carry them onward. He then crouched down so Jane could climb on top of his back once more. The last time anyone road his wolf form in such a way was when the young boys in training to be priests begged for him to play in their games.

To feel her hands weave through his thick mane and her body pressed flush against his broad back, Tor did not feel burdened any longer. Quite the opposite. He felt as if he could finally carry the load with pride. Not just her, but the expectations of the expedition and his responsibility as their guide.

Tor took off, leaving a trail of dust kicked up in his wake. He came upon the slope and could feel the earth incline under his paws as they beat against the sand. When he reached the rocky base of the cliff, his claws dug in and continued to propel him forward.

The scent of water and the ethereal pull of the unknown became stronger. Air huffed from his flared nostrils at the tip of his muzzle and his tongue lolled out around the staff he carried between his jowls. Whenever he felt Jane's hold begin to slip, he bucked his hips to keep her on.

He could see the edge of the plateau ahead, taunting him to reach it. Tor pushed harder, his instincts driving him to run faster, climb higher, and leap farther across the ridges that twisted down the slope. Jane let out sounds of distress each time he defied the odds, each time they could have fallen to their deaths, but he kept them safe and moving up the cliff.

His paws gripped the edge of the plateau and he launched himself over. The indescribable force that called to him had not disappointed. Before him, less than a mile or so off, lay a town. No, a city. Its stone walls towered high above the sands, some massive stones dislodged and lying half-buried around the edge of the perimeter. The wooden gates, preserved by the dry air, lay propped open and waiting for them to pass through.

"Arnathia," she gasped. "It's really here."

Tor wasn't too sure it was Arnathia, but the scent of water was coming from deep within that city. That was enough reason to explore it. He detected no humans, no other signs of life within the abandoned walls, so he hurried forward at top speed, the canteens knocking together around his neck.

There was a new energy in Jane that fought back the life-sapping sun. Her fingers gripped his fur and she sat up a little straighter to gaze upon what she believed to be the fated city for which they had been searching. As Tor grew closer, he wondered if it just might be. That, however, was not his first concern.

Tor skidded to a stop just before the gates and lifted his head to study the deep gashes and claw marks that scarred the thick wooden panels. Where the two halves would have met, a giant and jagged hole had been made. Perhaps the lingering reminders of a battle or war? It was not a promising welcome into a city that was supposed to be the center of peace.

Looking to each side along the city walls, he could now see that they angled off, somewhat curving to give the city's footprint a more circular shape.

Jane elected to climb down from Tor's back and dashed ahead of him to enter the city. Tor ran after her and stopped her from proceeding any further. If this was a trap or there was danger lurking within the crumbling structure, he would be the first to discover it, not Jane. He rose onto his hind feet to stand and took the staff from his mouth to wield in one of his massive paw-like hands.

The inside of the city reminded him of places in his ancient homeland. Tall, brick and stone buildings with open doorways and large apertures in their walls lined the sandy streets that curved with the city's perimeter and forward. Tor admired the way so much natural lighting filtered into the rooms, how open it was to nature despite still resembling something that belonged in a civilized world. His wolf appreciated the design.

Tor led the way to the left and looked upon the cracked and decrepit buildings that stacked higher in two, three, and sometimes four levels. Their thatched and straw roofs were caved in by in-blowing sand from past storms, but he could sense the life that must have existed here before the place was left to be consumed by nature.

Upon closer look, he found that the homes did not have one entrance, but two. The first and most obvious one, permitted inhabitants into the part of the homes that they could see from the street. The other went deeper, beneath the earth.

Tor went first, poking his muzzle around the corner of the doorway to find a hall that emptied into a cooler, darker part of the home. Jane followed and let out a sigh of relief. Inside the basement of the home, there was no light. Nothing of the sun shined past the hall and perhaps the builders specifically designed it that way. The walls that made up the hall served as a sort of light barrier that gave the room its dark ambiance.

Apart from the sand that had made its way inside to coat the floor in a thick layer of dust and dirt, the cellar would have been a perfect home for a vampire. Perhaps this *was* Arnathia. Vampires and werewolves could have easily lived side by side in these homes.

While Jane leaned against the cool earth wall to rest, Tor left the confining space to follow the still elusive water.

The streets of houses and homes were occasionally broken up by stretches of structures that looked like market booths, though they had been abandoned long ago. What could the Arnathians have possibly sold here?

He spotted a bit of a broken bowl around the doorway to one home and lifted it out of the sand. Its painted and carved patterns were simple, yet beautiful. A ring of running wolves circled just below the rim.

It took a moment, but Tor finally detected the blood and raw meat that had been served in the dark clay bowl. Wolves would have never devoured such a high concentration of blood, though the meat would have been more than acceptable.

Was it possible that the vampires and wolves ate together? Side by side, using the same bowl?

Tor continued on around the edge of the perimeter, avoiding the center of the city for now. What he came upon puzzled him. Against the inside of the city wall was a round tower that dwarfed the other buildings.

Yet what drew his attention most was the massive carving of a wolf head above the main portal to the tower that had been all but worn away by time and possibly the same violent vandalism that marred the gates. He passed through the entrance, unsure of what he would find.

There were no stairs, only wooden ramps wide enough for even him to easily walk upon. They led from level to level that was lined with empty racks and shelves. Spears, swords, and lonely arrows littered the floor. The air was dusty and seemed to carry the residual energies of those warriors who had come here to arm themselves for battle. Pride for one's city and their people, hatred for those who opposed them, and fear of the coming devastation.

In a corner on the third floor, Tor spotted a helmet too large to belong to any man. He sniffed it and detected the signature scent of his kind, of werewolves. The metal was tarnished and slightly rusted from the sweat and blood that had been caked upon its surface for centuries.

With hesitant paws, Tor set down his staff and took up the helmet and raised it over his head. His pointed ears slid easily through the notches that had been cut for its previous owner and no edge or point impeded with the shape of his wolfish snout and eyes.

He didn't let the helmet stay on his head for more than a few seconds before he knew that it was not meant for him, even if it fit him perfectly. None of these things, the weapons or the armor, represented him or his values. War and violence was sometimes a necessity, but if he had lived here millennia ago, he would have never been a soldier of Arnathia.

Tor quickly set the helmet back where he found it and exited the armory. Jane was in the streets, gazing up at the buildings and the tower. They rejoined without a word and carried on.

To the western edge of the city, they found another gate that was just as battered and beaten as the other. The scent of water led him to look toward the innermost portion of the city. They took to the path that wound through the many buildings and apartments until another structure loomed overhead.

A segregated part of the city from the rest, but different from the city's perimeter. The corners were squared, not rounded or angled to a lesser degree. Yet the gates were remarkably different.

Two imposing and identical statues stood guard over the gate to either side. The figures of a woman, stared with her eyes wide open to danger, looking toward the outer walls of the city and over the dwellings of the citizens.

Her long hair draped over her shoulders, her body covered by a flowing dress, adorned with carvings of beads and tassels. Her bare feet sat upon the stone pedestal that was just higher than Tor as he stood beneath the magnificent effigy. Her face retained a regal look with high cheekbones and eyes that not only could spot danger, but see through to the very soul of it.

An inscription was carved in massive letters on the pedestal, but it was in a language that Tor did not recognize.

"Tor, look!" Jane cried as she ran from the base of the monument to a place along the wall to the north.

He followed and found her leaning over the edge of a fountain. Hope kindled in his chest for just a second, but then died as soon as he saw the bottom to be just as parched as the desert that surrounded the city. Still, the scent of water was strong. In its prime, this fountain might have supplied many residents with water. A dozen feet wide at its greatest, it was just large enough for Tor to lay across the bottom.

Jane pounded her fist on the stone edge that came up to her waist. Tor set aside the canteens that still hung around his neck, then hopped into the fountain and tapped the bottom of his staff along the floor of the dry fountain. The water must have come up from somewhere. If he could just find where the earth was thinner or the reservoir that fed the fountain in the ancient times, perhaps he could reawaken it.

As he listened to his staff rapping the ground and felt the vibrations beneath his feet, Tor edged closer and closer to locating the source. Once he thought he found it, he dropped down to all fours and dug away the soil and sand.

The deeper he went, the more mud caked around his claws and between his digits. Tor scratched away the layers until the cool water spilled out over the fur on his paws. Yet he kept digging, widening the path for the water to flow through.

Soon, the bottom of the fountain was submerged in a thin puddle that steadily grew with each second that passed. Jane uncorked each of the canteens, flasks, and bladders to fill them.

Tor stepped out of the fountain and shook the water from his legs and tail, spraying some on Jane in the process. She squealed and flung some of the water from the fountain into his face. They could afford to be playful and waste their resources now.

With one challenge out of the way, Tor felt as if he could breathe a little easier. Hunting desert game would be no trouble for him once they were settled in the city, and as long as the underground water supply didn't deplete too quickly, he knew the party would survive.

Yet, looking around at the sea of buildings, monuments, and ancient language that seemingly appeared to be written everywhere, Tor knew their journey was far from over. If this was Arnathia, there would be many more days of discovery, research, and enlightenment ahead.

CHAPTER 8

ARNATHIA, 1570

From the moment Michael, Giovanni, and the rest of the expedition party arrived to Arnathia, the scholars barely slept. Every waking hour was devoted to studying the city, mapping out its walls and exploring the many buildings and houses.

What they found was a complex and interconnected design. It didn't take them long to find the four libraries and record archives hidden away in four of the twelve towers along the city's inner perimeter walls. In each scroll and codex that lined the dusty shelves of the libraries, they found ancient texts written in numerous languages. Tor assisted them with the translation of some, while Michael worked with Giovanni to compare the parallel texts, so they could read and understand the Arnathian language that was inscribed everywhere around the city.

What they learned was both fascinating and astonishing. Every aspect of the civilization, from the number of towers to the statues, had cultural meaning.

There were four gates into the city, representing a cardinal point on the compass, each with a name. The city was shaped by the high, twelve-sided, brick wall that protected it from the outside world.

On the interior angle of the outer perimeter was a tower devoted to a certain aspect of Arnathian life. Between each of the four gates stood three towers. One dedicated as an armory, one to knowledge and the records of the city, and the last was deduced to be a meeting place for the community with tables and benches for congregating. Giovanni reasoned that it might have been a religious center, but they found no relics in the sand around the entrance or inside to confirm it.

Not all three tower clusters were the same, however. Two sets seemed to be constructed to accommodate the werewolves of the city, with their open doorways and expansive windows to let in light and air. They were positioned between the north gate and the western gate, and between the eastern and southern gates. Opposingly, the remaining sets were closed towers with no windows and only a single doorway, similar to those that led to the cellar portion of the dwellings that filled the open space within the city walls. They reasoned these towers must have been exclusively maintained by the vampires of Arnathia.

What Tor found most intriguing was what lay in the center of the city. A four-storied building, the most ornate and grand in architecture of all the structures in the city, was guarded by stone deities. Giovanni was the first to learn from the ancient scripts that they were gods and goddesses, each with their own stories and purposes.

The woman, the first of the twin statues they had come across when they first arrived, was that of the vampire Erisitia, goddess of mercy and vitality. She faced to the northern Claedan gate, while her male counterpart, Oxthalo, god of knowledge and wisdom, faced to the south Plaora gate. The other male, Nuvdalo, was the werewolf god of war and strength. His mate, Amagitia, goddess of fertility and motherhood, faced to the east gate of Smesia while he watched over the western gate of Uthusan. Together, they had founded the city of Arnathia to be a home and refuge for werewolves and vampires. Peace and cooperation reigned as long as these four presided over what took place within the walls they guarded since immemorial times.

The building they guarded, referred to in the legal texts as Lavtio, was described in detail in the political and legal records that Michael studied. With its great stone columns that held up the domed roof, it served as the place of council for an extensive and complex government system that controlled the lives of vampires and werewolves everywhere. Within the Lavtio, the officials from both races decided on territory borders, laws, and settled disputes between alphas and coven leaders.

Inside, the assembly hall was set up with row upon row of stone benches and seats that circled around the center where a speaker may stand and recite minutes or present their case to the council. Tor stood in the center once and when he spoke, it could be heard from every point in the massive chamber.

There existed a network of judicious council leaders who made the laws and kept order between the races, but the king and his queen were the ultimate rulers. Tor recognized this system as a proportionate mix of his Egyptian heritage with its pharaohs, and the mighty Roman Empire that Michael boasted about with its republic and elected senate. Such similarities begged the question if Arnathia was a precursor to these great civilizations.

Arnathia was the capital, much like Rome in Italy or Memphis in Egypt. It was a place of pilgrimage, a place of communion and prosperity. Trade and commerce did exist within the walls and spilled forth into the outside world as the residents traveled across the known world.

Within just a few days, Michael, Giovanni, Tor, and even Yaverik, read through mountains of documents and records to find out more about the people who once lived in Arnathia. They encountered countless translation fallacies, along with many surprising facts. Unlike much of what they knew of history up to that point, there were no slaves in Arnathia. The majority of the population was made up of those who were staying temporarily within the city, and the officials and their families. No slavery or servitude existed, hinting that the vampires might have fed on their werewolf neighbors or that there was some co-dependency agreement between the races.

Women were afforded the same rights and privileges as the men, while the children were educated equally and with the utmost care. Leaders, philosophers, engineers, and clergy all played their roles within the society and the scholars were just scratching the surface. Giovanni and Michael worked tirelessly to translate the script, while Tor explored along the perimeter walls for more clues or hints to what exactly happened to these people to make them feel as if they had to abandon this great city.

Michael requested that the blood servants learn everything as well, but Tor could tell from the few times he had stepped in on a lesson that the only one who seemed interested was Marco. He suspected it was because Marco had been with Michael for so long and might have shared in his ideals about cooperation among the races. If he didn't, he wouldn't have been a devoted blood servant.

Francesca and Angelo, on the other hand, were far more interested in seeing the ruins of the city. Tor had seen them alone together and heard them laugh and talk around the gates during the twilight hours.

Now that they were able to relax and recoup from their long journey, everyone took time to themselves. Jane was no exception. She studied the scripts as well, but she wasn't as interested in the political and cultural aspects of Arnathia as much as she enjoyed the legends and myths that were recorded in their sacred texts. After Giovanni and Michael learned the language, they taught it to Tor, who in turn taught it to Jane. As soon as she knew how to read the scrolls, she would steal away a few volumes and retreat to the top of a building whose roof was still intact.

One night, Tor was scouting along the perimeter and found her perched atop the highest tier of the Lavtio, leaning back against the dome roof as she flipped through a leather-bound codex. He maneuvered around the other side, upwind from where Jane reclined, and scaled the columns, quiet as a mouse as it scurried across a stone floor.

He crawled atop the slick surface of the dome, stalking closer. A playful attitude had emerged after they first arrived to Arnathia. With food and water no longer a pressing issue, Tor felt as if he could ease back. Giovanni even made the observation that the werewolf smiled and laughed more than he ever had since they began the journey from Egypt.

What exactly brought about this change was anyone's guess. Tor's first visceral assumption was that it had to do with Arnathia itself. There was an unmistakable energy within the city. Apart from the dark and forbidden sensations he had perceived in the armory towers, this place was ancient and lively with the ghosts of its former residents.

Tor, like the others, hungered to know what happened here and who the people were. That hunger created some sort of bond between him and the city to the point that he couldn't understand why anyone would ever want to leave. They must have been forced out. That was the only explanation he could fathom.

He came closer to Jane and held his breath so she might not hear him.

"Do you expect me to fall for that?" she said, never looking up from her book.

Tor chuckled and slid down to sit next to her on the ledge. "It is not a crime to try, is it?"

Jane smiled sweetly and looked to him, a special sparkle in her eye. "I suppose not."

Despite the initial embarrassment of what occurred on the way to Arnathia, she and Tor had become fine friends. She did not flirt and he tried his best not to encourage the idea that he might have changed his mind. His wolf might not have cared about the age difference, which was a dangerous revelation, but Tor still could not bring himself to love her in the way she might have wanted before.

He peeked at the text and read a few lines. "More myths?"

Jane shrugged and tossed her blonde hair back over her shoulder. "Of course. My father can read council transcripts all day, but they put me to sleep. This is far more interesting."

Tor stretched out his legs and leaned back against the dome to copy her relaxed pose. "Tell me what you're reading today."

Jane closed the book and placed it squarely in her lap. "It's about their origins. *Our* origins. The origins of all vampires and werewolves."

"Truly? And what are our origins?" Tor asked, his heart light and willing to hear her speak, even though he might never subscribe to any belief other than the one in which he had been raised. Wepwawet, though Tor could finally grapple with the fact that he might have been a werewolf just as he was, remained the god of his childhood and the figure that he devoted his life to serving. He knew he was a descendent of Wepwawet and that was good enough for him. Michael's open-ended question of where Wepwawet might have come from didn't interest him nearly as much.

Jane grinned. "The two gods that guard this place, Nuvaldo and Oxthalo, they were once brothers, born from the same human mother and father."

"They were not born vampire and wolf?"

"No," she replied, excitement sizzling in her voice. "They didn't change until they were older. Oxthalo was a warrior and fought in many battles. One day, he was fighting off invaders that threatened to enslave his people. He was the last defender standing and he slaughtered the invaders. It was hot that day and he couldn't find a drop to drink. In his exhaustion, he thought to drink the blood of his enemies. It changed him into a vampire because he acquired a taste for blood. When he realized what he had become, it was too late and he hated what he had done. But, Oxthalo could not reverse his mistake. So, he hid from the world under the cover of night and loathed the taste and smell of garlic because the site where he first drank blood was in a field of garlic just outside of his home village. He repented of his violent ways and turned to the teachings of wisdom."

Tor listened, suddenly more intrigued than he thought he would have been. "So, is Erisitia his daughter or wife?"

"His wife. She was human when they met and she could feel his sorrow. In her native land, she was something like an oracle with powers. The text says that she wept aloud the first time she laid eyes upon him because he was so beautiful and so tragic all at the same time. Erisitia wanted to help Oxthalo, but he continually pushed her away because he didn't want to hurt her. She could also see into his memories. She saw what he had done and pitied him."

"Then how did she become a vampire too?"

Jane held up her hand as she continued, her face alight with a kind of fanaticism that he wouldn't have expected of her. "One day, Oxthalo was so distraught by his own sins that he tried to kill himself by not drinking blood at all. He made it three days without drinking, and then Erisitia came. He bit her and nearly drained her dry. She was nearly dead by the time he realized what he had done. He killed a deer from the nearby forest and tried to get her to drink its blood to replenish what she had lost. But, it did nothing for her. Then he killed a human and that human's blood sustained her. She revived and became what he was, forever needing to drink blood to survive. Their children, my ancestors, retained a mix of both Oxthalo and Erisitia. That's why we can feel emotions and see memories just as Erisitia did."

Tor looked toward the south, toward Oxthalo's towers where Michael and Giovanni were busy studying. "Yaverik doesn't have these abilities. What of that?"

Jane shrugged. "Yaverik was bitten, not born. In the ritual for a human to turn into a vampire, they must drink the blood of another vampire for three days. I suppose it's because the powers of empathy do not pass through the blood, but through the mind."

Tor turned to the north and stared at the back of Nuvdalo's stone head that guarded the Lavtio. "And werewolves? How did they come to be?"

Jane pulled up her knees to hug them to her chest, the book pressed tightly against her. "While Oxthalo went on to be a warrior, Nuvdalo chose to abandon humanity altogether. He hated the company of people and spent much of his time in the woods. Eventually, he was adopted into a wolf pack. He ran with them, ate with them, slept with them, and played with them all day long. As a man, he wanted to be more than just part of the pack. He wanted to be the leader of the pack. To do this, he had to become the alpha, but he was a man and the wolves did not completely respect him as an equal.

"So," she continued after a sigh, "Nuvdalo killed the alpha. In an act of revenge, the wolf's spirit merged with Nuvdalo's spirit and they became one. He could turn into a wolf to lead the pack or walk as a man amongst the human community."

This was not the story he wanted to hear. "Surely Nuvdalo regretted what he had done, just as Oxthalo did?"

Jane shook her head. "Not exactly. It doesn't say anything about him being remorseful. Nuvdalo envied the wolves and prized the abilities that he lacked, so becoming one was more of a blessing. The cost of murder wasn't a concern. He did, however, long for a mate. He turned into a man, donned clothes, and entered the village to find a wife that could run with him and the pack. He found a fierce and independent woman, a woman who could fight like a man and sing a beautiful melody that soothed the beast inside of him. It was Amagitia. He brought her into the woods and the pack immediately loved her, except for one."

A mischievous grin split Jane's face. "There was a she-wolf in the pack that wanted to be Nuvdalo's mate. You want to know what happened to her? Amagitia killed the she-wolf and the same thing happened to her as it did to Nuvdalo."

Tor's eyebrows shot up. "There were women werewolves?"

"Evidently."

"Where are they now?" Tor sat up on his elbows. "I've never seen one and even daughters who were born from the priesthood couldn't change."

Again, Jane shrugged her shoulders. "I don't know. Perhaps my father will find something of that in the records. All the myth does is explain how Amagitia became the first female and set a precedent for all females born after her. They were fierce, cunning, and tirelessly devoted to their families and mates. That's why she's the goddess of fertility."

"So, all the gods and goddesses were once human," Tor mused, looking back to the statues that surrounded the Lavtio.

"Yes, but they were the first of our kind, the fathers and mothers to our race. They came together and built this city so that their children and their families could live in peace with one another... Do you want to know my favorite story so far?" Jane asked as she looked to the heavens. "It's one about a princess. Her name was Tanatia and the book says she was the most beautiful and most gentle princess of all the royalty that came before or after her. She was the daughter of a werewolf king and vampire queen."

Tor smiled. It shouldn't have been surprising that such a story was her favorite, given all they had been through already. He had to remind himself that there was no prejudice or inequality between the races before the time she spoke of. Arnathia was built upon the foundations of peace, it made perfect sense that the king and queen might have been a mixed pair.

"Because she was the offspring of a werewolf and a vampire, she had traits from both. She could drink blood, but she didn't rely on it. She could change into a wolf, as well as sense the emotions of others. She was a perfect blend of both races, but that made her more powerful. A few council members feared her, and what she would do when she came to the throne, so they had her assassinated."

"And this is your favorite story?" Tor laughed.

Jane giggled. "It gets better, I assure you. The king and queen found out who had assassinated the princess, and they planned to have the council members, along with the assassins, executed. But, when the execution day came, Tanatia's spirit appeared and stopped it. She asked for her parents to have mercy on the men because they only did what was in their nature to do. They feared change and what they couldn't predict. So, instead of being executed, they were ripped of their titles and exiled from Arnathia."

She rolled onto her side to face Tor and let the book slide down onto the ledge at their feet. "From that day on, the people revered Tanatia as kind of a canonized spirit of peace and they held a moment of prayer to invite Tanatia to reside over every decision of the council, so the judgment would be fair to all."

Tor nodded. "Yes, I'll have to say that is a nice story. If only all the world behaved that way. Perhaps there wouldn't be as much war."

Jane's gaze became distant and pensive. "In the beginning, there was no hate or discourse, just as my father suspected. That didn't last forever, though."

"Then, what happened? What changed?"

Jane looked toward the south, just as Tor had done a moment before. "I'm sure he will find out any day now. There has to be some explanation. People don't just become enemies for no reason. And if this myth was true and they prayed to Tanatia for guidance, perhaps something terrible happened to make them give up their peaceful ways."

Tor hoped, deep in his soul, that whatever that reason was, it was a good one. Shame belonged to those who tore apart families and entire civilizations over petty disagreements.

Giovanni raked his hands through his hair and gripped the locks around his temples, pulling until some of the pain of his headache subsided. What was worse than reading a cryptic and ancient language for hours on end, was reading it by unsatisfactory candlelight. Though Michael did not need any aid to read in the near pitch-black darkness of the tower, Giovanni struggled to keep the flames at an adequate distance from the delicate paper of the scrolls and codices pages so that he could read without singeing them on the heat of the lantern panes.

Their situation in Arnathia, as far as anyone else was concerned, was favorable. Tor kept them fed with desert game and the fountain near the Lavtio continued to bring them fresh, cool water to drink. There was no lack of tasking, as every aspect of the civilization was copied into notes and the layout of the city was mapped in meticulous detail.

Whenever they left Arnathia, they wanted to be sure that they would never need to make another trip back. Scrolls and documents were already being set aside to be brought back to Italy with them.

It was a daily struggle to stay calm in the face of his padrone. During the daylight hours, it was easy to escape the tower and fret over the coming doom of their journey, away from the vampire who could sense his unease. Yet, during the night, when he was nearly held hostage within the tower until his head was pounding with new knowledge and his eyes burned from straining to read in the dim light, Giovanni could think of nothing else but where his contacts could have been.

Perhaps they died somewhere in the desert? Perhaps they were waiting for the troupe to return to the southern edge of the sea before they made their strike?

Giovanni had told his contacts of their intended path, but nothing had prepared him for what they discovered.

This place, this ancient city that might as well have been Michael and Tor's Eden, was the foundation of their race. It was their ancestors' birthplace and from everything Giovanni read, it was the ideal model of the perfect civilization.

Their system of government wasn't tyrannical, but surprisingly self-sufficient, despite the establishment of a monarchy and a quasi-republic senate. Besides the minor disputes, there was practically no dissention between the races. Being in the middle of the desert, they had no enemies who dared to cross the sands to disturb them, and even though they were so remote, they still managed to trade and become integrated with the outside world in the intellectual sense.

They found scripts and texts from nearly every ancient language from Egyptian hieroglyphs to Latin to Sanskrit and even Oriental glyphs. Even art had made its way into Arnathian life. Homes were painted with murals and depictions of daily life, much like the villas in the golden age of the Roman Empire. Irrigation, plumbing, and other modern innovations had been in existence here for thousands of years.

Arnathia might not have been just the birthplace of a race, but the precursor to all healthy civilizations that would carry on long after it dissolved.

In all respects, Giovanni could put Arnathia on the pedestal as one of the greatest cities to ever exist. The only reason he continued to study the texts over and over again, besides not wanting to anger his padrone, was to discover what could have happened. He only hoped that he could discover it before they left, or before his contacts arrived, whichever would come first.

In the darkness, Giovanni heard his padrone let out a moan, so laced with agony that he wondered if Michael had fallen ill. He quickly stood and carried his lantern to the other side of the tower where Michael sat on the floor, surrounded by volumes, tomes, and scrolls waiting to be devoured.

Michael had his knees propped up, an open book in his lap, and hand covering his eyes as if he had just read the most disastrous passage in the history of written language.

"What is it, signore?" Giovanni asked, kneeling in front of his padrone and lifting the lantern so he could see the vampire better.

"I found it, Giovanni," he muttered. "The reason why Arnathia fell." He took a stuttered breath, his chest quivering with the effort as if he were ready to weep aloud for the terrible thing that had happened probably centuries ago.

Giovanni set down his lamp on the sandy stone floor and took the bound book from his padrone's lap. Skimming over the first few passages, he sighed. "A feud," he whispered.

"Not just a simple feud. It was idiotic!" Michael uncovered his eyes and motioned to the book. "How could a people so grounded in their mutual affiliation, give themselves over to such hearsay!"

He looked to Michael, his eyes burning. "It says something about land, though."

Michael stood and stormed across the floor, waving his arms about as he recounted the tale. "Land was just the underlying tension. The true catalyst is what happened next. The piece of land they were disputing over hadn't been claimed. It was newly discovered to the north and no one could decide who should occupy it, werewolves or vampires. Felix, a vampire council member from the west, hadn't cast his vote to break a tie in the senate.

"He went home to think over the matter and was found dead in the neighboring territory of a wolf pack. The council cried that it was sabotage on the side of the werewolves, though they continually denied it. The werewolf in question was only a pup and didn't realize what he was doing."

Giovanni could see how such a misunderstanding could raise suspicion of treachery, but could it completely dismantle a great place such as Arnathia? He had never seen his padrone so animate, so furious at the men and women of the ancient past.

"From there, the senate took sides. What was worse, the king took a side! The king called for investigation after investigation, but no one could give an answer for the crime. Even looking into the memories of the dead politician proved useless. They were too scrambled and all they could make out were roars, fangs, and fur."

"That might suggest that the werewolf did kill him," Giovanni offered, hoping to quell Michael's fervor.

"Yes, but the werewolf had no political alignment, no reason to want Felix dead. His pack didn't even know about the land dispute. Reaching into the wolf's memory did nothing because it was completely blank, thanks to how young he was. None of it made sense and soon, word of what happened spread through the city and out into the nations. Feuds broke out everywhere and the story became twisted with each new telling. By the time the council and the king could give any kind of ruling over the matter, the whole world had erupted into chaos. Brother fought against brother, families were torn apart, and soon, Arnathia was under siege."

Michael pointed toward one of the city gates that lay beyond the tower. "Those claw marks were made by werewolves. The king at the time was vampire. If prejudice and dissention continued, they must have been coming for his head. Those statues of the founding gods would have done little to protect the Lavtio from being overthrown."

The tower went deathly silent as Michael stood in the middle of the floor, surrounded by the history and records of a people who had destroyed their own selves because of hatred and embitterment toward their friends and neighbors. Giovanni wished he could have given some sage advice or consoling sentiment to help his padrone reason through the tragedy. Yet, he remained silent.

In the history of man and God's creation, war and hatred were ever-present factors that no one could eliminate. Peace, as beautiful as it was, had a tendency to be fragile. It was a miracle that Arnathia lasted as long as it did. It might have been inevitable. If the feuds hadn't begun, Arnathia might have lasted another few hundred years, maybe a thousand, but it wouldn't have lasted until the present time.

It might have been fortuitous that Arnathia fell when it did, but Giovanni would not say any of that to Michael.

With how much the world was growing and expanding through trade and exploration, the city would have been discovered. Creatures like Michael and Tor would have been exposed and hunted down more so than they are now. Their futures would have been irrevocably different if Arnathia continued to stand as a shining star amongst the ancient constellations.

CHAPTER 9

Jane's hands trembled as she set the book down onto her lap and stared with wide eyes into the darkness of the tower. It was close to dawn now, and her father and the others had already gone back to the home near the fountain to sleep for the day. She elected to stay here, in Nuvdalo's tower dedicated to knowledge and literature to read just one more volume before retiring during the daylight hours.

The book she held in her lap had been filled with soldiers' accounts of battles and wars during the time just before the fall of Arnathia and the time immediately after. Michael had gathered them together the night before to share the unsavory truth about the people they had esteemed as enlightened and culturally superior to their descendants.

Having absorbed what knowledge could be gleaned from the towers that had been built to honor the other god and goddesses, Jane decided to indulge in what the god of war and violence could offer her in the way of stories and myths.

Much to her dismay, she found little fantasy and too much horror to comprehend. The warriors of Nuvdalo were brutal and savage in the time of the feud. They destroyed villages and cities that were controlled by the vampires, and these records told of how they came to control Arnathia for a brief time. Reading of their methods sent a cold chill down Jane's spine, and yet she continued to read.

She also read about the atrocities the vampires had committed in the name of strategy and necessary ethnic cleansing. Finally, she learned what happened to the females of Tor's race. They had been slaughtered. Every last daughter, wife, mother, and virgin of the werewolves had been systematically killed.

When the vampires struck a pack, they left no surviving women to carry on the legacy of their kind. As a result, only men could father sons that retained the gift of transformation. Their daughters, because they were born of human mothers, could not change and lived as mortals.

It was all in an attempt to control their numbers and curtail their breeding. Werewolf mothers could easily give birth to three or more children at a time, which would cause their race to grow exponentially. The texts said that the vampires couldn't allow such growth any longer, not as long as the werewolves were the ones who contaminated the world with their beastly violence.

Jane shuddered at the truth, hating it just as much as she hated the feud her father had told her about. It was all senseless. It was no wonder the races despised one another.

It wasn't until she came to this one last account from a young werewolf warrior that she realized she could read no more. It had nothing to do with their brutality or even the devastation. It was the promise of further destruction and turmoil that startled her.

She had to tell someone what she had learned. Heedless of the consequences, Jane tossed aside the book, letting it slide across the sandy floor, and darted down the ramps of the tower to step out into the street. It was later than she had anticipated, but there were still plenty of shadows for her to jump between to make her way across the city toward Tor's apartment on the east side.

One advantage of their stay in the city and great trek across the desert was that her father was more lenient with how they all should dress. Modesty was retained, but Jane was permitted to cast aside her heavy skirts and rigid corsets in favor of better maneuverability. Most of the time she wore one of her thicker chemises and a lighter gown overtop while her hair flowed down her back, unencumbered by ribbons or ties. Likewise, the men donned looser trousers and tunics that kept them cool. No one would have suspected they were part of Italy's elite class.

Panting and still stricken with fear over the prophecy she had read, she slipped into the upper story where Tor lay sleeping by one of the open windows that stretched from floor to ceiling. She could see the sun begin to sparkle in the fountain just a short distance from the house, so Jane crouched behind a wall next to the opening that blocked the light from striking her skin.

"Tor," she whispered.

The werewolf, sprawled out upon the dirty floor with his head resting upon his arms, grunted in response, but did not open his eyes. Her eyes skimmed over his broad, naked back and hated the way she lusted after it, even now after finally succumbing to the fact that they would never be together.

"Tor, please, wake up."

His eyes cracked open and rolled around for a moment before they found Jane sheltered and huddled against the stone wall. He sat up on his elbows and looked out to the coming morning. "Jane, you should not be here," he croaked out, probably fighting back grogginess.

"I know, but..." She could barely contain her composure as she remembered the story that was far from fiction, though she wished it had been. The alarm in her voice made him sit up a little straighter, though he didn't flee to her side just yet.

"What's wrong?"

Jane swallowed hard and tried to calm herself. She felt like a silly child who ran for the safety of a parent after having a nightmare. Though she had wished this had been a bad dream. The accounts in that book had been alleged as true, so there was no reason for her to disregard it.

"I just read something and... I wanted to talk about it."

Tor crossed his powerful legs and faced her as he rubbed at his eyes. "Another fairytale?"

"No, this one was true. It was about a monster... It was practically indestructible. It took the form of a werewolf, as you do, but bigger with red eyes like a vampire. It killed everything in its path and wanted to destroy the world."

Regardless of her frenzy, Tor cracked a smile. "That sounds like a fairytale to me."

"It was in a book of soldier's accounts of battles around the time Arnathia fell. That's far too recent to be a myth," she pleaded. "They said the beast was the last creature to be born of mixed blood, but they don't say what his lineage was exactly. But because of the mix, the man went mad and couldn't control his powers. He turned into this monster and went on a rampage. The vampires could not take him alone and the werewolves weren't powerful enough in number to defeat him. They had to unite and it took a league of werewolves and vampires together to stop him. Do you know how many people that is?"

Jane could feel the cold tears peek out from the corner of her eye and Tor was no longer smiling. A grave and somber expression looked back at her and she could sense that he was taking her seriously now.

He nodded to her question. "That's quite a lot of men," he said. "But, why are you so afraid? It was in the past and as you said, they defeated him."

She moved closer to the edge of the shadow she hid within. "Because when they finally killed him, his spirit drifted up from his body and vowed that he would return to scourge the world and destroy everything in it. He killed werewolves, vampires, men, women, children, everything. Imagine if he returned within our lifetime. How devastating that would be..."

The tear trailed down her cheek and she hated the way that only he witnessed her vulnerability. She hadn't cried in front of Francesca, or even her father in such an intimate way. Her tears were reserved for Tor alone, it seemed, and she hated it almost as much as she hated the way she still felt for him.

Tor let out a sigh and came into the shadows with her. In an unexpected move, he enveloped her in a tight hug and held her close. The fear that had consumed her just moments before melted as she pressed her cheek against his shoulder and let herself drown in his peace.

He was not worried about the monster that they called the War Beast. He didn't feel the same dread and terror that she did when it came to what the future may hold for them.

As soon as Jane had romanticized about the idea of another Princess Tanatia coming into the world, a figure of peace and gentility with a mixed couple for parents, she thought that a union between a vampire and werewolf might have been an advantageous thing. Yet if a creature like the War Beast should return because of the same type of union, she wondered if it was worth the risk. One could give birth to a leader or a destroyer, and they would never know until it was too late.

Though another Tanatia or War Beast might not come in their lifetime, Jane still feared for the fate of the world. Everything they loved, everything they had achieved, could be wiped out by one hateful creature. Who was to say if the vampires and werewolves would unite once more with a common enemy? What if neither of them cared or knew of the War Beast? What if the War Beast was roaming the earth today, looking for his chance to strike?

In his arms, though, Jane wouldn't think about those things. It would have been foolish to think that Tor would protect her from the grisly truth, or that he would protect her if the apocalypse came before their death. After they returned to Italy, he might go back to his home country. He certainly wouldn't stay with her. That was too much to hope for.

Yet, knowing that there was such a man as Tor in the world eased her troubled mind. If the War Beast ever did come, she knew he would be on the front lines, ready to defend and protect, just as he had done before.

Tor padded around the tiny footprints and sniffed at the lightly disturbed dust. In his full form, he could travel farther to search out prey, even to the eastern coast of the Caspian Sea. His keen nose could lead him on the trail of a rabbit or small desert deer just from one trace scent from a mile or two away.

Yet the game had become smart over the last few days. Since Tor had been hunting for the party, the animals of the desert had steered clear of Arnathia, despite the promise of water from the newly replenished fountain. Searching for game became more and more difficult and he pushed himself to travel further east toward richer, more fertile lands that the animals couldn't stay away from.

The sun had risen over the horizon by now and Tor had to keep his head ducked low to keep the blinding light out of his eyes. He had been hunting for a couple of hours, finding it hard to go back to sleep after Jane awoke him just before dawn.

Her anguish alarmed him at first, but as she told him about the War Beast and the kind of havoc it promised to wreak upon the earth when it returned set him at ease. Just as he thought, it was another of her fairytales. The way she felt, however, could not be easily pushed aside and that was when he did the only thing he knew to do. Tor held her between his strong arms to chase away the demented thoughts about the end of the world.

It seemed to work, but when he ushered Jane out of the apartment and into the vampires' den below, a new revelation came upon him and the hug was its catalyst. Despite her cold skin and lack of a beating heart, he enjoyed the embrace they shared.

Apart from their near disaster outside of Amol, Tor hadn't been with a woman in ages. Serving his time in the temple, he had no need for a woman or companion of any kind. Holding Jane changed that. He wanted to return with a meal for the blood servants so he could check on her and make sure that the War Beast was not tormenting her with nightmares. He loathed the sun for coming each day and chasing Jane back into hiding. He wanted her to stay above ground so they could spend more time talking of fairytales and Arnathia before it fell.

Tor's wolf encouraged all of it, coaxing him to feel what they had been fighting all along. Though his wolf despised the thought of making love to Jane, at least for now, it wanted to know her, to comfort her and be there as she learned so they could learn together.

The journey from his lonely temple in Egypt to this mysterious and remote city in the desert had been long, difficult, and frustrating on all accounts. Yet when he looked back, Jane was always there and he had to accept that she made the experience all the better.

He wasn't sure when exactly it happened, if it was truly because of the hug, or if it had started long before, when they first met. Either way, Tor knew that something had changed in how he thought of Jane. He didn't just think of her as Michael's daughter, an unnecessary burden, an ambitious girl with unrealistic expectations about where their relationship was going, or even as a friend. Tor wasn't completely familiar with the sensation, but he might have mistaken it for love.

He lifted his head and looked to the east, squinting at the horizon to spot the hare that evaded his grasp. A twitch of movement caught his eye and he darted for it, his claws digging into the earth for maximum traction.

Then, the wind shifted and blew against his fur enough to make his skin crawl. Dust blew over his head, but the wind carried something else. Another scent, less animalistic and more human, caught his attention and he skidded to a stop.

It was illogical to think another band of humans would travel this far. They hadn't seen another soul since they left the well-worn trade routes to the south and there were no villages or towns anywhere close by to draw humans to them.

Tor turned and looked to the west. More scents greeted him. Metal, leather, camels, some food, and worst of all, gunpowder. He recognized the scent from when he was shot by the hunter outside of Istanbul. Guns were not completely uncommon amongst traders, as he came to learn from their dealings between Istanbul and Amol, but that didn't make him any less wary of those who wielded them.

He ducked low and peered closer at the horizon, his ears pricked forward to listen for the sounds of the men. Soon the jingle of harnesses, the grunts of the camels, and the creaking of stiff leather told him that his nose did not deceive him.

Though he couldn't tell properly from this distance, he knew by the strength of their smell that there were more than a few men astride the camels. His first instinct was to run and avoid them as much as possible. He could be mistaken for game and though he was impervious to normal arrows and bullets, they might give chase and find they could not kill him easily.

Then again, Tor wondered about the soundness of running. What if he inadvertently led them to Arnathia and to Jane? He couldn't allow that. If he could
attract their attention long enough to make them more interested in him than
their current path northward, then they would be safe.

Tor charged forward until he could just make out the figures of the caravan.
Ten men he distinguished, their saddlebags bulging, and guns and sabers strapped
to their hips. By the looks of them, the men dressed as if they belonged in the
desert, but their skin color told another story. They were slightly paler than
the men Tor had encountered on the way to Arnathia. The way they sweated
profusely and constantly wiped their brows, verified they were not native.

Tor slowly circled until he was directly in their path, and then ducked behind
a low ridge in the landscape so he could watch their progress and determine who
these men truly were. The closer they drew, the more distinct their scents became.
Though it was a little more difficult to tell exactly where they came from.

They carried the scents of many places, just like a traveler or trader might. The
smell of silk from the orient, spices from the east, the salt of the sea, and just a
hint of wine from their flasks, and still more that he couldn't identify.

He listened to their conversations and he could only make out a few words
through his limited knowledge of the languages of the east. *Kill, hunt, search*, but
it was the names they uttered that made him growl. Giovanni and Michael.

There could be only two reasons for this. Either they were friends of Giovanni
and Michael, or they were enemies. By the way they spoke of killing within the
same breath, he knew they were not the vampire's allies. Who they were or why
they had come all the way out into the desert to find them wasn't certain. All he
knew was that if they were coming for his friends, they would have to answer to
Tor first.

Then he knew, he could not stay hidden. He leapt from his hiding place and
charged toward them at full speed, kicking up a cloud of dust and sand as he went.
The man reared their camels to a stop and one by one shouted in alarm.

Two men from the rear pulled out crossbows and aimed them at Tor. He managed to dodge a few, but one struck his foreleg and sent him tumbling. The silver tip of the arrow seared his flesh as it pierced between the bones.

Tor yelped and rolled back to his feet and gnawed at the shaft to get it loose. Another arrow grazed his shoulder and he realized he had to keep moving, though slowed by the pain and encumberment of the crossbow bolt that stuck out of his leg.

The men dismounted from their camels and began to load their guns as the two other men continued to fire their crossbows. Tor tripped on the shaft in his leg and an arrow finally found purchase in his hip. He wailed in pain as the silver imbedded into his muscle and flesh. He limped and tried to change back into his human form, where he could more easily yank the arrows from his body, but the men would give him no reprieve.

More arrows struck him. One after another stuck in his shoulder, side, and chest.

How did they know to use silver? These couldn't have been the hunters from Istanbul. Tor had killed them all, and they did not know Giovanni or Michael. This couldn't have been the same group of hunters. Had he been spotted by a merchant who spread rumors to more hunters, just as what happened long ago in Egypt? Did they deal too closely with a trader to make them suspicious of him?

He dragged himself as close as he could get to the hunters, his blood mixing with the sand and dirt beneath him until a thick, muddy trail formed. The silver burned, scorching his flesh from the inside and refused to heal. At this rate, he couldn't change back and each movement sent waves of agony through his body until he couldn't even grasp at the arrow shafts to break them.

Tor fell to the ground, arrows quivering as he strained to move and continue to breathe. The men surrounded him, their guns and crossbows trained upon him. He growled and snapped his teeth at them, trying feebly to push himself up.

He had to kill them. He had to protect Jane and Michael. The men, if they had tracked them this far, would surely find Arnathia and he couldn't allow that. What of the blood servants and Giovanni? They were in danger too.

Tor shakily rose to his feet and stumbled toward one of the men, determination burning in his eyes. The man pulled the trigger and the bullet struck his chest. Tor couldn't even make a sound; it hurt too much. He simply crumbled back into the dirt as the rest of the men fired their volleys into him.

He kept his eyes open, willing himself to stay alive as the silver poisoned his body and soldered his insides. The voices of the men became hushed and dark, their words barely discernable as his heartbeat roared in his ears.

Once more, he had been struck down by men who knew too much about his weaknesses. This time, he didn't save the day or rescue anyone. Again, it was his fault that his friends would die. With bullets and silver-tipped arrows slowly stealing his lifeforce, the men walked away back to their camels and continued on, leaving Tor to be taken by death.

Giovanni set his jug of water on the edge of the fountain and stretched his arms over his head. The afternoon wasn't as hot as it had been in the days before, though the sun was a constant, unrelenting presence. As far as he knew, he was the only one awake.

When he awoke in the apartment he shared with the other blood servants, Marco was the only one present. Francesca and Angelo were nowhere in sight, which wasn't all too surprising. They made no pretenses about hiding their affair and they could hardly ever be found when they were needed after the vampires took their daily feed just after nightfall.

He took a look over his shoulder to Tor's lofty apartment that faced the fountain and Lavtio. The werewolf wasn't lying in the window as he usually did, so

Giovanni assumed he must have been out and about around the city, or perhaps hunting in the desert as he sometimes did.

Giovanni was alone at the fountain, but that didn't last for long. Sucked into his usual anxious thoughts, he hardly heard the men come up behind him.

He turned and nearly dropped his jug when he came face to face with a band of men with murder in their eyes. Their guns and crossbows were already loaded and ready at their sides.

"Giovanni Dinapoli?" the man brandishing two pistols on his hips and another rifle in his hand.

The skin just under the thug's eyes and around his cheeks looked burnt, accentuating a vicious scar that stretched across the bridge of his nose and down to his jaw. He was slightly taller than the others, with broad shoulders and a pair of dark eyes that seemed to emanate vengeful intent.

He wasn't sure whether he wanted to be himself just then or not. Then, it occurred to him that this must have been the men he had been waiting for.

"Si," he said with a nod.

"Where are the vampires?" the man asked in perfect Italian, though he knew the hunters to be from farther north in origin. This nomadic band of vampire hunters traveled the world, fulfilling contracts with informants, and when Giovanni got word that they were rumored to be in the east at just the right time, he had jumped on the chance to employ them.

Much had transpired from the time he first contacted them until now. Jane was here. So was Francesca, and Giovanni had been vacillating between the decision to forget about the entire arrangement or carrying it to term. He knew once these men came, none of them would leave Arnathia alive, except for him.

Giovanni took a tighter hold on the jug. "Signori, I hate for you to have come all this way, but – "

The man with the scar charged forward and seized Giovanni by the front of his vest. "Where are they, Giovanni?"

The scholar trembled and felt his arms grow weak as fear swept through him. Surely, they wouldn't kill him, too, if he didn't tell them? What if they would?

Would their righteous hatred for vampires go so far as to kill anyone who stood in their way?

His voice failed him, so Giovanni jerked his head toward the house where Michael, Jane, and Yaverik were soundly sleeping in the cellar. The brute tossed him aside and Giovanni tripped over his feet as he tried to stabilize himself. The jug sloshed with water and finally fell from his hands, shattering on the ground.

The men spread out around the house with their leader standing off to the side, pulling out smooth clay orbs topped with fuses from the sack that hung across his chest.

"Wa... Wait," Giovanni stammered. "What about the blood servants?"

The man didn't even give the courtesy of a look. "They have been tainted by the vampires and will have to be killed as well."

Giovanni swallowed hard. "And Tor? The werewolf?"

"He has already been dealt with."

His blood ran cold as he imagined Tor's mangled and lifeless body lying somewhere in the desert. What had he done?

"I suggest you get your things together and leave this place, Signore Dinapoli. If things get messy, we wouldn't want you to be hurt." The man finally looked over his shoulder. "Thank you for your cooperation."

Giovanni looked between the tiny bombs in the man's fist, then to the house where Michael and his family slept. "What are you going to do?"

"We're going to do what we do best."

CHAPTER 10

When Tor awoke, he was blinded by a glaring whiteness that seemed to have no source. The void was open around him, with no end and no beginning. There was only the light and he was somewhere in it, alone and confused. There were no scents, no sounds, nothing to orient himself.

All his life, he had memorized the tenets of his faith down to the last word and parable. He knew what to say to each demon he came across in Duat and the path he needed to take to reach the end of his seemingly immortal life. He knew what was expected at the final checkpoint when his heart would be weighed against the feather of Ma'at. With providence on his side, his soul would not be devoured by Ammit, but welcomed into the eternal land of joy and plenty, the Field of Reeds.

This was not what he had been raised to expect. This was nothing. Absolutely nothing. There were no demons, no gods, no line of souls waiting to be weighed, nothing. If this was not the afterlife that he had been raised to believe, then what was this?

"Tor."

The voice, deep and echoing in the void, called to him from behind. He turned and saw his father, standing proud and tall in the white linen robes of the priesthood. His long dark hair was pulled back and dark eyes watched his son with the same stern look that he remembered from childhood.

He wasn't angry. His father was hardly ever angry. This gaze was a silent command for respect and obedience. As a child, he cowered at his father's feet and listened to his words. As he grew older, he learned that he could mimic this look and demand the same respect from others. As a man, standing before his father, who appeared just as he was the morning before he died, Tor had to hold firm and meet his father with that same solemnness.

Though, all Tor wanted to do was grovel at his father's feet and beg for the forgiveness he had never asked for in the final moments of his life. A silent second went by and Tor wondered why his father would be here in this void that was so unlike the afterlife he had preached. Was this an illusion? Or perhaps this was the Field of Reeds and Tor was privileged to bypass the usual rites and rituals.

"What is this?" Tor asked, his voice far less booming than his father's, adding to his feelings of insignificance in his presence.

His father did not answer, but only lifted his chin and let his eyes drop to appraise Tor from head to foot. "You have come a long way, son."

Tor straightened under his father's praise, his chest aching and heart heavier than it should have been. To see his father in front of him, alive once more, Tor should have been grateful and overjoyed. They arrived to whatever this place was, and it was far from the dangerous and evil hell they had spent their lives trying to avoid.

His thoughts drifted back to Michael and Jane. What had become of them by now? What would those men do? If they knew how to kill a werewolf, then it was likely they knew the weaknesses of a vampire.

He looked down to his bare feet, so dark against the whiteness beneath him. Another thought, far more troubling, entered his mind. If this place, this world that awaited the dead, was not Duat or the Field of Reeds, then what was it? Had his entire life been a lie? Was his religion and worship of Wepwawet as false as the outsiders believed?

If his mighty god was just a man, and this afterlife was not what they had been taught, then what was true anymore? Did it even matter? Tor gritted his teeth, rage and regret boiling over until he could barely contain it anymore. All the years spent in the temple, performing ritual after ritual to a lifeless statue of a werewolf who was nothing more than a historical figure, all of it for nothing?

"Why?" he asked. "Was it all a lie?"

His father stepped forward and placed his hand upon Tor's shoulder. "My son, look at me."

Tor did as he said, meeting his father's hard expression. "There is no time to explain the universe in which we live, though I tried to do so in life. You must return."

He blinked back his confusion. "Return? How can I return? No one returns from Duat."

Unexpectedly, one corner of his father's mouth tilted up in a half smile. "Son, look around. Does this look like Duat to you?"

Tor didn't need to look into the white void once more. He only shook his head. "So, this is not Duat? Is this – "

"'This is not Aaru either. That will come when it is your time. For now, you must go back. Protect the balance of Ma'at and chaos."

Now, seeing the smile on his father's face and feeling the warmth of his touch, Tor could not repress the need for absolution. "I have neglected my duties, father. I left the temple to see more of the world outside our country."

"I know," he said with a nod. "For now, your duties lie outside of the temple. Protect the balance. I have seen what the future is to be and you cannot let chaos win this day."

All his life, Tor had tried to appease Wepwawet so the world would not fall into the hands of chaos. As the last in a line of ancient priests, the responsibility rested solely upon his shoulders. Knowing that this place was not clearly associated with his view of what the afterlife should be, gave Tor a bit of consolation. Yet how much more of his life had been wasted on things like ceremonies and rituals that weren't necessary? Who was right in the end?

"You're asking me to protect Michael and the others?"

His father gripped his shoulder tightly. "Yes. At all costs. They must live." His hand released and as soon as Tor could no longer feel his father's hold, he was thrust back into the world of heat and color, full of vibrant smells and sensation.

The white void faded away and once more he looked upon the desert horizon. The pain flooded back over him, but he found the strength to grope and pull at the arrow shafts. With slow, aching movements, he ripped the arrows from his flesh. More blood spilled to the ground, but he healed once the silver was removed.

Protect the balance.

He repeated those words over and over in his head with each arrow he dislodged. Even if his religion was a lie, even if his devotion to Wepwawet was unfounded, Tor would obey his father's request. Still in his wolf form and the image of his father's face burned in his mind, he rose to his feet and turned to the north, to Arnathia.

Michael first awoke to Francesca's pleas for mercy. Then, as his senses adjusted, the scene began to take shape behind the stone wall that divided them from the sunlight. He could hear the multitude of feet shuffling in the sand, the clinking of metal and rustle of fabric as a crowd seemed to form around the building.

Marco and Angelo fought back against the intruders and he could smell their blood spilling onto the ground.

"What's going on?" Jane asked as she rubbed her eyes and sat up on her bedroll.

Yaverik bolted awake and went to the edge of the barrier to try and peak around. As soon as he did, Michael heard the hissing, sizzling noise and a few soft taps against the stone. The scent of gunpowder.

"Yaverik!" he shouted.

It was too late. In a great flash of light and explosion, the wall was nearly reduced to rubble. Yaverik flew back into the room that had once been their shelter. Now it would serve as their prison, lest they venture out to a worse fate.

Michael shielded his daughter from the blast as rock and pebbles rained down upon them. The blood servants continued to argue and fight against the men who came for their masters, but they would not be deterred.

This was what he had feared would come to pass, what Giovanni had planned for so long. He had hoped that it wouldn't have come so soon. They had gone so long without an incident that Michael wondered if the hunters would ever come at all, or if they had gotten lost in the desert. He should have known better than to let his guard down. If he had known, Michael wouldn't have let his family stay here for so long. They would have moved on from Arnathia.

Sunlight poured onto the floor of the room, but they were still safe against the far back wall. When the dust settled, Michael looked toward the gaping hole in the barrier. Two men in desert garb stood just outside the demolished stone wall, with crossbows in hand and aimed straight for Michael and Jane.

Yaverik, half-buried in debris, was now beginning to stir and push away the wreckage. Jane huddled closer into Michael's embrace and he hissed at the hunters, as if it would do any good. They had the clear advantage as they stood in the bright sunlight. The vampires couldn't touch them as long as they maintained such a vantage point.

One of the men pulled the trigger on his crossbow and the bolt shot out with a cord attached to its tip. Michael grabbed at the shaft and tossed it to the side, but he couldn't dodge or deflect the second arrow that was fired in quick succession.

It stuck through his shoulder, shattering bone and splitting muscle. Before he could yank on the cord, the hunter pulled first. Jane held tightly to his hand as the men reeled Michael into the light. Her strength alone held him back just long enough for him to find his footing again.

Michael then took hold of the cord and gave it a quick, firm tug to bring the two hunters to their knees. They called for help and soon, it was Michael against five men as they continually pulled on the line. He ordered Jane to stay back and she obeyed without question.

The arrow in his shoulder twisted and bent, sending pain shooting through his arm. He felt his grip loosen, but he would not relent. Yaverik joined in and took the line with both hands. The hunters didn't have a chance.

As soon as one hunter had the misfortune of stumbling into the shadows, Yaverik struck with swift force and brought the hunter deeper into their domain. Michael ignored his apprentice's bloodlust as he heard the wails and snapping of bones behind him.

Another hunter came behind the four that were left and raised his pistol to shoot Michael.

In the time it took for Michael to blink, the gunman vanished. The scent of fur and old blood met his nostrils just before the screams and gunfire erupted in the street.

"Tor!" Jane screamed from behind Michael.

His feet began to slide on the floor. With one more burst of strength, he drew the hunters deeper into the room. Yaverik was still immersed in devouring his previous victim, oblivious to anything else.

A blur of fangs, claws, and dark fur swept into the cellar one more time. Tor in his full werewolf form, grabbed the men and threw them into the street like they weighed nothing at all. The cord, still connected to Michael, pulled him into the light along with the hunters.

He cried out as the sun seared the skin on his face and hands. In the midst of the battle between beast and man, Michael struggled to stand after being knocked off his feet again. The owner of the crossbow that tethered him lay dead in the street, his head and torso ripped apart by Tor's rage.

Michael scrambled, not knowing which way to go as the bright sun blinded him. Somewhere in the midst of the fray, a pair of hands grabbed him by the back of his vest and hauled him in one direction. His senses debilitated by the pain of having his flesh nearly burned from his bones, Michael kicked and screamed wildly against whoever held him, thinking that it was a hunter ready to finished the job.

Soon he felt the coolness of the shadows surround him. His daughter came to his side and pulled him deeper into the curing darkness. His eyes soon healed and the first sight he was met with was Giovanni, standing in the center of the room, out of arms reach from the vampires.

Michael didn't have the strength or the will to be furious with him. He only nodded as Jane went to work to break the arrow shaft so they could free him from the tether. Giovanni turned and ran into the street where body parts and blood were flung in seemingly every direction.

It took some time to heal, but when his skin no longer looked charred, the screams of the hunters could not be heard outside in the streets. Instead, the air was filled with the scent of blood, bile, and seething hatred.

Michael looked to Yaverik who stood just at the edge of the shadows, the front of his shirt drenched in blood that rolled off his chin. From outside, Francesca's soft whimpering and Angelo's whispered words of assurance met Michael's ears. The tightness in his chest eased, now that he knew they were safe.

Marco and Giovanni exchanged some harsh words as Tor padded into the cellar, stepping over the rubble of the destroyed barrier. His fur was caked in his own blood and the blood of the hunters, his paws and muzzle dripping. Golden eyes probed into the darkness, assessing them one by one until he was satisfied that they were well.

Michael didn't yet have the strength to stand, but if he could, he would have hugged the beast and thanked him. However, Jane jumped at the chance. Soiling her clothes with the blood on Tor's fur, she held him close and wailed out thanks after thanks to the werewolf.

Tor stood and returned her hug, lifting her into his arms with a kind of affection that shocked Michael. Apart from the fading anger he felt toward their attackers, another current of emotion rushed in that he hadn't expected to ever sense from the Egyptian. True, unabated fondness for Jane. It wasn't quite love, but it was certainly the beginning of it.

After all he had learned in Arnathia and all he had experienced with Tor on the way to this place, Michael knew for a fact that if his daughter wanted to marry a werewolf, he would give his blessing. Hate and fear had surrounded their races for thousands of years. If she and Tor could spark a revolution, a renaissance of peace for the world, then he would not stand in their way. Their world had been submerged in the darkness of ignorance for long enough.

One month later, Florence Italy, 1570

Tor paced a short distance in the vestibule in Michael's villa. The sun would rise soon and the vampires would only have a limited window of time to see him off.

The journey back to Italy seemed much shorter than before. With the added supplies that they gleaned from the hunters' packs and saddle bags, they traveled north. Their camels had been loaded with scrolls, books, and all manner of other artifacts and documents that Michael would study in more detail in the comfort of his villa.

Giovanni revealed that the plot to have Michael killed was his doing. Yaverik needed the most restraining as the poor, misguided scholar groveled for mercy and pardon from his padrone. Michael had every right to be furious, but extended the hand of benevolence and forgave the defector. He had kept it a secret from the others, but the vampire knew all the time what would happen. He only refrained from telling anyone else because he knew how the others – especially Yaverik – would react.

Like a true optimist, Michael wanted to believe that Giovanni would change his mind before it was too late. Though Giovanni did return to Arnathia after attempting to flee, he admitted that he had been too much of a coward to stop the hunters before they took their mission too far.

They all were in agreement, though. If Tor hadn't come when he did, they would have all been killed. Francesca suffered a broken ankle that Tor deftly set, while Marco lost a fair amount of blood in his attempt to fight off the hunters. It left them crippled for a time, but not decimated as the hunters intended.

Their trip had been enlightening and perilous. Tor hated that he had to leave them.

Giovanni had been released from Michael's services, achieving what he had wanted all along. There was no true ill will between them and now that Michael knew how desperate Giovanni had been to serve other padroni, he gave him leave to seek other venturing enterprises. A wealthy baron in Verona sought Giovanni for a trip around the southern tip of Africa to seek trading alignments along the coast of India and the far east. Giovanni offered a place on the voyage to Tor.

With his appetite for exploration wetted by their excursion to the Caspian Sea, Tor could hardly refuse the invitation. Yet what he would be leaving behind created a storm of conflict within him.

Not only would he most likely never return to his temple in Asyut, there was the matter of a certain young woman he had grown fond of in Italy.

He and Jane had grown close on the trip back to Italy and though their future had never been determined, Tor imagined that she pictured them side by side for a little longer. He wasn't sure how long he would be away from Italy. It could have been months, perhaps years. Who was to say that when they met again, their friendship would be sustained? What if Jane found a husband and had a family? What if the growing ember in Tor's chest was snuffed out by the distance between them?

Tor would miss their long midnight talks and the way she laughed. Jane had an exuberance for life that he severely lacked and he was sure that he would be leaving a part of himself with her in Florence.

He heard her footsteps patter down the stairs and across the tiled floor. Michael stood on the landing overlooking the vestibule as Tor and Jane embraced for what might have been the last time.

"I wish I could go with you," she whispered against his neck.

"It would not be safe."

She giggled. "When did that ever stop me?"

Tor pulled away and gave her a look. "I will check the cargo holds before the ship pulls away from dock, just in case."

Tears glimmered in her eyes, despite the forced smile spread across her lips. "Promise me that you will write?"

He nodded. "I promise."

"Even if your ship is destroyed in a storm and you're stranded in the jungle?"

Now it was his turn to laugh. "You have been reading too many fairytales."

She lifted one of her slender shoulders in a half-shrug. "I suppose that's the romantic in me."

Tor looked up to Michael who chaperoned their farewell. "I will return to Florence as soon as I am able."

Michael waved his hand in dismissal. "Take your time. We are not going anywhere any time soon."

It was the truth. All three of them still had many more centuries to live, more adventures to have, and there was still more for them to learn and explore. The world was becoming an ever-smaller place, just as Michael had told him. It may not have been long before they would fail to hide who they really were. So, now was the time to seize the opportunity.

He took Jane's hand in his and kissed the back of her fingers. If anyone had told him months ago, living alone in his sandy temple, that he would be standing in the center of a wealthy Italian vampire's villa, kissing the hand of his daughter while horses waited for him outside to take him to another far-off place, Tor would have thought them mad.

He remembered the words of his father, that he needed to protect the balance. In his own way, he would, by leaving his past of ignorance and solitude behind. Tor would make friends, see the world, and feel far more than he would have allowed himself to before.

With her face still fresh in his mind, Tor turned and strode out into the courtyard, ready to face a new and promising future.

The Frenchman

Legacy Series Book 3

Sheritta Bitikofer

MOONSTRUCK WRITING

CONTENTS

CHAPTER 1

WARMINSTER, WILTSHIRE COUNTY, ENGLAND, 1623

"Darren, put that down!" his mother, Martha, screamed from the second story window. "That's not for you to concern yourself with. Let the serfs carry the load."

Try as he might, Darren's thin arms finally gave out and he dropped the wheelbarrow back onto its iron legs. His palms and fingers burned a bright red from the effort he had put into gripping the wooden handles tight enough to push the wheelbarrow a measly yard.

With his arms sore and face hot, he looked over his shoulder to see his mother leaning out the open window. She was still dressed in nothing, but her chemise and long brown hair draped like a thick curtain in front of her chest.

She waved her hand wildly at a servant who happened to be making their way out to the fields. "Arthur! Take that away from my son before he hurts himself."

Darren turned and puckered his lips in a seething scowl that he didn't want his mother to see. He despised his rangy build and the unerring fact that he was useless for anything more than stealing the air that rightfully belonged to those who could do more than him. In his own eyes, he was a waste of space, without skill or purpose.

Arthur, an elderly serf who had served the Dubose household since Martha's first husband passed away, came to Darren's side with a look of utter pity. He had to be well into his sixties, the son of another tenant farmer from Scotland who had moved to England in hopes for better work. Even this old man, whose skin had been darkened by years of toiling in the sun, could carry the wheelbarrow brimming with cattle feed with ease. Yet, Darren, who should have been in his prime, was hardly capable of bringing the load to the baiting place where the cattle took their twice daily meal.

"It's all right, Master Darren," Arthur said in his wiry Scottish brogue. "You just rest yourself."

"Rest yourself. Rest yourself," Darren mocked breathlessly. "That's all I ever do is rest."

Arthur shrugged his bony shoulders. "Enjoy it while you can." With that last word of advice, he hoisted the wheelbarrow off its legs and carted it down into the fallow field to the south.

As Darren listened to the single, squeaking wheel roll away, a gust of wind whipped across the estate, making his lightweight shirt and vest ripple against his frame. He shivered as the chill crept along his skin.

"Come inside, son, before you catch your death of a cold!"

Darren felt his lungs seize as he inhaled the cold air. He quickly pulled out his handkerchief from his trouser pocket and coughed into the fabric until his throat grew raw, which didn't take much at all. He had been coughing all morning and all through the night.

The window his mother had been hanging out of latched closed and, once more, the yard in front of their home was silent, besides the occasional groan from a milking cow or the bristling of wheat stalks in the adjoining field. Darren pulled the cloth away from his mouth to see it speckled with crimson blood. He scorned the metallic taste on his tongue and swallowed some of it back, wishing it had not come to this again.

Ever since he was a boy, Darren was chronically sick. Whether it was a cold, pneumonia, or a simple case of severe fatigue, he was laid up in bed for one reason or another. As a result, he had become a frail and bitter young man. Many times, he tried to be productive, even if it was helping his mother balance the books or riding into town to conduct some trade. Yet, he longed to ease the burden of the serfs that served on the estate.

The four fields that surrounded the sizable home was just a third of Martha's late husband's ownings. Upon his passing, it was rightfully willed to her and it provided an amiable income. Wheat, barley, livestock, and the newest crop of potatoes, kept their plates filled and coffers bursting. Martha, the mistress of the house, had been used to living lavishly, having come from an affluent French family of her own before she married below her station to a French farmer with a dream to become a wealthy landowner in England. She never made the same mistake again and chose her lovers with the utmost care, being mindful to check their pocketbooks before inviting them to bed.

At least, until Darren's father came. All he knew of the mysterious man was that he and his brother had come to England on some expedition of knowledge. His father had regaled Martha on the details of their many travels, but she could have cared less. The man was handsome and though he couldn't provide for her in any way that would suit her, she boasted that he made her feel the closest thing to true love that she had ever felt before.

Ten months after they met, Darren was born, and two years after that, his father and uncle disappeared from England altogether. A bastard in their world wasn't too uncommon. Darren knew a few in Warminster alone. However, there will never be a more broken-hearted woman than Martha. Arthur often talked how she simply fell apart after his father left her the way he did, without word or warning. Ever since, she kept her heart guarded, but her bed was never empty.

He would have been ignorant to not know that the villagers considered his mother to be a whore and a harlot. Not to Darren. To him, she had always been the caring and doting mother that he often didn't deserve. Even when her lovers demanded her attention, she would rush to his bedside in the middle of the night to ease his suffering with a fresh blanket or cold cloth to press to his flushed forehead. She never once complained about Darren's convalescing periods. Martha sacrificed much for her son and told him that she loved Darren more than her own life. No son could be dissatisfied with that.

His father left them fourteen years ago and if the man was to be blamed for Darren's constant ailments, then he hated him with all his soul. As far as he could remember, his mother was never sick. It was a miracle he was still alive at all.

Darren stuffed the handkerchief back into his pocket and hustled inside before another coughing fit would send him into convulsions. He had been putting off a visit to see George, but it was becoming clear that he couldn't wait any longer.

Donning a wool waistcoat and knitted scarf, Darren slipped out of the house once more to retreat to the stables. Two of the three stalls were empty, and the horses were on loan to another farmer on the other side of Warminster. The only steed left was a brown and white mare Darren had humorously named Gollumpus because of the mare's abnormally large size and unsure footing. They were much alike, Darren and Gollumpus. Both were nearly useless and were kept around the estate out of mercy.

They trotted along one of the balks between the tilled rows of barley until they reached the border of the farm. Looking over his shoulder, Darren could see his brick home in the distance with its dark thatched roof and creeping ivy that covered the outside almost completely.

His mother often complained about the spreading vines, saying that it was an affront against man's efforts to civilize and cultivate the land they claimed. Darren, on the other hand, admired the appeal it gave to the home and begged her to keep it growing until nature came busting through their windows. If he were anywhere near healthy, he would have asked permission to grow a small garden on the side of the house. It would have kept his hands busy while he failed to contribute to the farm and give him a little piece of wilderness that he could control and call his own.

He kicked Gollumpus in the ribs and steered her to the north. He had lived outside of Warminster all his life, their estate situated between the sprawling town to the east and Longleat House to the west. Darren had never seen the outside of Wiltshire county, or traveled anywhere outside of five miles from their home. The two paths he knew well were the road to get into town and the road to get to George's hovel.

The man they called George the Hermit might have been Darren's only friend, apart from his mother and the many servants and serfs they employed on the farm to tend the land. The only way he knew of the man everyone in town scorned and ridiculed was because one merchant's wife had sympathy for Darren's plight.

When he had come into town, coughing and hacking one evening while on an errand to fetch his mother some fabric for a new dress, the woman pulled him aside and told him of the miracle cures George had concocted for her own daughter when she fell ill. Darren was ready for a miracle and ever since his first visit to the hermit, he continued to come back for his salves and tonics.

Beyond Longleat Forest and around Cley Hill, George's hut was nestled deep within a strip of wooded land that belonged to no one. There, nature was his only company, and the burly man with a scarred face and long dark hair preferred it that way.

His hut, which to Darren's mind was a poor excuse for a home, was little more than one room made of mud walls and a roof comprised of straw and branches that must have leaked during rainy nights. A sloping stack of firewood was piled against one side of the house with an axe stuck into a stump not far from it. A mud brick chimney emitted a swirl of dark smoke that didn't help Darren's sensitive throat. He coughed a few times just before dismounting Gollumpus, which announced his presence to the hermit.

A tall man, dressed in clothes that were a little torn, but otherwise clean, ducked under the doorway to greet his visitor.

"Darren," he said. "I didn't expect to see you back so soon."

"I didn't expect I would need to come," Darren replied as he came forward and pulled the soiled handkerchief from his pocket to show his friend the blood he had coughed up.

George took one look and shook his head. "I told you not to exert yourself."

Though Darren wanted to retaliate with some harsh words about how everyone tries to limit him, he kept his lips shut tight. Not only would it do no good to argue with the man who was over twice his size, but he didn't want to risk upsetting the only person on earth who could make him better.

The countless nights spent tossing and turning because of his aching joints, the endless burning and rawness of his throat, and the numerous spells of sickness that plagued his life were more than Darren could bear. If he knew it wouldn't send him straight to hell, he would have killed himself long ago, so he could be rid of this perpetual state of suffering. None of the doctors his mother called for could find a cure or answer for her son's frailness, nor could they offer the kind of relief that George did.

"Come with me," the hermit said with a sigh and passive wave of his hand.

Darren followed him into his hut and the conflicting aromas of spices and herbs welcomed him. Against the far wall was a tiny bed with a mattress made of hay and soft down feathers. A deep indent had been made in the center where its owner slept at night. Beside it, a wobbly table with a single rickety chair whose seat appeared to be far too small for George's hulky body. The rest of the spacious interior was reserved for shelves and tables that were littered with bottles containing various powder and granule elements that George had never taken the time to identify to him, despite Darren's probing curiosity.

Swatches of various herbs and leaves hung at the end of twine that extended from the roof rafters. On the other side, the odious fire that billowed the smoke that tormented Darren's lungs, continued to burn. Though, inside, the acrid fumes were not as bothersome as the scents of the spices that wrapped around his head like a warm embrace. Just being inside the hut had a calming effect on his nerves and sickly disposition.

George donned a pair of sheepskin leather gloves and tied a mask over his nose and mouth. When first asked, he explained that it was to keep Darren's illness from afflicting him as well, but Darren told him that he didn't think the illness could spread. It wasn't the plague - that he knew of - but still the hermit took extra precautions when mixing up his usual remedies.

Darren watched as he pulled down bottles and oils from his collection, taking the time to read each label that he had scrawled out in not-so-perfect penmanship. The rest of the townspeople believed George to be many things. Uneducated was just one of them, but Darren knew all too well that the hermit must have been raised by a wealthy family for him to know how to read and write. He had never asked, but Darren suspected that he was not forced into this life of solitude, but chose it for himself.

George was rarely seen in town, and if he did venture that far, he did not stop to socialize - as was expected of most. He went there to do his business and return to the safety of his home. In some ways, Darren envied him, not only because of the carefree life he lived, but for his brawn and sturdiness. George was never sick, just like Martha. Darren wanted to resent their healthiness, but knew better to be grateful that another human being did not have to suffer what he did on a daily basis.

"What else are you experiencing besides the cough?" George asked.

Darren took a quick assessment of his body, though it was hard to determine what was normal and what had become *his* normal. "I feel cold and my chest aches. I also haven't been able to eat much because my throat hurts."

George nodded and snatched a branch of some herb from one of the baskets that hung beside the fireplace. "How are you sleeping?"

"Not much," Darren replied, though he thought George should have known that by now. It was rare that Darren slept all through the night. When he was violently ill, he would be awoken several times by the need to vomit or relieve himself in his chamber pot. Darren knew for a fact that this symptom was not normal.

"Are your muscles still giving you trouble?"

He referred to the more recent development of Darren's muscles turning so rigid that he couldn't move. It was a new symptom to his existential disease. One of his teeth had cracked when his jaw clamped shut and would not open, no matter how hard he tried to force them apart. It lasted for a few minutes and then Darren was left weak and breathless.

"No, not since before we last spoke. Your tonic helped."

George nodded again and moved to his crowded work table in the middle of the room to begin mixing everything together in his mortar and pestle bowl.

Some of the townspeople muttered about witches within the same breath as the hermit's name, but Darren doubted it all. No matter how hard the clergy pushed their hysterical propaganda about the infiltration of witches and devils into their community, Darren saw differently.

What George did was not witchcraft or magic. Darren saw his ingredients and watched him blend it together with water and sometimes fire, but there was no blood, no mystic words of enchantment, and no familiar to help him in channeling the demonic powers of Satan. This was nothing but pure alchemy, or perhaps a type of medicinal practice that the other doctors and physicians of the world would not yet accept.

Even if what George practiced was some sort of magic, Darren would have still gladly accepted his help. Anything to give him some relief.

"How is your mother?" George asked, rather unexpectedly. He had never asked about Darren's personal life outside the context of his illness.

"She is well, as always." Darren could have gone on and on about her newest lover, a baron visiting Warminster from another county. He had been at their home for three days now and disregarded Darren as little more than a nuisance. He stayed out of his mother's way and let her have her fun, but if any of her suitors dared to hurt her, then Darren would not hesitate to push aside whatever ailments he had to defend her. Such an occasion never came up, but Darren was certain that was how he would act.

"That is good," George said. "It's good that she isn't falling ill as well."

So that was why he was asking. If his mother became ill, then George would know that there was something new emerging about his condition. Darren crossed his arms over his aching chest and watched George's deft hands at work.

Darren's visits were never long, and there was never any conversation on any topic apart from what ailed him. He knew nothing about George and anything he thought he knew was pure speculation, such as his presumed education and reason for segregating himself from the rest of society.

Within moments, George corked two flasks and handed them to Darren. "This is a salve to rub on your chest at night," he instructed, pointing to one as Darren took them. "This one is to drink whenever your throat feels the least bit sore."

Immediately, Darren uncorked the second flask and took a swig to wash the sickness from his gullet. It was like drinking fire, but once the burn subsided, he felt he could take in a breath of air without the need to cough. George turned away to shed his mask and gloves as Darren hurriedly took some of the buttery salve from the first bottle and rubbed it on his chest behind the loose flaps of his tunic collar.

"Have your cook make you soup with chicken broth and plenty of vegetables from the town's market. Drink that every afternoon and evening for the next week." The hermit turned to Darren with a serious look in his black eyes. "And rest in bed for a few days. Try to sleep, even if you have to board up your windows to keep the sunlight from waking you."

Darren took a deep breath as if it were the first one of his life. "Everyone tells me to rest, but it's the last thing I want to do. I've rested my whole life and I'm through with sitting it out."

George tossed his gloves onto his thin and ratty bedspread. "If you do not rest, you will not get well. It's that simple."

Darren held out the two flasks as if to show him the immense weight of his struggles. "What if I never get well? What if I have to come to you for the rest of my life? What happens when my mother dies and I have to take care of the farm and estate? The serfs will not take orders from a bedridden master."

A new look dawned on George's face, as if he were considering Darren's words carefully. He scratched at his bold, clean-shaven jaw and looked around to the menagerie of ingredients and herbs that had more living space than he did.

"I suppose," he began, "that I will not be around forever as well. If you are to be ill until your last breath – whenever that may be – it might be good to show you exactly what it is I do."

Darren froze, hardly believing his luck. "You'll teach me all of this?" he asked, gesturing to the contents of the shelves and tables.

George made a grumbling, dissenting sound, but then nodded and waved him over. "It would make the most sense to do so. I've seen the way you watch me and you seem like a bright young man. You'll learn quickly."

Darren beamed, smiling for what seemed like the first time in weeks. George had never even let Darren touch the herbs, much less learn about their medicinal qualities. If he could learn to make these salves, lotions, and tonics on the estate, then he wouldn't have to risk his health riding to George's hut every so often. Perhaps, if these ingredients could be grown, Darren could finally start that garden he wanted and it would serve more than just one purpose.

There was little joy in his life, but when there was, he recognized it immediately and held firm to its promise for a - hopefully - healthy future. When his entire life revolved around the pursuit of wellness, any glimmer of optimism thrilled him to no end.

Chapter 2

Night had fallen over Wiltshire County and Darren knew it was time to make his way home as George was lighting his modest lanterns that sat amongst his scattered herbal remedies.

"Thank you again for teaching me," Darren said as he made his way toward the humble door that hung loosely off its hinges.

His head was spinning with long Latin names of plants and berries that he would most likely forget by morning. He would, however, remember what they looked like and their purposes. Now that he knew what was good for an aching belly and what was a quick aid to reduce the swelling of wounds, Darren was far more knowledgeable than he had been before that evening. A few more lessons and he would be more than equipped to cure his own ailments from now on.

"You're most welcome," George replied. "Do you require assistance returning home? There is no moon tonight, so it will be difficult to navigate the forest."

Darren peeked outside into the darkness and sighed. "No, I'll be all right. Might I borrow a lantern, though?"

He looked back to George as he searched for a spare, unlit lantern amongst his few personal belongings. His entire hut might as well have been dedicated to his art, judging by how little he owned at all. Such a simple life was deserving of admiration.

Finally, the husky man found a tiny lantern that was just right for Darren to carry for the few miles he would have to travel to return home. Anything bigger might have worn out his scrawny arms. Using one of his candles, George lit the lantern and passed it on to his new apprentice.

"May I return in the morning for another lesson?" Darren asked with a spring of excitement that puzzled the hermit.

"If I am here, you may. If I am not here, wait for a while and I shall return. There are some errands I must attend to."

Darren nodded. "Very well. Until tomorrow."

With that, he hurried away from the hut and mounted Gollumpus who had been patiently waiting by a patch of rich grass, munching occasionally to stave off the horse's hunger. Martha would be worried about her son and Darren knew there was no time to waste. With invigorated speed - thanks to George's medicines - Darren mounted his horse and took off into a steady canter to the south.

The night air was colder than it had been all season, indicative of the coming fall and winter months. Harvest time would be soon approaching and Darren held onto the fleeting hope that perhaps with George's help, he would be well enough to help the serfs in the field as they cut down the wheat stalks. At the very least, he wanted to alleviate the stress on his mother by supervising their progress without having to take a break to catch his breath or cough into his handkerchief every few minutes.

Driven by the need to return home and explain away his absence for most of the day, Darren kicked his mare to go faster as they rounded Cley Hill and into Longleat Forest. It was impossible to hear much beyond the jingling of the saddle harness and the huffing of Gollumpus as she sped onward.

Part of the way through the forest, however, Darren was stricken by a churning sensation in his gut. Thinking it had to do with Gollumpus' bounding stride afflicting his stomach, he reared the mare into a slower walk. He swallowed back the bile that rose in his throat, but the illness would not subside.

Within moments, it was accompanied by a piercing, sharp pain through his chest, unlike Darren had ever felt before. He winced and pressed his hand against the pain, as if that would make it ease. Gollumpus must have sensed his discomfort, because without his consent, she stumbled to a stop and turned her head wildly in every direction, searching for what ailed her master.

He patted her thick neck and shushed her fears, but it only proved to agitate her further.

The pain increased, spreading through his limbs and into his skull where it exploded like when a bale of hay met an incendiary spark. Darren groaned and let go of the reins to squeeze his temples. Gollumpus nickered and whinnied in fright, spinning and stumbling all around the clearing they had stopped in. The lantern fell from Darren's hand and he heard the glass shatter on the ground. The light was snuffed out, plunging him and his horse into darkness with the only light coming from a few stars that began to emerge against the black canvas of the sky.

The pressure began to build and his muscles convulsed and seized until he couldn't move. Gollumpus, too mad with fear, threw off her rider and darted through the trees to escape. Darren tumbled to the ground, but the pain of the fall was nothing compared to what afflicted him now.

This went beyond mere discomfort. This was far more, as if a searing iron were traveling through his blood, scorching and burning as it went until nothing in his body remained untouched.

A terrifying thought entered Darren's mind as he tried to breathe and fight whatever new sudden sickness to which he had fallen prey. Was this the moment of his death? Never in his life had he felt such excruciating, blinding pain.

What would happen to his mother? Would they find his body twisted and mangled on the forest floor, half eaten by the wild animals that would take him as an easy meal? He had heard of homeless beggars who died amongst these trees and had their bowels devoured by beasts. Would Darren become a tasty meal for some bear or feral dog?

Was this George's doing? Was this some delayed aftermath a product of the tonic he drank or the salve he had rubbed on his chest?

Darren writhed and cried hot tears as the pain continued, increasing in magnitude with each passing second until he felt he could bear it no more. His heart pounded in his ears, drowning out his muffled whimpers as his tears streamed down his cheeks and splashed into the cold earth that would soon receive his lifeless body.

His bones popped and quivered within his flesh. His heart stopped for an indeterminant amount of time before Darren's vision went black and he could remember nothing else but the agony.

Martha stared out the window, ignoring the slight dinginess of the paned glass, and watched the dirt path that led between the fields toward the house. Without the moon to guide her, she had no way of knowing what hour it was. The baron lay asleep in her bed chamber, but she slipped out some time ago to impatiently wait for her son to return home.

That evening when he didn't come in for his supper, she had sent her maid-servant to fetch him. He was nowhere to be found on the estate and even Arthur couldn't tell her to where Darren had run off. Her chest tight and limbs aching, she knew she should have gone to bed. Surely Darren would turn up in the morning.

He had never confided in her about the clandestine trips he took to the hermit's hut beyond Cley Hill, but she had known about it for quite a while. Each time he returned in good spirits, so she didn't have the heart to scold him. As long as her son was happy and healthy, she didn't care if he had to worship devils or sacrifice an animal to pagan gods.

That was what the townspeople thought of George, though none could confirm it. He had never brought a curse upon anyone as far as they could tell, so they let him be. Martha had heard rumors amongst the gossiping wives, though, that something was brewing over the hermit's little hovel. Something devious.

When Martha asked, fearful for her son's wellbeing, they turned up their noses and walked away. Their reactions were none too surprising.

Such rumors and hearsay were what kept her awake that night, full of worry that her son had been caught in some terrible and foreboding chaos that George might have been creating. Darren had left so suddenly earlier, without even leaving her a few last words to which she could cling. Not a single promise that he would return, or a passive lie to cover where he was really going. Now, she was left with nothing but the long wait.

Darren's eyes snapped open as the morning sun burned through his eyelids. He could feel his limbs twitch and tremble, as if he had run for a great distance. Sounds and scents bombarded his senses. The earthy smell of dirt, leaves, tree bark, and even the murky water of a stream not too far away, all crammed up his nose in a confusing, but vivid array. He could hear the tiny squeaks of field mice scurrying in and out of their burrows, the chirping of baby birds high in the treetops, and the rhythmic babbling of the stream.

If he listened closely, he could even hear the soft voices of men muttering unintelligible words. It was their voices that startled him awake. He rose from the forest floor, a few leaves sticking to his damp skin. The next thing he noticed was his pure and unabashed nakedness. He looked all around, but could not find his clothes anywhere.

In fact, this didn't even look like the clearing he had fallen in the night before when Gollumpus bucked him. This place was new, and the woods denser than he remembered.

After that, he noticed how his body was sprinkled and matted with mud and dirt. It was only then he realized that something was not right. His body.

He looked to his bulging calves, then to his thick, muscled thighs. Upward he inspected, his nerves rattling as his eyes widened. His limbs seemed to have grossly swelled overnight. Yet, was this swelling? He flexed his hand and saw the way his tendons and muscles bunched under his skin. No, this wasn't swelling at all. His biceps were four times the size they had been, giving them an intimidating appearance.

Then, he took in his new torso. His pecks were hard and chiseled like the famous naked statues of mythological gods and heroes from ancient times. His stomach, as well, boasted a set of tight, rippling abs that were certainly not there the evening before.

It was as if Darren's mind had been put into the body of a young and able field hand. He was no longer a thin and weak excuse for a human being. The fact that he was naked and covered in dirt didn't matter anymore.

His hands trembled as he flexed his new muscles, a smile curling across his lips. If the pain he experienced the night before had brought about this change, he was glad for it. And if George was the one who made all of this happen, Darren was forever in his debt.

Beyond the shock, Darren felt fantastic. The constant ache in his bones had disappeared, along with every other slight nuisance that came with being an invalid. No more congested nose, no more weak lungs and heart, no more upset bowels, no more dull headaches or anything else. Instead, he stood tall and strong, pushing himself off the ground with little need for assistance.

He took his first step, then another, making his way through the trees to find that stream he knew must have been nearby. It had to be nearby for him to hear it trickle so loudly. However, he must have traveled half a mile before he stumbled upon its winding current.

Darren fell to his knees and checked his reflection to make sure this was truly his own body. The face that stared back at him through the watery surface was certainly his, though something new had appeared. His jaw and lips were covered in stubble, something he had never seen on his face before. By his ailments or perhaps a cruel turn of fate, Darren had never been able to grow a beard. Now, it appeared that he would finally have to purchase a razor to keep his face clean shaven. Though, he was sure that he might never want to shave, lest the beard never grow back again.

As he dipped his hands into the cold water and splashed his face and arms to rid himself of the soil that was speckled across his skin, the thought occurred to Darren that perhaps this was temporary. Would he lose these muscles and the beard if he didn't constantly take the tonic George had given him? What if he would experience that same pain each time he drank it? It was worth it to look upon his reflection and see that he was no longer helpless.

He spotted a massive rock imbedded in the shallow banks of the stream. Testing if these muscles were simply for show, Darren gripped the edges of the boulder and heaved it out of the ground. It took little effort to rip it from its deeply inset home on the banks and toss it clear to the other side of the stream.

No, these muscles were not just for show. Darren let out a laugh of disbelief, feeling his heart hammer with unimaginable joy in his chest. He could lift a thousand wheelbarrows or plough a field without the leading aid of a horse. The possibilities were endless and he gave a great shout to the heavens.

To clean the rest of his body, he dove into the stream and let the frigid waters flow over his legs and chest, somehow knowing that he wouldn't get sick from it later. When he climbed out, he checked himself just once more to make sure he didn't wash away the miracle that had taken place.

Still unsure of where he was, Darren took a chance and ran to the north, hoping that he hadn't fallen unconscious too far from where he fell. He had to see George and tell him what happened.

Yet, as soon as he took off, he found himself colliding with a tree. Darren fell flat on his back and looked around, baffled. He was so far away from the stream that he could just barely make out the glittering sunlight along the surface. Darren only remembered taking a few steps and suddenly he was running into trees that weren't there? Or was it there all along?

He rose to his feet and dusted off the back of his legs before he started again. Once more, he nearly crashed into a pine, the prickly bark biting into his skin on impact. This time, he couldn't even see the stream. Darren looked to his legs. Perhaps he could run much faster now, at a blinding speed that not even he could keep up with.

He rose again and this time took off at a light jog instead of a full sprint. Sure enough, this speed was more manageable and he could easily weave through the obstacles in his path, but it still felt as if he were faster than he had ever been. His old stamina barely let him run for less than a quarter of a mile before he had to stop and rest. Now, he could jog at a steady pace for so much longer.

It must have been half an hour before he finally saw a break in the trees and realized that he was much farther from Longleat Forest than he anticipated.

Before him was Longleat House itself, the grand estate that was home to the politician Thomas Thynne. He could see the gardeners tending to the front lawn and expansive maze of hedges. These were the voices he heard from the forest, the mumbled conversations that woke him from his sleep. Closer now, he could hear them talk and gossip about estate affairs, but he was nowhere close. He couldn't even make out the details of their faces, so how was it possible that he could hear them from so far away? Could everyone hear in this way?

With a cleared path, Darren tested his speed once more. He took off at a run just around the perimeter of the estate, far enough from the eyes of the groundskeeper so that he wouldn't be seen in all his nakedness.

He managed to stop just before reaching the other end of the property where the woods continued. Looking back, he must have conquered several acres in a matter of seconds. This was impossible. How could he run so fast for such a long distance and barely break a sweat?

Now he knew that he had to see George.

He snuck onto the estate and swiped a pair of trousers from one of the laundry lines a maidservant was tending and rushed back to the safety of the woods. He directed himself a little to the east and continued on, until he reached Cley Hill with its rolling mounds and thick shrubs. It took him less time to arrive on foot at the strip of woods where George's hut was situated than it would have taken him with a horse. Poor Gollumpus would be out of a job as long as Darren's new body didn't fail him.

He smelled the herbs and spices before he even saw the plume of chimney smoke. He could even detect the slight whiff of George's personal odor that he remembered from the evening before when they stood close to converse over a certain plant he was lecturing about.

As he came into the clearing, George did not come out to greet him as he usually did. The planked door to the hut remained closed, but Darren could smell a bowl of stew steeping over the fireplace inside. His stomach rumbled in response to the savory scents.

"George?" he called out, only successful in disturbing some birds from their nests in the trees around the hut. He heard no response, and no one came out.

The hermit had mentioned that he might not have been there in the morning. With every inhale of the delicious aroma of the stew, Darren could feel his hunger worsen.

Surely George wouldn't mind if he took a sip? Cautiously, Darren made his way inside the vacant hut – realizing he must have also grown in height overnight since he had to duck under the doorway just as George had to - and found a bowl to fill for himself. It was a struggle to ignore the overpowering herbs and the acrid smoke from the fire.

The first few sips of the broth seemed to satisfy his appetite. But, upon the fourth sip, Darren knew something was not right. His stomach felt as if it were flipping within his core, and soon, the soup made its way back up.

Darren hurried outside of the hut in just enough time before the soup came spilling out of his mouth in a vehement storm of vomit and broth mixed with a bit of blood. He had thrown up his meals many times, but never as violently as this, or so soon after tasting it.

When it had all been expelled from his body, the nausea quickly abated and all that was left was a sense of utter perplexity and a more vicious hunger than before. New strength, new stamina, new senses, and a revulsion to simple stew? What did George give him?

He wiped his mouth on the back of his arm and tossed the soup onto the ground before going back into the hut to retrace his steps. He carefully went back over what George had put in his salve and tonic and rehearsed each of their purposes and meanings, though he still couldn't quite recall their names.

As long as George was telling the truth, none of these contents should have been able to give him these abilities. The only explanation was that when taken in conjunction with one another, they produce these unbelievable results.

Whatever the reason, Darren was not going to protest about a simple upset stomach. This new body, this new life that he had been blessed with, was surely worth a picky palette. Still, he needed to find George and thank him.

He made his way out of the hut and called out into the morning once more. Through the myriad of smells, he could still perceive George's distinct scent. At first, he thought he was imagining it. Then, as he veered toward the direction from which the scent seemed strongest, he knew it wasn't a mistake. Darren picked up George's scent, much like a bloodhound would, and was able to follow it right out of the clearing and to the east, toward Warminster.

Without questioning his nose, Darren followed it, hoping that it would truly lead him to George and a possible reasonable explanation for his new body. If anyone knew what had happened, it would be George.

Chapter 3

When Darren entered Warminster, he didn't consider the attention he would draw. Every one of the townspeople knew who he was by reputation, either of himself or his mother. They all knew him as the bastard child who could barely lift a basket full of grain. Even though he snitched a shirt from another farmer's clothes line on the way into town, it did little to hide the change that took place in him.

Heads swiveled in his direction and he could feel their shocked and frightened gazes as they assessed his new body. What he didn't expect was to hear their whispers. Every word they said, whether in hushed voices or simply masked by their own hands as they talked to their neighbors, he could hear them loud and clear, even if they were across the street or behind closed doors.

"Look at him!" they silently jeered. "What happened to him?"

"That's not the same boy."

"That can't be Martha Dubose's son."

"What did he do to himself?"

"It must be the work of the devil."

"An angel must have blessed that poor boy."

Darren's steps slowed as he turned to listen to each of them with a fluttering heart and uneasy stare. Their voices of dissention, ridicule, and disbelief crowded in until he was ready to give up on finding George and run for the quiet safety of the forest. He could scarcely hear himself think through the cacophony of noise from the townspeople's chatter to the rumble of carts and stamping of horse hooves on distant streets.

He could hear the merchants toiling away in their shops and laborers talking with their fellow workers. Children's laughter and baby cries screamed in his ears as if they were close enough to touch. Smells of all kinds, from the putrid stench of dung to the perfumes of ladies in their homes, strangled his mind, and sometimes made him retch and cough for cleaner air.

The town had never seemed so odious, so revolting and unkind a place as now. Darren thought he could take no more, until a new sensation pierced through the chaos. A tight and prickling feeling in the back of his skull. He sometimes felt this when he rushed out of bed too quickly or took one sip too many of the brandy that Arthur offered him to ease his stomach ailments. This, however, was much worse and more intense than any of that.

He touched the back of his head to make sure he wasn't bleeding or hadn't been inadvertently struck by something. Darren did wake up on his back, so perhaps some bug or insect had bitten his scalp during the night. However, there was no blood or bump to indicate an injury.

"Pssst," he heard coming from up ahead, a harsh sound that seemed to break through all the distracting noises.

Darren looked up and saw a man standing just outside the door of the bakery. His sharp blue eyes fixed on Darren and he waved him forward. As he obeyed the summons, Darren could feel the sharp needles in his skull dig their invisible points deeper into his skin.

Yet he bore the discomfort long enough to join the man at the door. The baker's cheeks and tunic were dusted with a decent layer of flour that offset his dark hair. As soon as Darren was within arm's reach, the baker pulled him into his shop and shut the door.

The yeasty scent of unbaked dough and fire from the ovens that met him was a pleasant smell compared to what he encountered on the streets of Warminster. All around, trays and bowls of rising dough and bushels of golden brown loaves were scattered over the floors and surfaces.

Before Darren had a chance to adjust to the sudden lack of congesting noise, the baker grabbed him by the arm. "Were you bitten?"

Darren looked to the frantic man and blinked back the fresh wave of confusion. "What are you talking about?"

The baker quickly let go. The tingling in Darren's skull began to ebb away, giving him some relief as he grew accustomed to the feeling.

"Were you bitten or born this way?" he clarified as he pinched the bridge of his nose.

Darren, still lost in the question, shook his head. "I don't know what you mean."

The baker's brows lowered and he gestured to Darren's body. "This. What made this happen?"

Taking a look at the hysterical baker, Darren didn't think that he was looking for the secret to his strength. Though the baker's profession might have been innocuous enough, the man looked as if he could crush bones easily between his hands. In fact, their statures were not so dissimilar.

"I... I just woke up like this," Darren replied, not wanting to give away George or make the baker suspect that the hermit had anything to do with this just yet. The rest of the townspeople already believed him to be a sorcerer or witch of some sort. If they thought that George had created this new body for Darren, their suspicions might be confirmed.

"So, you were born one," the baker said with a relieved nod. "That is good. At least we know that there isn't another of us running around somewhere. Where is your father? Or is what they say true, that you have none?"

Darren took a step away from the offending baker. "Born what? If you don't start talking sense, I'll... I'll..." He held up one of his fists, something that never used to be intimidating. "I won't hesitate to –"

The baker let out a hearty laugh, cutting Darren's threat short. "Boy, you can do nothing to me."

He had enough of their contempt, enough of being disregarded. He used to be defenseless, but no more. Darren used his fist and threw all his weight into the punch, sending the baker to the floor.

With his chest heaving and heart thrumming heavier in his chest, Darren stood over the man and shouted, "Don't laugh at me! Tell me what you mean! What am I?"

He was expecting the baker to call him a bastard, a coward, or a fool. Instead, Darren watched with horror as the baker took his jaw and popped it back into place. A trickle of blood oozed from the corner of his mouth and he wiped it on the back of his arm, smearing flour across his lips and chin in the process.

If Darren had broken the man's jaw in that way, he shouldn't have been able to talk or even push himself off the floor so quickly. He hadn't even expected to throw that much force into the punch.

"You, boy, are a werewolf," the baker said and he shoved a baffled Darren backward a step or two so he would have room to straighten out his tunic.

"A... a what?"

"Werewolf," the man repeated. "Just like me." He offered out his hand. "Bartholomew," he introduced.

Darren wasn't sure whether to take the man's hand or run out of the bakery screaming. He didn't move, he didn't accept the gesture of friendship offered by the man who just realigned his own jaw, and he wouldn't believe anything the baker said.

"Werewolf?" he questioned. "The beasts that mothers tell stories about to make their children behave?"

Bartholomew lowered his hand. "Not the exact same, but the general idea. There are many differences, of course."

"Such as the fact that they don't exist," Darren replied. "No man can turn into a beast."

"Yet, you changed forms overnight," Bartholomew stated. "I've seen you in town and you were not like this before. So how much more fantastic is it to believe a man can change into a wolf?"

Darren shook his head. "It's not the same."

"Isn't it?"

They stared at one another for a long, tense moment before Darren broke in. "What proof do you have? If you are a werewolf, prove it."

Bartholomew looked toward the paned window that gave him an ample view of the street beyond and moved away so anyone who might have peeked in couldn't see his face. When the baker turned back to Darren, his eyes were no longer blue, but a brilliant shade of gold. Darren staggered backward, but could not look away as his hands trembled.

"This is the easiest way to show you," Bartholomew said, a note of apology in his voice as if he didn't want their first meeting to have come to this.

More startling than the change in Bartholomew's eyes, was the change in Darren when he stared into the gaze of the wolf. Something deep within his chest began to stir, as if some whirling mass was coming alive beneath his ribs. There was no pain, just a sense of comfort and affinity with the pair of golden eyes.

The rational, reasonable part of his mind could not comprehend any of it, shunning any possibility that this was real. Perhaps he had been dreaming this entire morning? The change in Darren's body was slightly less difficult to accept than a man's eyes turning an unnatural color that belonged on an animal. Yet, what if this were all a fantasy? What if these muscles and those eyes were nothing but a figment of his imagination, concocted by whatever George put in that tonic? This all led back to George in some way or another and it reminded Darren that he still needed to find him.

First, he needed to see if this really was a dream. He shook his head and squeezed his eyes shut to block out the false reality. "This isn't real," he repeated to himself over and over again, as if it would do him any good.

The baker grabbed him by the arms and shook him. "I assure you, this is real. Look at me."

Against his better judgment to ignore the fictitious figure, Darren opened his eyes. The wolf in Bartholomew's gaze was gone now and the blue had returned.

"Where did you wake up? What happened last night before you fell asleep?"

Darren saw no point in lying to the baker, since this was only a dream. He would wake up soon enough when someone found him in the woods. So he told him about riding his horse through Longleat Forest, how he fell under tremendous pain, and blacked out in consequence.

"Yes, you were certainly born a werewolf," Bartholomew mused as he let go of Darren. "Do you know where your father is?"

"Neither I nor my mother have seen him for years. He was not a werewolf."

"Can you be sure of that?" Bartholomew's brows arched and Darren wasn't positive anymore.

"For the sake of argument, what if he was? What does that matter?"

Bartholomew crossed his strong arms over his chest. "A werewolf can either be born or bitten by another werewolf. If you were not bitten, then your father must have been a werewolf. Those are the only two ways. It is preferred that fathers stay with their sons until they reach maturity, as you have, but it seems to be a rarity now. I've met many more like you who change and have had no guidance. Most unfortunately, I cannot give you such guidance. Only your father or an alpha can."

It was all too fantastic to believe and Darren gave the baker a mirthless smile and looked heavenward. "This is absolutely ridiculous. I'm not a werewolf."

"Then how else can you explain your enhanced senses and your new strength and speed?"

Darren had mentioned none of that to Bartholomew in the short few minutes they had known one another. "How could you –"

Bartholomew grinned and tapped one of his ears. "I am a werewolf too, re-member? I've been around for centuries. I know how unusual it can seem, but you must believe I'm telling the truth."

"I do not believe it, sir, and I will not," Darren snapped. "It's preposterous all together and I don't know how I could have ever thought any of this to be real. I'm still unconscious, somewhere in the forest and this is all a dream. Good day to you,"

Darren stormed toward the door, but faster than he realized, Bartholomew blocked his path. "You can try and deny this all you want, but as the days, weeks, and months drag on and you haven't woken up, you'll know I am not lying to you."

Darren's skin crawled as a fiery anger welled in his gut. "I am not a werewolf and my father was not a werewolf. I am not some murdering beast that prowls around in the moonlight. You, sir, are insane and I've had enough of this!"

He forced the baker aside with one sweep of his arm and charged into the street without so much as a look backward. He slammed the bakery door shut behind him and stood in the street, immersing himself back into the biting words of the women and snide remarks of the men who watched Darren from a safe distance. He almost preferred the smell of dough over the suffocating city odors, but he could not bear the company that came along with it.

Bartholomew did not chase after him as Darren hurried to find George's trail again. Even as he did, the thought occurred to him that he was tracking, just as a wolf did, using a scent to find his target.

No. Darren shook his head. He would not give in to such temptations. He was not a beast. This was all either a terrible and misleading dream, or a hallucinogenic effect of the tonic George prescribed. He had to make sense of this somehow. There had to be a better explanation than werewolves and monsters.

Down the street, a commotion erupted. He turned to watch a cart careen down the lane, led by two mad horses who were not too concerned with trampling everything and everyone in their path. Darren jumped out of the way as the wagon loaded down with wooden crates, came rattling past him. Undeterred by the interruption, he carried on.

Then he heard something else. A woman's scream. Considering that the horses were plowing their way through the center of a crowded square, it wasn't surprising to hear. What she screamed was more important and it snagged Darren's attention.

"My baby!"

Darren turned and saw just the faintest flash of blonde hair down the lane, lying right in the destructive path of the rampaging horses. Without a second thought,

Darren did what he knew he had to do. Being careful not to overshoot, he dashed forward, little more than a blur to anyone else's sight.

He quickly passed up the horses who were at a full gallop, and positioned himself in front of the little girl who had fallen onto the cobblestone streets. He could smell a bit of blood from her skinned knee. Looking back to the horses, he felt a primal and inexplicable shift in his chest.

Without even meaning to, a deep growl rumbled from his throat and his eyes went cold as if wind were blasting them, but they didn't go dry nor did they warm themselves again when he blinked. Instead of grabbing the girl like he had intended, Darren stood his ground and braced himself to take on the horses himself.

What had come over him?

The horses spotted Darren, their crazed eyes rolling in their skulls as their necks and haunches frothed up a good sweat. They reared and quickly turned to escape the man who blocked their path. They skittered to the side and he thought he could smell something emanate from them as potent as the stench of dung that floated through the streets. It was a peppery, savory smell that only encouraged the rising of this primitive notion that he could easily tear these horses apart if he wanted. Some intuitive sense told him it was fear that he smelled. Fear of death from the human who dared to step in front of them.

Darren's lips curled up in a snarl as the horses turned. The wagon, however, could not be stopped so easily. The hitch that kept the horses strapped to the cart snapped against the force of their change in direction.

The wagon wheels first skidded along the stony streets, and then caught at some point, causing the contents to tumble out, barreling toward him, their sharp edges spinning with each turn. Darren turned his shoulder to the crates and crouched down to shield the child he endeavored to protect.

Oak collided with flesh and splintered into his skin, but he stood firm as the little girl screamed beneath him. When the collision was over and the dust had settled, Darren and the child were surrounded by crates that were cracked open and broken apart, their contents spilled onto the street. With a few great thrusts,

Darren pushed the heavy crates away from them and sent them flying in the square. Shrieks and gasps of alarm exploded among the nearby citizens.

Onward the horses sped, dragging the remaining parts of their harnesses as men tried to wrangle them to a stop. A crowd had gathered to assist in pulling the crates off, and the mother of the child rushed forward to claim the girl.

With tears in her eyes, the woman gathered up her frightened and confused daughter. She did not offer a thank you or a promise to repay the debt she now owed to Darren for saving the life of her child. Instead, she took one glance at him and fled with a horror-stricken look on her face.

The animalistic urge to growl and snap his teeth disappeared, but his eyes still felt cold and his muscles tensed to danger. He looked to the townsfolk, shards of wood sticking out from his tunic with dribbles of blood seeping through the cloth.

With each pair of eyes he met, disturbed sounds of alarm poured out of their mouths. Women ran away and men gaped, their hands reaching for the hilt of their daggers that were strapped to their belts. If the men didn't have a weapon, they picked up whatever they could find to wield.

"Beast!" they cried.

"Witch!" gasped another.

Darren picked out the splinters as he backed away from the mob that accused him of something he did not do. He pried each of them out, but when he inspected the wounds, he found no holes or puncture wounds. Yet there was blood all the same.

"I'm not a beast!" he argued, sweeping the last bit of dust from his tunic.

Still, they persisted and one man pulled out a gun, the shaking barrel pointed at his chest. Once more perplexed and frightened, Darren hurried from the scene at a fast pace, but not a supernatural one as he had before. He needed to disappear, to become inconspicuous somehow before these men were out for his head. What had he done? Yes, it might have been unnatural the way he blocked the crates from crushing the child, but shouldn't they have been cheering instead of scorning him?

Bartholomew emerged from his shop, probably hearing the disorder in the square. Darren made to steer around him, but the baker quickly grabbed him just as he had before. Their eyes met, but he did not have the same reaction as the others. "Run as far as you can from here and keep your eyes down until they're warm again."

It was then that Darren looked to the darkened window of the bakery. Between the framed panes, he could see his face and the golden eyes that stared back.

It couldn't be. He rubbed at them, trying to erase the truth he could not accept. This was just a dream. Just a dream.

"I will come to you this evening. Go!" Bartholomew pushed him further down the street as the shouts of men grew closer.

There was no time to protest. Darren lowered his head and hustled away after he regained his footing. Taking the shortest path out of town and ducking through alley after alley, Darren finally arrived back to the spacious, rolling hills of the farmlands that surrounded Warminster.

He breathed in the fresh air, but nothing would ease his troubled mind. His eyes had turned gold, just like Bartholomew's. Was that why they were cold? It had to be why the townspeople ran and shouted the way they did. What made them gold?

Darren remembered the way he felt staring down the horses, how he had been completely prepared to wrestle them to the ground to keep them from trampling the little girl. Such heroic impulses were not new to Darren. There were many times when he wanted to step in and stop a fight or help a man who was being robbed on the streets, but Darren had been unable to do anything about it because he wasn't strong enough to contend with such brutes. Now, he was the brute, and he could do so much more than toss rocks over rivers. He could help people and save lives, just like he saved that girl, but was it worth it?

What if every time he stepped out to help someone, he turned into a beast with wolfish eyes?

Darren caught himself on an oak tree and pounded his fist into the bark until his knuckles bled. Angry tears leaked from the corners of his eyes. What was he to do? Who had the answers he needed so dearly?

No, he was not a werewolf. They didn't exist.

Back and forth, his mind warred against him, battling for one truth over the other. Monsters were not real, not like those spoken of in fairytales and folklore. Surely, there were evil people in the world, tyrants and warlords who killed people for the pleasure of it. But it was not possible that a man could change shape and become an animal. He couldn't... could he?

CHAPTER 4

"M istress!" shouted one of the maid servants. "Your son is back!"

Martha bolted from her chair, knocking it clean to the ground as she hurried out of the study and into the hall. The maidservant continued to blubber about something, but Martha wasn't paying attention. When she reached the top of the stairs that overlooked the foyer, she found a man standing there that she almost didn't recognize.

Her trembling fingers found her lips somehow as her knees went weak. This couldn't be her son. This wasn't the same boy that left the estate in a hurry the evening before. It couldn't be. She took one step down the stairs, but Darren hurried to meet her instead.

No servant was in sight, no other person to confirm the man's identity. Yet, as he came closer, she knew it was indeed her son. She would know those brown eyes anywhere, the same eyes of his father, the same eyes she had fallen in love with years ago.

She ran to meet him and felt dwarfed in his strong embrace.

"I didn't know where you had gone," she whimpered, stricken by joyful tears. Darren was home, that was all that mattered for the moment.

"I'm sorry, mother," he said, his voice somehow deeper than she remembered. "I didn't mean to be away this long."

She pulled away and patted her thin hands upon his arms, her smile wavering for a faint second. "That's fine, son. Come, let's get you something to eat and we can talk, yes?"

Martha moved away to shout for a servant to bring them whatever was left over from breakfast. She might have to get cook started on their noonday meal sooner than expected. Before she could open her mouth or wander too far, Darren tightened his grip over her hand.

She looked back into the eyes she had loved since she first held her son in her arms. Yet these eyes, as familiar as they were, held a new emotion that she had never seen before. Grief. Utter mortification and grief. It was then she realized that she wasn't the only one trembling. This was not just one of his moods, either. He had his days when he moped about the estate, wishing he could do more. This, however, was something new entirely.

"What's wrong?"

Darren took a deep breath, his broad chest rising and falling. "Mother, I don't know if I can stay. Something happened in town and –"

Martha waved her hand to silence him, just as she did whenever he would go on about some melancholy thing that she didn't care to hear. "None of that. We will have a meal and we will talk. We have many things to discuss." Her eyes flitted from his feet to the crown of his head.

Yes, something certainly had happened. Even his hair, which had been matted and oily, seemed to have adopted a healthier luster. His face, now half-covered in a layer of stubble that she thought he couldn't grow, took on a bolder shape, more masculine and strong. Just like his father.

Martha gave her orders to the servants and led her son to one of the chambers that she reserved for their quiet evenings alone. The baron had gone out on business, so they wouldn't be disturbed. She seated Darren on the sofa, confident that his weight might crack the legs of his usual chair, whose fabric had been worn thin by years of sitting.

Darren's hand fidgeted over his knees as he sat like a boy who was ready to receive bad news or a reprimand. Martha would give neither. Yes, she had been angry that he left without a word the day before, but the total bliss of seeing him alive and more than well was enough now.

"Did George do this?" she finally asked, unable to keep the question at bay for much longer.

Darren's eyes went wide. "You know about George?"

Martha tried to laugh in that carefree way she did when asked a silly or troubling question. "Everyone knows about George, my dear. I know you've been going to him for help. I never minded because you would always come back better. But, this..." She gestured to his body. "It's a little remarkable, isn't it?"

In the back of Martha's mind, a war took place that she would never let her son see. She knew the fanatical rumors about George's practice, how it could be considered witchcraft. Martha hoped against everything that her son had not given into some black magic. She knew his frustration with being unable to do the things that everyone else could, but would Darren stoop to such sinful lows as to make a pact with the devil?

The other faction, her motherly nature, wanted to disregard such assumptions. Darren was still the same boy she raised, the same one she had cared for and loved all these years. Even if he did sell his soul to Satan, Martha would still love him. Even at the cost of her own soul, should God deem to not have mercy on her for accepting such blasphemy.

"Mother, I... I don't know if George did this or not," Darren confessed, offering his hands out in supplication to her. "At first, I thought he did. It was the only thing that made sense, but I'm not so sure now. I spoke with Bartholomew, the baker, and he –"

"Bartholomew?"

"Yes, he said this has something to do with my father."

Martha froze. No, this couldn't have anything to do with Hugo, could it? There were many strange things about the man who had stolen her heart and left her just as quickly as he had appeared. He, too, was strong, but strong men begot strong boys. It could not explain Darren's sudden growth and coming into himself, so to speak.

There was the way that Hugo sometimes disappeared at night and wouldn't come back until the morning, just as Darren had done. No matter how much

Martha begged him to stay, he refused. When he was with her, however, every-thing in her world was all right. He often said he would take a thousand arrows for her, run across the country just to bring her anything she wanted. Hugo would have gathered the very stars of the heavens into his arms and given them to her if she had asked.

Then, he left. Without a word, without warning, he and his brother, Geoffrey, had left her alone with their child. Perhaps his demeanor had been warning enough. Martha recalled the solemn look in his eyes, the way his voice dropped when they spoke of the future that they could never have. Darren was too young to remember the last time Hugo visited them.

If she married him, like they wanted all along, she would lose almost everything she had from her first husband's inheritance. Hugo was poor, a lowly scholar just like his brother, but he could not bear to bring her into his poverty, neither would she wish it.

They were once comfortable in their unholy arrangement. Hugo visited when he could and stayed for days, maybe weeks at a time, then he would have to go away for a while. When he left the last time, Martha assumed he would return. Weeks passed, then months. Slowly the years trickled by and Darren grew up without his father, and she without a true lover to keep her warm at night.

Whatever Darren believed, whatever the villagers gossiped about, Martha had never known a real love quite like Hugo's. All the rest were just play things, distractions for the lonely nights when she worried about the fate of the farm or the health of her son. Hugo had been her rock and when he left, he dashed her into innumerable pieces.

To hear that Hugo might have committed some other heinous act without even being in Warminster, Martha didn't know how to respond.

"Your father did nothing," she whispered, hoping to convince herself as well. Perhaps George wasn't the sorcerer, but Hugo. Could that even be possible? Nothing in her recollection could verify such a claim. Though, she would never deny that he had indeed bewitched her beyond mortal understanding.

"Bartholomew said... he said that my father might have been something unnatural and I have inherited whatever it was." Darren swallowed hard. "Was my father... a werewolf?"

Martha gasped. "Certainly not. Darren, werewolves don't exist. Don't you know that?"

He ran his hands through his hair and gripped at his scalp in agony. "I know they're not, mother, but please humor me. I don't know what has happened." Darren looked to her with imploring eyes. "Please, do you know where he is?"

Martha straightened in her chair, her delicate hands folded neatly in her lap. "I don't know where your father is, Darren. I'd advise you to not find him, though."

"Why not?" he pleaded. "If he has the answer to this, then –"

"Promise me you won't try to find him!" she snapped. "My heart cannot bear to lose you, too."

Before Martha even realized she was weeping, Darren had clasped his hands around hers and knelt at her feet.

"You won't lose me, mother," he said, his voice a soothing balm to her broken heart. "Can you tell me anything about him? About my father?"

Taking stuttered, sniffling breaths, Martha shook her head. "There is nothing to tell beyond what I've already told you."

Darren's hands gripped tighter over her fingers. "Can you even give me his name? Perhaps Bartholomew will know him."

"Bartholomew?" she questioned as she peered at her son quizzically. "How would he have known your father? He's only been in Warminster for a few years, long after your father left us."

A pained look came to Darren's face, as if he regretted telling her the truth. "The reason Bartholomew says my father might have been a werewolf is because he is a werewolf too, and must sense that... that I'm a werewolf as well."

Martha couldn't stand that word any longer. "You are not a werewolf, Darren. Neither was your father and neither is Bartholomew. They do not exist!" she cried, more frustrated tears brimming in her eyes and blurring his features. Witches and devils were easy enough to believe, but werewolves? Simply out of the question.

"Mother, I know no other explanation. It's ridiculous, I know, but –"

"That's exactly what it is," she interrupted again, feeling her heart pound ever faster beneath her breast. "It's ridiculous and I won't have any more talk of it." Martha took a breath that was meant to calm, but her tone suggested the opposite. "I will call for the doctor and he will prove that you are not a werewolf. There is a logical explanation for all of this and –"

Now it was Martha's turn to be interrupted as one of her maid servants rushed into the chamber, unannounced.

"What is it, Bessie?" Martha reproached, but neither she nor Darren moved from their place.

It was only then that she heard a slight commotion building outside the walls of their home.

"Mistress, there's trouble outside. They're demanding to see Master Darren."

Darren was the first to rise from his knees and start toward the door, but Martha nearly tripped over her dress hem trying to grope for his arm.

"No, don't go to them!" she insisted. They came into the hall and Darren went still. The maid servant waited by the door, nibbling on her fingernails with nervous eyes shifting in her sockets. Martha's frantic hands finally found purchase on her son's shirt sleeve.

"I can't stay," Darren told her as he turned to regard her with a new, frightened expression that conveyed the utmost pity and regret. "Neither can you, mother. They've come to take me. I can hear them. They won't stop until they have me."

The front doors were hammered upon and angry, unintelligible shouts floated up to them. How could he possibly understand any of that mob?

Martha squared her shoulders. "They can take all the wheat and the cattle, but I won't let them have you."

Darren turned and took his mother by the arms. "Mother, they think I'm –" for a fleeting second, he looked to the maid and back to Martha again. "They think I've committed a crime."

It took her a few heartbeats to realize what he truly meant. Darren wasn't the only one who thought he was a werewolf. The people did too. He had tried to tell her about something that happened in town. She could easily see how such a superstitious people could mistake her son's newfound health as a sign of witchcraft or other demonic influences.

"What happened?" she demanded.

"I... It's a misunderstanding, I assure you. They saw something. If I told you, you wouldn't believe me."

Martha turned to her quivering maid servant and flapped her hand. "Bessie, go away. Make sure no one leaves the house." The maid servant curtsied and hurried away before Martha turned back to her son. "Tell me. Now."

"My eyes," Darren said, trying to find the words. "They changed. They became like a wolf's and were gold."

"That's impossible," Martha insisted as she shook her head with a tendril of hair slipping from the pins that held it back from her face. "No one can change their eye color. It must have been a trick of the sun. Your eyes did always look lighter in the sun."

"No, mother," he asserted, his word thick with severity. "They were gold. Bright gold. I saw them in my own reflection and the villagers all saw it. Bartholomew's eyes changed in the very same way."

Martha could feel her composure slipping like loose sand through her fingers. "Prove it. Make them change now and I will believe everything you say."

Darren winced at the command. "I don't know how, mother. It happened so suddenly in town and I –"

The banging from the first floor persisted, their shouts growing louder and more urgent. Martha could hear some of the servants argue back that Darren wasn't in the house. Loyal, every one of them, even in the face of an angry horde that was out for blood.

Martha took her son's hand in hers, marveling how large it had grown since the day before. "It doesn't matter. You're not a werewolf and I won't let them take you." Thinking quickly, Martha pointed toward the other end of the hall. "Go through the servants' corridor and run to the woods. Hide there. I will come for you when they are gone."

Darren refused and his nostrils flared. "No. I won't leave you to them. God only knows what they'll do to the mother of a..." He paused to pick his words. "The mother of a man who destroyed a lot of merchandise by accident."

She was glad that he didn't utter that word again. Martha might have screamed otherwise. "I will settle it then," she said, giving his arm a reassuring pat. "Go, now. I will see you this afternoon."

Her son grabbed her about the shoulders and kissed her cheeks. It had been a long time since he had kissed her in such a way and the scratch of his stubble was unexpected. Though, each touch was laden with immense love and appreciation for her.

Darren rushed out of sight, down the hall and through a corridor that would lead to the kitchen where he could make his escape. Martha watched him go, her heart bursting with both sadness and joy. Finally, her son was well; how was of no consequence. Werewolf, witch, alchemist, it didn't matter. This time of turmoil and confusion would pass, she was sure of it. The truth would be known either way and she welcomed it, whatever it was, as long as it didn't have to do with monsters and fairytales.

First, she would deal with the real wolves at the door.

Darren ran as fast as his legs could carry him, through Longleat Forrest, past Cley Hill, and toward George's hut. If his old friend could not give him an answer, he would turn to Bartholomew and the elusive father figure whose name he didn't even know. If he could probe his mother a little more, demand the facts from her, perhaps she would confess that there was something not quite right about his father and confirm one of the only theories he had in his possession.

Still holding out hope that there was a simple, scientific explanation for everything, Darren broke through the dense underbrush, following the clustered scents of herbs and firewood smoke. Amongst them, he could smell George and the fading aroma of the stew Darren tried to ingest earlier that morning.

Darren slammed his fist against the hermit's door to knock and make his presence known, but inadvertently bashed the wooden panel off its rope hinges, taking bits of the mud plaster with it.

George let out an expletive and soup spilled onto the dirt floor of his hut as he started to his feet.

"What in God's name... Darren?" The hermit's wide eyes roamed over his young friend's body from toe to brow. "What happened to you?" he asked, a bit of soup drooling from the corner of his mouth.

Darren came forward, arms outstretched. "Do you not know?" The harried inflection of his words told the story of a young man who had been through hell all before noon. "What did you give me last night? What caused all of this?"

He lifted the edge of his tunic to show George the sculpted muscles of his torso. George let out a long whistle and let his jaw drop. "I didn't do this," he muttered in a daze. "No natural thing on earth can produce this overnight."

Darren had been afraid of that. George was his last hope, the only string of reason left before he had to resort to the fantastic and insane. He let his tunic drop to conceal the miracle once more, this new wretched body that he had been glad for now seemed like such a burden.

"You didn't..." Darren began, feeling the world around him grow dim and lifeless. He had this sensation before, just before he was about to faint. Yet the release of unconsciousness did not come. He remained standing, though all he wanted to do was collapse in a heap and sob.

George took a few bounding steps forward and set his bowl down upon his work table. "What happened, Darren? Tell me."

He shook his head, gaze distant and unblinking. "I hardly know. I woke up this way, I swear it." Darren went on to tell George about the pain, the extra abilities, the incident in town, Bartholomew, everything he could.

"Can you help me?" he finally asked, ready to fall upon his knees and beg the man for another miracle, another elixir or lotion to rid him of this cursed nightmare.

George shrugged and blabbered out a few inarticulate mumbles, but it had seemed the man was on the edge of madness. "I can't help you, because I don't know how this happened. You should go to Bartholomew. He might have answers."

Just as George finished his suggestion, a sound met Darren's ears, as clear and piercing as anything he had ever heard. A scream. A wailing of pure agony and terror that heralded the end of his life as he knew it.

Without a word to George, who wouldn't have heard the desperate cry, Darren fled from the hut and ran back into the woods. The smell of smoke was thick in the air now, though the sky hadn't yet been blackened by the harsh reality of what must have been unfolding on the farm.

Shouts, taunts, the screaming of women, and the crackling of wood as it was burned to cinders joined the pandemonium. By the time Darren ran the few miles back to the estate, the house and barn were already engulfed in the flames of hate.

The superstitions of the people had disrupted their lives, calling for the blood of the man who showed himself to be different, to be something that was perhaps not human. Their frenzy amassed into a rally of fear and loathing so powerful it had spilled onto the farm, the estate, and his family. They didn't know his story and they didn't care. All they wanted was the threat eliminated.

Darren watched from the other side of the farrow field, concealed in the hedges as he watched his home make its way to becoming nothing more than a memory.

It wasn't the house that bothered him. It wasn't the sobs of the servants as they were pushed and harassed that made the bitter rage boil in his blood. It was the sight of his mother being dragged by her hair into the open that brought the cold golden shade back to his eyes.

A firm hand grabbed him, but he already knew who it was that detained him.

"Don't," Bartholomew growled.

No matter how hard Darren tugged to get away, Bartholomew was stronger and held him back from running into the field to save his mother from the mob.

He listened to them question her, berate her, call her a whore and a conspirator. They demanded to know where Darren was and what pact he had made with the devil to give him the strength and imperviousness of a man possessed.

Tears stung at his eyes when she refused to tell them anything, claiming that her son hadn't come home since the evening before. They pushed her further, asking if she was in league with the witch. They asked about George and how Darren could have grown so strong overnight. Still she would not tell them anything.

Darren fought harder against Bartholomew, the evil and primal essence in his chest fuming with wrath. Still the simple baker, who was more than he seemed, restrained him with hardly any effort.

When they had enough of her obstinacy, the mob seized her and approached the flames that ate away at his home.

"No!" Darren shouted, but he was too far from the riot for any of them to hear.

His mother screamed, crying for help and mercy. They didn't care. One of the men who carried a pitchfork drove the butt of the staff into the charred front doors while the rest brought Darren's mother to the threshold. With one sweeping motion, they threw her inside the blazing home as beams and walls came tumbling down around her.

Darren twisted and pulled against his captor, but Bartholomew would not give an inch. The dying screeches of his mother rang in his ears louder and louder until it was all he could hear. His mouth opened to let out a monstrous roar of anguish to drown out the tragedy before him.

Servants rushed to the aid of their mistress, but found themselves on the dangerous end of makeshift weapons. The mob cheered as they chanted for Martha's speedy demise for consorting with demons and witches. All the while, they reveled in the murderous thrill of their insurrection.

They came for a witch and instead, they settled for his mother. He heard rumors that they were going to George's hut next. Darren's roar died away into a shrill, weeping whimper. He fell to his knees, defeated and shaken by all that had happened.

All the while, the aching and swirling chaos in his soul would not rest. It shuddered and wailed with him, mourning just as he did. Somehow, it understood him and as if he were truly possessed, Darren understood it, too. The nameless entity, which he had not recognized before that day, became a storm of feeling within him. It frightened Darren, but somehow gave him solace as well. He was not the only one to suffer, not the only one to come undone. Yet what was this thing inside of him? Why was it there? What was happening to him?

Now, more than ever, he wished this were a nightmare. He wanted to wake up in bed, wracked with a fever, as his mother mopped his brow one last time. No matter how he tried to awaken, Darren continued to stare up at the fiery anarchy in front of him, wishing that he were inside the burning wreckage instead of his precious mother.

CHAPTER 5

Night fell over the county a few hours after darkness had fallen over Darren's life. Clouds obscured his view of the stars and the bright sliver of moon above as the rains came. It was as if nature itself was trying to wash away this nightmarish hell that had taken residence in Warminster.

Chaos erupted in the town as the hunt for the witch continued. They would not find him. Instead, they settled for the blood of innocent men and women who did not conform to the image that society had set for them. Old women with disabilities, grumpy men, and reclusive spinsters were targeted, dragged from their homes and thrown into the dank and dirty jail. Some citizens were impatient to see the misshapen lives blotted out and took a few into the square to lynch them.

From his place, sitting under a sheltering elm in the dense woods outside of Warminster, Darren could hear their cries for mercy and pardon for living. Cold and dead inside, he did not come to their rescue. Why should he go to them when he couldn't even save his own mother?

Bartholomew did not restrain him now, but stood close by in the open air where the rain dumped upon his head and shoulders. Both of them were soaked, their tunics and trousers drenched and clinging to their bodies. Darren's hair hung heavy to his scalp and forehead as droplets of rain found their way past the canopy of branches to soak him through.

As the heavy raindrops crashed into the leaves above, making them quiver and rattle with terror for the torrent that had been unleashed, Darren seethed in his own quiet rage. He hated the people, hated their ignorance, hated whatever it was that he had become, sparking such a riotous change in the people, and provoking them to become murderous, single-minded fiends.

He wanted to hate Bartholomew for holding him back while his mother's flesh burned to ash inside the ruins of their home. After they fled the farm, he tried to tell Darren that it was for their own safety. If he had gone to his mother's aid and rescued her from the flames without being hurt himself, it would not help his case to convince the villagers that he was human and not in league with the devil. If he went to kill those that murdered his mother, the authorities would come to investigate the slaughter and it would put them both at risk.

They were selfish reasons in Darren's mind. Whatever he intended to do, it might have all led to his death or the revelation of some dark supernatural secret, but at least his mother would be alive. At least he could have seen her one last time.

Even George had fallen prey to the mob. Hours earlier, they had gone to his hut and ransacked its contents. From his safe hiding spot in the forest with Bartholomew, he did not hear the hermit's cries or shouts. Perhaps he knew what was to come and left the area before he would be next.

Only Darren and Bartholomew remained untouched by the witch fever that inflicted the townspeople. They had been waiting there for what seemed like an eternity and Darren was sure he hadn't moved a muscle except to blink and breathe since they came there to hide.

Bartholomew spoke, of course. He told Darren about werewolves, about the unholy beasts that they turned into once a month under no duress from the moon. He talked about silver, wolfsbane, and the need to stay inconspicuous in society.

He, himself, had traveled around England and Scotland, moving his bakery every ten or so years to avoid detection. They did not age as humans did, but slower and more gradual. He was hundreds of years old, but there were others far older than him.

The werewolf baker spoke of alphas, betas, omegas, and packs. He spoke of their strengths and weaknesses and the dangers of what would happen if they were discovered. The world already had a vague idea of what werewolves were, but it was not all true. If it were possible, the human race would never know the truth. What little they did know was dangerous enough.

Witches were the craze now. Towns all over the country buzzed with rumors and suspicions of so-and-so casting spells and curses upon unsuspecting children. Just as Warminster had fallen under the vicious, red glare of the obsession, plenty more had fallen to the hysteria. Each one became graveyards for the odd, the recluse, and the unwanted.

Some witches who were burned were genuinely benign. They were humans who had the unfortunate luck to be put under scrutiny by the neighbors and they paid for it with their lives. Others, Bartholomew said with a definite air of regret, were werewolves such as they were, who would not die so easily. It was those cases when hanging a man was not enough and they resorted to the pyre to snuff out their unnatural lives. It was a slow, agonizing death, but it was possible, even with their quick regenerative abilities.

Darren's life was no longer simple. His health may not have been a concern anymore, but there were greater fears and greater enemies. Death would have been a happy release, if only he had the courage to face the same fire that killed his mother.

Yet he was not the only one who would have his life upended. Bartholomew now had to seek a new home since the witch hunts had come to Warminster. He said he would travel farther north, perhaps to Scotland where the witch hunts were slowly dying off after decades of ravaging the pocketbooks of the townsfolk. Burning a witch and putting them on trial had become costly when dealt with properly. Now, the children of the generation that condemned witches were more concerned with other things. Scotland would have been a safer place than England, to be sure.

Bartholomew did not extend the invitation for Darren to join him. Instead, the baker simply turned to the distraught youth glaring into the distance and said, "You can't stay in Warminster."

Darren would not speak to him, would not even look at him. Of course, he couldn't stay. What a stupid thing to say after what had taken place that day.

"You need to seek out your father, or perhaps an alpha who can teach you better than I can."

For the first time in hours, Darren moved. His muscles tensed and trembled as his hands balled into fists on his thighs. "I don't even know my father's name," he mumbled. "I wouldn't know where to look for him."

Bartholomew took a few steps forward, but Darren stopped him with a single look and something entirely new came over him. From within, a force, as strong as the pull of the ocean and as fierce as the all-consuming flames of a wildfire, seeped from his chest and core. It was as if a bit of his essence, his soul, were reaching out and seizing Bartholomew, though such power was invisible to his eyes.

Nevertheless, the results were clearly seen. The werewolf stood still and a look of worry and intrigue spread across his face. Darren didn't know what he was doing, but there was a certain satisfaction in the way he could freeze a man where he stood without speaking a word or assaulting him in the physical.

Bartholomew lifted his hands, palms facing the earth as if he were trying to pat down the embers of Darren's rage before they could burst into maturity.

"If you can't find your father, you need to find an alpha. I don't know where one would be in England, since we're so scattered, but I do know of one in France."

France. The place of his ancestry, where his mother's family came from and where his surname originated. He did not know the nationality of his absent father, but he had taken what pride he could in his French roots, just as his mother did. He might have been born in England, and have the tongue of an Englishman, but France had always been on his mind. On those days when he was a young boy and couldn't rise from bed because of his sickness, he dedicated himself to learning the French language and their history. He could faithfully recite the names of the kings and monarchs from Charlemagne's time and forward. Though he never had the chance to step on French soil, it was something Darren had always wanted.

He had extended family in France, but none that he could visit without an introductory letter from his mother or anyone closer in relation. It would be an expedition purely for his own personal benefit, and to find this alpha of whom Bartholomew spoke.

"Who?" he asked, feeling the aggressive power return to his body and release Bartholomew from its malicious grip.

"His name is John Croxen. Don't forget it. The last I heard, he was going to Albi, but that was nearly seventy years ago. He might have moved since then."

"How can I find him if he isn't in Albi?"

Bartholomew came closer as the rains continued to moisten the ground beneath them, turning it into a thick, congealing mud. "You'll have to ask and search out other werewolves. That feeling in the back of your head will guide you. That is how you'll know that another of our kind is near. Follow that. There are more werewolves in France than there are in England, so you should have a better chance of finding someone who knows of John. He had the makings of an alpha when I last met him, but he was naïve and uneducated in our ways, just as you are now."

Darren looked away. From his studies of French maps, he knew that Albi was along the River Tarn in the southern provinces. It would be a longer journey from Wiltshire County, but there was nothing left here worth staying for. His farm had been ransacked, his mother killed, his only friend was missing and considered him a freak of nature, not even his new ally would stay in the country.

France was the only place left he could go and John Croxen was the only name he had.

"How do I get to France?" he asked, realizing how bare his pockets were and how disheveled he must have looked. No ship would take him on as a passenger and the channel was too far to swim... Or was it? The water would certainly be cold, but would it really be too far for his new strength and stamina? It could be possible.

Bartholomew reached into his pocket and fished out a few coins, all of which were of smaller value than what would have been sufficient for any passage to

France. He sighed and assessed the coins as they became sprinkled with raindrops in his palm.

After a moment of consideration, he offered them to Darren. "Take this."

Darren, understanding the kind of trials that awaited Bartholomew, shook his head. He could use the money to start his next bakery. "No. You need it more than I do."

The resentment he felt for the baker was strong and seemed to cover his heart like a thick, black sludge, but Darren did not wish him ill. He was not the one who killed his mother. He was the one who tried to look out for Darren's well-being through detestable means. To blame Bartholomew for his mother's death would be like blaming the rain for making the mud that the dog rolled in to sully its fur coat. He was faultless in the events that unfolded, though that didn't make Darren like him.

Bartholomew stuffed the coins away without protest. "Very well. Night will cover our escape. Stay clear of villages, and if you can avoid farms and cottages, do so. If you absolutely have to, only stay with a family for a night and don't give them your real name. If you find yourself hungry, don't put off hunting or foraging. Only eat meat and fruits. Berries will sustain you for a time, but you need meat to survive, so don't ignore the wolf inside you. He will be your guide through all of this. Don't resist him."

Darren looked away, hating the way Bartholomew made it seem as if some other entity were living within him. Though that was exactly how it seemed, he didn't have to like the idea. If any of this was true, Darren would be living with this wolf for many years, perhaps centuries. How could he make peace with something that he couldn't see, couldn't speak with, and what might have been the ultimate catalyst for his life torn asunder?

"Another thing," Bartholomew continued. "In one month, you'll begin to feel the way you did last night. It'll be painful and you won't remember anything. You'll wake up just as you did this morning. If you can find John before that time comes, you'll be much better off. He will help you through the change."

The blood beneath his skin chilled at the mention of changing. Out of all the legends and fairytales, the one true claim upon the werewolf was that they turned from man to beast. The wolf, that thing inside of him that he had to contend with and yet somehow trust, would take over his body. To know that it happened the night before was bad enough. Now, he knew it would happen every month from now until death would lift this curse from him.

Darren did not confirm anything Bartholomew advised, but he heard everything, whether he wanted to or not. When Bartholomew did not receive an answer, he turned to the north.

"I wish you luck in your journey, Darren," he said. "I hope John can help you make sense of this and that you can find peace with yourself."

He began to walk away and Darren wasn't sure if it was the wolf who might have appreciated what little knowledge Bartholomew could impart, or if it was his own guilty conscience for despising a man who only wanted to help him. Either way, he muttered a soft and begrudging, "Thank you."

Bartholomew paused in his step, but did not linger long before he ran and disappeared into the woods. Darren sat still, listening to the baker's hasty footfalls fading into the distance. Once more, the calamity in Warminster came to him, wrapping around his head like a tormenting reminder of what he had lost and what kind of unsure future awaited him.

Whatever was across the English Channel, whoever this John Croxen would turn out to be, Darren had to face it, no matter how much he dreaded it. To go to France might have been accepting that he was a werewolf, but he needed the help of a werewolf alpha. To go was to leave behind his place of birth and possibly never return. How long would he be under the care of this alpha? A few months? A few years? Centuries? What kind of a life could a monster like him live?

With stiff movements, Darren pushed himself to his feet, his pants soiled by mud and dirt from the forest that he would never step foot in again. He took one step, then another, headed south. And that's how he continued, walking until he could no longer hear the screams and smell the rancid stench of death that devoured his former life.

Southern France, three weeks later

Darren had long forsaken his constant alertness for the tingling sensation in his skull in favor of another sense. His nose brought him to a village far to the east of Albi.

The journey had been long, trying, and lonely. Walking through the forest, avoiding the well-worn roads that merchants and other travelers used, Darren was forced to traverse through dense underbrush and weave his way around obstacles, even when the most logical path would have saved him time. Sometimes, days had been wasted skirting around towns and farms teeming with laborers.

Passing around Paris was especially difficult. The temptation of food, culture, and people was so strong that Darren nearly cried when he had to take a long detour to the east.

Now, near the River Tarn and so close to his goal, his soul became weary and tired. From what Bartholomew had told him, this country should have been swarming with other werewolves to help guide him on his way. He hadn't met a single one. Either he wasn't searching hard enough, or there simply weren't any.

He wondered if Bartholomew had been lying. Perhaps, he just wanted Darren to leave Warminster, because he had been the one to bring so much destruction and social dissidence. However, he had come too far to give up on finding John Croxen. In his tired delirium, sometimes he spoke the man's name, committing it to memory as if to urge him onward, to take one step after another until he had arrived in Albi.

It had been three weeks since he left his home in Warminster, and two weeks since he dragged himself onto the sandy shores of France after swimming the entire breadth of the frigid English Channel. He hadn't changed clothes or bathed since he began, and only when the hunger gnawed at his empty belly would he resort to catching small game like birds and rabbits.

Though his inner wolf was ready to dig into the bleeding carcass of his prey, Darren would not stoop so low and did his best to strike a fire to cook his meat. With nearly no experience in the way of true wilderness living, Darren struggled on a daily basis. When he couldn't create the fire he needed, he left the food to the scavenging animals of the forest. More than once, a vulture or other feral thief stole his catch right from under his nose.

Injury was not a concern, as he healed from every twisted ankle that resulted from a fall, and every wound closed up when sliced open by sharp rocks or prickling brambles he traversed through. His body, however, became malnourished and his mind soon followed. He hadn't had a meal in a day or two, but the incessant ache deep in his belly drove him to madness more than a few times.

That was where he was now, delirious with hunger and insane from the solitary hours spent going over and over in his head every heart wrenching event that led him to this place. Though his skin could heal, his clothes were torn where he had been cut, revealing the kind of depravity to which he had been subjected. Hardly an inch of him was clean, but, instead, covered in dirt and grime. The same nose that carried him dangerously close to the village had become accustomed to the stink of his own body.

His scalp crawled with the presence of bugs that he could not scratch away, so he left them there to perhaps pick his hair clean of the oil and dirt that matted it.

He looked toward the village street, a dirt path that led between two rows of houses with steep roofs and potted plants in the windows. It was a quaint hamlet, and he could hear the townspeople go about their day, just as he had heard that long ago morning before his world fell to pieces. It was the sound of civilization, of company, of real people. Besides the occasional traveler that he had to hide from, Darren hadn't seen a soul in what seemed like much longer than three weeks.

Better yet, the village promised something else. Food.

He took a few halting steps forward, acting the part of a true penniless beggar. Then he shook out his limbs and walked straight, forcing himself to stand upright. If he drew attention to himself through his stumbling walk, then anyone he passed might have given him a second look, which he couldn't afford.

Onward he went, not meeting the eyes of the citizens he passed and ignoring their muttered abhorrence to the way he dressed and smelled. Their words did not matter. What mattered was finding the good, hearty meal that he needed, that he deserved.

A few blocks from the edge of town, he came to the source of the delicious, meaty scent. A butcher shop with the latest cuts displayed in the window, salted and ready for purchase. Darren knew he had no money, but there was one other thing he couldn't afford besides the prized cut of lamb he salivated over. He couldn't afford the morals that told him that he shouldn't steal. He either stole or he died. His muscles could not stand another day without the nutrition they needed to keep going.

With one last burst of energy, he would take that side of lamb, ribs and all, and flee to the forest. No one would be able to catch him. Then, once he had the lamb, he would come back and perhaps find a lantern or candle that was still lit from the night before and use it to cook the meat with. If he could not find a fire, however, Darren might have to debase himself once more and eat the raw, juicy meat anyway.

He slipped inside the shop, careful to not make a sound. The butcher was not at his station, but somewhere out back, perhaps cleaning a new batch of cuts for his customers. Darren quietly snatched the rack from the window display and darted out of the shop as quickly as he had come in.

Darren dashed down the road and pushed pedestrians aside, the lamb clutched tightly to his chest. He wasn't running nearly as fast as he would have liked. In fact, he sprinted like any normal man. His supernatural speed had failed him when he needed it most, all because he did not have the energy. For the first time since he turned, Darren felt himself inferior, crippled.

They shouted for him to stop, probably suspecting that he had stolen the meat. Why else would a vagabond be running so quickly with a prime cut such as that? Distracted by the burning in his legs, Darren glanced behind him and didn't feel the prickling in his skull. He thought it must have been another symptom of his starvation and the exertion of so much energy when he clearly had none to spend.

He wanted to make sure that no one was in pursuit of him. When he looked back, he collided with a stranger who did not budge against the impact. All the other men and women he shoved out of the way were cast aside easily, but not this man.

Darren fell flat on his back, sending a plume of dust from under him as he met the ground. The man stood over him, tall and broad in frame. His dark brown eyes looked him over as the wind played in his equally dark, long hair. He wore the clothes of a gentleman of middle class stature and carried a simply crafted cane in his hand.

It was only then that Darren took the time to realize that the feeling in his head was not what he thought it to be. The man who had stopped him so effectively was no normal man. He was another werewolf, just like Bartholomew.

Breathless from the collision and stunned to finally meet his second werewolf, Darren didn't say a word. Neither did the stranger. They both acknowledged one another and knew what the other was. There was no need for an introduction yet.

The stranger tapped his cane on the hard ribs of the lamb that Darren held so tightly. "Did you pay for that?" he asked in fluent French.

Darren shook his head and the stranger made a rueful face. "Get up," he commanded as a crowd began to form around them.

Curious spectators twittered and gossiped in French just as another man burst through the throng. Clad in an apron that was heavily stained with dark splotches of blood, he began to shout at the two werewolves, though Darren was sure if he knew what they were, he wouldn't have confronted them in such a way.

Darren scrambled to his feet and hid behind the stranger under provocation by his inner wolf. This man, who appeared older and more assured than even Bartholomew, had to be a prominent werewolf, perhaps even an alpha.

The stranger put on a smile and stepped forward to ease the concerns of the butcher whose lamb had been filched from his shop.

"How dare you protect this petty thief, John!" the butcher shouted, pointing his fat finger at the trembling youth.

"Easy, monsieur. This is my cousin. He's a little touched in the head," he said as he tapped his finger against his temple to make a point. "I apologize for his rudeness. Here, let me pay for the meat. It will be a lovely feast for our table tonight."

With that, he untied the money purse from his belt and dumped out several gold coins into the palm of the butcher. He took the money gladly, seeing as it was far too much for one side of lamb, and walked away after giving Darren a contemptable sneer.

The crowd, seeing that the drama was over, turned away to go about their business.

"John Croxen?" Darren asked, speaking the name for the billionth time since he had first learned it.

The stranger turned back to Darren, brows raised. "Excusez-moi?"

"Are you John Croxen?" he repeated, his voice faltering with exhaustion as he tried to formulate the question in French rather than English.

The stranger came closer, but did not touch him. "Do not say that name here," he advised in a hushed voice, so soft that he was sure no one else on the street could have heard them. "Come with me."

The stranger, whom Darren could only identify as John based off what the butcher said, hurried past him. He obediently followed, hoping that wherever they were going, there would be a fire so he could finally eat what he had stolen. The relief of finally finding someone who knew John Croxen was dwarfed by his need for food. Perhaps once his belly was full, he could properly celebrate.

CHAPTER 6

They returned to the mocking forest with its faceless trees that had kept Darren company for the last few weeks. He wanted to return to the town, where there were people and streets and buildings for him to walk into and take shelter. Here, in the wilds of France, there was no reprieve, only the incessant chirping of birds and rustling of leaves when animals scurried away from him in fear. It had been a lonely journey from England and the one thing he was entirely sick of was the forest.

John, however, did not seem to dread these woods as Darren did. He took a deep breath before coming to a stop. Then he turned and regarded Darren with a certain look of curiosity. "Why have you not eaten yet?" he asked in perfect English with no hint of a French accent. In the village, they spoke nothing but French to one another and Darren easily mistook him for a French native.

They had been traveling for several moments outside the village and were well away from the prying eyes of the townspeople. Darren could have eaten the raw meat if he pleased, but the last shreds of his humanity still clung to the standards on which he was raised.

Instead of answering his question, Darren's eyes widened a bit. "You're not French?"

John gestured the tip of his cane toward him. "Of course, not. I'm no more French than you are."

Darren straightened. "I am French, sir. On my mother's side."

The man squinted at the youth's features and pulled his lips in such a way that told Darren he was only mildly convinced. "Very well. Why have you not eaten? You look as if you're starving."

"It's not cooked."

John passed his hand over his face and sighed. "Dear boy, it is better for us to eat it raw rather than cooked. Please eat, before I am forced to carry you over my shoulder, because you can't bring yourself to move."

Darren looked down to the rack of lamb that was still held tightly to his chest, the dirt from his hands and tunic spotting the rich red meat. The wolf in him approved and continued to salivate for the taste of it, but it took a few heartbeats before Darren brought it to his lips and bit down.

John continued, beating a path through the bushes for them to follow. All the while, Darren feasted upon the lamb. After the first bite, he couldn't help himself. As he cleaned each bone, he let it drop to the ground so the ants and other creeping bugs could pick away the scraps that he couldn't.

The cold wash over his eyes returned and he knew they must have turned gold, however he didn't have to conceal it from John. Nor did he have to close his lips over the sharp fangs that seemed to elongate the more he ate, providing him ample tools to shred the meat and pull at the tough parts with ease.

When he came to the last rib, Darren was still ravenous. The lamb did little to quell his hunger.

"If you are French, then why do you speak like an Englishman?" John asked, not even taking the courtesy to look over his shoulder.

"I was raised in England," was all Darren said. He still didn't know for sure if this was the John Croxen for whom he had been searching. Bartholomew's warning to never reveal his true name continued to ring in his head and he frantically thought of a false identity to tell John before he finished licking the last of the juices from the rib.

"How long have you been loup-garou?"

Darren paused at the word. He understood its translation to be roughly the same as werewolf, but if this man was English, why didn't he use the proper term like Bartholomew did?

"You mean werewolf," Darren corrected as he deposited the last bone as an offering to the forest.

"It is the same, but we use loup-garou here," John said, as he finally looked to assess Darren's clothing and appearance. "How long?"

"Three weeks or so," he replied.

John nodded and turned back to the path without a word.

"You said 'we'. Is there more than just yourself? Are you taking me to John Croxen?"

He stopped to face Darren once more and stamped the end of his cane in the earth. "First of all, I am John Croxen. I go by John Dumonte in the village, which is why I told you not to speak my true, given name. Secondly, yes, there are more, but I will explain that once we've arrived."

Silence stretched between them, werewolf regarding werewolf, each with an edge of suspicion and wonder.

"Where are we going?" Darren inquired. The question burned in his belly as strong as the hunger.

"My home. It's not much farther... May I have your name now that you know mine?"

Darren narrowed his eyes upon John. "Are you really John Croxen?"

A slow smile crept across his lips. "Why should you doubt my word?"

There was every reason. Though he was also a werewolf, how did Darren know that he wasn't lying? How could he know that this man wasn't working with people who wanted to kill him? If the last few weeks had taught him anything, it was that no one could be completely trusted.

When he didn't receive an answer, John approached him. "Here is your first lesson. Do you know how you feel when you tell a lie?"

Darren shrugged, at least willing to play along. "I suppose my hands sweat."

"Yes," John said. "Your heart also beats just a little faster. You'll either look away or stare too fixedly at the person you're lying to. These are just some of the ways, but even if the liar is a good one, you can always tell by the heartbeat. Listen closely."

Darren did his best to focus on the muffled thump coming from John's chest. "My name is John Croxen."

There was no pitch, no sudden flux or break in the way his heart continued to steadily pump beneath his ribs.

Darren gritted his teeth and decided to take the plunge. If John wasn't who he said he was, heartbeat or not, what would death matter to him? At least he would be with his mother again.

"My name is Darren Dubose."

John gave him a short bow. "It is a pleasure to meet you, Darren Dubose." He turned once more and waved him on. "Come. We will be just in time for the noon day meal and you can meet the others."

Darren hurried to catch up. Instead of trailing behind like a stray dog in need of a few more scraps, he came to John's side. "So, there are more in France? I haven't been told falsely?"

"Who told you that?" he asked, sliding a glance Darren's way.

"A werewolf I met in England, before I left, told me that I could find you in Albi."

John grabbed Darren's arm and pulled him to a stop. "His name?"

Darren blinked away his surprise at John's sudden insistence. "He was a baker. His name was Bartholomew."

A look of utter relief came over John's face and he nodded. "It's good that he's still alive. I haven't seen him in many years. England is not a safe place for our kind anymore."

"When we parted, he was going to travel north to Scotland." Darren wasn't going to mention the fact that it was his fault the baker had to leave Warminster. It was clear these two men esteemed one another enough to remember each other after all that time.

"It might be safer in Scotland, but I wish that he would come here," John remarked as he let go of Darren's arm and walked on.

"He also said that you could be an alpha. That you had the makings of an alpha."

John gave Darren a pleasant smile. "I suppose he saw great things in me when few others did. Yes, I am an alpha."

Now it was Darren's turn to be relieved. He was in the presence of an alpha, a possible mentor and guide to controlling this thing he had become. It was hard to hold back the assurances that he wouldn't let John down, that he would be an excellent pupil, and that his years of private education would ensure that he wouldn't be an ignorant apprentice. Though his clothes probably didn't profess him to be the scholar he longed to be, John knew he would tell the truth.

Yet he bit his tongue and kept his grateful groveling to himself. John exuded a certain confidence and intolerance for such stupidity. That was clear when Darren told him why he hadn't eaten the raw meat. Like he learned through one of his many tutors, it might have been wise to simply shut his mouth and let the alpha teach. God knew there was so much he needed to know, so many questions he needed answers for.

When they arrived, Darren was met by a wall of new sensations and scents. It was as if he had stepped into another world, filled with werewolves in such a contemporary setting that it confused him at first.

He had expected John's home to be a little hovel in the forest, much like George's. At the most, perhaps a farm house. What greeted him instead was a towering chateau with many rooms and a landscape to rival that of Longleat House back in Warminster.

Hedges were trimmed and neatly cut into geometric shapes of grand design. Flower beds sprawled across the grounds like rivers of vibrant colors, only severed by the gravel pathways that allowed the residents to walk through and enjoy its beauty.

The house, built with stone the color of sun-ripened wheat, was larger than his first home had been. There was a gentleness in the way its slate roof and the way the tops of the windows were rounded to avoid the sharp angles he had been accustomed to seeing on many homes. Brick chimneys peeked up from the roofs, letting their smoke swirl and climb into the sky, carrying with it the sweet promise of meat.

The front walk parted to the left and the right to lead toward steps that curved up to the front terrace and the massive twin doors. They were already propped open, receiving the fresh autumn air and any weary traveler who might stumble upon the home.

The solid doors were crowned with a piece of Grecian design that might have seemed out of place with the rest of the façade, but Darren saw it to be fitting. A stone carving of men and wolves running alongside one another was trapped within a triangular pinnacle frame. An ironic depiction, if there ever was one. Any human who noticed the artwork might never think twice about it.

From inside, he could hear the voices of men and women alike, some arguing, others laughing and a few seemed to be in a heated discussion of some topic or another. It only proved to complement the rest of the estate, and Darren felt at home for the first time since the evening before his transformation.

John led him up the walk and pointed out the features of the home as a way of introducing the two. "These gardens were first planted by my wife and I when we built this place," he said. "I have my students tend them for three hours every morning."

Darren smiled at the thought of spending solitary time fostering something so aesthetically pleasing. Finally, he would have the garden he always wanted. Out of all nature, he preferred these flowers and hedges over the uncultivated and uncivilized forests. Though, he supposed that would have to change with time.

"Behind the house is a forest where I've constructed a course of sorts, designed to keep the body fit. We might be supernatural beings stronger than twenty men, but we cannot allow ourselves to become lazy."

His smile widened. Darren couldn't decide where he would spend the most time, with the flowers or with his new strength that he now prized.

"Of course, if it's time for one of the boys to shift, you'll be expected to join them," John continued. "You won't have to be concerned about anyone outside of the pack seeing you. We travel farther south to the forest beyond where no human lives. There are mountains, streams, and meadows to run through, so you'll get plenty of exercise and fair game."

The smile weakened and the corners of Darren's lips turned down at the thought of shifting. The concept was still foreign to him. How could a man shift into a beast? He had no doubt that John would teach him everything he needed to know. So far, the alpha did not appear to be the harsh headmaster that he might have expected. It was clear that he could administer a firm hand if needed, but there was nothing malicious in the way he talked or instructed Darren. Thus far, he seemed to be the caring mentor that Bartholomew promised.

"We have twelve other boys here who are learning just as you are. They have been loup-garou for only a few years or less. My son, Bart, is their beta. We have others who are still in training, but they have their own betas and reside all over the province. They are just a short distance away and join us for our runs, just as we join in theirs on occasion. We have enough loups-garous in our pack that we meet almost every night of the month. Our bunch do not go with them all the time, unless our shift nights coincide. We do this to avoid excessive conflicts between members. Though, it is always better that a wolf run with his pack." John looked to his future pupil and grinned. "You will never be alone here, Darren. I can assure you of that."

Darren's head swam with the idea that there were so many other werewolves – loups-garous as John called them. Bartholomew had talked of betas and alphas, but he never imagined that there would be multiple betas within the same pack. If there were so many, why hadn't he sensed them earlier? Perhaps they were all in the villages, just as Bartholomew had been. Perhaps some of them lived in these immaculate homes and could become part of society like any other normal citizen. If that were the case, it was no wonder that he couldn't find them.

"Let's get you cleaned up and in a fresh set of clothes. Evangeline will help you. She only speaks French, but it seems you have no difficulties with the language." John walked Darren to the open doors and gestured for him to precede. "Then I'll have Noelle bring you a meal. I'm sure you're still hungry after that lamb."

For the first time, Darren took the lead and walked into the foyer ahead of John. The sound of tramping feet and the turning of book pages added to the full effect of the home's ambiance. The smells of cooking meat intensified, along with the usual scents of hardwood floors, patterned wallpaper, and an assortment of artistic decorations such as paintings and crafted sculptures perched upon table tops and pedestals along the walls.

It was nothing like what he expected. Then again, nothing had been. Down the foyer lined with doors that led into multiple rooms on either side, he could hear them brimming with life and activity. A hush fell over the house as he entered and the pattering feet fled to the doors. One by one, heads poked through to investigate their new visitor.

Eyes of every color focused upon him, all full of questions and curiosity, just as he was. Some wrinkled their noses, probably repulsed by his stench. Their faces were unique, but he knew they all had one thing in common. They were all loups-garous.

"Go back to your studies, boys," John ordered. "You can meet him later."

Without question, they turned away and retreated to the rooms, which must have been libraries or sitting rooms. He could hear their whispered questions and gossiping about Darren's shabby rags, but his attention was diverted elsewhere.

The sharp rap of heels on hardwood approached, bringing with it the sweet scent of lavender. A young woman dressed in the usual gown of a servant entered from a corridor at the far end of the hall, from where the delicious aroma of food originated.

She looked up from the tray she carried, laden down with porcelain cups of steeping tea and a pot to match. Green eyes met his and her thin lips parted in a gasp. All in seemingly one move, she let go of her tray and John sped forward to catch it. He covered the distance of more than a few yards in less time than it took to blink, just to save the tea.

The servant let out a string of exclamations in French of which Darren didn't even understand the translation. He knew the common language, but curses had been conveniently left out of his education. Then she turned her wrath upon John.

"Why did you let this boy come in the house with his filthy bare feet when you know I already cleaned the floors this morning?" she cried, stamping her heel like a cross housewife.

John chuckled, but did not offer her back the tray. "Evangeline, this is Darren Dubose. Since you clean so well, I thought you could take him to the washroom and scrub him down."

Darren swallowed hard and felt his stomach quiver with anxiety. The lady that was to strip him down and wash him was certainly beautiful. Though his experience with women was limited, he was sure there were no girls like Evangeline in Warminster. He also noticed, with a kind of wonder, that she was not a werewolf as the others were. She was purely human, if his senses did not lie.

The servant looked from John to Darren and made a face as if she were to dread the task of cleaning up the wreck of a man who stood on her pristine floors. "Very well. Allons-y," she said as she turned back down the corridor from which she had come.

John jerked his head toward the fleeing Evangeline and Darren hurried to catch up.

"By the way," John said as they passed one another, "she's married to my son."

Darren wasn't so impulsive to try and steal another man's wife, especially when that man was a beta. Bartholomew said that betas were sometimes the strongest and most capable of werewolves within a pack. They enforced the rules set down by the alpha and kept unruly pack members in line. Darren wouldn't want to be on bad terms with a beta, especially if he was John's son.

Down the corridor and through several doorways, he and Evangeline silently walked until they came to what resembled something of a room that his old estate used to use for washing clothes. A large tub sat in the center with a pump beside it to dispense water, while the edges of the room were lined with counters and bins of linen and clothes. A door led to the outside where clothes lines stretched from one pole to another to allow laundry to dry.

"Take off your clothes and throw them outside," Evangeline instructed as she set to work on the pump. "There's no saving rags like those."

With apprehension, Darren shed his garments to do as she said. Standing bare in the washroom, shielding his manhood behind shaking hands, Darren tried to look anywhere else but at her. He had heard of the French's loose sense of morality, but he didn't want to think it to be true.

Evangeline filled the tub and tossed in a few slivers of soap. Without a hint of shame, she turned and jerked her thumb toward the water. "All right. Get in."

Just then, Darren heard someone approach down the hall and felt a new spike of tingling in his skull, though the scent told him it wasn't John.

Another man, tall and with a darker complexion, entered the room and looked straight to the stranger. "Who are you?" he asked in French, his dark eyes accusing Darren and his nakedness of some unspoken crime.

Darren stuttered in his presence, both intimidated and too startled by the strange scene to give an answer.

Evangeline rolled her eyes and propped her hands on her full hips. "Bart, this is Darren. He just arrived with your father. The boy looks like he's been through hell, don't you think?"

The man, Bart, eased back and the tension in his body seemed to lessen. So, this was the beta. He was not as finely dressed as his father, but Bart did not carry himself like a commoner either. Like the loups-garous on the other side of the house, he wore a pair of trousers and a loose tunic with billowy sleeves that still showcased his robust physique.

"You're one of our new loups-garous?" Bart asked.

Darren simply nodded, the ends of his matted hair jiggling with the motion and dislodging a few granules of dirt from his locks to fall to the floor.

"Very well," the beta said with a nod. "I knew a stranger was here and I wanted to make certain you were all right, mon chéri." Now, he addressed his wife, who strutted toward him and planted a long and meaningful kiss upon his lips.

Darren suddenly coveted their happiness. Perhaps not Evangeline, though. He was certain beyond the shadow of a doubt that Bart could turn his skull to dust between those two powerful hands, if he caught him philandering with his wife.

"I am fine, mon amour. Did John bring you and the boys your tea?"

They continued light conversation while Darren stood, shivering and naked by the back door. He wasn't sure whether to hop in the wash basin so that he would be somewhat concealed under the water, or perhaps step outside to allow them a moment of privacy.

The answer came when Evangeline looked to him and pointed to the tub again. "I told you that you could get in."

He didn't waste time in dunking his lower half under the water. Evangeline bid her lover goodbye and set to rolling up her sleeves. Bart gave one last look to Darren, his eyes passing along a cautionary message to not displease his wife, and then disappeared down the hall.

"I assure you, I can bathe myself," Darren said as he saw Evangeline take a wash cloth and soap bar in her hands.

He had said it in French, but she didn't seem to hear him at all. She proceeded to wash and scrub away the dirt from three weeks of travel. Washed away the many miles he conquered to get from England to this chateau. Darren ignored the way her fingers felt on his skin. The first time a woman had ever touched him besides his mother, and even then, she never touched him in all the places Evangeline did.

After his face had turned beet-red with embarrassment, she pulled out a few cloths for him to dry himself, and a change of clothes similar to what the others wore.

"These belong to my husband, but they might fit. John will have better clothes made for you soon, I'm sure."

With that, she dried her own hands and left the washroom, as if she hadn't just toyed with Darren's manhood both physically and mentally. The water was tainted a deep brown and the bottom was now covered in a thick layer of soil. The tiny bugs that had taken residence in his hair floated along the smooth surface, their thin legs kicking at the water.

Darren jumped out, spilling some excess water over the edge to seep between the floorboards. Not only had a thousand miles been washed away in mere moments, but it felt as if the old life had been wiped away as well. He was in a new place, a new home, and with a new group of people he could trust and rely upon.

Dirt, mud, and bugs were not the only things left in that tub. The old Darren, the memory of the sickly child without a father, had drifted to the bottom with the rest of the reminders of his journey. What emerged was the reborn Darren. This new Darren, was loup-garou.

Darren found John on the back veranda, his cane positioned in front of him as if he were the king, surveying the far reaches of his kingdom with a chest full of pride and heart gladdened at the sight of it. He could see why. The late afternoon sun caressed the fields before him, trees and flora dispersed in patches as far as the eye could see. The chateau was situated atop the crest of a gently sloping hill, the highest point where one could gaze for miles and miles. He could just barely make out the obstacle courses that John spoke of, hidden amongst the elms and oaks.

They stood beside one another on the civilized side of the stone banister that divided them from the wild nature beyond. Neither spoke at first, but simply took in the sight of such wondrous beauty. Darren could feel the feral side of him stirring within his chest. Inducing him with the need to run into the midst of it and become one with the forest he had despised for the last few weeks. Why now, of all times, might he actually want to be part of it, rather than before?

The dark brown in his eyes morphed into the bright amber once more and he tried to keep his breath steady as the tide of such desires nearly carried him away. It was John's touch that brought him back to the world of man.

Darren looked away and cleared his throat, unsure why he might be embarrassed to show such emotions in front of the alpha. His alpha.

"It's splendid, isn't it?" John said as he kept his firm and grounding hand upon Darren's arm.

"It is... Was it the..." He began the question, but was unsure of how to end it.

"Yes, it was the wolf in you," John answered. "Many boys who come here have never been outside of their towns. They've never seen the world that is open to them and every other loup-garou. Each one reacted in the same way you did and there is no shame in it."

Slowly, he looked back toward his alpha, his eyes still glowing their wolfish gold. John gave him a warm, encouraging smile and let go. "My wife and I came to this place after we fled England. Her uncle, who was also loup-garou, taught me all that he knew. He still resides in Albi, but I wanted to create a place for new loups-garous to come and be free from the constraints of town living."

John turned his eyes back to the fields. "When I changed as a young man, I didn't know what had happened to me. I, like so many who have come here, did not have a father to explain these things to me. I wandered all across England for a century with the idea stuck in my head that I was possessed by a demon. It took my wife, Annalette, to show me that I was not possessed, but blessed.

"She told me all about loups-garous. In fact, it was Bartholomew who told me that her uncle was in Albi. I named my son in his honor." John turned to face Darren as he continued. "Our world is becoming smaller and smaller with each passing year. Discoveries are made, countries are expanding their borders with colonies, and yet superstitions still wreak havoc in our communities. I wanted to create a safe place where loups-garous could come and learn what their families could not teach them. I assume this is why you're here and why Bartholomew sent you to me."

Darren nodded, entranced by his story. "My father left my mother when I was too young to even know his name. I had always thought werewolves or loups-garous were the stuff of fairytales."

John's smile never wavered. "There are still many fairytales in the world, but you will learn that some of them are more true than others... Your situation is not new, Darren. It is the sad misfortune that some loups-garous fathers are no better than human fathers. Here, we can't change the past, but we can make a better future for you."

It was a touching sentiment, a glorious dream to pursue. Darren needed exactly what John offered. After the hell he had been through in England, he could get used to a little piece of heaven, such as this.

CHAPTER 7

For the first few days after Darren arrived at the chateau, John kept him confined indoors to rest from his long journey. When the rest of the pack was away, training in the valley behind the house, tending the gardens in the front, or running as wolves through the night, Darren kept to himself in the library and devoured book after book on all manner of subjects: philosophy, mathematics, history, and the newest publications in scientific developments.

He found that he could read much faster than before, comprehending everything he read with a startlingly accurate recall of all he learned. These studies were reserved for the boys who lacked the kind of education that he did, but that didn't stop Darren from working his way from one bookcase to the other, pouring over the manuscripts with zeal.

When Darren asked John how it could be that they were able to retain so much knowledge without the aid of study, John only told him that it was one of the many gifts of the wolf. Their minds could hold an infinite wealth of information. Darren thought this was perhaps the best advantage of being loup-garou, apart from the strength and preternatural abilities.

When the others were inside, taking a meal or settling down to their studies, Darren became acquainted with each of them and their personal stories. Though he left out many of the details of how his own journey as a loup-garou began, the other boys were more than willing to divulge the gruesome specifics of their turnings.

An aspect, he noticed, was that there were no female werewolves at the chateau. There were only two women, Evangeline and Noelle, who cooked and cleaned for the pack. However, they were the only humans on the estate. When Darren asked John about this, he informed him with a heavy heart that there were no female loups-garous in the world and there never could be. He explained how their fragile frames and gentle temperaments could not contain the spirit of the wolf with the same effectiveness that men could.

Darren did not believe this, because Evangeline had more fire in her than some of the younger boys put together. And Noelle, a hefty woman of color, could carry three or four baskets of dirty clothes without breaking a sweat. The female sex certainly was strong enough to be loup-garou, but John warned him to never try and turn a woman by way of the bite, which was a lesson for another day.

One boy named Edmund, who seemed to possess a certain edge that unsettled Darren, had turned while visiting family in Italy. He, too, was from England and could never return, lest he be charged with the murder of his mother and grandparents. The way he retold the tale, Darren saw no remorse in his eyes. Either he found pleasure in the suffering of others, or he had come to terms with his demons long ago and decided not to waste any more time feeling sorry for his actions. Darren doubted it was the latter.

Another boy, Fermin, who was a native to France, seemed to be a natural leader and John often spoke as if he might become an alpha one day, or perhaps a beta for one of the other factions within the pack. From the stories Darren overheard, he was the first to lead in running the course and at the head of every run they went on as wolves.

Though he could admire Fermin's passion for leadership, he still lacked a quality that Darren thought was more than necessary. In fact, it should have been a requirement. Compassion. Fermin was the best in everything, but he would not help those who struggled like Johannes, a loup-garou from Germany.

Johannes was smaller than the rest in height, but Darren knew he was strong enough to take the lead if he just had the right encouragement. Because of this, Darren often made a point of sitting with Johannes during meals and they shared one another's language with the other. He knew no French and he knew no German. Yet, within the few days, they could switch back and forth fluidly. No one had offered to teach him French in the short time he had been there, but John and Bart instructed him in German to accommodate.

Johannes had been an orphan on the streets of Amsterdam, without mother or father or relatives to care for him. He ran with other orphan boys, much like a wolf pack would, but he was the runt, and bullied because of it. When he turned, he fled the city in the same way Darren had. They shared many common traits, but the difference between them was the fact that Johannes hadn't learned to rise up with his new gifts. He stayed low, meek, and unoffending, just as he had as a street urchin. Darren wanted to change that.

The more he socialized and talked with the others, the more Darren began to abandon his preconceived notions of what a werewolf was. He didn't even call them that anymore. They were loup-garou and, somehow, calling himself this new name added another facet to his character. There were too many ties to the term "werewolf" and too many negative perceptions of its meaning. Loup-garou was new, fresh, different, and seemingly harmless.

So, too, did the image of the loup-garou become. He hadn't seen them yet, in their true form, but he knew he would soon. From what Bart and John briefly described, they sounded nothing like the horrific and vicious beasts of legend, but some mythical blend of man and wolf. John often said the loup-garou form was a symbol of the perfect harmony in nature. His wife, Annalette, whose name was spoken in reverent whispers as if she were a holy saint, taught him to appreciate everything a loup-garou was and could be.

On the night before Darren was expected to join the others in training, he found himself restless and eager. Lying awake in the dormitory where his other pack mates slept in beds resembling military bunks that lined the walls, Darren could not sleep. Johannes insisted that he try, though, because the trials that came with dawn would demand it of him.

Darren did not heed his warning.

When the sun rose, Darren was the first to rise, even before Fermin. The pack took breakfast in the dining hall and Darren was given the seat of honor beside John near the head of the long banquet table that should have belonged in a palace, rather than a humble chateau. Some boys, including Johannes, were sequestered at a round table in the corner. Darren usually sat with Johannes at this lesser table, but not this morning.

Across from him sat Bart, the beta. They discussed the plans for the day and how each morning's routine would become ingrained in him after some time. It was a pattern of living that John wished to foster in every loup-garou. Part of the day was devoted to calming one's mind, which took the form of gardening that Darren looked forward to. Then, there was the physical exercise that would keep his body fit. The evenings were devoted to study and sharpening that calm mind. Then at night, if the rest of the pack was willing and the opportunity was available, they would take to the woods as loups-garous and shift with the rest of the pack.

That night was Fermin's time to shift. Darren paused, his fork stopping halfway between his plate and his mouth. The library, the obstacle course, the fellowship with other loups-garous, the garden, it was all something he could enjoy day to day without growing bored. The shift, however, was another thing entirely.

For most of the boys, they remembered nothing about the shift except the pain and passing out from exhaustion. Darren remembered on the night he had arrived, going to bed in a practically empty house while the rest of the pack went out. When they came back with the dawn, John allowed them to sleep for a few hours before resuming their daily routine. In real life, they would have no time to recuperate. With families and jobs, they would have to recover quickly after a shift night.

What bothered Darren the most wasn't that the pack was going to go shift, but that he didn't know how to shift at all. Neither did he want to. The thought of fur sprouting from his skin and face extending into a muzzle was far less than appealing. If he could have just stayed human, Darren would have gladly gone with them. Perhaps, since Darren didn't have much training, they would reconsider making him go.

After breakfast, they went to the gardens and Darren somehow felt in his element. Some of the others had come from farming backgrounds, just as he did, but they only understood planting and cultivating crops. They didn't understand that weeds were the enemy of the flowerbeds and pruning was necessary for growth.

He gave advice where it was needed, especially to Johannes who had a nasty habit of pulling up the flowers with the weeds. Sometimes, he couldn't quite tell the difference. He showed him how some weeds only needed a gentle tug, while others needed to be pried up from the roots. John told them pulling weeds would help in controlling their strength and mastering it on a finer level. Loups-garous like Fermin and Edmund snapped the stalks of the weeds too quickly, applying too much force.

When it came time to practice their agility and speed, they took to the valley behind the chateau. Fermin boasted that he was the fastest of the pack, but Darren had seen the way Johannes snatched the last slice of roast from the communal plate during meals. Fermin was not the fastest at all.

"Why don't you show them what you can do?" Darren asked, jamming his elbow into Johannes' ribs.

The boy, whom they teased and called the "omega" from time to time, simply shrugged. "I don't want to make Bart mad."

Darren glanced ahead to the beta who led the boys down the worn path through the forest to the training ground. "Why would Bart be angry?" he asked, keeping his voice low so the beta wouldn't hear. Against John's wishes, many of the boys kept their conversations private by dropping their voices so low that not even his alpha ears could pick up the words from across the room.

"He doesn't like it when we break rank. He may be the beta, but Fermin has his eyes set on becoming an alpha one day. Bart doesn't want any of us to try and take that title from him. It doesn't make for good pack dynamics to try and compete."

"John is still alpha, though. That can never be taken from him."

Bart glanced over his shoulder to check on the boys, then turned his eyes forward again.

Johannes walked a little closer, his blue eyes nervously watching the superiors. "There can still be squabbles among the mid-rankings like us, but like I said, Bart doesn't want us to fight. Don't upset the balance."

It didn't seem right to Darren. It was a poor excuse for making Johannes feel like he couldn't rise above, like an omega could never become an alpha, and it didn't settle with his wolf. He knew this because it made him squirm without quite understanding why.

There were still many things he didn't understand about being a loup-garou, but the one thing he could grasp was that his emotions and mind were not entirely his own anymore. The wolf spirit in him, which John referred to often, had a soul of its own. It was complete with everything it needed to be a conscious, living entity within each loup-garou. It had feelings, instincts, desires, and those things should never be ignored.

They arrived in a meadow of rich grass that rippled like a green sea blown every which way by tempest winds. On the opposite side, nearly half a mile away, was their target. A stuffed sack that was once used for holding flour, suspended from a low-lying branch by rope. He had watched this game from the back veranda at the chateau. The boys would run and touch the sack, then run back. It was simple enough, but much harder in practice.

They all took turns, running forward and running back. Edmund and Fermin, of course, were able to touch the sack without plowing straight through it or missing their target completely in the mad dash. Some skittered to a stop too soon, undershooting so they wouldn't collide with the sack. Others completely disappeared in the woods beyond the sack altogether.

When Darren's turn came, he made sure not to go at top speed. He touched the sack successfully because he could see where he was going, and came back only to receive an unexpected blow from his beta.

Bart struck him across the chest and sent him flat on his back. Darren caught his breath and looked up into his dark, glaring eyes.

"You did not do what I asked. You run your fastest and that was not it. The goal is precision. Do it again."

Darren was certain something in his chest had cracked, a bone perhaps. Yet, he stood and shook off the pain, knowing that if the rest saw his weakness, they would remind him of it later. He ran as fast as his legs could carry him, the same way he ran that first morning in Longleat Forest before he realized the kind of abilities he had been endowed with.

Just as before, he crashed into a tree and splintered the wood. Bits of bark fell around the protruding roots and Darren staggered away to recover. He heard them snicker, but he ran back anyway, a failure in their eyes. For now.

Johannes was next and he ran, but not as fast as Darren knew he could. Yet, he didn't call Bart's attention to it, lest his friend receive the same beating that he did. If Bart thought Johannes could move faster, he would be yelled at for deceiving his beta all this time.

They did this for what seemed like hours, running back and forth in turns. None of them tired, though. Their stamina proved to be remarkable and if Bart had his way, they would do this well into the evening without break until every single loup-garou could run and touch that bag without fail. Yet, even some of the boys who had been doing this almost every day for months, hadn't quite figured out how to stop with such accuracy.

Despite his previous offense, Bart proved to be a competent teacher. Some of his instructions made the difference between Darren crashing into trees and crashing into the target sack itself.

If he made a mistake in the next exercise, however, it would be far less forgiving than the tough bark. For the next drill, the boys were to climb the trees and jump from branch to branch at least twenty feet off the forest floor.

It was clear as soon as Bart ordered them up, that many of the boys loved this training and treated it much like a game. Darren, however, did not. He had never climbed a tree in his life, nor was he ever given a chance. He had missed out on the playful adventures of childhood in exchange for a sickbed.

Darren stood at the base of the tree and looked up to the first branch that was well out of his reach. The others were already scaling up into the canopy, but he couldn't find a way to even begin.

"Darren!" Bart barked. "Are you waiting for an invitation from the tree?"

The boys tittered in the same way they did when Bart had struck him earlier in training.

"I... I don't know how."

In an instant, Johannes leapt from the tree he had claimed and came to Darren's side. "I'll help him, monsieur."

Bart accepted this and turned his attention away for the moment. Johannes took Darren's hands and without a word, pressured his thumbs into his palms. Darren winced at the sudden pain and watched in amazement as the second manifestation of his curse became visible.

Sharp talons, a deep and grisly brown shade, grew in place where his fingernails once had been, extending from his fingers as if being drawn from their sheath by the force of Johannes's touch.

"You'll learn to make them appear on their own after a while, but this will get you up the tree for now. Just latch on and get up that way. The wolf will take over the rest."

When he was done with the second hand, he left a stunned Darren to scurry up his tree once more with his own set of claws. Darren wasted a little too much time marveling at his claws before Bart yelled at him again.

He didn't understand how a wolf would know how to climb when Darren didn't. Wolves didn't dwell in trees, but in dens beneath the earth. Following Johannes' instructions, he reached up and dug his claws into the trunk and pulled with all the strength he could. The nails did not bend or break against his weight, but only pulled and strained against his fingers and the tiny bones that he relied on to climb higher.

He propped his feet against the trunk and climbed, first with one hand reaching up, and then the other. Sure enough, just as Johannes said, his wild instincts took over and with each foot of tree he scaled, it became easier, more natural.

He came to his first branch and the others were already far ahead of him, jumping and leaping from one tree to another. His footing wasn't sure and his sense of balance wanted to fail him, but one look down told him that he couldn't miss his mark. The fall alone could break his body, but how well could he heal from a fall like that?

Darren aimed for a closer tree and jumped. Just barely, he grabbed the limb and pulled himself up, but that wasn't how the other boys were doing it. They were jumping from one branch to the other as if they were hopping across river stones. Some, like Fermin, didn't even crouch before a leap and seemed to be running through the forest up in the air.

It was slow, terrifying work, but Darren got to the point where he could jump and not feel the need to regain his balance. All the while, he wondered what any of this had to do with being a loup-garou. At what time would any of these skills become useful? The gardening and the shifting he could understand, but this was a new level of ludicrous that he couldn't comprehend.

In the treetops, far behind the others and unable to keep up, Johannes doubled-back to join Darren.

"You have to go faster," he said.

"I know," Darren grumbled. "This is harder than it looks."

Johannes jumped to his branch and it bounced with the added weight. "Don't think too much about it. If you take time to think, you lose ground."

"How does Bart expect everyone to go at the same pace?" he complained, watching the beta keep up with the others from the forest floor.

"The pack is only as slow as its slowest member," Johannes explained. "If you are running from hunters, you have to know how to keep up with the rest, so we all survive."

Darren's brows furrowed. "Hunters?"

Johannes shivered and nodded. "Yes, they're humans who seek out our kind to kill them. I've never seen one, but the others say that they're monstrous, hateful men. They live their lives believing the stories their ancestors have told and they hunt us, thinking that they're doing the world a service by exterminating loups-garous."

They sounded terrible, indeed. Yet, how many other types of men did the same to their fellow humans? Wars were a prime example that men had the hearts of devils. How much worse could a hunter be than a man who sought revenge?

The creaking of branches and taunting of the boys faded ahead, many of them vanishing behind leaves. Darren couldn't even spot Bart's gleaming white shirt on the woodland path. They had fallen so far behind that it seemed no one remembered they were there. Would it be so in a harried escape from hunters or a rival pack? Would Darren fall behind just as easily and be forgotten?

Beside him, Johannes swayed a bit, his blonde hair tossed in the breeze that made the leaves around them quiver.

"Are you all right?" Darren asked.

Johannes snapped to attention and nodded. "Yes. I am fine. I'm just hungry."

A defiant idea that would satisfy them both entered Darren's mind and he jerked his chin to the forest path. "Let's go get you some food, then."

"It's a long walk back to the chateau."

"No," Darren said. "I mean, let's try to hunt for something. Something small, of course. Just for you."

Johannes looked to him with a mix of excitement and apprehension in his eyes. "We need to try and stay with the others."

"You can't stay with the others if you're starving and don't have the energy to continue."

Darren's logic seemed to break through the rigid rules and structure that John's institution had ingrained in him. His friend gave a quick nod and together, they hopped down onto a soft bed of leaves alongside the path.

They waited a little longer until the rest of the pack was gone, and then set off on their hunt to find food. Darren had plenty of experience hunting small game after spending three weeks in the wilderness, but no matter how hard he looked for the signs in the earth, he couldn't find the trail of a rabbit, a fox, or even a snake. It was as if all the other animals had sworn off this piece of land, knowing it was inhabited by predators.

Perhaps the forest took pity on Johannes, because they did find something much better than a hare. When they came upon a stream some distance from the path, Darren grabbed Johannes and held him still, his gaze fixed across the water.

There, lapping up water and her legs spread wide to help crane her neck down, was a doe, unaccompanied by a fawn or buck. Darren took a quick survey of the area, smelling and watching for any other signs that the doe was not alone. None. She was free to take.

In a move that he didn't expect, Darren summoned forth his wolf, asking it to help him catch his prey. He hadn't done anything like it in the entire month that he had been a loup-garou. His eyes turned golden, muscles tensed, and claws extended on their own without persuasion.

Johannes whispered something, but Darren wasn't paying attention any longer. He rushed forward with blinding speed, leapt straight over the creek and pounced upon the deer. She didn't even have time to raise her head from the surface of the water before his claws and fangs sunk deep into her neck.

Blood spilled out and drenched the front of his shirt as it ran over his lips and chin. The doe's fur scratched at his face, nearly rubbing it raw as she struggled to get free. Darren wrestled it to the ground and pinned it there, all four hooves kicking wildly at her assailant. Her feeble cries for help were too short and too raspy to be heard by any other creature around. Within just a few moments, it was over and the doe lay lifeless beneath him.

Johannes rushed to the stream's edge and tried to cross it as Darren had, but his jump came short and the hem of his pants were dampened by the slow-moving water.

Darren straightened and looked to his hand, shaking and dripping with the bright red blood of his quarry. The boundary between man and beast had been crossed and Darren thought he would exult in it. He did not. He might have caught a meal for Johannes, but what was he given in return? A racing heart and a mind that couldn't comprehend or cope with the thoughts that he had when he had taken down the prey.

In the moment, he had gloried in the kill, wanted to snuff out the life of that animal like it was fate and his hands were the procurers of it. That deer would have been hunted down one way or another, but Darren had to be the one to kill it. That's what his wolf believed, what it wanted his human side to believe as well.

Yet, for the first time, he truly became horrified and disgusted with what he had become. He wasn't just a man with golden eyes and claws, or a boy who could run fast and throw boulders across rivers. He was a beast. A monster whose two halves warred over whether to pity the carcass he straddled over or devour it.

Johannes, his eyes golden as well, dropped to his knees by the belly of the deer and tore into it with little hesitation. Darren staggered away, stepping over the rivers of blood that snaked through the blades of grass to taint the clear water of the stream.

His stomach lurched at the sight of the deer's intestines spilling out in Johannes' hands and the way his friend bit into the flesh, sullying his clothes just as badly as Darren's. He was sure he would never forget such a stench as long as he lived.

Through the haze of trauma, fear, and sensory overload, Darren did detect something new. Another loup-garou was near. In an instant, he appeared by the deer and attacked Johannes. The smaller of the males cowered under his assailant.

When Darren had taken a heartbeat to realize it was Bart who had tackled Johannes. A hideous and frightening roar erupted from the beta's throat and Darren snapped into motion. Without a single thought to his own safety or the fact that this was insubordination of the worst kind, Darren leapt on Bart's back and wrenched him away from Johannes with such force that even he was surprised.

They rolled together, away from the carcass, fangs and claws ripping into immortal flesh in a flurry that lasted little more than a moment or two. Bart pushed Darren off with his feet and sent him tumbling away toward the edge of the creek.

Darren stood and faced him, eyes still blazing gold and the blood of two loups-garous and a doe mixed on his chest and torso. His cuts were beginning to heal already, but the battle wasn't over.

A familiar sensation consumed him, claiming his body in a way that harkened back to that first night when he and Bartholomew were in Longleat Forest. The essence of his savage spirit reached out and lashed at Bart with tempestuous vigor.

Bart stopped and snarled at Darren, his own gold eyes rife with fury.

"How dare you!" he bellowed.

Then, as if two Titans clashed in the heavens, a force stronger than his own pierced through and smacked Darren with such strength that he crumbled to his hands and knees. Once strong and daring, his wolf had stuck its tail between its legs and begged for mercy. Darren unconsciously hunched his shoulders inward, attempting to appear smaller and less threatening to his superior.

Bart charged forward and that unforeseen force that subdued Darren nearly crushed him into blind subservience. Is this a taste of what Bartholomew felt when Darren had treated him so?

The beta gripped the back of Darren's neck and pushed his face into the soil until he could taste it, feel the grains of dirt go up his nostrils, and sting at the edges of his eyelids.

"You will never get in the way of my discipline," Bart growled. "Do you understand?"

No, Darren didn't understand. He didn't understand why Bart would punish Johannes for taking care of himself. He didn't understand why, when Darren was the one to kill the deer, that Bart would go after Johannes instead.

He heard the rest of the pack stir in the trees and watched the scene unfold. Johannes moved from his place by the deer and in a surge of courage which Darren couldn't help but be proud of, the loup-garou spoke up for himself.

"I was hungry and Darren caught the deer for me," he said. "He did nothing wrong."

Bart loosened his grip on Darren's neck, but wouldn't relent as he snapped at his subordinate. "You should not have eaten first. Darren should have taken his fill before you. You are at fault for that, but he defies my authority." He looked to the others as Darren's lungs burned with the need for air. "Let this be a lesson to you all. Honor the order of the pack. If you stray from it, there is only chaos. Those who are stronger and more dominant go first. Those who are weaker go last."

The beta wasn't even upset that Darren and Johannes broke away to go off on their own. He was upset because of the order in which they ate and that Darren tried to defend his friend. As he lay in the dirt, unable to struggle under the weight of Bart's heavy power, all he could think of was how backwards it all seemed. How wrong and unfair it was that loups-garous like Johannes, who could be strong if he chose to, were terrorized unnecessarily.

Darren might have hated what he had become and despised the feral beast within him, but he had to agree with the wolf that this was not the way of the loup-garou.

CHAPTER 8

John could hear the whispers of the boys that trailed behind him and Bart. They simply could not stop themselves from talking about what happened earlier that day at the stream.

Though they thought he would be fooled by their low tones and hushed words, he heard every single one of them. They were not the first boys to try and trick him with their secret conversations and they wouldn't be the last. As an alpha, he heard every utterance from their lips, even those spoken by Darren and Johannes in the far back of the group. He let them believe they could keep their secrets, but he was more than dismayed to hear about the occurrence from them rather than from his own son.

The sun was close to setting now and the French sky came alive with shades of violet, crimson, and deep blues that put all the flowers in his gardens to shame. Man was fortunate to watch a sunrise or sunset, but so much more was the loup-garou who could enjoy it for a thousand lifetimes.

Each evening, almost ritually, John stood on the veranda that overlooked the valley and watched the sunset, so special and unique to that day. In that moment when the light sank below the tree line, he would whisper a good night to his beloved. Annalette had been gone for many years now, leaving him with a son he could be proud of and a legacy of hope for all loups-garous.

He remembered how she insisted that the chateau and the academy was his dream and his alone. John knew better than any that none of it would have been possible without her. If she had never come into his life with her wild soul and

Romani spirit, he would still be in England, ignorant and blind to the truth of what he was.

That was why he led these boys deeper into the forest, toward the rest of the pack that waited at their usual meeting spot. Each of them donned their dark trousers in preparation for the shift night, though those would have to be shed shortly before. Their chests were bare to the evening winds that slivered through the trees, but John did not worry about their health the way Noelle did. Somehow, she expected them to come back with terrible colds during the winter months when they trudged through the snow without shoes. She knew what they were, but had only been employed at the chateau for a little over a year. She was not used to their ways just yet.

John glanced over his shoulder to check on the youngest members of his pack. He spotted Darren's dark shock of hair beside Johannes' blonde and watched how they talked and smiled to one another. The tales that the other boys spun were far more exaggerated. They had to be. At least, John hoped.

"Would you like to tell me what happened in your own words?" John asked his son who walked beside him.

He could hear Bart grinding his teeth together, a sign that told John he did not want to speak, but he would anyway. "There is nothing to tell. They disobeyed and I put them in their place."

John smiled. "Are you too prideful to tell me the rest, or do you think I'd scold you for not keeping them all together in the first place?" When Bart didn't reply, he continued. "I don't mind the boys running off to catch their own game every once and a while, especially if they're hungry. I don't intend to starve them."

"It wasn't just that," Bart replied. He turned his dark eyes to look upon his father, the eyes that so resembled his mother's, and there was a hint of concern in the way his brows tilted. "Darren... he has dominance."

John quickly looked back to the boys once more and Darren met his gaze for a fleeting second before he turned back to Bart. "You know this for certain?"

His son nodded.

"How was it?" John asked, intrigued and partly thrilled by the aspect of having a true potential alpha in his pack. Fermin certainly had the qualities of an alpha, but he had not shown the dominant trait yet. He was still a follower, trailing after Bart or John. He had the better likelihood of becoming a beta than an alpha, unless he began to show other signs.

"It was untamed, unrefined. He slung it at me with barely any control or precision. But, the power was still there. It took a bit for me to bring myself to fight back."

"Darren has only been a loup-garou for less than a month," John remarked. "It seems almost impossible that he would know how to summon such strength so soon."

"What's more is that when he caught the deer, he took no part of it. After he killed it, he just let Johannes take what he wanted."

John narrowed his eyes upon Bart. "No," he denied, stricken by the queerness of it all.

"Truly. He just stood there. I think he was in shock. I saw him take the kill and it was... for lack of a better term, beautiful. It was perfect. Some of the other boys struggle to catch rabbits without tripping all over themselves like newborn pups."

"He did have to survive on his own for three weeks. Perhaps he learned to hunt then," John offered. He was perplexed by the notion that this new loup-garou could have the spark of dominance great enough to send his son, a seasoned beta, scrambling for control.

What was more disturbing was Darren's lack of selfishness. If his wolf was in control when he took the kill and he has the dominance of an alpha, he would have denied his friend to even get near the carcass before he took a share for himself. Yet, he let Johannes have first pick. It didn't make any sense.

He didn't have much time to think, because a skitter of tension made its way from the very back of the line, right up to John and he froze in place. No others would feel that change because they did not have his experience, but he knew what was about to happen.

The rest of the boys stopped with him and he looked to Fermin, whose night it was to shift. He showed no signs yet, nothing but the usual nervousness that came with knowing what was to come.

No, it wasn't Fermin who was about to shift.

He looked to Darren and saw his face contort with discomfort. John wedged his way through the group of boys, parting them like Moses parted the Red Sea. Bart stayed close behind him just as Darren let out the first groan and nearly crumbled to his knees.

Johannes helped him to the ground when John came to him.

"Darren, look at me," he said, taking the youth by the shoulders. The young loup-garou looked up, his eyes glowing gold in the waning light. "Just relax and let it happen. The more you tense, the more you'll suffer and the longer it will take. Do you understand?"

He nodded as the first wave came and he cried out. The rest of the boys behind him shuddered and backed away from the scene.

"Bart," he ordered, "start the shift in the rest. We'll have to shift a little earlier than expected."

It was unorthodox, considering that the sun's light hadn't fully dissipated yet. They still had a few miles to go until they reached the meeting place, but if they could all cooperate, they could reach there in time to join the rest of the pack.

Bart nodded and turned to face the boys, who knew what would happen next. One by one, he went through the ranks and squeezed that tender part of their shoulder to induce the shift as they took off their pants to stand naked on the path. Annalette had shown John this trick even before they arrived in France to seek out her uncle.

When the loup-garou couldn't shift at will, they could be forced by finding that special nerve around the meaty part of their shoulder where their neck began to slope down. It was painful, but not any more painful than a willing shift.

That was how John knew the boys were ready to move on from the chateau, when they could shift at will. It took years sometimes, but once in a while he would come across a prodigy who could master it more quickly than others.

"Johannes, go to Bart."

The German loup-garou nodded and left his friend in the capable hands of the alpha.

Darren let out an agonized scream as his bones and joints began to pop out of place. John stayed by him, serving as a constant presence to assure him. This would have been his second shift and it wasn't until perhaps the one hundredth before the typical fear and uncertainty would subside.

The other boys began to voice their own torment, their screams segueing into roars and growls. He could see Darren's eyes go wide as he beheld the sight of his first loup-garou turning. John faced away from the scene. It was nothing new to him, but the sight of so many dark fur pelts and massive wolf heads with their gnashing teeth would have sent any mortal man running.

Darren watched them morph and John could almost see their reflection in the youth's eyes. The human bodies grew nearly twice their size, fur sprouting from their skin, becoming that perfect combination of man and beast. Muzzles extended from their faces, becoming long and pointed like a wolf's, their hands growing rough pads along their palms and tails lengthening from the bottom of their spines to dust the forest floor.

The display was almost enough to distract him from his own pain, from the truth that he was about to become what he saw. John brought him back to focus with a tiny pulse of dominance that made the boy shiver.

"Just relax, remember. Everything is going to be all right."

Sometimes, that's all the encouragement they needed. Sometimes, it wasn't enough. Darren did not look convinced, but he did relax as John commanded and the fearful tears spilled down his cheeks as the shift took its final hold.

Darren changed in front of John, ripping the pants he had neglected to take off. While the youth was in the throes of his agony, John slipped off his own pants and shifted. The boy was fresh, unbroken, and with his reputed dominance, he would not take orders in his loup-garou form easily.

Just like with all the others, John would have to break Darren like a man broke a wild stallion. He had learned this hard reality the first time he took a pupil. He ran wild and savage, without discipline or regard for any other living creature. He killed without mercy and John had to clean up the mess.

The boys were not conscious of their condition as the wolf took over, meaning they would have no logic beyond what the wolf wanted. Breaking was the only way to bridge the gap and give back a piece of their human soul. It would not restore their consciousness, but they would obey their alpha. Only after decades of discipline, would the two minds meld to share a consciousness during the shift.

John shifted and stood tall as the other boys followed Bart toward the meeting ground. The alpha's fur bristled as Darren opened his golden loup-garou eyes and snarled at the stranger in front of him. His fur, black as the night that was closing in around them, stood on end as his lips curled up over his fangs and snapped at John.

His fur may have been a little lighter, denoting his age, but John was ready to give Darren a thrashing that his wolf would never forget.

It had been a week since Darren first joined the rest of the pack, but there was still a part of him that didn't feel quite right. He remembered turning for the second time, but that time seemed so drastically different than the first. When Darren turned that night in Longleat Forest, he didn't know what was happening. He thought he was dying. When he awoke, the idea that he had turned into a beast was the last thing on his mind.

The second time, on their way to meet with the rest of John's expansive pack, Darren was well aware of the harsh reality of what he had become. He saw the other boys shift into dark beasts of the night, saliva dripping from their muzzles and eyes rolling inside their wolfish heads.

After a certain point in the pain, it all went black, but he didn't need to be conscious to know what happened to him. He turned into one of them. He had turned into a loup-garou. When dawn came, it brought a whole new level of soreness and aches that he hadn't experienced in his first shift.

Not only that, but something was different in his wolf. It no longer yearned to rebel against Bart or John, but seemed more docile, more meek, and submissive to their whims and orders. In the days following, Darren didn't question when Bart told him to do something. He didn't second guess John's intentions for a certain test or exercise.

One thing Darren did understand was that there was no fear in the wolf when he obeyed. Only a kind of respect for his beta and alpha. He gladly did as he was told because it was his way of honoring them.

Darren fought it in the small ways by staying awake an hour past curfew, or slacking off during training when he knew he could do better. Sometimes, he didn't put so much work into pulling the weeds and trimming the garden as he had before.

His friendship with Johannes hadn't faltered, but some of the other boys began to flock to him, especially after the incident at the stream.

It was one night, when the moon was high in the sky already and its blue and silver rays slanted through the tall windows of their communal dormitory, that Darren received a harsh shake in his top bunk. He jolted awake and rolled over to see two pairs of eyes watching him.

Fermin and Edmund gripped the edge of his thin mattress and stood on their tiptoes on the bunk below, Johannes's bunk.

"Darren, come with us," Fermin invited.

He rubbed the sleep from his eyes as Edmund clarified, "We're going out to try and shift. Come with us."

They were insane. Not only because it was the middle of the night, and they could never leave the chateau without someone noticing they were gone. Who in their right mind would want to shift at will? Darren was well aware that it was the key to leaving the chateau and returning to the outside world of humans, but he was far from interested in such a concept at this point.

"You're daft," Darren grumbled as he readjusted his feather pillow. "Go back to bed."

"So, that's a no?" Fermin asked, a note of dejection in his voice.

It had become clearer with each day that Fermin was slowly losing popularity amongst the others. Darren was the new favorite, both with John and the rest. He retained his place of honor near the head of the table and everyone worked to mimic the newest member of their pack. Perhaps Fermin wanted to claw his way back to the top by associating more and more with Darren, rather than putting him down, as he knew jealous men would do.

Why everyone seemed to admire him that much more, Darren might never know. As far as he knew, he had done nothing special, nothing unique or praiseworthy since he arrived. Yet they flocked to him anyway.

"That's a no." With that, he rolled over to turn his back to the two and tried to fall asleep. It was in vain.

He listened to them sneak out of the dormitory, past all the bunks full of sleeping loups-garous and down the hall that led to the foyer and dining hall beyond. John and Bart's chambers were on the other side of the chateau, but they would surely hear the front door open. Then, the two insurgents would be caught and thrown back into the dormitory where the boys would laugh and mock them for trying to sneak out.

Only, that never happened. Even Darren heard the front door creak open and the two boys slip onto the front landing to skip down the stairs and toward the front gardens.

Darren couldn't believe it, nor could he allow it. The gentle prodding of his wolf assured him that he needed to go after them. Perhaps not to join in their efforts, but to ensure their safety or convince them to return. John should have been the one to bring them back, but if John wouldn't, then he would.

Being careful not to make so much as a whisper of sound, Darren followed their paths and found his way outside into the night air. He wore nothing but his warm sleeping shirt and a pair of knickers to fight off the cold as he tracked down their scents. It didn't take him long to realize they had rounded the chateau and escaped toward the forest and the training grounds.

When he came upon them in the meadow where they practiced their precision running, he saw how Fermin watched Edmund as he squeezed his eyes shut, looking more constipated than on the verge of a shift.

"Do you realize how foolish this is?" Darren scolded as a brisk wind snapped at his tunic, pulling it tight against his chest and torso.

Fermin waved him off. "You're going to break his concentration."

Darren came up and shoved both of them in the shoulders. "You need Bart or John here to look after you. Why sneak out?"

Edmund turned to him with flashing green eyes and his strong, English jaw set in a scowl. "Well, you're here aren't you? That's good enough."

Darren didn't have a notion why he would say something like that. "I'm not an alpha or a beta. You two have been here longer than I have and should know the rules better."

The French loup-garou rolled his eyes. "We all have heard what John says about you. That's why we knew you'd come out here. You're like an alpha just by coming after us, aren't you?"

"Serve and protect, that's what John always says an alpha should do," Edmund added.

Darren didn't want to be an alpha any more than he wanted to be a loup-garou at all, but he had no time to argue. "I didn't come out to protect either of you. I came to bring your miserable hides back. We need to go back to the chateau before someone sees we're missing."

"Too late," a deep voice rumbled from the trees behind them. The wind had been blowing his scent away from Darren's nose, but as soon as it shifted in his favor, he knew Bart was the one who spoke.

He could just barely see the beta's dark skin amongst the shadows as he approached. Fermin and Edmund groaned.

"Did you let him follow you?" Fermin asked, jabbing his finger at the beta as he glared at Darren.

"I didn't know he was following." Darren shrugged.

Bart towered over the three boys and folded his arms over his thick chest. He could easily beat every one of them into the ground if he wanted. He had done it before. Instead, he simply smiled, as if he was amused by their attempts to thwart his authority.

"What were you two thinking?" he asked, pointedly excluding Darren from his accusations.

They explained their endeavor to shift at will, but Bart seemed far from mad. He listened to their rushed excuses and occasionally threw Darren in with them, but he was unfazed by it all. If only Bart were so amiable during the daylight hours, training might not have been so demanding.

When they were finished and left waiting for their punishment, none came. Bart looked to the three of them, then jerked his head toward the forest. "Follow me."

Darren did not, even though his wolf was curious to see what the beta had in store. He was having none of this. He didn't want to shift and didn't want to see the others shift. He only wanted to crawl back into his warm bed and sleep until dawn. Unlike Fermin and Edmund, he wanted to be well rested for the following day.

When Darren turned to the north, toward the chateau, he felt what he came to recognize as the dominance in a loup-garou tickle down his spine. He turned and saw Bart regard him with an expecting look. It was clear he would get no sleep that night.

Under the threat of a lashing from Bart's dominance, he followed them back into the woods. The beta took them to a far secluded spot in the forest, a place none of them had been before. The underbrush was so thick. One could hardly walk through it without thrusting aside the dense branches and brambles that guarded this secret place.

"The key to shifting at will isn't to completely force it. You must summon the wolf forward, bringing it into the open. You must coax it from within yourself. That's the only way you can shift at will. It is by *your* will that you shift, not the wolf's."

Fermin pointed back to where they came. "So, why take us from the meadow? Why here?"

Bart opened his arms as if to display the obvious reason before their eyes. "Can't you feel a deeper connection with it when you're surrounded by the forest instead of in the open field?"

Darren couldn't. The forest, the meadow, or the chateau made no difference. He kept his wolf at a distance, always out of arm's reach. The wolf seemed to prefer it that way too. They were aware of one another, but not did not interact except for the last two times he shifted.

"That's it?" Edmund questioned. "Just ask it to come out? Why not teach this to everyone?"

Bart dropped his hands and Darren moved a little further into the shadows to lean against a nearby oak, still within sight of his beta but separated from the others.

"Because you actually want to shift. Many of the others still fear their wolf and can't bring themselves to turn. The wolf will only come when it doesn't smell your fear. So few are ready for the shift, but you are."

Fermin already had his eyes closed, putting into practice what Bart had just told him. Darren folded his arms over his chest, his face telling a different story than what he truly felt. He didn't want to be there when they shifted, but what else could he do? He knew he wasn't ready for what they wanted, yet Bart wouldn't allow him to leave.

For nearly half an hour, both Edmund and Fermin tried to shift on their own. That time was punctuated by several moments of meditation, ending in an exasperated sigh from either boy when they simply couldn't bring their wolf forward. Bart told them to have patience and try a little harder.

Surprisingly, he did not pressure Darren to join them. He remained a bored spectator, watching and waiting with a kind of worried expectancy. After a while, his senses wandered, scoping out the forest around him. Nocturnal critters scurried through the treetops as bugs sang their nightly lullaby to the moon above. Everything was calm, pristine, and the four loups-garous were a part of nature, as it was a part of them all the time.

Yet, there was something amiss. A subtle, but nagging scent that didn't seem to mesh with the rest of the forest. Darren took one last look at Bart and the rest before slipping away to follow it. It was foolish, perhaps even dangerous to do so. Darren couldn't just stand there against the tree trunk for the rest of the night while the boys continually failed in their mission to become one with their wolf outside of their cycle.

He came to a certain clearing, one he hadn't been to before. There were no markings on the trees to tell him where he was in relation to the chateau training grounds. He could still hear the soft voices of his packmates not too far away.

Darren stood on the edge of the clearing and sniffed for the source of the foreign scent. It was metallic, he knew that much. It was something that didn't belong amongst the wild earth and the living things of the forest. Metal was manmade, like guns and arrowheads and armor. Loups-garous had no use for armor or blacksmithing of any kind.

Yet, even in the moonlight, he couldn't see any glint of the metal he smelled. Perhaps he was mistaken and it was beyond the clearing?

He took a few steps into the open before he realized his mistake. So swift that he didn't have time to jump out of the way, a net enclosed around him and a thousand sharp edges cut into the skin of his arms and legs. The metal he smelled burned his flesh when it poked through the fabric of his shirt.

Searing pain like the embers of a popping fire nearly covered his body. Whatever this strange metal was, it was woven into the netting. Darren pulled and tugged at the ropes to snap them, but found himself recoiling and writhing to escape the poison metal.

He shouted for help and it seemed to take an eternity for Bart to find him. In reality, it might have been seconds. The pain blinded him to the passage of time. Darren continued to struggle and fight against his bonds. He could feel the metal lacerate his skin with every motion. The cuts healed slowly, only to be sliced open once more as he thrashed about.

"Darren, stop moving," Bart ordered. "This is silver. I know it hurts, but you need to stop moving."

"Silver!" Fermin exclaimed from the safe edge of the clearing where the vicious metal couldn't hurt him. "That must be a hunter's net!"

"All of you, calm down!" Bart's dominance flooded through to each of them and Darren slowed in his struggle, though it wasn't because of his beta's orders. The pain was almost too intense for him to bear any longer.

Blood soaked into his ripped pants and tunic, dripping to the ground. Bart couldn't reach where the edge of the net closed around Darren and suspended him off the ground. So, he began to take his summoned claws and cut around the silver pieces to make a hole for Darren to fall through.

Bart stopped cold and his nostrils flared. Darren smelled it too. A stranger, a human. He was clearly not loup-garou because he didn't bring with him the tingling sensation that followed every loup-garou. He smelled of foreign, stringent things and more metal.

The stranger must have appeared on the other side of the clearing, because Fermin and Edmund took off running to the north, disappearing from view. Bart roared and charged at the intruder that Darren couldn't see coming up behind him. He heard the twang of arrows loosed from a bow and the dull thud as the arrow tips imbedded in flesh.

Bart growled and roared, both in pain and rage, but Darren's consciousness began to slip from him. The fiery, intense pain of the silver against his skin became too much, he couldn't escape it. He was aware of a sudden silence in the clearing and then the euphoric sensation of falling as darkness enveloped him.

CHAPTER 9

When Darren's senses returned to him, he became keenly aware that he was no longer in the forest. The smells of metal, stagnant water, stone, and poison blasted him, instilling a terror that he couldn't shake. His eyes, burning and sore as they were, finally opened to search in the dim light.

He was trapped in a cage, its shiny metal bars like the ensnaring fangs of a beast. The padlock appeared to be clamped tight around the swinging end of the door. Beyond the bars, he could see further into the room though there was no light to aid him. A long table sat a few yards away. Its surface speckled and stained by old blood that gave its finish a darker shade than what it might have been when it was first made.

Strange tools of all kinds, with blunt and sharp edges, were littered across the tabletop. More contraptions, all bizarre and menacing in their construction, lined the damp stone walls of what he assumed to be a cellar. There were no windows and only one door that remained closed on the opposite side of the room.

Water dripped from the ceiling to create tiny puddles of standing water across the floor. The rafters and wooden planks that made up the roof of his prison were old and rotted out in many places, the boards cracked through. Darren wondered if the earth above would cave in at any moment.

When he turned to look beside him, he was shocked to see another person in the darkness. Not just a person, but a woman. No, a girl, he realized as his eyes further adjusted. She perhaps looked a year or so older than him, if at all. Clad in a long, dingy gray dress whose hem was stained by the dirt and muck from her own private cage. She paid no mind to him.

Her eyes, as pale and gray as her dress, were fixed on the door, as if she were intently waiting for it to open. Long blonde hair trailed down her back and over her shoulders, the only radiant thing in the entire cellar.

Darren couldn't help but noticed she was attractive, in a sophisticated and elegant sort of way.

As his strength returned, he pushed himself to sit up, but she still did not turn to him. He inspected his body, expecting to see the many scars created by the silver that had nearly torn him to shreds before he passed out. His skin was clean and spotless, without a single blemish. His sleeping clothes, however, were still torn and wrinkled. Noelle would not be pleased with him after she took one look at the blood-spotted garments.

That was, if he could even get back to Noelle and the chateau. Fear, more stifling than he had ever experienced, took claim over his heart and mind.

"What is this place?" he asked the mysterious woman, crawling closer to wrap his hands around the bars.

"You don't want to – "

It was too late. The metal coating on the bars burned Darren's palms and he shrank away to allow them to heal. He hissed at the stinging pain and watched as his seared flesh began to stitch itself back together again.

How did she know the bars would hurt him?

"Who are you?" he asked, still puzzled why she would not look at him. He became furious when she didn't answer his question.

He repeated it, a little louder this time.

The girl rolled her pretty eyes and finally acknowledged him. The very breath froze in his lungs. When he saw Evangeline for the first time at the chateau, he had thought she was beautiful. Seeing this stranger, he knew that he had been wrong. This fair-skinned lady in the cage beside his might as well have been the definition of true beauty. A goddess incarnate.

"My name is Jane. Jane Gennari... And you're in hell."

Darren looked around, hating to tear his gaze away from her. By her accent, he could immediately tell she was Italian. "This isn't hell. Where am I?"

He knew exactly what hell was. Hell was the black, empty void of his memory when he had no control over his body or senses. Hell was succumbing to agonizing pain without source or reason, that threatened to tear him apart. Hell was being thrown into this new life, watching the old one burn to ashes, and somehow survive. Hell was breathing when all he wanted to do was stop.

"It's close enough." Her eyes grazed over him, thick lashes batting with each blink as she assessed the man with whom she was trapped. "You haven't been a luppo mannero for long, have you?"

One of the boys at the chateau was Italian and sometimes used the term interchangeably with loup-garou. Darren's gaze turned hard. She might have been in her own cage, but who was to say that she wasn't in league with the man who brought him here? The one who set the net that was purposefully made to contain a loup-garou. It might have been unthinkable to believe that such a wondrous beauty might have been so evil, but Darren was leaving nothing to chance.

"I beg your pardon?"

Then, she grinned and Darren couldn't decide which stole his heart first; her smile or the way her eyes seemed to hold their own kind of luster. "It's all right," she said. "Perhaps you're more accustomed to the term 'werewolves'?" Jane must have seen the way his shoulders went rigid at its utterance. "Yes, you haven't been turned for long at all. Poor thing."

A low, threatening growl rumbled in his throat. He hated that term. Hated the very way it sounded, with that pitiful tone like he was some creature to feel sorry for. He heard it whispered when he passed villagers in the streets, back when he was an infirm child. Not anymore.

"Oh," she crooned playfully. "You're a proud werewolf too."

"I am not proud," he challenged. "I'm just not poor and I'm not helpless."

"Except that you are in a cage of which you can't get out. You appear pretty helpless to me."

Darren's nostrils flared. "You're in the same predicament. You're just as helpless as I am."

She held up a pale, slender finger. "That is where you're wrong. I have a plan. You do not."

"So, you know where we are?" Darren took another look around, closely inspecting the walls as if there could be some detail that would help formulate the perfect plan.

"Yes," she said. "We are beneath the house of a madman."

He waited for her to explain herself or to elaborate on her wonderful, fool-proof plan. She did neither. If it weren't for the constant dripping of the water and the whistling of the wind somewhere above them, the silence would have rung shrill in his ears.

That was when he realized something was not right. He didn't hear her heartbeat. Even in the soft silence of the dormitory, he heard the heartbeats of those around him, as well as his own. Here, he only heard one. His own.

He looked to Jane and narrowed his eyes, listening hard for any sign that she was actually there. Surely, he hadn't gone insane so much as to imagine someone to be there when there was no one. He didn't hear a heartbeat. Not even a single breath was expelled from her delicate nostrils.

"Touch me," he ordered.

Jane looked to him as if he had just asked for an obscene favor. "I beg your pardon?" she shrieked.

"Not that way," he growled and offered out his hand as close to the bars as he could without touching them. "Touch my hand. I want to make sure you're real."

She simmered down and shrugged before slipping her hand and arm through the two sets of bars to touch the tips of his fingers. Her skin was cold, but she was certainly real.

"Why can't I hear your heart?" he asked, their fingers still barely touching one another in such a way that knotted his stomach and made his wolf shiver. He had never been so close to a woman so exquisite.

Jane blinked and seemed stunned for just a moment before withdrawing her hand from his and pulling her knees to her chest. "You don't know?" When Darren didn't so much as flinch, she said, "I'm... I'm a vampire."

Darren took a second look at her, considering her features. She was pale, but she hardly appeared to be the succubus of the dark, cautionary tales. Then again, neither was the loup-garou. It was completely possible that vampires were not the beasts they were rumored to be.

"Vampire... So, you're the undead?"

Her slim shoulder shrugged again, such a human and lively quality for a lifeless body to display. "That's not quite the right term, but it'll do. I drink blood, too. Just in case you were wondering."

If he had met her months ago, Darren wouldn't have believed her. Even if she could prove it, he wouldn't have reacted with such calm. He simply nodded in understanding. "So, a vampire and werewolf find themselves in the custody of a madman... Why?"

It was clear that Jane couldn't fathom how he could be so composed either. Yet, now that the elephants in the room had been addressed, they could set to the more pressing business of escape.

"The man, Richard, he has something of mine. I ran away from my father in Italy to get it back. From what I understand, he's been feeding off the blood of vampires for over a century. It doesn't turn him into a vampire, but it does give him immortal life." She scooted closer to the bars. "From what I've heard in rumors, he takes something from each vampire he kills. I allowed myself to be caught so I can take back what he stole from my mother."

Darren's heart sank into his stomach. With each word, she poured out the passion and determination that led her miles from her home, just for a family heirloom. Her bravery in the face of danger and death was remarkable. This might have been the very place her mother was killed – if he was assuming correctly – and yet she came here willingly to take back something she believed rightfully belonged to her.

Once the amazement of her resolve passed, Darren was able to put the conversation in reverse. "Wait," he said. "This man drinks blood, but is not a vampire?"

Jane rolled her eyes once more. "It's much more complicated than that, but that is the result. It gives the drinker nearly immortal life, but it also rots the brain, which is why he's gone insane. To become a vampire, he must be on the point of death and then drink human blood. Vampire blood is not the same, just as werewolf blood is not the same. Why you're here, I don't know."

Darren passed a hand over his eyes, as if it would erase this terrible nightmare. When he looked around again, he was still in the cellar. He would have cursed the spark of life in his chest if a lady weren't present. Vampire or not, Darren had been taught better than to speak foul language in front of a woman.

"How far away is this place from Albi?" Darren asked, as if Jane would even know.

"I don't know, but his home is about two days' walk from the Italian border."

Darren hung his head in his hands. That was so far from Albi, practically on the other side of France. Surely his pack would be looking for him. What became of Bart, or Fermin and Edmund? They weren't in the cellar, but that didn't mean they were alive either.

If he remembered correctly, Bart had been shot multiple times with arrows that may or may not have been made with silver tips. The beta could very well be dead. What if the pack couldn't find him? What if Jane's plan to escape didn't work? What if this madman killed him or tried to use him just like he had used vampires?

Every inch of his body quivered as his muscles bunched and tensed beneath his skin. His wolf, as calm as it was from Jane's presence, writhed and bucked against the confines of his prison. Darren couldn't take it anymore and grabbed for the bars one more time.

Jane screamed for him to stop, but he wouldn't. He had to get out, he had to escape and breathe fresh air. Darren roared against the pain as he stretched and bent the bars. Quickly, the nerves and muscles in his hands lost strength and his body rebelled against his own will. He let go, letting the bloody and charred skin fall from his palms.

Darren crouched and rammed his shoulder into the opening he had created, but it wasn't enough for his bulky frame to squeeze through. If he was the small, weak, frail boy he had once been, he could have slipped through easily. Now, he could barely wiggle the bulk of his arm through the close-set bars.

The silver found the tears in his tunic and fried his skin just as it had his hands. "Stop it!" Jane cried. "You're going to kill yourself!"

More from the pain than her pleas, Darren fell back away from the bars, fresh blood seeping through the fabric of his shirt. Darren pounded his throbbing fists on the floor of his cage. "I can't just sit here and do nothing!" he bellowed, his golden eyes glaring.

Jane came closer and he saw her reach through the bars out of the corner of his eye. "Please, you must calm down or you'll wake Richard and my plan will be ruined."

Darren turned on her, his fangs and claws making an appearance as his heart, the only beating heart in the room, thrummed louder and harder with fear. "Does this plan even include me? You're just going to take your trinket and leave me here?"

Jane gave him another look of pity, but this time it did not conjure resentment toward her. He almost regretted his words and wished he could have said them again slightly less reproachful.

"Yes, it can involve you." Her hands wrapped around the silver bars. "See? Silver doesn't hurt me. I can easily get you out of this cage."

"Then do it!" he pleaded. "Why wait if Richard is asleep?"

"Because he will come after the both of us, or perhaps another vampire or werewolf. We need to ensure he never hurts anyone ever again."

Darren knew he could manage that much. The way he felt at that moment, he would willingly rip out the throats of any man who stood in his way to freedom. "We could kill him in his sleep. Can you get out?"

"I'm not as strong as you are," she replied. "I have to wait until he opens my cage. Then, I can kill him and free you."

Darren ran his, now healed, hands through his hair and gripped at his scalp, wishing he didn't have to wait until daylight. It was an indeterminant amount of time before Jane finally spoke again and Darren realized she was still holding the silver bars to his cage.

"Please calm yourself," she insisted in a soft, almost angelic voice that might have been enough to soothe a wild boar.

"I... I feel like I'm coming undone," he admitted.

"That's your wolf reacting to the cage. You need to put your mind away from this place. Take deep breaths."

Darren looked to her. "How do you know so much about loups-garous?"

She smiled at the word, but did not ask him for a translation. She must have known its meaning. "My father knows more than I do, but I met a loup-garou once before. He was older than you. I've never met one so young, but no matter the age, all loups-garous are alike." She rested her head against her own bars. "Tell me about yourself? You're clearly English, so what brought you to France?"

He knew exactly what she was doing. Distracting him from their current situation might have proved effective, but Darren doubted it. How could he take deep breaths when each one resounded with the reminder that he was not free? Like a sickly child, he was bound to a place and fate that seemed inescapable. How long would it be before Jane could enact her plan? Hours? One second was too long as it was.

Yet, he indulged her. His guard completely dropped, he told her his name, about his family, his childhood, and how he came to be loup-garou. Once he began, it was hard to stop the flow of truth spilling from his lips. Reliving the memories and speaking it aloud seemed to steal some of its power over his soul. He would never forget those terrible, earth-shattering moments when he lost his mother, but it did not seem to sting as much. He relinquished his secrets to Jane as easily as handing her a parcel that meant nothing to him.

He continued to talk and she listened attentively, smiling at the comical parts and sighing in sadness when he spoke of the ghosts that followed him. When he was done telling her all about the chateau and the pack, and how it was his curiosity that lured him into the trap Richard had set, Jane went quiet.

Her stare, as beautiful as it was, bore into him like a vicious wolverine digging its den in the earth. It was as if she were looking for more, and finding exactly what she wanted.

"It's your turn now," he said, breaking her concentration.

Jane blinked a few times and whatever she had mentally latched onto fell away. "My turn?"

"Yes, I just told you more than anyone else alive knows. Not even my alpha knows everything. You must return the favor."

She let go of the bars and let her hand settle in her lap. "I suppose I should start by saying that I am much older than you."

"How old?" Just like that, Darren did feel himself farther away from this cellar. He could not forget that he was a prisoner, but the ache of confinement did not hurt as badly as it had moments before.

"I turn one hundred and one years this winter."

Darren's brows shot up. "You don't look a day over eighteen."

She smiled. "Thank you for the compliment. Just like loups-garous, vampires do not age the way humans do. Yet, we do seem to age a little more slowly than loups-garous."

"Is your father also a vampire?"

With that simple question, it seemed that Jane had lowered her defenses as well. The quiet, demure lady who sat beside him divulged details of her life, her family, and their unique curse. They had a few things in common. They both lost their mother, too soon, to fates and men who did not understand what they were doing.

Her mother, Caterina, was stolen from them by Richard, and by the time they found her body, she was too weak to survive more than a few minutes. Bled dry and starving, she could barely lift her head, as Jane told him. Darren couldn't help but notice the way Jane's eyes misted when she spoke of her mother. Even after so many years, the pain was still fresh and it made him pessimistic for the centuries ahead that he would have to live with his own mother's memory.

Jane stopped and gave a mirthless laugh.

"What is it?" he asked.

"Your alpha never told you, did he?"

Darren was now sitting cross-legged, leaning his elbows on his knees. "Told me what?"

Jane looked to him, still grinning. "He never told you that vampires and loups-garous don't get along?"

John had once said that there were still some fairytales that held a shred of truth, but he never explained what he meant. Darren simply assumed that there were other things hidden in the dark, but never had he guessed that vampires existed, let alone that he should be at natural odds with them.

"No, he never mentioned it. I only learned about hunters the other day."

Jane shook her head. "It's just as well that you learn now, I suppose. If any other loup-garou were in your place, they would never have spoken to me, much less carry on a long conversation. I pray you never adopt such prejudices."

"Why should our kind hate one another?"

Before Jane could answer, she went still and the smile faded from her lips. Darren heard it too. A faint stirring above their heads, the rustle of fabric and creaking of bed rails as someone was awakening. Darren waited, his breath quickening with anticipation. Finally, he would lay eyes upon the man who had captured him.

CHAPTER 10

The same guttural growl that rumbled in Darren's chest returned when he heard the soft tap of Richard's shoes upon the stone steps as he descended toward the cellar door. The damp air around him became saturated with a kind of evil that Darren had never felt before. Not even when the mob stormed onto his farm did he sense such a powerful tide of malignant intent.

Yet, the man that stood in the threshold was not what he had expected. Somehow, Darren thought he would be faced with an older, ugly man with ragged clothes and disheveled hair. He expected to see the look of a madman, but he was met with something far more devious. Instead of looking the part of a murdering psychotic, Richard appeared as a man dressed in clean, fashionable clothing. His facial hair was groomed and trimmed, his body clean and smelled fresh as if he had just bathed.

Richard was a wolf in sheep's wool, a murderer in disguise who could walk through a crowd and never be seen as anything suspicious. He might not have been a vampire or a loup-garou, but he was certainly a monster akin to them.

Beside him, Jane became a completely different person. Instead of the strong, independent woman with a plan, she reduced herself to a sniveling, frightful child who huddled in the back of her cage and sobbed at the very sight of Richard.

Darren played along and did not give her a look of disbelief as he wanted to. This must have been part of her scheme. Richard would never think a coward would fight back. It was too bad that Darren could not do the same. He growled and bared his teeth, his body tensed as if ready to pounce, even though the silver bars separated them.

Richard entered the cellar and moved around the room, ignorant of his two captives, to light the lanterns and sconces along the walls. The room became bathed in the amber glow of firelight that flickered in the puddles and cast deep shadows along the floor. Then, he finally turned to the two cages with his dark eyes that were as black as coal and just as heartless.

"Oh, my dear," he said to Jane. "Must we go through this every day?"

He stepped forward and picked up a long instrument with prongs at the end, ideal for grabbing. Darren rammed against the cage bars to make a point that he wasn't afraid of the pain, but Richard did not pay him any mind. So sure in the protection the silver offered him, the madman walked right past his cage and squatted in front of Jane's, displaying the tool for her.

"If you don't come to me, I'll have to drag you out," he threatened in such a sweet, but condescending voice, as if he were talking to an insolent child. He unlocked and opened Jane's cage door, but as long as Richard's body was blocking the way, Jane could never get out.

"Leave her alone!" Darren yelled.

Richard did not even flinch, but turned to regard the loup-garou with eyes that could have killed on the spot. Darren did not budge.

"You'll have to wait your turn," he said. "I have something special in store for you."

It was then that Darren knew he had to be taken seriously. He continued to ram his shoulder against the bars, his flesh blistering and sizzling with each impact. He gripped the bars and tugged as hard as he could, inflicting as much damage upon his body as possible.

Richard was in the business of using them, wasting the body until there was nothing left. If Darren could make the madman fear for the safety of his newest prize, perhaps he would take his focus from Jane just long enough. He hated to see her whimper and cower like a fool with no nerve.

Just as he suspected, Richard stopped groping for Jane's arm with the instrument and came to his cage.

"Stop it!" the false nobleman screamed. "Stop it this instant!"

"What do you want with me?" Darren snarled as he winced at the intense pain that riddled his body. Swollen and charred flesh began to heal, but so slowly.

"You, my little friend, will complete me."

"What are you talking about?" Darren had to pretend as if he and Jane hadn't been talking while the madman slept.

Richard pointed his prongs toward Jane, who continued the charade, pressing herself against the back wall of her cage with her face twisted in feigned fear. "Do you know what that is? It's a vampire, a creature of the night. She is immortal and her blood makes me immortal too." He then pointed to Darren's chest. "But, do you know what you can do for me? You may be immortal as well, but you can give me so much more. Invulnerability. Your strength, your speed, your healing abilities, I want all of it."

Darren bared his fangs, his golden eyes flashing with pain and anger. "You think my blood will do that for you?"

"No, not your blood," he laughed. "Your bite and hers."

"What!" Jane screeched.

If Darren's nose did not lie, it told him that Jane was no longer faking her terror. Something in what the madman said inspired true, unadulterated fear in the vampire and that was enough to give Darren pause. If something was about to happen to make Jane so afraid, then it should have terrified him as well.

It was already clear that she knew far more than he did.

"We can't both bite you," she insisted, fresh tears streaming down her perfect cheeks. "It... It will kill you!"

Richard was not convinced and neither was Darren. Something much more diabolical would happen if they both bit him. Her reasoning of death was a lie.

"You're talking about the bite that can change you, aren't you?" Darren asked.

Richard nodded, a wicked grin splitting his face. "Indeed, I am. If both of you bite me and change me, I can become something far more powerful than both of you combined."

"I don't even know how to change anyone," Darren said. "And if you slip your arm through these bars, I'll just rip it off."

The madman chuckled. "If you don't cooperate, the pretty bloodsucker will get hurt. Do you want that?"

What Darren had said was the truth. He didn't know how to change anyone. Why should Jane be punished for something he was incapable of doing? "I'm telling you, I don't know how to change you!"

Richard dropped the prong tool and went back to the table. Darren looked to Jane for any sign that she was ready to move, but she seemed to be immobilized by some haunting thought or vision. She simply stared, gray eyes wide and unblinking. This would have been the perfect time to carry out her plan while their captor had his back turned. Yet, she stalled and Darren wanted to scream to snap her out of it.

The madman turned back to show Darren a sharp, tapering dagger longer than his forearm. In his other hand, was a bottle of some thick, milky and chunky substance. As soon as he uncorked the bottle, the fresh scent of crushed garlic permeated the air.

"Vampires, like werewolves, have a particular weakness to something so simple," he explained as calmly as if he were giving the time of day. "Instead of silver, they cannot stand the taste or touch of garlic." Richard slowly poured the mixture over the shiny flat of the blade. "If I pierce her chest with this, she will die."

Darren looked to Jane again and he could already see her eyelids grow red and puffy. The very smell of garlic was already having an affect over her. She sniffled, but the harsh awakening of the garlic seemed to bring her out of whatever delirium she had fallen into.

Richard walked toward her cage with the dagger. With every last bit of strength he had, Darren lunged through the widened gap in the bars and grabbed for Richard's leg. His claws sunk deep into his calf and the man yowled in pain.

With one good yank, Darren brought Richard to his knees and dragged him closer. Even with the silver branding into the skin around his shoulder and chest, he managed to hold the madman there until Jane darted out of her cage.

Richard, unconcerned with the loose vampire, reeled back and slashed at Darren's arm with the dagger. Before the blade could make contact with his skin, he grabbed Richard's wrist and snapped it backward. The dagger clanged to the floor and the blade became submerged in one of the shallow puddles to wash away the garlic he had slathered over it.

Jane found her opportunity and took Richard's head between her hands and bit down into his neck. Richard screamed and grabbed at her blonde hair to yank her mouth away. Her fangs must have been in too deep, because she would not give an inch.

Darren dislodged his talons from Richard's wrist and plunged them into his abdomen, slicing through the thick fabrics of his vest and tunic to feel the soft and unprotected flesh beneath. Blood poured from the belly of the murderer as his screams and cries were slowly muffled into the last gurgles of life still hanging by a fraying thread.

The wolf, through the pain and anguish of the silver burns, reveled in this victory as he heard the last few heartbeats of the man who sought what man should never seek at the expense of others: power and immortality.

Jane continued to drink long after the spark of life died away in Richard's chest and Darren pulled his hands away from the corpse. Somehow, killing this man who had murdered so many others did not faze him as killing the innocent deer. Both kills were justified in their own way, but there was a sweet satisfaction in the way he watched Richard's skin turn ashen and pale. The madman would not hurt anyone ever again, human, loup-garou, or vampire.

The blood on his hands didn't matter so much as it had before. He simply wiped the sticky substance on the seat of his pants and patiently waited for Jane to finish her meal. Once she was finished taking back the blood that had been stolen from her and all the others of her kind, she let go of his neck and pulled away to revealed the gnarled and grisly revenge she had exacted.

Her chin and upper lip were covered in the dark liquid and she would not meet Darren's gaze. After she wiped her face clean, she moved toward his cage and broke the padlock with her renewed strength that must have come from the feeding. Darren emerged and stood tall to stretch out his legs and back that had been cramped inside the cage which would have been a better fit for a large dog than a man.

Without a word, he stepped around Richard's body and moved toward the door. Jane followed close behind.

"It might be morning," she said. "I can't go into the sunlight."

Darren nodded as they hustled up the stone stairs. "Where is this thing you were searching for? The thing that belonged to your mother."

The promise of fresh air was ahead of them, seeping through the cracks of the wooden door that led to the topside world of the living and sane.

"It was a ring. It might be in his chambers. We'll have to search for it."

Once they came to the door, Darren noticed something else. Not only did cool, clean air greet him from underneath the door, but a sliver of sunlight pierced the darkness and created a sharp dividing line that a vampire could not cross. Behind him, Jane stood well out of its range.

"You wait here and I'll try to take care of the sunlight," he assured.

Unexpectedly, she hurried up the last few steps to grab his arm. "Promise you won't leave me here?"

When the soft sunlight fell across the skin of her neck, he saw its devastating power. Just as the silver had burned his flesh, peeling it back to expose the raw and bloody contents underneath, so did sunlight destroy the defenses of the vampire.

Darren stepped in front of her to shield the light. "I promise I won't leave without you."

He would have never suspected that a hand that could kill could also instill such peace and joy. The tiny touch of her fingers just a couple of hours ago did not do her justice. Feeling her grip, so gentle and yet powerful, made Darren feel so much more than he dared to before.

Jane swallowed hard and he could sense a small sample of the fear she had shown before. This time, she wasn't afraid of death or some nameless catastrophe. She feared that he would truly leave and never return. How could he ever abandon her?

She descended the stairs to wait in the murky darkness before Darren opened the wooden door.

Once again, he was surprised by what was waiting for him. The home of this madman was nothing like his cellar. The polished wooden floors and high ceilings were fit for a king. Stunning wallpaper with intricate, yet elegant patterns covered the walls of the chamber he entered.

The door that led to the cellar was masked by the wallpaper that matched the rest of the room and cloaked this secret entrance from the public eye. Expensive furnishing filled the room, chairs with their colorfully embroidered cushions, and hand-crafted tables. Tall windows lined one wall, letting in the treacherous light that consumed the room, that same light he had to block out for Jane.

He shut the door behind him and quickly went to work drawing the thick velvet curtains, but even then, he could not keep the morning from beaming around the edges and through the gaps that he could not close.

If Jane walked across this floor, she still would have been blasted by the sunlight that refused to be hidden. Darren passed through the chamber and explored the rest of the mansion to find something he could use to his advantage. In every immaculate chamber, he found more tall windows with inadequate curtains and no shutters or spare boards to block the light.

The house, surprisingly, was empty. No servants, no maids or slaves, no one to tend to the needs of the nobleman or take care of such a grand home. Outside, the grounds and gardens stretched on for acres upon acres, not quite as beautiful as John's estate, but more on the same level as Longleat House in Warminster.

Scouring through the rooms, both upstairs and downstairs, Darren was running out of convenient options. Finally, he resorted to the unthinkable. A groundskeeper shed behind the home supplied him with a hammer and bucket of nails and he brought them inside. He started in one of the rooms he thought they would not have to search through, and began to dismantle the smooth, wooden floorboards.

One by one, he ripped them from their place and piled them in the rooms that would need to be boarded up. The task took a few hours, but when the project was done, not a shred of offending light slanted through the windows.

He opened the door to the cellar and found Jane waiting patiently on the stairs.

"It's safe now," he announced, tired and more than a little hungry. While Jane searched the house for her mother's ring, he knew exactly where he would go. The kitchen. If there was no meat there, he would take to the woods. He needed meat and the bloodless corpse in the cellar would not do the job.

Jane cautiously eyed his handiwork. "Where did you get the wood?"

"From an obliging floor."

She smiled and set to work, rifling through the drawers of desks and tables. Knowing that they were finally out of immediate danger, Darren let the relief wash over him. Neither of them would die this day, nor suffer any more harm at the hands of the dead man in the cellar. Jane might have been fully capable of finding a way out herself and take on Richard alone, but it might have been twice as difficult.

Gratification swelled in his chest and he could walk to the kitchen with pride, knowing that he had been able to help her. He hadn't been able to help his mother, or the townspeople that fell prey to the ravages of the manic crowd, but he helped Jane. That seemed enough to right the wrongs of the past, though it was a far cry from absolution.

After procuring a hefty chunk of ham from the kitchen, Darren scouted the area around the house. His nose worked, testing the air. What he found puzzled him just as much as the mansion and the enigmatic madman. There wasn't a hint of civilization for miles. Even at the chateau, he could faintly smell the smoke from cottage chimneys some distance away.

Here, there was nothing but the wild forests and a string of snowcapped mountains so far off that Darren could hardly judge their true height. How could a man maintain such an estate by himself with no readily accessible resources? Unless Richard did it all himself, it simply didn't make sense that such a magnificent home would be situated so far from everything.

He returned inside and determined that Jane was upstairs. Darren thought now would be the ideal time to dispose of Richard's body. If left to rot in the cellar, the stink would become too unbearable for his nose. There were still several hours to go before nightfall and only then could they leave the mansion safely.

When he arrived in the cellar, lanterns still flickering along the walls, Darren did not find a body. In the place where they had left him, bloodied and his face frozen in the last horrific moments of his death, there was not a corpse to be found. Instead, a long pile of soggy, dark dust and bones blotched with the darkness that had consumed his soul.

There was no flesh, no organs to toss to the crows outside, nothing left of the man but an empty skull where a demented brain was once housed. Still, Darren picked up each of the bones, one by one, and cradled them in his arms. There were still many things he didn't understand about the preternatural world. One thing he remembered from legends was that the body and bones of evil people must be burned and buried so they will never return.

Darren found a cleared place on the grounds and managed to light a pyre. He stood vigilant, watching the bones crack under the heat and shrivel into the soil. He did not mourn the man, nor did he feel any guilt for what they did. Yet, he could not help but wonder who this man was. Apart from the mad pursuit for eternal life and power, did Richard once have a family? What drove him to such extremes and how did he come to live in such a luxurious place? Flames danced in the hollow eye sockets of his skull, and Darren tried to imagine why a man with such fortune and privilege would throw it all away for the chance to be something so unnatural.

"Darren!" he heard from the second floor of the mansion. "I found it!"

Leaving the last shards of white bone to burn, he sped inside to join her in what he assumed was Richard's bed chamber. The red canopy bed was laden with his scent, as well as the other belongings within the room.

Jane stood in front of a vanity littered with all manner of grooming tools with a mahogany jewelry box open in the center. Inside, jewels and gems from necklaces, bracelets, and rings seemed to sparkle in the darkness, without the need of any other light around it. Pinched in her fingers was the object of her obsession, the Holy Grail of her long quest.

She offered it to him and he inspected it. "All this way, for such a small thing?" he questioned her as he turned it over in his hand.

It was of a simple design, yet beautiful in the way the pure sapphire gem was nestled into the golden band that featured intricately chiseled details. There were greater rings, to be sure, but how many of them could hold such weight within a woman's heart? How many of them were so precious that a young girl would leave the safety of her home and risk death to acquire it?

Jane took the ring back from him, holding it so tenderly within her hands that no one would ever doubt its importance in her life. "It's the only thing I have left of my mother. It belonged to her mother before her, as well." Jane smiled. "One day, if I have a daughter, I'll give it to her."

Darren nodded in approval. Women weren't allowed the indulgences and freedoms they deserved. Heritages and wills often passed from father to son, with no inclusion of the female sex. His mother was an exception because she possessed some of her own wealth. But if she had had a daughter instead of a son, the farm wouldn't have been in her inheritance.

This ring, and others like it, signified the one shred of autonomy women possessed. They could own something and have the complete freedom to give it to their daughters. Darren could not scoff at such an ambition.

"That's quite a legacy," he said as he watched the way her eyes danced with delight over the fact that she found exactly what she had yearned.

"It will be mine, at least," she replied as she slipped the ring onto her right ring finger. As if it had been made for her, it fit perfectly.

CHAPTER 11

Darren dove for the rabbit and the tips of his fingers grazed the soft hairs of its tail as it scurried away into the bushes. It had never been this difficult to catch his meals before. He had managed to leap upon a deer with complete stealth and precision, but he couldn't nab a tiny rodent? It must have been because Jane was watching him from the shadows.

Any other man might have been embarrassed to fail in front of a lady, especially in something that should have been his expertise. He was a loup-garou and he couldn't even catch a rabbit? Yet, Darren did not feel ashamed or angry at his momentary short-coming. Jane's giggles were well worth it.

He pushed himself up and brushed off the dirt from the fresh shirt he had pinched from Richard's wardrobe. They weren't quite the same size, but it was better than the blood-stained tunic he would have to give back to Noelle.

"Would you like me to help?" Jane asked as she approached him.

Darren looked to her, noticing the way the moonlight seemed to glow off her pale skin. She seemed out of place amongst the trees and wilderness. A beauty like her belonged in elegant gowns, dancing with all the handsome and wealthy men of the court. She had told him about her slightly extravagant lifestyle in Italy and how her father could pay for anything and everything she desired.

Still, she did not falter among the protruding roots or stumble over the uneven terrain. If it were possible for her to be loup-garou, Darren wouldn't have doubted it.

He gestured in the direction that the rabbit had darted. "Be my guest," he offered. "I've had enough tries for one night."

Jane giggled again and knelt beside him, her slender hands placed upon her knees and eyes focused ahead. Darren watched her, both confused and intrigued by the way she simply sat, as if waiting for the rabbit to come to them.

It did. It took a moment, but when Darren looked back to the bushes, the same rabbit that had eluded him for the last hour came bouncing over the distance between them. It sat in front of them, well within arm's reach with its nose twitching vigorously as it tested the air for the danger that was so near.

"What did you do?" he whispered to her.

"Take it," she replied. "I don't know how much longer I can hold it."

Darren's hand snapped out just as the rabbit seemed to comprehend where exactly it was, but by then it was too late. With a quick jerk, he snapped the critter's neck and the wildly pumping, long hind feet went still.

"How did you do that?" Darren asked as he set to work spreading the feet out so he could skin the rabbit with the talon he had learned to extend from his finger.

"It's something all vampires can do," she replied, placing her hand over his to stop him. "Wait. Let me first?"

Slightly stunned by the brush of her skin onto his, it took Darren a moment to realize what she meant. He nodded and Jane took the rabbit from him. She sank her teeth into the soft underbelly and fed. A tiny trickle of blood leaked out from the corner of her parted lips, but Darren couldn't look away. Even feasting upon the blood of their prey, she was lovely.

When she was finished, she handed the bloodless rabbit back to Darren and wiped her mouth with her sleeve.

"So, you can control minds?" he questioned as he continued his work. It turned out to be surprisingly easier to gut the hare now that there was little to no blood left to get in the way.

"Not minds, but bodies," she explained. "And I'm only just learning how. My father can control several men at once, but I seem to only have luck with the tiny, weak-minded things like rabbits and birds for now."

The thought troubled Darren as he tried to focus on stripping skin from flesh. How terrifying would it be to be under the manipulation of a creature that thirsted for blood? He had thought loups-garous were powerful beasts, but it seemed that vampires could be just as deadly.

"Of course, my father only uses the skill in self-defense. He's never killed a man for blood."

It was as if she could read his very thoughts, but Darren didn't reply. His belly was far too empty to bother with what her father was like.

They had been walking for quite a while to the east, further from his pack and further from Richard's mansion. As soon as the sun had sunk below the horizon and ceased to cast its deadly light upon the earth, they set foot in the general direction of the Italian border where they knew Jane's father would be.

Darren could have left her on her own. Jane was fully capable of crossing the countryside by herself, but he knew that if they parted ways at Richard's mansion, he would constantly think about her, wondering if she made it safely into her father's hands. He was at no risk of changing into his uncontrollable, unmanageable loup-garou form, so there was no danger on her part. Though, he would have been in much greater danger of growing too attached to the vampire.

What would his alpha say when he told him the whole story about Richard and the mansion and Jane? What would Bart say? What would the rest of his pack say? If vampires and loups-garous were truly at odds with one another, they might not have approved of his decision to escort Jane home. Then again, what if John was like Jane's father and seemed to desire peace and goodwill toward the opposite race? Would he applaud Darren's ignorance of their differences?

When Darren was finished with his meal, he found that Jane had not wandered far. Not once since they met, had she given him any indication that she cared for him in the same way that he did her. It was as if he were her equal, or close friend, but never anything more, which frustrated Darren.

His wolf, however, sang a different tune than it first had in the cell. Away from the stench of death and evil, Darren finally realized that Jane did not smell like a lady at all. The subtle odor of something rotten clung to her and he wanted to believe it was something on her clothes. Whatever it was, it repulsed his wolf and they were no longer in agreement over Jane.

Darren's heart beamed with one emotion, while his loup-garou soul bristled with another.

"You said you met another loup-garou before," he said as he tossed aside what was left of the rabbit, so the buzzards and bugs could pick the bones clean.

Jane turned to him, eyes bright and glimmering with a certain emotion that he never wished to see on her again. Regret.

"Yes, once. Many years ago."

Darren smeared the excess juices from his meal on the seat of his pants. "Your voice tells another story," he remarked and they set out in the direction of the Italian border once more.

A corner of Jane's lips turned up. "It's hard to talk about sometimes."

"If you wish to not – "

She turned to him and touched his arm. "No, no. It's all right."

Once more, Darren cherished the moment, while his wolf quivered as if the very touch of her should have made his skin crawl. Perhaps sensing the contradiction in him, she pulled back her hand much too soon.

"We spent weeks together, traveling with my father and we... I thought our hearts beat as one, but I was wrong. He sailed away, but never returned, even when he promised he would." Jane sighed. "He told me he would write, but I only received a few infrequent letters before he stopped replying to mine."

"Perhaps he..." Darren didn't want to say it, though he would gladly think it. Jane was still clearly infatuated with this first loup-garou she met, and in consequence, she did not care for Darren. He wanted to tell her that her first love would not return, so she should move on to a loup-garou who was closer.

It was all selfish and that was not the kind of heart-wrenching reality that she wanted to hear. It would make him the villain, not her hero. So, he offered her another alternative.

"Perhaps he's been busy or in a place where he could not send word to you."

"I had held out hope for it," she said, "but the days and weeks and years dragged on and he still never came back. Whatever became of him, I'm sure he's happy."

Darren carefully weighed his words, then said, "He is at a terrible disadvantage, though."

Jane regarded him with a look of wonder. "Why is that?"

"You are not by his side."

Jane smiled and looked away, a tiny hint of color rising in her cheeks. "You are kind," she muttered as she gripped her elbows. "But, as I said, the man did not want me in the same way. He might have thought of me as a little sister, but nothing more."

"That is his loss, then," Darren countered quickly. "I don't know how every man who lays eyes upon you wouldn't fall madly in love with you."

She slid a sly glance his way. "Oh? Have you made this mistake?"

Darren thought quickly and clasped his hands behind his back. "I am not every man," he replied. He hoped to sound as if he was immune to her charms, though he had fallen for her oh so quickly.

"I see." He could feel her eyes roam over him, then looked away. "Well, it would be a shame if every man did fall in love with me."

"Why is that?"

"My father wants me to marry for love. If every man fell in love with me, I'd leave scores of broken hearts in my path, because I cannot love them all."

Darren chuckled. "Your father is lenient. Not every man would wait to give his daughter away to the right man."

"Yes," she replied. "My father is wealthy and powerful enough that he doesn't have to use me as a bargaining chip. It's a blessing and a curse, because now I have to decide my own future."

"That is not so bad," Darren said with a shrug. "My future was decided for me. It's a terrible one, but at least I wouldn't have to wonder what my life would be like. Now I know for certain."

Jane looked to him and smiled sweetly. "No, your future is still unwritten. You are loup-garou, and that will shape the days to come, but it will not decide who you marry, where you live, or what you do with your time. It can only add context."

Darren thought on this. Not every loup-garou that came into John's care stayed at the chateau. They moved on, to the surrounding villages to lead their own lives, but were never out of reach from their alpha and mentor. What happened if one of them wanted to break away from the home they had known for so long? What if they wanted to travel just as Jane's first loup-garou love had?

It led him to think where he would be in five years. Ten years. Five hundred years. Would he still be in France with John, helping other loups-garous understand what they were, or would he move on to start his own pack? As a loup-garou, the possibilities were endless. The years stretched on before him like a wide road with many turns, forks, and obstacles that he could not yet see.

Darren had never needed to look farther ahead than the next harvest season. Now, he was faced with far more than he could ever imagine.

"Jane?"

The voice trembled through the fading darkness. The sun was close to rising, but that didn't matter so much now. They had finally arrived at the tiny Italian village where Jane knew her father would be waiting. It must have been his voice that called from some unseen place.

Beside Darren, Jane fingered the sapphire ring that she had traveled so far to find. He could see the joy and hesitance mix in her gaze as she searched the lit windows of the homes. They hadn't stepped foot in town yet, but somehow her father could sense her approach.

It had been a long two days, filled with pleasant conversation that Darren thought he would never have with a woman as unique and extraordinary as Jane. The hours of philosophical debate and contemplation, about the wonderful and terrible things they would see in the coming centuries, almost made him ready for his life as a loup-garou. If he was even half as wise and brilliant as she was at one hundred years old, Darren would be content to live so long.

The moment of departure was upon them and as much as he wanted to go with her to Italy, she refused.

"You belong with your pack," she told him. "You still have a lot of learning to do."

And she was right, unfortunately. If this manic excursion proved anything, it was that Darren had much to learn about the preternatural world and those who were hell-bent on destroying it. It would be a long journey back to Albi and he wished with every fiber of his being that he could have her company with him, but just like he belonged with his pack, she belonged with her family.

"He's waiting for you," Darren said, breaking the silence between them. If they prolonged their farewells much longer, it would be even more difficult to leave. Perhaps not for her, but for him.

Jane turned back to him and in a split second, her arms were around his neck, body pressed tight against his. For an ephemeral, blissful moment in time, Darren couldn't breathe or move. As the shock wore away, his arms encased her. It was the first hug he had received since he left his mother. The first hug from a woman other than his mother as well.

He ignored her vampire scent, ignored the way he somehow knew her father was watching them. He wanted to enjoy this moment, savor it and remember the way her cold skin suddenly felt hot for the first time.

"Thank you for everything," she whispered, her breath feathering his ear as she spoke.

Darren could have said a million things. *Don't go. You're welcome. Thank you. I love you.* Instead, he did something he might regret for the rest of his unnatural life.

He pulled away for the briefest of seconds and pressed his lips against Jane's. She went rigid at first, then melted into his arms as if she were meant to be there, and he wondered if he did the right thing. Perhaps one kiss was all it took for her to realize that she could want him in the same way.

He could feel her fingers begin to thread through his hair, but then she paused and eased her lips away from his by the tiniest bit. "My father's watching," she whispered and he could almost taste her breath on his tongue.

"Let him watch." It was a daring move, so bold that he hardly recognized the man he had become in that moment with a woman in his arms.

This time, Jane came to him and they were tossed into the throes of a passionate kiss that he never wanted to end.

"Jane!" the voice demanded from the village, dragging them both back into the world that wanted to tear them apart. It might have been centuries before they could find one another again and it seemed so unfair.

She pulled away for the last time and their fiery gazes met. "I have to go."

Darren's hands balled into fists on the hips he had been cradling close to him. With every ounce of strength he had, he let go and nodded. "I know."

It took even more courage than he thought he had left to let her body, now warm with desire, fall away from him. Not another word was spoken as she worked her way through the bushes to stand on the edge of the road that led toward the village.

Jane looked back at him, her eyes misting. Inside, Darren felt the same way. He wanted to scream at the heavens. He wanted to pound his fists into the earth, until it would yield to him what he wanted so badly. Yet, he stood tall, chin up and jaw set. He might have been falling apart to see her go, but he couldn't let on. Not for an instant.

She looked away for the last time and hurried down the path to disappear through the narrow streets of the village. With his loup-garou memory, he would never forget the way her eyes reflected the moonlight, or how every move she made was graceful and perfect. All the way back to Albi, he played Jane's memory over and over in his mind.

It was foolish, he knew. She was one girl, the first in a history that would go on for centuries. There would be other women, other lovers, and perhaps even wives.

Darren knew, however, that Jane would hold a special place in his heart that no one could claim. She was his first kiss, but she would not be his last.

Morning dawned over the chateau as Darren dragged his feet up the stone steps to the front door. Noelle and Evangeline were there, but he could sense no loups-garous inside or in the training field. The rotund servant spotted him through the window and he heard a plate drop from her hands as she gasped and hurried to the front door.

Wiping her hands on her flour-dusted apron, she stamped her foot. "Darren Dubose!" Noelle scolded in French. "They have been looking everywhere for you and you have the nerve to show up while Monsieur John is away!"

Darren expected no less from Noelle and simply shrugged. "I'm sorry I've caused so much trouble," he said without a hint of remorse in his tone.

She waved him inside. "Trouble! You've terrorized the whole pack. Come in and I'll get you something to eat."

Noelle and Evangeline catered to him, gave him a fresh shirt and pair of trousers, but neither of them could answer where John and the others were. The women only knew that the pack had been gone for four days searching for him. He had half a mind to go after John himself, but Noelle would have none of it and insisted that he stay put. They would be back soon enough.

The unending silence that engulfed the few days before they arrived back gnawed at Darren's sanity. After he had read and reread every book in the library, he resorted to assisting the women with their chores and weeding the garden while the team of loup-garou gardeners were away.

Darren was on the back veranda when they finally came home from their search. The boys, of course, were both furious and thrilled that he was well. They were given a reprieve from training for almost a week while they looked, but it had all been in vain.

John, of course, was beyond relieved and Darren was elated to see that Bart was alive. The silver-tipped arrows had taken a toll on his body, but as soon as he recovered, the pack set a plan in motion to find their missing brother.

"Whoever took you masked your scent well," John explained as the women tended to the rest of the weary and hungry boys. "We only picked up your trail to the far east and followed it to the Italian border."

It was completely possible that he had passed right by them on the way back to the chateau, but Darren's mind didn't stall there. Bart chimed in with a more important question.

"What happened to you?"

Darren told them about Richard and his scheme to acquire immortality and strength by inheriting it from the bite of a vampire and loup-garou. Upon the mention of vampires, both of them stiffened. That was when he knew that what Jane said must have been true.

"If you escaped, why did you go to Italy?" John asked.

Darren braced himself to tell them about Jane. "I wasn't the only one Richard was keeping prisoner. There was a girl with me. A vampire."

They waited for him to continue, both with a cagey look in their eyes, as if they were ready to attack or reprimand him for even being in association with Jane. He knew that he couldn't tell them about their kiss, but he did reveal that he had gone to Italy to return her to her father.

John and Bart looked to one another and Darren recognized that look. It was the same look his mother donned just before she would reproach him for doing something he knew he shouldn't have done.

"Darren," his alpha began, "vampires are dangerous creatures. You must not go anywhere near them. Do you understand? They will kill you if given the chance. They are no better than hunters."

For the first time since he arrived at the chateau, he completely doubted John's words. He had wondered, questioned, and disregarded it at times, but never doubted that the alpha was far wiser than himself, until now. "Jane didn't want to kill me. She told me that she and her father were friends of the loup-garou. When I brought her to her father, he could have killed me on the spot, but he didn't."

Bart stepped forward and Darren saw a muscle jump in his jaw. "If the vampires that we encountered at the Italian border were who you speak of now, then your little friend was lying to you."

"What are you talking about?"

John moved between them, ready to intercede. "When we followed your trail to Italy, we were confronted by a small coven. We were attacked and some of us were injured."

A chill gushed down his back and his stomach twisted into tight knots. "No," he said, shaking his head. "It couldn't have been Jane's family. She said they were peaceful. She didn't hurt me at all."

"Her family nearly killed one of our own, Darren!" Bart sneered. "What more proof do you need that they can't be trusted?"

Darren didn't want to believe it. He couldn't. They had to be different vampires or perhaps it was a misunderstanding. There had to be a simple explanation. He swallowed back the bile that wanted to spew up his throat. "Was there a young girl there? Blonde hair, blue eyes."

John shrugged and shook his head. "I didn't see any women who attacked us, but that doesn't mean anything."

"Then it might not have been her or her father," Darren declared, hope fluttering in his chest, though everything else told him to be cautious of it.

"You're not listening to – "

John held up a hand to stop his son from continuing his outburst. "Let's just be glad that the boy is safe and we are all well. It could have been much worse, but it isn't. The threats are gone and we can return to our lives."

There was plenty of truth in his words, but Darren could not put this behind him and there would be nothing usual about the weeks and months to come as he would second guess the testimony of his pack and the kind, sweet words of a beautiful vampire that he only knew for a few days.

Nothing about his life was simple anymore. Love, family, loyalty, and trust were all called into question, put through the fires of adversity. Some came out scorched and ashen, while others would come out stronger. It was these things Darren leaned upon as he continued to make sense of his new life as a loup-garou. He was a boy tasting the first fruits of what it was to be a man.

The Prophecy

Legacy Series Book 4

Sheritta Bitikofer

MOONSTRUCK WRITING

CONTENTS

TERMS TO KNOW

Signore/Signori – Gentleman/Gentlemen in Italian

Gospoda – господа, "Gentleman" in Russian

Salt Riot – The Moscow uprising of 1648 (Russian: Соляной бунт, Московское восстание 1648), sometimes known as the salt riot, started because of the government's replacement of different taxes with a universal salt tax for the purpose of replenishing the state treasury after the Time of Troubles. This drove up the price of salt, leading to violent riots in the streets of Moscow. The riot was an early challenge to the reign of Alexei I, eventually resulting in the exile of Alexei's advisor Boris Morozov.

Boyar - A boyar was a member of the highest rank of the feudal Bulgarian, Kievan, Moscovian, Wallachian and Moldavian and later, Romanian aristocracies, second only to the ruling princes (in Bulgaria, tsars), from the 10th century to the 17th century.

Tsar – Russian equivalent of a king or monarch.

Kremlin - The Moscow Kremlin, usually referred to as the Kremlin, is a fortified complex at the heart of Moscow, overlooking the Moskva River to the south, Saint Basil's Cathedral and Red Square to the east, and the Alexander Garden to the west. It is the best known of the kremlins (Russian citadels) and includes five palaces, four cathedrals, and the enclosing Kremlin Wall with Kremlin towers. Also within this complex is the Grand Kremlin Palace.

Spasibo – Спасибо, "Thank you" in Russian

Madám – мадам, "ma'am" or "madam" in Russian

Sér – сэр, "Sir" in Russian

Mal'chikov – мальчиков, "Boys" in Russian

Myshka – мышка "Little Mouse" in Russian

Izmenyat' – изменять, "Shift/Change" in Russian

Wawakalak – Werewolf cursed by the devil to roam the earth as a wolf and beg for food from loved ones. Considered friendly.

Bodark – Werewolf by choice. Chants an incantation after stabbing a tree and morphs into a wolf.

Chapter 1

Small Russian village, a day's travel from Moscow, 1648

"I'll make a bet with you," Hugo said as he looked around at the growing flames that slowly consumed the bundles of hay and branches at their feet. "Fifty rubles says the fur on my collar will catch fire before my beard."

Geoffrey rolled his green eyes heavenward and caught a glimpse of the first few stars appearing in the Russian sky. "You know perfectly well that neither of us have fifty rubles. I hardly think you're in the position to make such a bet."

Beside him, tied to his own post with his hands behind his back, Hugo shrugged. "Fine. Five rabbits then."

Geoffrey shifted his hands against his own bonds, but the silver beads woven into the rope seared his skin as harshly as the fire would in a few moments. "How can you compare fifty rubles to five rabbits? That hardly seems a fair trade."

Hugo chuckled, such a strange sound coming from a werewolf who was about to burn alive. "If I promised you the meat of fifty rabbits, I'd be in your debt for a hundred years. You know how terrible I am at catching the blasted things."

All around, Geoffrey listened to the village folk shout their curses and obscenities at the two brothers. While they spoke in the language of their mother country, Russia, Hugo and Geoffrey preferred English. It was an advantage when they didn't want the locals to know what they were talking about. Certainly, if any of them could understand their banter now, they would think them doubly mad.

"You just had to confuse the *bodark* and the *wawkalak*, didn't you?" Geoffrey chided his younger brother. "We have been here for five – "

"Five years," Hugo cut him off, rolling his dark eyes. "Yes, I know. You're usually the one to talk to the locals and I take the notes. If you hadn't been busy with that blonde, farmer's daughter, you might have been there to say the right thing."

Geoffrey didn't even know where the young lady had gone since they were seized by the mob. He hoped she wouldn't suffer because she was caught romping around with a werewolf. The flames licked around his ankles and he could feel the heat seep through the leather of his boots. June in eastern Russia wasn't outrageously cold, but the temperature had dropped once the sun sank below the horizon. If it were any colder, the fire might have been comfortable. Yet, how comfortable could they really be when the fire would slowly eat away at their flesh?

As werewolves, they could heal faster than a human, but burning alive was still a concern. Their bodies could not regenerate fast enough to compensate for the destructive force of the flames. That still didn't give them much time to escape. If it weren't for the blasted silver in their bonds, it might have been easier to break free.

Still, Geoffrey worked at the ropes that had been especially made to contain them, trying in vain to loosen the tight knots.

"Are you free yet?" he asked Hugo, not bothering to look his way.

"I was hoping you were working on that, brother."

Geoffrey growled in frustration as the first of the flames finally caught on the fabric of his pant leg. "Damn it, Hugo! This is serious."

"I am well aware of that," his brother replied. "No, I am not free yet. This silver is hurting me more than the fire."

"It will soon be the other way around if we can't get off this platform."

Geoffrey tugged one last time and the rope fell slack around his wrists. "I'm loose!"

"Me too."

Hugo snapped his hands around and together they bent low to undo the ropes that tied their feet. Though the silver bit into their fingertips, it was nothing compared to the searing flames that brushed at their cheeks and hands.

Geoffrey fully expected the crowd to scream and run away after the two were-wolves jumped from the burning platform. Yet, not a single one interrupted their shouting or waving of angry fists to even look their way. Not willing to question it, Geoffrey and Hugo darted through the crowd that still faced the pyre.

Their burns quickly healed as they escaped into the cool forest. Their baggy tunics and coats reeked of smoke, though he knew a good bath in the river was long overdue anyway. Yet, there was another scent on the wind that he did not recognize. Either they had come much closer to the depths of hell than he realized, or something else was amiss.

Once they were a good distance from the village and hadn't heard the mob chase after them, Hugo and Geoffrey stopped in a dense cluster of trees. He lifted his nose and took a deep whiff, but coughed and sputtered at the foul stench. Sulfur. His inner wolf growled, but Geoffrey would not let his lips curl up in the same way.

"Did you breathe in some smoke?" Hugo asked.

Geoffrey wondered if his brother's senses had been impaired by that same smoke. "Can you not smell that?"

Hugo sniffed and his brows puckered together in a concentrated look. "What is that?"

A twig snapped to their left and the brothers turned to see a man emerge from the shadows. Was it a man? Geoffrey listened, but could hear no heartbeat. As the figure drew closer, the smell became stronger.

"Do not be alarmed," he said, his voice laced with an Italian accent. It had been a few decades since they had been in Italy, but it was rare to see an Italian this far north. "Are you well?"

In the darkness, Geoffrey could make out the man's aristocratic features and dress. Compared to their dingy peasant's clothes and long beards, he was every inch the European noble.

"Who are you?" Geoffrey asked in Italian, which brought a fascinated glimmer to the stranger's brown eyes.

"A friend," he replied. With a great sweep of his arm, the man bowed low in greeting. "My name is Michael Gennari." When he straightened, he gave them both a warm smile. "And you two are the scholars, Hugo and Geoffrey Swenson. Word of your travels have reached even my inner circle of associates."

Geoffrey appraised the man in front of them, noting how his skin was paler than the moonlight. "Your inner circle?"

Though he was surprised that anyone would speak of them at all, Geoffrey made a point that they should never stay in one place long enough to make an impression. Given that they hadn't been to Italy in quite some time, he was skeptical as to whether the man was telling the truth. Without detecting a heartbeat, Geoffrey couldn't determine such.

When Michael's grin widened, Hugo was the first to notice the sharp tips of the stranger's eye-teeth and he let out a low warning growl. Geoffrey stiffened, bracing for a fight if this vampire should make a wrong move. He had been amiable up until now, but how far could one trust a sworn enemy of the werewolves?

"Please, *signori*," he said. "I have no quarrel with you. In fact, I wish to help."

"Help?" Geoffrey looked him up and down once more, this time searching for a weapon he could use against them.

"Si. In fact, I already have. Did you think those ropes loosened all by themselves? I also distracted the villagers for you. As far as they know, they're watching two witches burn in their town square."

Geoffrey's eyes narrowed upon Michael. "You were not there."

"Evidently, there are many things you don't know about my kind. One of which being that we're not all out to kill werewolves." Michael's smile faltered. "As I hope the same can be said for you."

Hugo took a step forward, but Geoffrey grabbed his shoulder and forced him back.

"No," he said. "We do not harm others unless they harm us first. Right, Hugo?"

His brother's muscles were tense beneath his grip and he could already see his claws sliding out from the tips of his fingers, as if he were ready to fight. As long as Michael proved himself to be an ally, Geoffrey would not allow it.

"That is good to hear." His smile returned again. "My camp is set up just a few miles to the west of here. I was on my way to Moscow when I heard you two were close. I hoped we could join efforts and, perhaps, we could help one another find what it is we're looking for."

Geoffrey lifted his chin. "And what is it you think we're looking for?"

Michael's eyes sparkled with enthusiasm. "The White Wolf of Peace."

Geoffrey continually looked over his shoulder to peer through the trees that partially masked Michael's small encampment. Not too far away, Hugo furiously scrubbed at his scalp that was dipped just below the surface of the water. The slow moving river served as the perfect place to wash up, conveniently close to where the vampire was patiently waiting with his blood servant.

They had talked briefly on the trek they'd taken to the camp, but Geoffrey continued to question the vampire lord's motives. He had never known a vampire to travel alone in this way. He knew they clung to their covens in the similar way that toddlers did to their mothers. They prided themselves on their sense of unity amongst their own kind, much like other werewolves.

Just like he had explained to Michael, Hugo and Geoffrey preferred their lives apart from the restrictions of a pack structure. They were considered rogue by many other werewolves, but they were hardly the savage beasts that myths had made them out to be.

With each passing moment, Michael also seemed to break the general vampire stereotype that Geoffrey had familiarized himself with. He did not seem arrogant, bloodthirsty, or vicious in any way. This only proved to make Geoffrey more skeptical.

He scooped up some water and let it run down his muscular arm and shoulder. The soot and smoky remnants of their brush with death washed away with the cool current. Hugo lifted his head and shook out the excess water, sending droplets spraying in all directions.

Geoffrey shielded himself and splashed his younger brother teasingly. They chuckled, though both of them could hardly wish away the tension they felt.

"Do you really think he wants to help?" Hugo asked, none too quietly.

Geoffrey shushed his brother and whispered at a volume that was barely intelligible over the sound of rushing water. "He can hear you. Vampires have just as sharp of hearing as we do." He took another look over his shoulder to see if Michael was hiding in the thicket. The scent of sulfur hadn't come any closer since they'd shed their dirty clothes and dipped naked into the river. "And I think he is certainly willing to help us. For what purpose, I don't know."

Hugo shook his head as he wrung out his long, dark beard. Wherever they traveled, both brothers made a point of blending in with the locals. Long beards were just one of the alterations to their appearance that they abhorred. What Geoffrey wouldn't have given for a razor to shave off every bit of blonde hair on his jaw and chin.

"I don't trust him," Hugo boldly stated. "Or the human. I say we take the clothes and disappear before we find out what kind of plan he really has in store for us."

As much as Geoffrey wanted to agree to such a plan, he shook his head. "Michael's abilities have proven to be useful so far. If he can get us into the Kremlin so we can search through the archives, we have to bear with him for a little while."

Hugo let out a short, irritated growl and crouched into the water so he could wash off his chest and torso that was covered in a streaked layer of dark soot. "Fine. As soon as we're out of Moscow, we're through with him."

Geoffrey only nodded and continued to clean himself off. Once he was satisfied, he made his way back onto the banks and used one of the clean towels Michael had provided to dry himself off. This was just one of the advantages of traveling with a wealthy patron. The other was slung over a low-lying branch. Two fresh sets of garments awaited them, both in the fashion that was suitable for the European middle-class. Though not as fancy as Michael's clothes, they would do fine for posing as part of his entourage when they walked into the Kremlin.

The brothers rejoined Michael at the campfire where he and his blood servant sat and talked about their plans. On the edge of the encampment sat a covered carriage, just big enough for one passenger, two in a tight squeeze. Two horses were tethered not far off, and grazed on the summer grasses.

Michael stopped abruptly as the two werewolves entered camp. He grinned and gave his nod of approval. "Very nice, *signori*. Though, I do think you should trim your facial hair. I don't know how long it's been since you were in Europe, but it is not the style anymore."

It had taken him years to grow it this long. However, if Michael could truly expedite their search, then perhaps he wouldn't need to grow it out again.

Hugo didn't need to be given permission a second time. Instead of waiting for the blood servant to fish out the razor from the pack beside him, his brother extended a long claw and began to trim away the dark hair. No doubt, it was all for show.

Geoffrey shot him a sidelong glance as he graciously took the razor and tiny looking glass from the blood servant. The fair-haired man, who appeared not too far into his twentieth year, did not seem the least intimidated by the vampire or the werewolves in his company. In fact, he behaved at ease, as if he weren't the only human in the party. By the snippet of accent that Geoffrey picked up on their approach, he assumed the man must have been of German descent.

"Geoffrey, Hugo, this is Reitz Faust. He has been my companion for these last seven years."

Geoffrey shot Michael a perturbed look. "Seven years? He's served you since he was a boy?"

Reitz finally spoke up, something that neither werewolf expected. Servants and slaves did not often speak for themselves in the company of their master. "Yes, Herr Geoffrey. My father served Michael first and I was trained to take his place."

Hugo gave a wary look to his brother, most likely thinking the same thought.

"You have my condolences," Geoffrey said with a nod as he sat himself down beside the fire to begin grooming his beard.

"Whatever for?" Reitz asked.

"For your father," Hugo answered.

Both Michael and his blood servant appeared confused, but Geoffrey was unwilling to explain. It took a moment for them to understand.

"Oh, no," Reitz laughed. "My father isn't dead. He serves another vampire within Michael's coven now. He is in Italy at the moment with Michael's daughter."

Geoffrey jerked at the mention of a daughter. It shouldn't have been a strange concept. Vampires could procreate as easily as anyone, but to hear that Michael had a family seemed to humanize him a little more than he was comfortable with.

The sudden motion of the blade in his hand cut into his cheek and he hissed at the pain. Reitz quickly grabbed for a handkerchief and handed it to his new traveling companion. Geoffrey took it and cleaned away the blood. The cut healed quickly enough and for once, he was thankful that he didn't have to hide his supernatural abilities from human eyes.

"I was just about to tell Reitz all about your prolific travels," Michael said. "But, now that you're here, perhaps you can tell him yourself."

The young man turned with a smile to the two werewolves. "Yes, please. Michael and I have been to a great many places, but is it true you two have journeyed to the orient?"

Geoffrey gave a sly smile to his brother, cueing him to take the lead in this conversation as he continued to scrape away the years of hair growth.

"We have," Hugo proclaimed with pride. "The orient, India, Africa, Italy, Spain, Norway. We've been in Russia for five years and if we can't find what we're looking for, we plan to journey to the New World next."

Reitz's blue eyes went wide. "Truly? Incredible. Michael said you're looking for the White Wolf of Peace, just as we are."

Hugo gave him a shrug. "Only recently. We've been collecting fables and legends about our kind from every culture and religion of the world. We go to each country and visit small towns and villages. If a family is kind enough to give us food and a place to stay, we ask them about the local legends."

"Fascinating," Reitz said. "How long have you been collecting these stories?"

Hugo pursed his lips in thought, then looked to his elder brother. "Would you say it's been two-hundred and... fifty? No, two-hundred and sixty years."

Geoffrey flung some locks of the trimmed beard into the grass. "I believe it's been two hundred and eighty years, give or take a few."

If it were possible for Reitz's eyes to widen any more, they would have popped out of his sockets by now. "You must age similar to Michael."

Geoffrey assessed the vampire. If he were werewolf, he would easily be placed around their ages. "Pray, how old are you?" he asked as he inspected some of his handiwork in the mirror.

Without missing a beat, Michael replied, "I was born in 1158."

Now it was Hugo's turn to stare in wonder. "No, you age much more slowly than we do. You don't appear a day over thirty."

Michael grinned. "I'll take that as a compliment."

"What made you decide to hunt down these stories?" Reitz asked, obviously enraptured by the idea of a scholarly werewolf.

Geoffrey wiped the flat ends of the blade against his thigh. "At first, we were looking for our father. Then, it turned into a quest for knowledge. We had no one to guide us in our youth, so we had to figure it out for ourselves. Seeking out those of our own kind seemed the easiest way."

Michael's brows furrowed with concern. "You had no one to teach you?"

Hugo gave a huff and Geoffrey knew he was about to start in on his righteous speech. "Our father left us when we were barely ten years old, several years before we turned. Our mother knew what we would become, but she was too distraught over our father's disappearance to show us anything. She died of a broken heart. When we turned, we tried to find him, but had to settle for a quick lesson taught to us by an alpha in Scotland."

The vampire nodded. "I understand, you must have had a difficult childhood."

Geoffrey would have scolded Hugo for his hypocritical slander of their father. His younger brother was almost no better, but at least they had tried to find Hugo's son around the time he came of age.

If their mission allowed it, Geoffrey would have gladly let him and his brother settle down in Warminster so they could be with the boy when he grew up. Yet, if they were to complete their catalogue of shifter myths, they couldn't stay in England any longer. Not only that, but Martha didn't even know what they were. Hugo never had the courage to tell her and Geoffrey didn't think it was his place. With the rising hysteria of witches, everything told them that it was their time to move on from England, with or without the boy.

When they came back to England with the intent to mentor Darren, all they found were the remains of a farmhouse and none of the townspeople would even speak the name of the widow who stayed there with her bastard son. If listening to the myths and legends of the world had taught him anything, it was that people could be downright superstitious about the silliest things.

Their father, on the other hand, had no excuse for his abandoning Geoffrey and Hugo, and he didn't even try to return to them. He could be dead and buried somewhere for all they knew. Hugo certainly didn't care.

"I've heard you never joined a pack?" Michael continued.

Geoffrey shook his head. "No. We never felt the need and our journeys don't allow us to stay in one place for very long. Although, we have stayed with packs for a short time in the past."

"I know of a werewolf who doesn't belong to a pack either and we haven't heard from him in some time. Perhaps you know him? His name is Tor, an Egyptian." Michael took on a certain eagerness, as if dearly hoping that one of the brothers knew of the werewolf's whereabouts.

"We've been to Egypt," Hugo said, "but we didn't come across any of our kind by that name." He took the mirror from his elder brother's hand to cut out the shoddy job he'd done to his beard with only his claws to aid him. Without a word,

Geoffrey passed him the razor and he took it to clean up the jagged bits. So much for intimidating their new acquaintances.

"He hasn't been in Egypt in about seventy years," Michael said, leaning his forearms on his knees. "The last we knew, he was sailing to India with a family friend who was also an explorer."

"We haven't been to India in over a century," Geoffrey replied. "I'm sorry, but we haven't heard of your friend."

Michael's shoulders sagged and nodded. "Very well. My daughter will be disappointed, but I fear that he may have been lost at sea. She still hopes that he is alive, but I do not share in it."

Geoffrey ran his hands over the rough stubble on his jaw, finding it strange to feel so much skin beneath the coarse hair. If things progressed in the way he hoped, he would be able to keep his beard this short for plenty more years to come.

"When do we leave for the Kremlin?" he finally asked, ready to get this business over with. They had spent longer time in a country before, but the last five years had proved to be more than a little tedious. Russia was a big country and it had taken them this long just to cover the western portion.

"As soon as you are ready," Michael replied heartily. "We have the rest of the night to travel and we should be able to sneak inside before daybreak."

Geoffrey had almost forgotten the vampire's limitations. The brothers were used to traveling at all hours of the day or night, whatever it took to get to where they needed to go. Michael and Reitz were restricted to the darkness and he inwardly cringed at all the time they would be losing. Yet, if they stuck to their agreement, they would only have to stay with Michael just long enough to find where the White Wolf roamed. Then, they would leave the vampire and blood servant behind.

CHAPTER 2

The inside of the Kremlin palace was beyond stunning. Even in the dim light of the torches, the gold embellishments and brilliantly colored murals that covered the walls reflected the candlelight throughout. The hard soles of their shoes rapped against the polished floors as they made their way through corridors and lavish chambers. The abundant amount of time and detailed craftsmanship that must have gone into creating such a glorious, unique masterpiece baffled Hugo's mind. It took more than a little restraint to keep himself from slowing to a stop just to admire the beauty of the palace. The intricate patterns alone were dazzling.

Ahead of him, Geoffrey and the vampire led the way. Guards and other royal delegates paid them absolutely no mind, as if they weren't simply waltzing through the private rooms of the tsar's magnificent home. They might as well have been invisible, just like when he and his brother escaped the angry mob in the village.

Despite his awe and reverence for the architecture, unlike anything he had ever seen before in Europe, Hugo still felt a sliver of unease in his gut. His wolf loathed Michael's presence and wanted nothing more than to run at the sight of him. He didn't trust the vampire, not as explicitly as his brother did. It was a means to an end, nothing more. Yet, after their long talk around the fire, Hugo was inclined to believe his brother was warming up to the blood sucker. Reitz might have been a good enough fellow, but Michael would take much longer to earn his respect.

"What exactly are you doing to make them look the other way?" Geoffrey asked as they passed through another doorway as casually as if they owned the palace.

Hugo snapped just inches from the nose of one of the guards standing beside the threshold and he didn't even flinch.

"I am manipulating their minds to ignore us," the vampire replied. "They don't see anything we're doing. It's the same technique I used to mask your escape in the village."

"So how do we know you're not manipulating our minds?" Hugo questioned. Geoffrey shot him a scathing look, the same one that he always gave when he wanted his brother to behave himself.

"I never use my abilities against a friend," Michael replied as he passed a smile over his shoulder to the two werewolves. "Besides, if I really wanted to manipulate your minds, you would have trusted me more readily. Since you still don't, you know that I'm not forcing my will upon you."

The vampire's logic seemed sound, but Hugo would continually question his own thoughts as long as they were close. He had to hold on to his brother's promise that as soon as they knew where the White Wolf was, they would leave Michael and Reitz. Only then would he be at ease again.

"You seem to know where you're going," Geoffrey commented as they took another twisting turn down a corridor half hidden behind a towering column.

"I reached into the memories of one of the guards on our way in and found where the library is hidden. Very few people outside of the Kremlin staff know anything about the archives."

Geoffrey nodded in approval, seeming to openly accept that Michael could simply read the minds of anyone he wished. Hugo, on the other hand, could feel the sweat bead on the back of his neck. What else did Michael know about them that he wasn't willing to admit? Obviously, the vampire knew that he was not trusted so eagerly, but what more did he see?

If it was possible for Hugo to have the discipline to shut his mind like a steel trap, he would have.

They came to a modest wooden door reinforced with heavy metal plating, held in place by soldered rivets. A thick bar, locked in place by a hefty padlock blocked their way. Michael examined the lock and then shook his head in dismay. "This is too much for me. Would one of you care to try?"

Hugo stepped forward, gripped the lock in his hand and ripped it clean from the loop. Michael thanked him and opened the door, but Geoffrey shot him another reprimanding look. His brother knew all too well that he did it as a show of force. However, his efforts to intimidate the vampire were for nothing.

Down a few flights of narrow stairs, they descended beneath the Kremlin, encountering not a bit of opposition. With no light or torches to guide their way, all three men had to use their preternatural vision to see their way down the stone steps.

Hugo stopped in his tracks when he detected a new, but familiar scent. It was the same pungent sulfur smell that seared his nostrils when they first met Michael, but there was a slight difference that he couldn't quite distinguish. They were not alone in the darkness.

Almost as soon as the new odor registered with Geoffrey as well, they were ambushed. A streak of something dark and fast blurred toward them. Michael was the first to face it and he reacted as calmly as if the charging threat were nothing more than a moth or darting animal.

He snatched at the blur and pinned it to the wall. Only then could they make out that the creature attacking them was a man, clad in the customary uniform of a Kremlin guard. Only, the fabric looked to be torn and stained by years of neglect. His eyes, however, did not belong to any normal man. They glowed a bright red that would have been clearly visible in the light, even without their keen senses.

The vampire snarled, baring his fangs at his captor. Michael managed to hold him at bay, but neither Geoffrey nor Hugo would dare approach. The guard pinned to the wall appeared much younger, probably a boy not far out of his teen years. His jet black hair was pulled back from his face and the sharp features of his nose and chin might have made him an attractive man.

A few long moments passed before Michael looked to the brothers, breaking his concentrated stare. "He needs to feed."

Hugo was the first to back away up the steps. Geoffrey only gave him a wary look. "Feed?"

Michael nodded. "I can see it in his mind. He's been kept down here for too long by himself. He's starving. Perhaps that's why the door was locked that way."

"You can't be serious!" Hugo cried, his voice echoing against the brick walls that closed in on both sides.

"Terribly serious," Michael replied with a troubled look. "He cannot drink my blood, but even if Reitz were here, I wouldn't want to risk his life. This vampire might take too much blood by accident and kill a human. I assure you no harm will come to either of you... Please?" It was clear he cared for this vampire, perhaps as much as either of them would care for one of their kind if they came to find one suffering in this way. That didn't convince Hugo.

The two werewolves looked to one another, but Geoffrey was the first to slip off his coat and roll up the sleeve of his shirt.

"Brother, you can't do this," Hugo hissed, ready to jump in and intercept if he needed.

"Short of killing him, we aren't going to get past any other way."

"Then kill him!" Hugo exclaimed. "I'll do it myself if neither of you can."

Michael's lips curled up and the vampire hissed at him. As if he had been struck in the chest by the dominance of an alpha, Hugo was stunned into silence, neither could he move. All he could do was watch Geoffrey approach the wild vampire and offer out his arm.

With Michael still in full control, he allowed the guard to feed on his brother's blood. Fangs dug deep into his flesh. Geoffrey turned his head away so he didn't have to look, but Hugo saw no betrayal of pain or discomfort.

"It doesn't hurt," he said to assure his younger brother. "Certainly an odd sensation, though."

"Our saliva numbs the skin when we feed," Michael said, his eyes fixed on the scene to ensure that nothing went awry.

Hugo found the will to move closer, slowly stepping down the steps until he could see the vampire's mouth latched onto his brother's arm. A dribble of blood leaked from the corner of his mouth and slid over the curve of Geoffrey's wrist.

There weren't many things that could make his stomach turn, but the sight of the vampire's hungry, wide-eyed stare made Hugo almost retch. Even his wolf cringed at the sight and urged him to continue on toward the library. His bond with his brother was stronger than any primal need to flee from the barbaric scene so Hugo stayed. He forced himself to watch the feeding, glancing to his brother's face to make sure that he was still well. Besides a slight loss of color in his complexion, Geoffrey seemed to be holding up just fine.

The tension in the vampire ebbed away and his eyes were no longer red, but a deep brown hue. Michael eased his new pet off Geoffrey's arm and Hugo tugged his brother away before he could be seized again.

The vampire nearly crumbled to the floor with relief and Michael tended to his slightly weakened condition.

"Will he be all right?" Geoffrey asked as he wiped away the excess blood on his skin.

"He should be. He just needs a moment to recover. Go on ahead to the library and we will catch up."

"We?" Hugo snapped.

Michael shot him a displeased look. "Yes. Anton will be joining us."

Hugo rolled his eyes. The vampire guard has a name now. "I presume you found that out from his mind?"

"Through the hunger and mangled thoughts, yes. I'll let him make the formal introductions once he's stronger. It shouldn't be too much longer."

Geoffrey and Hugo hurried down the corridor.

"I can't believe you let that thing bite you," Hugo murmured under his breath once they were a good distance away.

"What other choice did I have?" Geoffrey replied. "He would have died or killed us. At least Michael was there."

There was no amount of reasoning that would let Hugo believe there was anything good about this trip. If it weren't for Michael, they wouldn't have needed to be there at all.

"Let's just get this over with..." His last words trailed off as they arrived at the expansive library. The corridor opened up into the high-ceiling chamber. Bookshelves and mountains of scrolls lined the walls. Tables and chairs, that didn't look stable in the least, took up the floor in the center of the room. The musty smell of dust clogged his nostrils, rivaling the stench of the vampire who had lived between these walls for God only knew how long.

Hugo's shoulders slumped in defeat. Russia was certainly a backward, medieval country. The innovations in style, art, and architecture hadn't made its way this far to the east. When he thought of a library, he suspected a few bookcases and maybe some royal records, but nothing like this mess. Surrounded by such knowledge, he wondered how they would ever find anything about the White Wolf.

Standing next to him, Geoffrey must have fully felt the weight of the task at hand.

"You take the left side of the room and I'll take the right?" Hugo quipped.

That elicited a soft smile out of Geoffrey. "Are you sure you remember how to read Russian?"

"If I get confused, I'll ask for your help."

Geoffrey elbowed him in the ribs. "I might as well read to you then. You'll be asking for my help all night."

Two pairs of footsteps sounded down the stairs behind them and Hugo quickly moved into the room to make way for the two vampires who were ready to join them.

"You have my sincerest thanks and apologies, *gospoda*."

Hugo turned with a startled look to behold the once rabid and vicious vampire, standing upright with his chest out and sensible like any other man. If it weren't for his ratty garments, Hugo would have never guessed he had behaved with anything other than dignity and poise.

"Not at all... I think?" Geoffrey replied with a questioning tone as he looked from his brother to the former ravenous vampire. Without any prompting from Michael, he extended his hand in greeting. "Geoffrey Swenson."

The guard smiled, his white teeth slightly red with residual blood. "Anton Wiatrowski." He heartily shook Geoffrey's hand. "Thank you, truly. I can't remember the last time I was so contented."

At a loss for anything better to say, Geoffrey simply turned to his brother. "This is my brother, Hugo. You'll have to excuse his manners."

Hugo waved him off, not willing to play nice. "Charmed, I'm sure."

Anton looked to him and his smile faltered a little. "I'll try not to hold your offer to kill me against you."

Michael quickly stepped in. "Anton, I assume you're familiar with this place?"

The guard nodded and looked down to his clothes as if he didn't realize how tattered they really were. A look of embarrassment passed over his face before he replied. "Indeed. I've read everything in here, at least twice. Sometimes, it's the only way to distract myself. The tsar assigned me to guard this place from outsiders. I should kill you, but after the kindness you've shown me..." He gave a pointed glance to Hugo. "I suppose I can assist you."

Thankful they wouldn't be reading through mountains of scrolls, Hugo stopped and waited for them to get to the point.

Michael explained their search for the White Wolf and had to retranslate his request a few different ways before Anton finally understood exactly what they were looking for. The White Wolf of Peace wasn't just any *wawkalak* or *bodark*.

"It's a wolf that is said to embody the spirit of an ancient royal that was canonized as a deity, bringing peace to the community."

It took a moment for Anton to search his memory, but then he moved through the piles of loose-leaf manuscripts and scrolls to stand before a tall bookcase. "I believe there's a book here that mentions it. Only, I can't recall which one."

Geoffrey and Hugo fell in beside Anton and slipped out stacks upon stacks of the volumes, some bound in leather and others held together by leather cords with no formal binding. He might have hoped too soon for a quick solution.

Hugo chose to sit on the floor, away from the others as they brought their selections to the table and began skimming through the ancient pages.

"Why are you looking for this wolf?" Anton asked after they had worked through more pleasant, casual conversation that Hugo wasn't paying attention to. Once more, Geoffrey was opening himself up to a stranger. For being the older brother of the two, Hugo did not think him the wisest.

Michael was the first to respond. "When was the last time you left this palace?"

Anton didn't have an answer. "It seems like an interminable amount of time."

"The world is not a friendly place," Michael continued. "Wars, hatred, senseless feuds, murder, strife, and all manner of oppression have stolen the hearts of man. This Spirit of Peace may be our only chance to restore balance."

Hugo rolled his eyes and he was glad his brother didn't see or he might have been on the receiving end of another scolding. What Michael said wasn't untrue. The world had long been rocked by violence and anger. They had only recently heard of the legend and, though they might have easily been lumped with the countless other werewolves who were untrusting of vampires, they knew it was not the way to live. The dissention, greed, and general despicable conduct of the three races of the world were enough to make the most holy man lose faith in the goodness of the Almighty.

It wasn't just man destroying man. It was werewolf turning against werewolf over territories and rumors. Alphas battled one another for control over space. As if they didn't have enough to worry about with the vampires looking to eliminate their kind, they didn't need the threat from within. Perhaps that was the true reason Hugo and Geoffrey never longed for a home with a pack. Too much bickering, too much rivalry and discord. It wasn't worth it.

If they could find the White Wolf of Peace, perhaps they could reason with it to ease the strain, just enough so the world could breathe easy again. Evidently, Michael was just as displeased with the way their races lived. Why else would he wish to help them rather than kill them?

Hugo shook his head and hoped the vampire's mind-altering powers weren't starting to have an effect upon him.

CHAPTER 3

The last time Geoffrey's head pounded this hard, he was a young man suffering from a common human ailment that should have been unfamiliar to him now. That was over two hundred years ago and as a werewolf, Geoffrey shouldn't have gotten headaches. Bent over the manuscript resting on the table, his eyes straining in the dark, he had lost track of how many pages he had read.

The four of them had sat and paced across this underground library for what seemed like days. Geoffrey could feel his stomach growl in protest to the amount of time he had gone without a meal and he knew that if his brother was awake, he would have been feeling the effects of the hunger as well. Hugo leaned against a bookcase a few hours ago and had nodded off after his efforts proved fruitless as well.

When they first dove into the challenge of searching through the texts, Michael and Anton talked more than read. They hunkered down to their task only when Geoffrey mentioned that they were running out of time before any of the guards might discover the lock on the heavily guarded library door was torn off.

He rubbed at his red-rimmed eyes and let out a tired sigh. Anton sat across the table from him while Michael had been quietly wandering around the room with a volume between his hands. He was glad that both of the vampires were as veracious readers as werewolves, otherwise this task might have taken much longer.

"How many more books?" Geoffrey asked to his companion.

Anton lifted his head and regarded the bookshelf. "Perhaps only another dozen or so."

That was both good and bad. Good, in the sense that they were narrowing down the possible options for which book held the secret of the White Wolf. Bad, in that if they still couldn't find it in the last books from that bookcase, the four of them would have to move on to the rest of the library. Though Anton's memory seemed reliable, it was still likely that he was mistaken where he last saw the manuscript they were searching for. Geoffrey was determined to take a break before it came to that. He needed to eat something, and unlike the vampires, he didn't have such a convenient source.

Michael's footsteps slowed and then stopped completely. Geoffrey turned and regarded the older vampire, and saw the excited look in his dark eyes. With a snap of his fingers and a wide grin, he looked up to his friends. "I've got it!"

Hugo jolted awake, his wolf eyes nearly glowing in the darkness. Geoffrey quickly stood and met Michael in the open space in the middle of the library, Anton hot on his heels.

"You've found it?"

"I believe so," Michael said as he angled the open book for them to read. "It talks about an ancient Spirit of Peace that takes the form of a wolf and travels in the east."

Geoffrey's eyes skimmed over the passage and nodded with a smile. "Yes, this might be it."

Anton craned his neck between their shoulders to verify. "Yes! It is. I remember this." Then, he dodged around to take a peek at the title on the cover.

Hugo wiped the sleep from his eyes and hurried toward them. "Please say it's not far from here?"

Michael shook his head. "Afraid not. It says it's been commonly sighted in the far east, but not in the orient. Yet, it doesn't give an exact location."

"So, we'll have to search the entire country," Hugo groaned. "This told us nothing we didn't already know."

"Not necessarily," Geoffrey interrupted. "We can narrow our search down to one half of the country, the half we're currently not in, and then ask around if they have seen the White Wolf."

Michael pointed to the text. "It doesn't say the wolf is white. It actually doesn't signify a color at all."

"I'm sure peasants would recognize a wolf as unique as that, though," Anton added.

Geoffrey pinched the top of the page near the fold and gently ripped the parchment from the book. The younger vampire who must have prized these volumes let out a horrified sound as if the werewolf had just desecrated something holy. "We will need to refer to this," he consoled him.

With precision, he folded the paper and made his way toward the exit. Hugo followed close behind, probably just as eager to leave the library and dusty tomes. Geoffrey heard Michael snap the book shut and have a quick conversation with Anton before they trailed behind up the stairs.

"I can help you get out of the palace safely," Anton told them.

"Thanks, but no thanks," Hugo called over his shoulder as they took the stairs three at a time, ascending back to the mortal world.

The closer they came to the surface, the more Geoffrey began to realize that something wasn't quite right. Heavy footsteps sounded above their heads, men shouting in Russian as they went.

"He's coming with us," Michael announced.

While Hugo was inclined to turn and argue, Geoffrey grabbed his brother's lapel and hurried him forward up the steps in an attempt to silence him. What was one more to their party going to hurt? They couldn't simply leave him there to suffer from further starvation at the hands of the tsar, the *boyars*, and his council. He was put down in the library to guard it against intruders, and those intruders were the only source of nourishment he received. He couldn't allow Anton to remain a prisoner like that.

Geoffrey would be lying if he said that Anton's feeding had absolutely no affect upon him. At first, it was a means to an end. Michael wasn't going to let them dispense with him in the way Hugo wished, but they also needed his assistance. Even before he mentioned that he had read the entirety of the library, Geoffrey somehow knew that Anton could prove useful.

However, the more the vampire fed on him, the more attached he became. He had invested his blood into the young man and, however much he despised the idea, Geoffrey felt obligated to help him however else he could.

"What's happening?" Geoffrey asked, purposefully changing the subject to draw their attention to the activity within the Kremlin.

As they neared the door that led into the hallway, he could just catch bits and pieces of the frantic and panicked conversations. Anton pushed his way forward and listened, the torchlight from the corridor falling across his pale face.

"A mob has surrounded the palace," he said in a whisper, lest someone running by hear him. It was clear that in the growing hysteria, no one cared to notice that the door to the secret library had been broken into.

Hugo squeezed past the vampire and peeked out into the hall. "I don't see any sunlight. It should be safe to leave."

"Were we down here all day?" Geoffrey questioned.

"It appears so," Michael replied. "Anton, lead the way and I'll do my best to distract the guards we pass. Hopefully, they will be too preoccupied to notice us."

"Distract?" Anton asked, a confused frown forming between his brows. Clearly, he knew just as little as the werewolves did about the elder vampire's extraordinary psychic abilities.

Hugo shoved Anton through the doorway. "No time to explain. Just get us out of here."

The vampire, tattered uniform and all, paused in the middle of the empty hall to gain his bearings. The others waited, then followed him in the opposite direction from which they had originally come. Geoffrey half expected his impulsive brother to make a remark on the fact, but he seemed too busy listening to the shouts coming from outside the palace.

Geoffrey heard them too. The people were rioting over unfair taxes and something about salt. They wanted the heads of officials, but the tsar was not willing to listen to their demands. A riot would surely break out at any moment and he didn't want to be around when it finally happened.

A few guards ran past them and Anton flinched, but just as before, Michael did a fair job of masking their movements through his bizarre, but oddly useful mind tricks. Anton led them through the heart of the palace, through the grand golden chambers and decadent rooms. He led them down through the servants' quarters and out the back passageways that Geoffrey was sure Michael wasn't even aware of.

Within moments, they were outside the Kremlin, breathing in the fresh night air. The mob that clustered around the front of the palace wouldn't see their escape through the streets of Moscow.

The party arrived back to the small encampment just outside of the city. Reitz stood to greet them, but when his eyes fell on Anton, he looked less than enthusiastic. Michael took the time to explain everything to his blood servant and introduce the new vampire, while Hugo pulled Geoffrey aside, well out of earshot.

"We have our information," his younger brother whispered. "Let's leave them. We don't need their help anymore."

Geoffrey glanced over his shoulder and sighed. He remembered the promise he had given to Hugo before they left for Moscow, but something didn't settle right with the idea of leaving anymore. Not only because of their new addition, but because of everything Michael had said in the library.

Their goals and values were nearly identical. Past their obvious differences, Geoffrey found himself identifying with Michael's frustrations about the world at war. The mob around the Kremlin was evidence enough that this world needed the Spirit of Peace, now more than ever. Five heads were better than two – though

Geoffrey sometimes wondered if his brother's mind could only be counted as a half. If Michael was the traveler he proclaimed himself to be, his assistance in navigating through the harsh eastern lands would prove invaluable.

Geoffrey looked to his brother and did not take pleasure in what he would say. "I think we need to travel with them for a bit longer, just until we feel like we're close to finding the Spirit. Then, we'll part ways."

Hugo gave him a look as if he had grown three heads and sprouted a set of devilish wings. "I can't believe you're siding with them over us."

"That's not what I'm doing," Geoffrey growled.

"You actually think staying with them will benefit us at all?"

His brother balled his hands into tight fists as his eyes glowed their wolfish gold. Geoffrey didn't want this to end in a fight, but his wolf was ready for one if it came.

"I think it is pointless to leave them now," Geoffrey replied, stepping closer so his brother wouldn't mistake the light shiver of dominance he radiated. "If Michael could find us in an obscure village, he will find us in the forest. He would only follow, if he was truly set on all five of us seeking out the Spirit together."

A muscle jumped in Hugo's jaw and Geoffrey knew he had won his case. Hugo was eager to get away from the vampires, but fleeing wouldn't do them any good at the present. It would only create a strained conflict between them.

"When can we leave them? I won't travel all the way across Russia with that smell."

"If you're truly worried about the smell, we can stuff some cloth up your nose."

Hugo sneered. "Cloth you've wiped your ass with? No, thank you."

Geoffrey cracked a smile and playfully pushed his brother to make him stumble backward. The two chuckled and their eyes faded to their human color. "I promise, as soon as the time is right, we will part ways with Michael. Just, not right now."

"Traveling with them will slow us down," Hugo remarked as he glanced toward the campsite.

"The carriage will protect the vampires during the day, though I'm sure it will be slower than we are used to."

Hugo pursed his lips in thought. "Perhaps I can run ahead and scout the path. You know, make sure it's clear."

"And let you out of my sight?" Geoffrey said. "Not a chance. If I have to tether you to my hip with chains, I won't let you wander off. Who knows if I'll see you again."

For a moment, a hurt look flashed in his younger brother's eyes. "I would never leave you," he said softly. "Especially to them. Anton would bleed you dry, I'm sure of it."

Geoffrey rolled his eyes and draped his arm around Hugo's shoulders. "You needn't protect me, brother. I can take care of myself."

"Yes," he spat sarcastically. "Just like you could get free from the pyre the other night."

"I would have gotten free if I were given a few more moments."

They slowly traced their way back to the group. "What about the time that merchant nearly cut off your manhood for messing around with his wife?"

Geoffrey winced. "Well..."

"Or the time – "

"Okay," he cut him off. "We need one another. I understand."

Hugo laughed. "Ah, you need me, but I certainly don't need you," he said as he poked his brother in the chest.

"Weren't you the one to admit that you were a piss-poor excuse for a rabbit hunter?" Geoffrey teased.

"Rabbits, yes. But I am an excellent deer hunter. I specialize in big game. Which," Hugo held up an instructional finger, "I believe we are due for a meal. Shall we?"

Geoffrey looked to the vampires and blood servant who were still deep in conversation. "I suppose we can disappear for a moment or two."

With that, they steered away from the campsite and dashed into the forest to find their unsuspecting quarry. Hugo might have been obnoxious, arrogant, and downright cocky at times, but Geoffrey wouldn't have traded his company for the world. They were all they had left. They were each other's pack, each other's support. For centuries, they'd had to rely on one another and Geoffrey couldn't imagine a time when Hugo wouldn't always be close by. He wasn't sure what he would do without his brother.

CHAPTER 4

Days stretched on into weeks as they trekked across the wild and untamed country. As much as they could help it, they avoided towns and villages along the way. Skirting around farms and cottages until they reached the half of Russia that might as well have been hell itself. Geoffrey wondered who in their right mind would live in such a rugged, inhospitable place.

The answer became clear as they continued to pass by huts, cottages, and small clusters of villages, even this deep into the wilderness.

The journey became more and more difficult as the roads they took to accommodate Michael's carriage ceased to serve their purpose. The wheels constantly popped off their axels after taking a dip or unexpected bump, rocking the entire cabin and the vampires inside. During the day, Reitz and the two werewolves had to reposition the wheel and get the carriage back on track, only to be stalled in the same fashion, not an hour later.

Three nights into the east, Michael and Anton came to the decision that they could no longer use the carriage. They would have to bundle themselves against the light of the sun and travel in that way. The older vampire said they had done it before, but it proved to make the journey just as arduous.

However, Michael wanted to travel one more day with the carriage, so as to get the most out of it before they had to abandon the abused vehicle. It was on this final day, when Reitz was resting after being up all night, and the vampires were unconscious, that Hugo pulled Geoffrey aside.

"How much longer?" he asked his brother, fury and frustration plain in his voice.

Geoffrey ran his hand through his hair, hating the way the oils and grime felt slick on his fingers. They were due for a bath, but could hardly make the time for it between sleeping, walking, and fixing the wagon. Such simple things were so much easier and convenient when they traveled alone. "I'm not sure," he grumbled.

Hugo let out a suppressed growl that rumbled in his chest.

"I know you want to leave," Geoffrey sighed. "I do as well."

"Then, let's go while Reitz is asleep! If they find us again, we'll say we were following our instincts to try and find the wolf sooner. I've been itching to go farther north. The paths don't allow us to travel as we usually do."

Geoffrey nodded. He had felt the pull as well. Michael was set on following the roads, but the two brothers had learned long ago that no adventure came from sticking to the lines on a map. If their wolves were urging them to the north, then they needed to go, Michael or not.

Finally, he nodded his consent and Hugo didn't waste time. He oriented himself to the north and darted through the woods. His pack slapped against his hip and back as he went. Geoffrey followed as they dodged through the densely packed trees and leapt over the shrubs that dared to keep them at bay.

Their eyes glowed gold in the afternoon light as they followed their wolves to the north, uncertain what they would find.

It had been three days since they'd left Michael and the caravan behind. They had seen no sign of the vampires or blood servant and assumed they had resolved to let the werewolves go where they wished. At least, that's what Hugo hoped. Being far away from the stench of the vampires made him appreciate the smell of fresh air and open countryside.

They could run at their full speed for the first time since before they'd joined up with Michael and Reitz, and Hugo was glad to finally stretch his legs. His brother didn't fully share in his revel of freedom. Even now, as he sat on a fallen log and poured over the manuscript page again, scratching at the scruff on his cheek, Hugo wondered if Geoffrey could be having second thoughts about running away from the vamps.

He looked to the north and felt his wolf coax him into running again, but Hugo would go nowhere without his brother.

"Are you going to keep staring at that thing all evening, or are we going to get a little more ground covered before nightfall?" he asked, feeling his wolf tell him something else, but this was far more difficult to ignore.

Geoffrey glanced up briefly before folding the parchment and tucking it away into his coat pocket. "Yes, although I wonder if we should go a little farther to the east today."

Hugo tested that against his senses, sniffing the air and looking around as if his surroundings would give him any clue to affirm his brother's suggestion. "I suppose we can," he replied.

It was then, as his ears strained to hear for any threat or meal, Hugo heard it. A light melody, hummed by a woman. By the sound of it, she was older, far past her prime, but still had a lovely voice. Without telling his brother anything, he leapt into a nearby tree and scurried up the branches so he could get a better look.

"What are you doing?" Geoffrey called from below.

From a high branch, almost near the top, Hugo looked and spotted the sliver of smoke far in the distance. This high up, he could smell a roast cooking over a fire and his mouth watered. With nimble movements, he made his way down the tree and faced his brother.

"It's a cottage, a few miles from here. An old woman is cooking a roast." He grinned. "Didn't you say you wanted to talk to the locals? We can get an easy meal and ask her about the wolf."

Geoffrey gave him a wry look. "I think you're more interested in the easy meal."

Hugo shrugged. "Perhaps, but we can both get what we want. What's the harm?"

His brother stepped closer and eyed him suspiciously. "You know we can't stay long."

If he weren't so right, Hugo would have laughed at his elder brother's superb intuition. "You are right. If we hurry, we can stay with the hag for an hour or so."

With his silent agreement, they took off into the woods once more, bound straight for the lonely cottage whose chimney billowed the sumptuous scents of roasting meat and delicious herbs, promising a fine meal for the werewolves.

The humming of the old woman became louder to both of their ears as they came closer to the cottage. Staying just out of sight in the shades of the forest, they circled the quaint home, admiring the simplistic design that was typical of the peasant dwellings they had passed by. This house, however, seemed different. The sweet and savory scents of the meats were what enticed them to come closer, but there was something else in the clearing where the cottage was nestled.

Hugo likened it to the feeling when one stepped into a warm church on a cold, snowy night. There was a safety, a comfortableness about the place that made him feel even more drawn to go inside and meet the woman who continued to unwittingly serenade them.

Then, the humming stopped.

"Come closer," the withered voice spoke from inside the home. "There's plenty for everyone."

Hugo and Geoffrey exchanged puzzled looks, but before they could second guess themselves, they found they were in the clearing. They passed by budding flowerbeds and a tiny garden that was only producing enough to sustain one elderly gardener.

Geoffrey was the first to enter the cottage, not bothering to knock since the lone resident had invited them in already. The furnishing inside the one-room cottage was sparse and what furniture there was appeared to be old. Perhaps just as old, if not older, than the woman herself.

The elderly woman sat on a three-legged stool by the crackling fireplace. One hand stirred the copper pot over the flames while the other rested on her knee to support her weight as she leaned over. Beads of sweat dotted her wrinkled forehead as kind, green eyes looked up at them through greying brows. Her long, silvery hair was pulled back into a braid that trailed down her hunched back.

She smiled and they saw a few teeth had been rotted out from neglect. Yet, the sincerity could be fully felt and the corner of Hugo's mouth twitched in response.

"Come in, *mal'chikov*. Come in." She pulled out the spoon and hung the handle upon the nail beside the fireplace. "I wasn't expecting company, but please take a seat and relax."

Hugo looked to his brother, who still seemed skeptical. His first impulse was to believe this old woman was a witch. How else would she know that they were close by? Hugo didn't suppose they were that loud on their approach. She wasn't a vampire and she certainly wasn't a werewolf like them. He had never met a female of their kind before.

Geoffrey did not move from where he stood just in the doorway, but Hugo squeezed past him to take his leisure in one of the rickety chairs next to the dining table. The wood creaked and wailed under his weight and it was clear the furniture hadn't been used by someone so heavy in ages. Even though it held well, Hugo tensed his legs to rise in case it should collapse from under him.

"We don't want to trouble you, *madám*," his older brother assured.

"Please, close the door," the old woman asked. "It gets terribly drafty."

Geoffrey didn't question her and shut the door behind him. Still, he did not sit down. "We smelled the stew and thought if you had any to spare for two weary travelers…"

It was their usual line of greeting. Formal, polite, and borderline pathetic in Hugo's opinion. But it got them into the homes of many peasants and noblemen alike.

"How far off did you smell it?" she asked as a youthful twinkle appeared in her eyes. "Ten miles? Twenty miles? Don't be modest, I'd love to know."

Their brows shot up. "The wind is strong today, but not that strong," Hugo replied.

"We were just passing by your cottage when we smelled it."

She gave them an amused look. "Please, don't be coy with me. I know your kind can smell and hear over many miles. Please, do tell me."

Hugo looked to Geoffrey, who in turned looked to him. He wasn't about to wait for approval before he turned back to the old woman on the stool. "I first heard your humming from a few miles away. I only smelled the roast you're cooking when we came closer. In our defense, we were up-wind from your cottage."

"Brother," Geoffrey hissed at him, as if that would help matters at all.

Hugo shrugged. "She said that she knows what we are."

Geoffrey combed his hair back with his fingers and grumbled curses under his breath.

"Oh, it's all right, *mal'chikov*," the old woman said with a laugh. "My husband was one of your kind. I know what to look for."

Hugo grinned, thankful that they had no fear of being turned out or burned alive by this woman. She knew exactly what they were and seemed to be perfectly fine with it.

The old woman stood to her feet and hobbled toward a cupboard on the other side of the cottage. Passing between the two werewolves, she patted them both affectionately on the shoulder. "No, *myshka*. Don't worry a bit." Hugo nearly laughed as she called them her "little mouse" but out of respect for the one who fed them, he kept his lips shut tight. They had been called worse.

"Your secret is safe with me. Although," she grunted out as she tried to reach the top shelf that was just inches from her fingertips, "where is your pack?"

Hugo braced himself to stand, but Geoffrey was the first to come to her aid and snatched up the three bowls from the shelf for her.

"*Spasibo*, dear," she said as she took the bowls from his hand.

"You're welcome. We don't have a pack, *madám*," Geoffrey said. "We travel alone."

She passed them both a worried look. "Alone? Oh, that will never do. You should not be alone."

When the old woman turned her back, Hugo made a face as if she didn't know what she was talking about. Geoffrey didn't appreciate his snide look and made him know it through a look of his own.

"It's served us fine over the years," Geoffrey said softly and watched as she bent over the fireplace to ladle soup into the bowls. Her hands were unsteady and a few drops sloshed into the fire, emitting a light hiss. "Let me help with that."

His older brother hurried forward and took the spoon and bowls from her hand. The old woman straightened and propped her hands on her hips. "Thank you again. My, you boys are so kind."

Now it was Hugo's turn to feel sheepish. Geoffrey was the one being helpful, not him. He shifted uncomfortably in the chair and it creaked in response to his shame. He didn't care if his brother outshined him, but the reminder that he wasn't pulling his own weight was like a punch to the chest.

No matter where they went, what pack they visited, or what family they stayed with, Hugo always seemed to be the leech, sucking off the provisions of others while his brother did his best to be productive.

He let out a sigh and looked around for something to keep his hands occupied when the old woman came to sit with him at the dining table. The top rocked to one side as she leaned her thin, frail arms on the edge.

"What brings you two this far? You do not look Russian."

Hugo glanced to his brother, half expecting him to answer, but he was too preoccupied fishing out the chunks of meat from the broth that they couldn't drink. When he didn't speak, he replied, "We're looking for something."

Her old face split in a grin. "What is it you're looking for?"

Once more, Hugo looked to his brother, but decided to answer her to the best of his knowledge. "We're looking for a wolf that's said to embody the Spirit of Peace. We want to find it and petition it to help the world. I don't know what kind of news you receive way out here, but your country isn't exactly doing well. Neither is the rest of Europe and the orient. Wars, famine, disease, violence, it's all tearing the world apart. It's only getting worse now that we're discovering new places to conquer."

The old woman nodded as if she understood exactly what he was talking about. "I have seen my fair share of the terrible world we live in. Why do you think I choose to live so far from everything? It's much quieter out here. No one disturbs me, but then I have no one to talk to."

Geoffrey glanced over his shoulder and there was a pained look of sympathy in the way he regarded the woman. "I'm sure it must be lonely for you," he said. "What happened to your husband?"

She let out a heavy sigh and looked down to her neatly folded hands. The skin that stretched across her knuckles was so thin he could see her dark veins underneath. "He's been gone for ten years now. A hunter took him from me one night. If he hadn't led the hunter away from the house, I would have been killed as well. Somedays, I wish I had."

Geoffrey finished spilling the contents of the stew into the bowls and came to the table to distribute them. Hugo, heedless of manners, took his bowl and pinched the bits of tough meat between his fingers before popping them into his mouth. His brother went hunting for utensils in the cabinet hutch behind them.

"He didn't leave you with any sons to take care of you?" Hugo asked with his mouth full.

She smiled sweetly. "He did. Three boys and two girls, but they are all grown now and living their own lives. My three boys were taken in by a pack closer to Moscow when we lived there. When the tsar came to power, we left them behind. The girls are married with their own families. I could have never asked them to follow. It was just me and my husband for the longest time."

Geoffrey took a seat beside the woman and dug into his portion of meat. As meager as it was, Hugo considered it to be filling enough and seasoned well. It beat raw rabbit any day. The old woman didn't partake in her soup, not even after Geoffrey slipped her a spoon. Instead, she stared down at the grainy table surface, a faraway look in her eyes as if she were thinking of better times.

"I think you made the right decision to leave Moscow," the older brother said. "When we were there a couple of weeks ago, another riot was breaking out at the Kremlin."

She shook her head. "Such tragedy and hatred. Senseless. All of it."

"We agree," Hugo said. "That's why we're trying to find this wolf. Have you seen any around lately that might be traveling outside of a pack? Maybe a pure white one?"

Geoffrey shot him a harsh look, silently reprimanding him for pushing the subject too hard. He stuffed his mouth with meat again to keep himself from saying any more.

The old woman tapped her pursed lips with her fingernail in thought and then nodded. "I do recall one not too long ago. It came close to the house, but wouldn't come into the clearing at first. I had to coax it with a bit of meat first."

"Was it white?" Geoffrey asked, now suddenly eager.

"It was," she said with a nod. "I'm sure of it. I remember that clearly because most of the wolves around here are darker than she was."

"She?" Hugo mumbled.

The old woman grinned. "Yes. I believe it was a girl. There was a softness in her green eyes, just like a lady's would be."

Geoffrey and Hugo quickly looked to each other. No natural wolf had green eyes. That must have been the Spirit they were looking for.

"How long ago did you say that was?"

She flipped her hand dismissingly. "Oh, perhaps a week. Maybe two."

Hugo let out a disappointed breath. "It could be anywhere by now."

The woman turned to Geoffrey and patted his shoulder. "Not to worry, *myshka*," she said. "I'm sure you'll be able to track her down. It has barely rained since then."

Any rain was bad rain when it came to tracking. Drenching the earth in water was the best way to lose a trail. That wolf was as good as gone. Unless it decided to stick around and claim this territory as its own. Yet, would the wolf have the same instincts, given that it was the vessel for the Spirit? It might roam just as wild as a creature not bound to territory lines.

Hugo's stomach lurched and he did his best to hide his pain as Geoffrey and the old woman continued to talk about her children still living in the west. He set his bowl down, wondering if it was the stew that upset him. When his muscles began to ache and spasm, he knew this had nothing to do with the stew.

"Oh, no," the old woman said. "You're not well. Is it your night to *izmenyat*?"

Geoffrey stood from the table and moved around to help Hugo to his feet as his wolf began to barrage at the corners of his mind. "It is. Please forgive us."

The old woman nodded and gave them another dismissive wave. "Think nothing of it. My husband had to run out at the most inconvenient times as well."

His brother gave the woman a grateful nod. "Thank you for understanding."

Hugo growled at the pain as his eyes morphed into their werewolf gold. There was little he could do to stop the shift once it took hold. Pain tore at his body and much of his consciousness slipped away as Geoffrey jostled him out of the cottage and deep into the woods. He was old enough to have control over his beast once the shift was complete, but getting to that point was pure torture.

Bones and joints snapped out of place as his body grew in size. The front of his face elongated to resemble a muzzle, his ears lengthening to resemble a wolf's. Fingers became tipped with claws and the undersides of his palms grew rough. If his brother hadn't had the sense to help him undress, he would have torn his clothes to bits as brown and black fur sprouted from his skin. A tail extended from the end of his spine and dusted the ground as he dropped to all fours.

Geoffrey joined him in the change and shared in his agony, though it wasn't his night to naturally shift. Their cycles were a week or so apart. They never shifted alone, not even as young boys. They had learned quickly how to summon the change on command, so they wouldn't have to spend the night without one another.

When the last of the searing pain of the shift had subsided, Hugo looked to his brother. Unlike him, his pelt was a marbled mix of deep brown hues and beige like his human hair. Yet, their forms were nearly the same. They did not shift completely into wolves, but a monstrous blend of both man and beast.

The first few decades of their new lives as werewolves had brought with it many challenges, one being that they couldn't control themselves once the shift took hold. It took years of training before the two minds could meld as one. Once they did, once they could dictate what they would and would not do in this beastly form, Hugo and Geoffrey realized how terrifying they truly were. It was no wonder the villagers were afraid of the *bodark* - the evil werewolves who chose to make a pact with the devil so they could change into monsters.

Geoffrey, Hugo, and every werewolf in the world knew that this had nothing to do with the devil. This was what they were, not always by choice, but by fate. Those born into this existence learned to live with it and coexist to the best of their ability. If not, there were plenty of others who were willing to kill them. A silver bullet between the eyes or a silver blade to the heart would end their double-lives as man and beast.

But that was not how Hugo and Geoffrey wanted to live. There was still more to discover, more to learn and enjoy. They may have despised their father for abandoning them. They even wished they could have been born into a normal life. But they could never bring themselves to hate the wolves they were gifted with.

With a toss of his massive wolf head, Geoffrey instructed that they should return to the cottage. Hugo didn't argue and they lopped back through the woods toward the clearing. When they arrived, however, it was gone. The cottage, the woman, the stew, the chimney, all of it. The clearing they were once in was nothing more than a thick patch of wild grasses and flowers.

They sniffed for any trace of the old woman who had fed them, but found nothing. Not a single sign of anything remained. It was as if she were never there.

Hugo shivered in the early night air and turned with his tail between his legs to retreat back into the woods. His brother lingered and continued looking for anything. Finally, he snorted and trotted back to Hugo with a wooden bowl in his mouth.

It was one of the bowls they had eaten from, but this one was cracked and filthy. It was covered in moss as if it had been sitting in the dirt for ages before Geoffrey picked it up. Hugo's ears folded back against his head and he slunk away. Had it all been a mirage? An illusion? If so, to what purpose? Perhaps she was a witch after all?

He didn't want to stick around long enough to find out. Geoffrey tossed the bowl back into the clearing and the two werewolves dashed off into the night to escape the mystery of the old woman and the disappearing cottage.

CHAPTER 5

Hugo was still fast asleep in the shade near the lake. With a cushy bed of wild foliage and flora, Geoffrey thought it as good a place as any to sleep away the long night running as wolves. What he hadn't expected was the breathtaking view that became illuminated by the dawn.

In the late morning sun, he watched the flocks of birds fly across the bright blue sky. A few wisps of clouds rolled by with the wind, casting shadows over the pristine, dark blue water. He had heard that Siberia could be a harsh and unforgiving land, full of dangers in the untamed nature. It had conjured images of a barren wasteland, frozen at all times of the year. No one said a word about the rich, green beauty that covered the countryside in the summer seasons.

If it wasn't for the promise of a deadly winter ahead, Geoffrey might have been inclined to convince his brother that they stay in this part of the country. A werewolf could survive here with little trouble and no contact with the outside world.

Even the smells that surrounded them soothed his wolf in a way that civilization never could. Last night had been one of the best shifting nights in a long time. Besides the slight shock of the disappearing woman and cottage, Geoffrey and Hugo were freer than they had ever been. Not a single human for miles around and plenty of game to satisfy their bellies.

Geoffrey let out a long, contented sigh and closed his eyes as he basked by the lakeshore, his arms folded behind his head and bare chest drinking in the warm sun. He let his mind drift and though the sun was energizing, he could feel himself doze off.

A few moments passed before a scent crashed through the perfect morning. His eyes shot open and he pushed himself upright to listen. Someone was coming toward the lake. He sniffed and his suspicion was confirmed, much to his dismay. Geoffrey should have known it was only a matter of time.

He stood and slipped on the tunic he had discarded to the side. Still clad in his trousers, he set off into the thick forest to meet Reitz. The blood servant held a long dagger in one hand, slashing through the underbrush so he could make a clear path for himself.

The scent of vampire met him, but the scent was stale, as if Reitz hadn't been in Michael or Anton's company for some time.

"What are you doing out here alone?" Geoffrey asked, taking in the human's tired face. His garments appeared torn and stained as if he had been trudging through these woods for days on end without relief.

Reitz panted and nearly dropped his dagger with relief when he looked up. "Thank the Lord, I found you." The blood servant looked barely strong enough to stand and Geoffrey rushed to him, pushing aside the bushes with ease.

"What's happened?"

Reitz pointed in the direction he came. "Michael and Anton. They've become too weak. They can't even move. I can't provide enough for both of them and Michael refuses to feed as much as he needs. The sun, even if their skin is covered, weakens them to the point of exhaustion."

Geoffrey crossed his arms over his thick chest. "You came all this way because your masters need blood?"

He gave the werewolf a helpless look. "I tried to catch animals for them to feed on, but it wasn't enough. I'm not accustomed to this wilderness."

Looking over his tattered clothes, that was obvious. "How far away are they?" he asked.

"They're in a cave just to the south. Michael told me to travel this way to find you."

No doubt one of his vampire tricks. Geoffrey looked back toward the lake where his brother was still resting. If he left and Hugo woke up, he would be furious to find out what Geoffrey had done. Then again, if he waited for his little brother to wake up and told him what had become of Michael and Anton, he would be sure to balk at the idea of coming to their rescue.

He let out a breath and looked back to Reitz. "Let me get my brother. We will do what we can, but please don't mistake me. We cannot travel with you and Michael anymore."

Reitz's brows pinched together. "Why not? Michael wouldn't tell me why you left. Did you find the Spirit?"

"No, not yet." Geoffrey's lips twisted as if he tried to think of the best way to explain this to the human. "We are used to traveling at a faster pace. We don't take the conventional, easy paths, and you three were slowing us down. It wasn't our intention to abandon you when you needed the extra... resources."

Reitz shook his head. "None of us truly anticipated this. Anton is used to hunger, but the thirst seemed to come on them so suddenly, so strongly. I've never seen anything like it."

Geoffrey motioned his hand in a placating manner. He couldn't handle the blood servant's panic, not in a place so peaceful and serene as this. "All right. We'll come. Just give me a moment."

He walked back to the lake and kicked his brother's hip. "Hugo, wake up."

Hugo let out a grunt and cracked open his eyes. "What is it?" he grumbled.

"We need to go. Michael and Anton have found us... Well, more specifically, Reitz has. The poor human walked all this way to fetch us."

His little brother sneered and rolled on his side, his tanned and bare back sprinkled with the bits of leaves and flowers from his makeshift nature pallet. "They can burn in the sun for all I care."

Geoffrey grabbed Hugo's arm and hoisted him to his feet.

"Michael and Anton are weak, perhaps dying. There is no one else to help them."

He shoved Geoffrey away with a fierce, guttural growl. Hugo wasn't moved, just as Geoffrey predicted. "Why should you care? We agreed we wouldn't travel with them."

His hands balled into fists. "And we are keeping our agreement. I told Reitz we will go help, but we cannot stay. He understands and I'm sure Michael will once we explain ourselves."

"How do we know it's not a trap?" Hugo offered. "What if Michael sent Reitz to lure us to them so they can kill us? What if this is another illusion, sent to keep us from finding the wolf?" He folded his arms over his chest like the stubborn child that he was. "I'm not going."

Geoffrey felt the rage and indignation boil in his blood. Even his wolf couldn't bear with Hugo's stubbornness. "Fine. You can stay here," he barked. "I'm tired of your bickering, selfish, arrogant mouth. Stay here, puffed up in your own pride. You've never cared about anyone else but yourself anyway. Why should you care for two people who need our help? I'll come back to fetch you when I'm done."

With that, he turned and marched back to where Reitz waited. No doubt, the human heard their heated argument, but Geoffrey wasn't ashamed for his words. Ever since they were younger, Hugo could never own up to anything. He blamed the world and their father for his misfortunes, but he did nothing to lessen the suffering of others as Geoffrey tried to do.

When their mother fell into her depressive, almost catatonic state, it was Geoffrey that stepped in to take care of her. When they turned, it was Geoffrey who comforted Hugo in the midst of his own terror about the future. When their mother died, Geoffrey dug the grave while Hugo disappeared for days in the throes of his despair.

Every town they went to, every family they visited, Geoffrey poured himself into their services while Hugo tagged along and gleaned what truth he could find in the stories they told. When Hugo found love in that woman from Warminster, Geoffrey became incensed. Why should they stall their mission so he could enjoy himself in the carnal passion of romance?

When Hugo's son was born, Geoffrey had hopes that he would finally learn to care for someone beside himself. When they left England, he constantly questioned if Hugo wanted to return. Each time, he dismissed him, saying the boy and his mother would be fine.

They weren't.

When they found the abandoned farm, and learned nothing from the locals, Geoffrey feared that Hugo would slip into a state much like their mother had. He didn't. And that infuriated him even more.

Hugo was his brother. His stubborn, reckless, selfish brother, and he couldn't help but love him and care for him whenever he could. Today, Geoffrey had had enough. He would come back to retrieve Hugo, but he needed some time away to simmer down.

He and Reitz traveled in silence for nearly an hour as he brooded over everything he hated about his brother, wishing that somehow it would justify leaving him. It didn't and the ache in his chest was a testament to that guilt.

When he sensed Hugo's approach, Geoffrey had to restrain himself from turning to greet him with open arms and profuse apologies. Hugo hurried up and walked alongside him without a word. The human didn't utter a thing as he looked between the two werewolves, probably wondering if it was safe to ask if they were on better terms now.

Geoffrey wasn't even sure of that.

Was it something he said that made Hugo change his mind? Or was it the idea of being alone that scared him into running after them? Geoffrey hoped against the odds, hoped against the two hundred years they had spent side by side, that Hugo finally realized that his behavior was unacceptable.

He set them aside for another time. There were more pressing concerns to deal with at the moment.

It felt as if they have been walking for hours. Or perhaps that was the hunger talking. Hugo's belly growled angrily in protest, in spite of the feast it had received the night before. Even Geoffrey's stomach made its complaints known. Evening shades of deep purples and blues blended into the sky above them. Reitz's fear had abated the longer the three of them walked together.

He told Hugo how his masters had fallen so gravely ill from a thirst of their own, hence the reason he had come to find the two werewolves and plead for their help. There wasn't a human around for miles. At least, that's what Hugo had thought before he caught a whiff of something sweet on the winds that snaked through the trees.

Hugo and Geoffrey both stopped, the captivating aroma holding them in place as Reitz continued ahead. Only when he was a few yards away did he realize that he was walking without them. He turned and regarded them with a perturbed look. "What is it?" he asked.

The two brothers looked to one another and Hugo could see the torn look in his brother's eyes. They needed to eat, but his saintly attitude toward helping those who were less fortunate, must have been tugging at his heart.

"What's a few minutes going to hurt?" Hugo asked with a shrug. He could feel his wolf press against the surface, begging for a meal that seemed long overdue. After the long night running as a wolf and the lack of sleep to recover from it, Hugo needed some sort of nourishment or he would collapse. Or worse, his wolf might take over and go on the hunt. Yet, that didn't make much sense because of the bountiful feast he and his brother had devoured. Now, there probably was little to nothing to hunt. It was as if the forest had completely emptied itself of life besides the two werewolves and blood servant.

Geoffrey told Reitz to wait there for them as they set off to follow the promise of a meal. It didn't take long for them to catch something else carried on the wind with the scent. A child was crying in the same direction and her sobs troubled them.

They quickened their steps and found her in the middle of a clearing, her legs curled up to her chest and weeping on her knees. She couldn't have been more than six or seven years old at best. Clad in nothing but a thin peasant dress that must have reached to her knees. Her long dark hair a tangled mess around her ears. It was indeterminate how long she had been stranded out in the wilderness. There wasn't another town or village within miles of here. The last home they saw belonged to the illusion of the woman they had met the evening before.

Hugo and Geoffrey watched her, their faces colored with shock and wonder at the scene. Testing the air, there was no mistaking that this girl was the source of the delectable scent they followed. Never in his life had Hugo ever considered a human a meal. He and Geoffrey had known of those werewolves who devoured the flesh of the innocent. They were the true monsters of the fairytales that the peasants told.

Geoffrey took a few steps backward as Hugo did the complete opposite and drew closer to the edge of the clearing. His eyes fixed on the child as she continued to cry, oblivious that two starving werewolves were so near.

His brother grabbed at his sleeve and yanked him deeper into the shadows. "No," he whispered.

Hugo knew what his brother must have been thinking, but it wasn't true. Though he was starving, ravenous with hunger to the point that it was a struggle just to keep his wolf at bay, he didn't want to eat the little girl. Far from it. His heart bled for her. He could never stand to hear the feminine sobs, no matter their age. That was why he left Martha so suddenly. He couldn't bear to hear her wail and cry against the unfairness of losing her lover. If he had stayed or tried to explain himself, he wouldn't have had the strength of will to leave.

He ripped his arm from his brother's grasp and hurried into the clearing. The little girl's head shot up and looked at him with wide, green eyes that looked like glittering emeralds in the waning light. She watched his approach, her nose running and lips quivering with the need to burst into more weeping.

"What are you doing out here by yourself?" Hugo asked softly, crouching down to face the girl. Her scent made his mouth water, but he beat back his hungry wolf.

She sniffled and swallowed hard. "I got lost and I can't find my way back home. Now, it's too dark and I can't see."

Hugo gave her a reassuring smile as fresh tears brimmed in her eyes. "I'll tell you a secret," he whispered. "I can see really well in the dark. Maybe I can help you."

A hopeful looked dawned in her gaze. "Really? Would you?"

She was so adorable and innocent. Even if he wanted to eat her, Hugo couldn't bring himself to do it. He offered out his big hand. "My name's Hugo. What's yours?"

Her pretty eyes darted between his face and his hand. Then, she took it, placing her tiny, delicate fingers in his palm. "Tanatia."

"That's a pretty name. Come on, Tanatia. Let's get you home." He glanced over his shoulder. "My brother Geoffrey will help, too. Won't you?"

Geoffrey stood at the edge of the clearing, every line of his body tensed as if he were ready to lunge or run. Hugo wasn't sure which. He only nodded.

Hugo helped Tanatia to her feet and scrutinized her skinny body. There was hardly any meat on her bones worth eating. "How long have you been lost?" he asked.

"I don't know," she replied as she wiped her dirty cheeks on the back of her hand. "A few days, maybe."

Hugo's eyes went wide. "A few days. You must be hungry."

She nodded and gave a little whimper of an answer that made Hugo want to wrap her up in a tight hug.

"We'll get you something to eat," he assured.

When they came to meet Geoffrey, he could see the turmoil in his brother's eyes. "Geoffrey, this is Tanatia. We're going to help her get home."

Helping a little girl home was certainly preferable to going to have their blood drained by a couple of vampires. Geoffrey put on his bravest face and smiled at the little girl. Tanatia shied against Hugo's side and he could smell the potent scent of fear waft from her.

"He's friendly," Hugo said. "Just a little upset right now. Don't worry."

"Why are you upset?" she quietly asked the older werewolf, her voice so light and weak compared to theirs.

Geoffrey squatted in front of her. "Because we're in a hurry to get somewhere, but we're going to help you too."

Hugo was satisfied with the new smile his brother put on and together they went back to meet Reitz. Greetings were exchanged, and Hugo looked to Geoffrey for his call. To see the vampires first or help Tanatia get home.

"Is your house close to something?" Geoffrey asked her, answering Hugo's unspoken question. The vampires would have to wait. "A river or a mountain maybe?"

Tanatia nodded. "We live next to a little creek."

That would make it much easier to find. They could follow the scent of water and hopefully find the house within no time at all.

After a little coaxing, Tanatia let Hugo lift her onto his shoulders, so she wouldn't have to walk on the forest floor with her bare, blistered feet. With a firm grip on her legs and her fingers digging into his hair, they set off in the direction of the nearest river.

Whatever Geoffrey believed about Hugo's selfish tendencies, he had to know that helping this little girl was purely altruistic. He thought of his own son and what he would have been like at Tanatia's age. If he had been lost in the woods with no way to get home, Hugo would have wanted some kind stranger – werewolf, vampire, or human – to help him. Hugo had been useless in raising his son, in helping his mother, and in a multitude of other things, but perhaps he could start taking action now. He could set a trend and be like his brother, helping others in need. Geoffrey had always been his idol, his hero in youth and present day.

If only he could ignore the gnawing hunger in his belly. That would have made their efforts so much easier.

CHAPTER 6

Night descended and Geoffrey couldn't keep his eyes from glowing gold a moment longer. The hunger had become too great and his wolf raged within him. Never had he suffered from such blind, animalistic cravings. Reitz and the little girl atop Hugo's shoulders were in more danger than he would ever let on.

Though Hugo's eyes had turned gold hours before, he hardly showed a waiver in his convictions to help Tanatia. The little girl, who seemed so shy and insecure before, talked on and on about her family and their little farm where they kept chickens, cows, sheep, and grew all manner of crops. Geoffrey listened to her ramblings, but it was Hugo who interacted the most with her. He asked her questions about her life and family as if it truly mattered to him. Geoffrey suspected it was a trick to keep himself focused on anything but the burning hunger that made their bodies tense and ache. In the back of his mind, Geoffrey was thankful for the girl's constant chatter. It distracted him as well.

Reitz, too, seemed unconcerned about his safety, but only cared for finding Tanatia's home quickly so they could get back to Michael and Anton who were wasting away in their own strange, uncontrollable hunger.

Geoffrey was suspicious of it all, especially when they came to the river and found it was completely empty of fish. He had planned to catch one to feed themselves and the thin girl as well, but no matter how hard his eyes and nose searched, there wasn't even a minnow to scoop up from the water.

This phenomena couldn't have been a coincidence and after their run-in with the vanishing cottage, he continually looked over his shoulder, half expecting to see a witch or other magical being ready to catch them in some snare.

"Why are your eyes gold?" Tanatia asked, interrupting her own conversation with Hugo about a feisty tomcat that hung around her family's cabbage garden. Her little head was listed downward to peek at his face, her dark hair falling over her shoulder.

Without missing a beat, Hugo replied, "It helps me to see better in the dark, so we can find your parents."

Tanatia seemed to accept that reply with a childlike innocence and continued babbling.

Hugo's newfound cheerfulness when it came to helping Tanatia confused his brother to no end. Why did he want to help this little girl when he didn't even seem interested in helping the old woman in the cottage? It must have had something to do with Geoffrey's reprimand for his selfish behavior, but Hugo was a stubborn man. It wasn't likely that he would make such a genuine change within a few hours.

His first thought when Hugo made to approach the weeping girl was that Hugo's hunger was getting the better of him. Then, once he showed that he was truly adamant about helping her find her home, Geoffrey decided to let his brother have his moment.

The scent of wood smoke and animals mingled in with the salty tinge of river water made Geoffrey strain his eyes to see ahead of them along the banks. Tiny flickering lights, like the glow of a candle sitting in a windowsill, broke through the darkness to greet the weary travelers. This must have been Tanatia's home.

He breathed a sigh of relief, knowing their trial was almost over. They would leave Tanatia a safe distance away from her farm and go about their way to find Michael – and hopefully a sustaining meal. They didn't want to impose on Tanatia's family, nor stay in case they wanted to ask questions the brothers couldn't answer. Surely, Hugo would want to sneak away to snatch up a lamb from Tanatia's flock, but Geoffrey would have to cart him away.

The little girl must have seen the firelight and eagerly tapped on the top of Hugo's head, insisting he let her down. Hugo scooped her up and placed her squarely on her feet in front of him. As soon as she touched the ground, the little girl who seemed to have no strength when they first met, darted toward the house with the swiftness of a young fawn.

The men stopped and watched her dart away, shouting thanks and endearments over her shoulder as she went. Hugo gave her a wave and smile, but he didn't take his eyes off of her for one second.

"Now we can find Michael," Reitz said, the relief prevalent in his words.

Geoffrey peered into the darkness and wondered if the hunger was affecting his sharp night vision. The lights of the little cottage began to twinkle and fade away like stars in the early morning sky. Soon, the smell of smoke and sheep wool was replaced with something far less appealing. Sulfur.

Beside him, Hugo tensed and lowered his arm. The longer they looked, the more they came to realize that the cottage was just another illusion. Geoffrey couldn't hold the curse from spouting out from his lips as the true and unmistakable image of a dark cave began to take shape before them.

At the mouth, he saw Michael trying to restrain Anton – or whom he believed to be Anton. What the older vampire held in place was the vicious, red-eyed beast they had encountered in the corridor at the Kremlin. Michael's eyes gleamed a thirsty red, but it was clear that he still had control over himself enough to know that the little girl was not a meal.

Tanatia, however, didn't slow down.

Hugo and Geoffrey burst into a run to intercept just as Michael's hold over Anton was broken. The vampire charged toward the girl in a blur, his long fangs glinting in the moonlight. The werewolves let their wolves off their tethers and their bodies partially shifted.

They, however, passed up the girl and went straight for Anton with their own fangs and claws extended, ready to tear the vampire apart if he even came close to touching a hair on Tanatia's head.

The creatures clashed together, bones snapping and flesh ripping. Blood splattered onto the grassy shore of the river and snaked down into the steady stream to be carried away. Growls, snarls, yips, hisses, and roars erupted from the mass of thrashing bodies between the little girl and the mouth of the dark cave.

Michael joined the fray, both trying to restrain his ward and keep the wolves at bay from shredding Anton to pieces. Geoffrey hardly felt anything as claws and teeth serrated his flesh. The high of hunger and dire need to defend the girl numbed him. He wasn't even sure what Tanatia was doing. Perhaps running for her life in the opposite direction. He hoped so, anyway.

Just when he felt a pair of fangs sink into his neck, he let out a yowl of pain and tried to buck the vampire off. A chunk of his flesh went with it and he was sure the damage was too much to come back from. He tried to breathe, but felt his hot blood course into his mouth and lungs.

Geoffrey swung his arms wildly in a last attempt to gain purchase on Anton's own throat, but his vision went black and he couldn't see anything through the haze as he fell to the ground. He heard his brother growl his name and Michael's shouts of unmitigated anger.

He blinked and tried to speak, but too much had been ripped away. As the last of his consciousness slipped, he heard Hugo shift into his full beast form and charge toward Anton and Michael to continue the battle and avenge his brother.

A bright light flashed, piercing through the darkness of what he believed to be his final moments of life. The searing pain of his wounds dissipated, and the hunger vanished with it. But when he opened his eyes, he wasn't met with the heavenly realm of the afterlife as he had anticipated.

Above him, the night sky, alive with the moon and glittering stars welcomed him back to the earth. Around him, he could smell blood and fear so thoroughly mixed that it seemed to make a new signature scent all its own. Geoffrey scrambled up and saw Hugo, Anton, and Michael staring past him. They were civilized now, fangs and claws retracted and eyes their normal, human colors.

He swiveled around and instead of seeing the little girl, Tanatia, he beheld a woman, beautiful unlike any he had ever seen. The only resemblance between her and the child they had led to this place was her bright green eyes and long brown hair that now looked smooth and soft.

Yet, this was no ordinary woman. An ethereal glow caressed her skin from the top of her head to her bare feet. Clad in a gleaming white dress, she appeared every bit an angel.

His hand flew to his neck, checking for the huge missing chunk of flesh, to find it whole. His skin was sticky where the blood had spilled, but other than that, he was completely healed. His other battle wounds were also gone, though the evidence of their existence was in the tears of his garments where Michael and Anton had cut and bit him. Even the hunger, which had so consumed him just moments ago, was completely gone.

His brother and the two vampires were likewise completely healed, though their fight had been real.

"You have proven yourselves worthy," the woman said, her voice feminine and like the strumming of a perfectly tuned harp.

"Worthy?" Hugo questioned with a note of confusion.

"I have seen the devastation of this world," she continued. "The wars, the violence, the hatred. All of it is displeasing to me."

It was then that Geoffrey realized who this woman was. She was the one they had been searching for. The Spirit of Peace. Why would she choose to come in this form? Why not the wolf that she was professed to be? Then again, why did she come as a little girl? And if his suspicions were right, an old, lonely woman?

"You have shown me that humanity deserves peace."

Geoffrey let out a long breath. They did it. Somehow, through the fighting, bickering, and groping around in the dark for something that may or may not have existed, they had accomplished their goal.

"So, you'll take away the evil in this world?" Michael asked, hope springing in his question.

Tanatia's smile faded and she shook her head. "I cannot."

"Why not?" Geoffrey asked.

"There are other forces at work in this world that I cannot overcome until it is time."

The four men looked to one another, hoping that perhaps the others knew what she meant.

Hugo was the first to speak up again, "When will that be? How much longer do we have to wait? How many more innocents have to die?"

"I have limited power in this form," she said. "But I will come again in such a way that I may have dominion and walk the earth as I once did eons ago. There will be a child born who is both wolf and vampire. When the child comes of age, I will appear again and right the wrongs. I will heal the wounds and erase the scars that your war has inflicted."

"Our war?" Anton questioned.

"The war between the wolves and the vampires," she replied. "Your hatred for one another have driven the world into the state that it is in. You are as much to blame as the humans."

Shame welled inside of him. Geoffrey remembered the way they initially felt toward Michael and Anton, and every other vampire they had met. Disrespect, hatred, skepticism. None of those things proclaimed them to be men who desperately wanted to see a world at peace.

"You four, and your descendants, I will bless. When I come again, your valor, loyalty, selflessness, and courage, will aid me in cleansing the evil."

A few beats of silence stretched before Geoffrey snapped out of his daze. "Us? Why us?"

The pleasing smile returned to her lips. "You have shown yourself to be defenders of the innocent, champions of peace."

Geoffrey slid a glance toward Anton, who bowed his head. Out of the four of them, he did not show any restraint in attacking Tanatia, while the other three had at least tried.

Before a single ill word could be uttered against him, Tanatia answered their unspoken thoughts. "I have seen Anton's heart and the loyalty that lies there.

Though he is young, he shall accomplish great things and serve the cause well in the future. Michael, I charge him into your care."

Michael gave her a nod of understanding as her beautiful eyes turned to the two brothers. "Though you may not understand now, your roles will become plain in the coming years. Have faith and do not forget my words this night."

Slowly, Tanatia faded into the night, but Geoffrey would never forget her face, so branded into his mind like a beacon. She was right. He couldn't understand why she should choose them, of all creatures, to be her champions for peace. Geoffrey did as he saw fit, but he hardly thought himself qualified to be blessed by the Spirit.

Hugo, with unsteady legs, flew to his brother's side and checked him for the death wounds that were gone now.

"I am all right, brother," he assured as they embraced one another.

Reitz, who had been a helpless witness to the historic moment, staggered closer to address his master. Geoffrey heard them silently reassuring one another, but he didn't care what they said. His mind was still trying to process all he had seen.

Had they really done what they set out to do, or was this just the beginning? How long until Tanatia would appear again? What should they do to prepare for her second coming? How could they simply go on with their lives after learning that they and their legacy would never be the same again?

Bering Strait, Spring, 1649

"You're insane!" Hugo said for the thousandth time as he tossed his head over the railing of the ship and vomited into the frigid ocean water.

They had been at sea for weeks, skipping from port to port along the eastern coast of Siberia. Finally, they and their small group of fellow explorers had made the leap to find the connection between the old and new worlds.

They were well aware of Semyon Dezhnev and his somewhat disastrous expedition with his team of sailors, but Geoffrey and Hugo were no ordinary explorers. And though Hugo might have been right about his elder brother's crazy intuition that there was a shorter way to reach the new world that did not involve crossing Europe again, Hugo was just as insane for following him.

Geoffrey briskly rubbed at his back and Hugo didn't have to see his face to know that he was grinning. "Have faith, brother. I can almost smell the land ahead."

Hugo coughed and lifted his head back up to address him. "What you smell is the last bit of spoiled meat you made me eat last night." The fresh wave of insults that wanted to bubble up was cut off by his need to hurl the contents of his stomach over the side of the ship again.

He had never been this sick in his life. He hated sailing, hated the ocean, hated the meager rations they were forced to eat. And above all, he hated the confined quarters of the cargo hold where they'd had to shift in secret once already.

"Would you have rather followed Michael and Anton back to Italy?" Geoffrey asked, a lilt of jeering in his tone.

Hugo sneered. "I would have rather gone to the orient again and perhaps to Africa."

"We have already been there, brother," he said. "The New World must be conquered now."

"Forgive me if I'm not as enthusiastic as you are."

Geoffrey glanced over his shoulder at the bored sailors whittling away at bits of rope and wood to pass the time, while the helmsman steered them farther into the east. "I believe you aren't the only one unenthusiastic."

"You've heard their talks about mutiny, right?" Hugo whispered. "They've wanted to turn back for days now. And I don't know about you, but I don't think we could swim the rest of the way back to Russia."

Geoffrey didn't answer, but his gaze lifted to regard the horizon past the bowsprit. The waves crashed against the hull of the ship as the vessel continued to dip and sway along its course.

Hugo recognized that look. It had appeared every so often, ever since they'd met the Spirit of Peace in Russia. Geoffrey must have been thinking about the beautiful woman who had appeared to them and spoken her prophecy over their lives. Hugo dismissed it. He would have no descendants and his skeptic nature made him reluctant to believe that he would be around for her second coming.

Just like Christians who prepared for the rapture, Geoffrey seemed eager to prepare himself for whatever mystic, blessed future lay in store for them. Hugo could care less if he was caught unaware. His only son was probably dead and, after the fiasco with his first and only lover, Martha, he didn't want to risk endangering the lives of any more women. However, if Geoffrey ever decided to father his own children, Hugo would be the most doting uncle in history.

That is, if they ever made it across this stretch of ocean.

It was then that a strange, almost foreign sound met Hugo's keen ears. Over the roar of the waves, the scraping of knife against wood, and the many other ship sounds, like the creaking of ropes on their pulleys and flapping of canvas sail, Hugo could have sworn he heard the cry of a bird.

He lifted his head and gripped the rough rail, straining his ears to hear it one more time. Geoffrey had also heard it and leaned into the wind. They heard it again and the two brothers looked to one another with gleeful smiles.

Seagulls could only mean one thing. Land. Land and food, which Hugo and his wolf were certainly ready for. The constant bobbing and tight spaces of a ship were not the ideal climate for a werewolf. He would be glad for the moment when he seeped his paws into the raw, steady earth and breathed in air that wasn't so saturated with salt, sweat, and the stench of stale food.

Perhaps the New World would become a new home for them, just like it had for many more explorers and settlers. Maybe the New World was where Tanatia, the Spirit of Peace, would make her appearance again and do everything she had promised them back in the dense, dark forests of Russia.

AFTERWORD

Dear Reader,

I hope you have enjoyed reading the first four novellas in this series. You've read about the origins of pivotal characters like John Croxen and Darren Dubose, as well as epic introductions to important figures like Michael and Jane Gennari, Geoffrey and Hugo Swenson, and Tor. This small cast makes their grand appearance in my young adult paranormal saga, The Loup-Garou Series, and all have a special tie to the main heroine, Katey McCoy.

In the second volume, you'll be introduced to more characters, such as Dustin Keith, James and Will Croxen, and Adam Swenson. You'll also get to take a trip to more exotic lands such as Australia, Ireland, and the Caribbean.

I have always had a love for Europe and it's rich history, so when I first got the inclination to tell the backstories to my beloved characters, I knew there were endless possibilities of where I could take my characters and how much mayhem I could put them through. Hours upon hours were spent in libraries and combing through the internet to make sure every detail was as precise as I could get it. Though there were many aspects of each era and country that I left out for the sake of novella length, I believe I stayed true to the essence of the setting. Not only did I gain a new understanding of cultures and languages, but I grasped the reality of what it must have been like for characters like John and Darren to grow up in the kind of societies that they did. It was a blast writing this and I hope you enjoyed it just as much.

If you enjoyed this story, please take a few moments of your time to leave a review on Goodreads. I invite you to check out my social media sites for more

updates and sneak peeks into my progress. You can find me at my blog, www.m
oonstruckwriting.wordpress.com.

Happy Reading!

Sheritta Bitikofer

ABOUT THE AUTHOR

Sheritta Bitikofer is an author of paranormal and historical fiction. She lives for the deep, engaging stories that enthrall readers from cover to cover. As a wife and mother of eclectic tastes, she can be found roaming Civil War battlefields, haunting her local coffeeshop, or relaxing with a plate of chili cheese fries.

Follow her for upcoming novel releases

www.sherittabitikofer.com

www.moonstruckwriting.wordpress.com

ALSO BY SHERITTA BITIKOFER

<u>Bewitching Brews Trilogy</u>

Bewitching Fire

Bewitching Darkness

Bewitching Hearts

<u>The Decimus Trilogy</u>

The Beast of Verona

Amber Ashes

Saving the Beast

<u>Redemption Duet</u>

The Rose

The Lion

<u>Standalones</u>

Escape

Clouds

Passions

Silver Screen

By The Book

www.ingramcontent.com/pod-product-compliance
Lightning Source LLC
Chambersburg PA
CBHW020921020726
47495CB00002B/280